Pamela's mother . . . not the wrinkled, lifeless thing Pamela had seen in the satin-lined casket, but the former Jasmine, plump and full of energy . . . suddenly appeared in her bedroom, wearing her red paisley-patterned apron. She held a spatula in one hand, a large iron crucifix in the other. She asked Pamela if she would like some pancakes. Pamela sat up and pointed to the cross. "What's that for?"

"Demons been in the pancake mix again," was the irritated reply. "Don't do a bit of good to fry 'em . . . they'll go down hot right into your belly. Dad-gum witches been foolin' in my kitchen again, puttin' demons in the cereal boxes and everything else. Have to stick this cross down in there to drive 'em out."

The next moment Pamela was sitting at the breakfast table in pigtails, a stack of pancakes dripping with butter and syrup on the plate in front of her. Breathing, those pancakes. Yes, ever so slightly.

"Mom, are you sure you got all the demons out of this?"

"Of course I did, Sugar. Now eat 'em up before they get cold."

The first forkful made its way down Pamela's throat like a glob of scalding fat. The fire began to spread and she was on the floor, kicking and screaming as her eyes began to bulge. . . . And then she was looking down at her body on the floor, into the empty eye sockets through which a hellish fire began to glow . . .

Books by D. A. Fowler

What's Wrong with Valerie?
The Devil's End

Published by POCKET BOOKS

THE DEVIL'S END

D. A. Fowler

POCKET BOOKS

New York   London   Toronto   Sydney   Tokyo   Singapore

An *Original* Publication of POCKET BOOKS

POCKET BOOKS, a division of Simon & Schuster Inc.
1230 Avenue of the Americas, New York, NY 10020

ISBN: 0-671-72659-5

First Pocket Books printing April 1992

10 9 8 7 6 5 4 3 2 1

POCKET and colophon are registered trademarks of
Simon & Schuster Inc.

Cover art by Keith Birdsong

Printed in the U.S.A.

For Susan Scott

Acknowledgments

Many well deserved thanks to my editor,
John Scognamiglio, and to Dr. Stan Howard
for the priceless opportunity to pursue my dreams,
however demented they may be.

Prologue

A blustery September wind swept through the surrounding trees, filling the night air with the sound of countless hissing snakes. A storm was coming in from the north, announcing its approach with an occasional roll of thunder and forked streak of lightning.

Down a narrow path carpeted with pine needles, two elderly women followed the impotent beam of a flashlight. The one holding the flashlight kept glancing around nervously, as if expecting at any moment for an attacker to jump from the dark foliage. Her companion, white-haired and bent with age, trudged fearlessly behind the flashlight's beam, mouth set in a grim line.

"Where the devil is it?" she said, wheezing. "Are you certain we're on the right path?"

The other angled up the flashlight with a slightly trembling hand, eyes straining to penetrate the gloom ahead. "It's just a little further. I think I can see one of the markers." The wind whipped errant strands of her gray hair about her withered face, and a nearby clap of thunder brought her heart up into her throat. She could hardly believe the old woman hadn't read her guilty mind, discerned the real reason for bringing her up here in the dead of night. But maybe she had, and just wasn't saying anything, wouldn't say a word until the truth was manifested, guilt confirmed, and then . . .

She shuddered to think what would happen then, and cast a furtive glance over her shoulder. Her fear was taking large, ominous shapes around her, stalking her with all-knowing eyes and a smile that guaranteed she wouldn't get away with this. For the hundredth time since they'd left the house she reconsidered her plan, but concluded, as always, that it had to be executed. Or at least attempted.

They finally reached the end of the path and entered a clearing where the wind buffeted them with a vengeance. Before them lay a small cemetery, its leaning headstones testifying of abandonment, but a scattering of litter—crumpled paper cups, beer cans, cigarette butts, and used condoms—indicated that it was still visited, though obviously for reasons other than mourning the dead. In the unyielding darkness these irreverently discarded objects were unseen by the two women as they carefully made their way through the stones toward the single crypt.

Approaching its shadowed door, the older woman came to a sudden halt, snowy head cocked to the right. "I'll hold the flashlight. You go in."

Her companion's heart fluttered with fear. There had been suspicion in those words, and no attempt had been made to disguise it. She thought of the serrated steak knife hidden up the left sleeve of her jacket, and wondered in a moment of panic if she should pull it out and use it right now. But she meekly handed over the flashlight instead, avoiding the old woman's piercing black eyes, then stepped in front of her to the crypt's door and from one of her jacket pockets pulled a large silver ring holding one key.

"This isn't how it was to have happened," the old woman said, her feeble voice quickly carried away by the violent wind threatening to tumble her over. She muttered something else, but it was drowned out by the frantic rustling of leaves.

Having inserted and twisted the key, her companion reluctantly faced her, wincing in the upturned glare of the flashlight's beam. "How else would you explain it?"

"You still haven't explained why you came to look in the first place," the old woman countered, fighting to keep her balance.

"I told you, I was just curious."

"Curious." A skeptical smile touched the old woman's

puckered mouth. "Well go on, open the door before this goddamn wind blows me away."

If only it would, the other woman thought. Pushing on the crypt's creaking metal door, the tip of the concealed steak knife pricked her wrist. With the sharp pain flashed a vision of blood—bright crimson soaking into dark, dank earth. The grave she'd dug two hours earlier, shortly after sundown, was waiting less than a dozen yards from where they stood.

"Give me the key," the old woman suddenly demanded, holding out a bony hand.

The other quickly turned, eyes filled with alarm. "What for?" she asked in a tremulous voice, but she already knew the answer; the old woman intended to lock her inside the crypt and leave her to slowly die. So she did know; there was no question about it now. Odd that she would resort to something like this, considering what she could do. But that was hardly important. All that mattered at the moment was the knife hidden in her jacket sleeve and its purpose for being there. She began working it into her left palm as inconspicuously as possible.

The old woman thrust her hand out farther. "The key," she repeated, her words punctuated by another jolting thunderclap. A split second later the sky above them was momentarily brightened by a long, jagged spear of lightning that revealed the vengeful intent written in her expression.

"No." The other woman clutched the wooden handle of the steak knife and summoned all the courage she possessed, which had never been very much or she would have done this long ago. "I can't let you do it. Not this."

The flashlight beam wavered as the older woman suddenly began to laugh, a chilling sound coming from her, as always. "You ignorant fool! There's nothing you can do to stop it. Haven't you heard, where there's a will there's a way? Or that necessity is the mother of invention?" More laughter spilled from her lips, but her mirth was abruptly terminated by the knife blade's swift and deep introduction to her throat. The flashlight fell to the ground and she stumbled backward, mouth opening wide to issue a scream that came out as a strangled gurgle. The next moment the sky seemed to split in two as a deafening crack of thunder ripped through it, the accompanying flash of lightning illuminating her panicked attempt to pull out the knife. When she succeeded, a thick stream of blood spouted from the hole, spraying the face of her advancing attacker. Grimacing at the unappreciated taste of salty-sweet copper, the other woman grabbed the knife away from her and shoved her to the ground, falling upon her to plunge it again, this time deep into her left eye socket, assuming the wound would be instantly mortal, an end to both the will and the way. Blood surged to fill the sunken cavity, but the old woman continued to struggle, reaching up to claw whatever flesh her long yellowed fingernails could find.

"Die, damn you!" the other screamed, hammering the knife's end with the palm of her hand, driving it in up to the hilt. She began to fear that the old woman would survive no matter what she did, a fear that was reinforced by the inexplicable burst of strength in the bony, withered arms that fought to throw her off. With the fallen flashlight's beam aimed in their direction, she could see steam rising from the bloody throat wound that rhythmically opened and closed like a fish's gill, systematically vomiting another gout of blood with each expelled steamy breath. Another nerve-jarring crack of thunder tore across the sky, and seconds later a punishing rain began to fall. Soon afterward the old woman's body finally went limp, and the hole in her throat closed for the last time.

Weeping with relief, the other slowly rose to her feet and began dragging the body toward the grave she'd prepared, glancing back several times at the crypt's open door. *Where there's a will there's a way.* God forbid it in this case.

She rolled the corpse into the narrow three-foot grave, hearing the rattle of bones, then reluctantly returned through the driving rain to the crypt for the shovel she'd hidden inside it. She picked up the flashlight before going in, shining it around the decrepit graveyard with renewed apprehension. The beam cast long shadows behind the upright markers, and suddenly she thought she saw one of the shadows move in a way that couldn't be explained by her handling of the flashlight. Stopping abruptly in her tracks, she stood with her eyes glued to the spot, heart thudding with dread, until a raccoon emerged from behind the stone and scurried into the nearest trees. Releasing the breath she was holding, she proceeded to the crypt and quickly retrieved the shovel, then closed and locked the door. A part of her felt triumphant, but a dark inner voice reminded her that a celebration tonight would be premature. She couldn't be sure for several days yet, and those days were certain to be the longest of her life.

Soaked to the skin, she put the flashlight down near the mouth of the grave and bent to fill the shovel with dirt when she again heard the rattle of bones. She froze, terror raising gooseflesh over her entire body in spite of her silent insistence that the sound had been produced by nothing more than muscle reflex. But in the beam of light directed toward the grave, she saw a muddy hand appear, groping at the edge. For a moment she thought she was going to faint, and came very close to doing so when the old woman's body sat up, white hair pasted to her scalp, rain mixed with blood coursing down the crevices in her hollow left cheek. Her right eye was open and focused accusingly on the woman standing above her, whose automatic reaction was to dump her load of dirt and swing the shovel at the old woman's face. The impact knocked her back into the grave with a loud crunch of cartilage, and before she could get up again, the blade of the shovel was frantically positioned under her wattled chin.

Gritting her teeth, her mind filled with an unvented scream, the other woman placed her right foot on the back of the blade and thrust downward. The thin flesh parted easily enough, but she had to use all of her weight to break through the spine. With a final jump the metal tip burrowed into dirt on the other side, and the head rolled forward into the shovel. She quickly tossed it out, noting with horror when it landed faceup that the lips were curved in a hideous smile.

Shivering uncontrollably, working like a madwoman with much more energy than she normally possessed, she filled the grave, deciding just before she left to say a few words over it.

"Go to Hell, Mother."

One

Spiro Guenther ambled down the sidewalk in his typical leaning gait, eyes focused on the ground, arms pressed tightly to his sides. In one hand he carried a canvas bag weighted with school books; the other was clenched into a meaningless fist. The sharp curvature of his spine near the base of his skull robbed him of three inches in height, but Spiro didn't need to be any taller; even with his physical defect, he measured six feet, four inches, and at 265 pounds outsized most of the men in Sharon Valley.

He had turned seventeen the previous July. He was labeled a freak, monster, moron, dumb ox, and dozens of other derogatory titles, and he accepted them all bitterly. He'd seen himself in mirrors, in storefront windows, in the shocked stares of other human beings. So much for his outer qualities; his inner ones were just as defective. No matter how hard he'd tried in school, he'd always gotten low scores, so as he grew older his mind tended to navigate toward other, "inappropriate" subjects while lectures were being given. Seventeen years old and he was still a sophomore in high school. Still, mournfully, a virgin. Still and always the outsider.

He'd learned to live with the taunting; it had started back in the second grade. Had he been a bully, or possessed of the slightest bit of a temper, his size might have earned him respect, but it didn't take kids very long to figure out Spiro could quite easily be pushed around. Therefore his size only made him a bigger and better target, for rocks, spitballs, pennies; whatever was available for his tormentors to throw. They in turn suffered only in his mind.

Spiro's straight, sandy-blond hair was kept extremely short by his middle-aged mother, the one person on earth who might have loved him but never did, and despised him, perhaps, even more than the rest because of his reflection on her. Her husband, a policeman who had died in the line of duty—he'd stepped out to issue a speeding citation and was struck from behind by a passing truck—did so before learning the terrible truth about his infant son. The terrible truth: the German measles his wife had contracted during her pregnancy had caused encephalitis in the spinal cord and brain of her unborn child, and although the resulting retardation was not as severe as it might have been, Spiro was undeniably damaged. Being unable to accept responsibility for the tragedy, Bertha externalized her guilt, transformed it into anger and eventually hatred, which she directed at the living reminder of fate's abject cruelty.

Retarded. Tardo. Spiro wondered how many times those scorching words had been applied to him. Once for each star in the sky, he decided on his eleventh birthday. And he'd heard them a million more times since then.

But today was a special day, and he lumbered along a little faster than usual. Sam Weaver, the mail carrier and only person in Sharon Valley besides Spiro's English teacher, Ellen Callahan, who treated him like a human being, had promised a surprise would be waiting when he got home from school that day. Spiro had thought of little else since his waking moment, and his daydreaming in history class had earned him a half hour detention with the vice-principal. But Spiro hadn't really minded the extension of his wait; he'd been saved from his usual dose of after-school abuse.

As he turned onto his block he looked up, his attention captured by a large orange and white truck parked in the drive next door to his house. The new neighbors had been expected for over a week; the For Sale sign in the front yard had been removed Tuesday before last. This was Thursday, meaning, for Spiro, only one more day before the weekend—two days of cherished, isolated freedom. On the weekends, he would lock himself away in his small dusty bedroom, where he would intermittently work on his model airplane and draw dirty pictures.

He avoided looking at the people who were carrying items from the moving van to the house. People didn't like to make eye contact with him anyway; it seemed to make them extremely uncomfortable, for it was hard for them to conceal all the revulsion they felt, assuming they were polite enough to even try. Any smiles ever offered Spiro were brief and wavering, a thin mask of friendliness pulled over a gape of horror. Oh yes, he was an ugly one too. Hideously ugly, so that his classmates could say things like, "Your mother's doctors should have tossed you away and kept the afterbirth," and Spiro knew as well as they that he had no room to argue. Nature had cheated him out of everything but strength, and the power of imagination with which he constructed a tolerable fantasy world. Wary, silent passersby were unaware of the compliments he could quite clearly hear them say to him. His enemies begged for forgiveness. His mother sang sweet lullabies to him in the dead of night.

A real voice was calling to him now, saying "Hi there" with a Texan accent; the greeting came out as "Hah thair." Spiro continued up his sidewalk and paid no attention to it; his mind was again centered on the surprise promised by Sam. Besides, greetings were usually followed by scathing insults, and unless cornered, Spiro didn't hang around to hear them out. No reason he should stop to hear them begin.

"Hey, you stuck up or somethin'?"

He paused on the bottom porch step and tried to see who was talking without turning his head. He could tell it was a girl; she was standing in front of the truck next door, near the edge of the driveway, a blue and yellow blur with hands placed challengingly on her hips. Spiro was tempted to turn and get a better look even though it would cost him, he was sure, another ounce of his muddy pool of self-esteem, but a scratching noise on his right caused him to turn the other way. There was a large cardboard box on the ground beside the porch. His heart

9

leapt with excitement; Sam's surprise was in the box. Spiro dropped the canvas bag and scrambled around the peeling support pillar supporting the eave, forgetting about the girl next door. He knelt beside the box and eagerly opened the flaps.

Inside was exactly what he had fervently hoped for. His thick, moist lips pulled back into a huge grin, Spiro reached into the box and lifted out the squirming brown and black puppy. As he cradled it to his chest, accepting the puppy's affectionate licks on his chin, the girl's voice spoke again, this time directly behind him: "Hey, what'cha got there? A puppy?"

Spiro clumsily turned around and gaped openly at the fair-complected face upon which a smile, seemingly void of fraudulence, was planted around a row of perfect white teeth. She squatted down and said, "He's so cute! May I hold him?"

Spiro was reluctant to release his new treasure, but it wasn't his nature to deny requests made of him. His lack of assertiveness made him the perfect clown, the jester marionette that required no strings. *Pick up the pennies, Spiro! Hey Tardo, jump up and down! Go give Vickie Sebring a kiss; she's dying to go out with you, Ape Face!* No matter how degrading the order, he would typically do exactly as he was told. He handed the puppy over, eyes downcast.

The girl proceeded to delight herself with the animated bundle of fur, rubbing its face against hers like a powder puff, kissing its forehead, giggling as the tiny pink tongue lapped out to return the amity. After a few minutes she said without looking up, "My name is Lana; I'm your new neighbor. What's your name?"

Spiro wondered if the question was directed at him or the pup. He glanced up at the girl's face, her sculptured features framed by a halo of white-blond hair. Her wide blue eyes, now lifted to meet his, showed no hint of the anticipated abhorrence. "My—My name?" he stammered.

The girl rolled her eyes, playfully muzzling the puppy with a delicate hand. "Yeah, so who else would I be talkin' to?"

Spiro impulsively looked around. "Nobody, I guess." He was already aching to hold his new pet again; why didn't the girl with the strange accent get her teasing over with and leave him alone? "Can I have him back now?" He held out his massive hands in a pleading gesture.

"Soon as you tell me your name," Lana said firmly. She sat down Indian-style and nestled the pup between her legs.

Spiro's eyes bulged slightly; she was wearing a short yellow skirt, and the way she was sitting allowed him a brief view of her lacy white panties. The puppy didn't cover them completely, and if the girl was aware of it, she didn't seem to care. Spiro memorized the exhibition and then turned his head. "Spiro. Hardly no one calls me that, though."

"What do they call you?"

Spiro winced. "Tardo, mos'ly. Stuff like that." His eyes stole another peek at the tantalizing view being offered him; Lana was too busy petting the puppy to notice.

She asked innocently, "Tardo . . . ? What kinda name is that?"

"I'm . . . slow. It means retarded," he admitted with a heavy sigh. He reached again for his precious bundle, keeping his gaze averted when the girl handed it back. He could well imagine what she might do to him if she caught him taking advantage of her position. Yet, it was equally easy for him to creatively interpret the situation as a direct come-on, to hear her whisper softly, though her lips were sealed, *Would you like to touch me, Spiro . . . ?*

The puppy began to whimper. "I'm going to name him Sam," Spiro declared with a loose smile, his secret safe and sweet within him. He could hardly wait to sit at his desk tonight with paper and pencil.

"People sure can be assholes," Lana stated flatly as she rose to her feet. "Well, don't you pay any mind to that crap, Spiro. Just tell 'em, 'I know you are but what am I!' No matter what they say. They'll get mad an' give up sooner or later. Well, see ya. I gotta get back to work."

Spiro watched her walk back to her own property and disappear behind the truck, astounded that a girl—

especially such a pretty one—should be so nice to him. It had never happened before, and he didn't know quite what to think of it. He stretched his bulky frame out on the ground to play with Sam, but the illicit memory of seeing between the girl's legs lingered to distract him from fully enjoying the experience.

Two

In the northern foothills surrounding Sharon Valley, South Dakota, was a development called Cameron Estates, where the wealthy and influential of the community lived in homes of quiet elegance, most of them on three- to five-acre tracts of land surrounded by lodgepole pine, aspen, and spruce trees. A quarter mile west of this development was Beacon Hill, the highest point overlooking the bedroom community, and the site of a graveyard with some stones dating back as far as the eighteenth century.

In the center of the graveyard was a white marble tomb. The engraving on the upper front wall announced the silent inhabitants as Myrantha and Nathaniel Ober, both dead at the age of thirty on October 31 almost seventy years earlier. The fact that they had died together on All Hallows' Eve, or Halloween night, gave rise to diverse speculations about the couple, which were ritualistically repeated during adolescent slumber parties, or around the dancing flames of a midnight campfire made by Boy Scout troops roughing it in the "wilderness."

There were presumably no Obers left in Sharon Valley to give denial or verification to any of these speculations, but as time had not yet completely erased all traces of their existence, neither had it totally expelled the basic truth from which legend had been spawned. One remaining link was eighty-year-old Jasmine Annabell Colter, who claimed to have known the Obers' daughter, Morganna. But it wasn't until after Jasmine had been placed in a nursing home that she began to insist—and quite vehemently—that Morganna had been a witch from a long line of black art practioners, and thus her rantings were, for the most part, dismissed as senile fantasy. But not by her granddaughter Marla Mingee and her best friend, Nancy Snell.

Marla and Nancy were seniors at Sharon Valley High, and both looked forward to the day they would leave Sharon Valley for college; both had been accepted at Princeton, much to their parents' delight. But before embarking on their scholarly adventure, they conspired to do what apparently no one before them had dared: they planned to break into the tomb on Beacon Hill and open the coffins of Myrantha and Nathaniel Ober. If there were any secrets to be disclosed about the mysterious couple, that would be the sure-fire way to find them out. On the following Saturday night a substantial moon was promised, and Nancy had decided they'd kept themselves in suspense long enough. Marla had agreed, though somewhat reluctantly. The deed would be done then, only six days from the seventieth anniversary of the Obers' death.

The two friends, having successfully climbed the social ladder during junior high school, enjoyed the fringe benefits of their popularity, one of which was the slack they were allowed by their peers for delinquent behavior —in their case delinquent usually meaning mild obnoxiousness and brattish behavior designed to draw giggles from their friends. They had three classes together, which included second-year algebra during their last period. It was taught by Albert Montgomery, a sour-faced, balding, potbellied man in his early fifties who had written the book on teacher burnout. What Albert liked about his profession he could write on the back of a postage stamp; what he liked about teenagers he could write on the head of a pin. He was known as Dr. Doom to the majority of his students, and being aware of the nickname, made all the more effort to live up to it. His homework assignments went beyond cruel and unusual punishment—rumors persisted that they were originally dictated in Hell—and God help the kid who came to

14

class tardy or unprepared, or who was caught talking, passing notes, or committing any other infraction of Montgomery's Rules and Regulations for the Ideal Student, which he listed on the blackboard at the beginning of every semester and made his students copy. Marla and Nancy were convinced he simply changed the name on a pamphlet for the Hitler Youth faction.

Montgomery would have liked nothing more than to send Marla and Nancy to the gas chamber. But for their obstinate habit of passing notes to each other in class and giggling like inebriated chipmunks, he had to settle for sentencing them to longer periods of detention in combination with forcing them to grade his papers, relieving him of a considerable amount of the detested duty. And ah, yes, the homework. Tons upon tons of it, due in an impossible amount of time, though for some irritating reason they always got it done. Montgomery had his suspicions, but he couldn't prove anything, so he had to accept what they turned in as their own work.

It was a quarter to five that Thursday when they finally finished grading the tests he had given them. Nancy, the more dominant and strong-willed of the two, slapped the thick bundle of papers on Montgomery's desk and asked with her usual air of insolence, "Can we go now, Mr. Montgomery?"

Albert looked up from his book of poetry and studied the slightly plump, dark-headed girl with deep-set eyes, pug nose, and bee-stung lips which were always glistening with tintless gloss. "Sit down, Miss Snell. There is something I'd like to discuss with you two before I let you go." Beneath the patience in his voice ran a current of sweltering hostility, which could always be detected when he was speaking to an adolescent. It didn't intimidate Nancy. Very little did.

"Listen, if it's about that note—"

"I told you to sit down," Montgomery repeated sternly, gritting his teeth.

Marla tittered nervously as Nancy returned to her seat beside her on the front row, making a face Montgomery couldn't see. Marla and Nancy could have been sisters, with the same raven hair and rounded noses, but Marla was a good fifteen pounds lighter than Nancy, and her lips were on the thin side. High cheekbones hinted of Indian ancestry.

Montgomery opened his top desk drawer and removed a folded piece of notebook paper. He opened it and frowned as he read for the second time what had been written on it. Normally when he caught students passing notes he would force them to write their messages on the blackboard for the purpose of humiliating them in front of the entire class—which worked rather well on the less popular kids—but in this case the tactic would have backfired on him. He put the note down and glared intensely at Nancy, her smug expression doing little to dilute his rage. "Tell me, Miss Snell . . . why the preoccupation with my sex life?"

Marla clamped a hand over her mouth to keep from bursting into hysterical laughter, but Nancy had no trouble at all in keeping a poker face. She casually flipped back a lock of her shoulder-length hair, her chestnut eyes locked fearlessly into her teacher's. "I was just wondering, Mr. Montgomery, if the reason you're so crabby all the time is that you don't ever get any."

Albert, who was divorced and could barely remember his last sexual encounter—with a partner; there was always the Vaseline jar and his left hand—felt his cheeks redden; what had he hoped to accomplish with this inane confrontation? He said tersely, "The reason I'm so . . . as you say, crabby all the time, Miss Snell, is because I have to tolerate the likes of you year after year. What I'd like to know is why you and Miss Mingee seem so bent on setting the world record for being insufferable little monsters?"

Marla snickered derisively behind her hand; Nancy simply cracked a wry grin and answered flippantly, "I didn't know there was a world record for that."

Montgomery stood up, gripping the edge of his desk, his knuckles turning white. "I've had quite enough of you two," he spat, glowering at them with dark intensity. "And I'm sure you realize what flunking this class would mean to you. It would mean summer school, which I also teach, by the way—and if you fail summer school, you won't have the required credits to graduate and therefore

16

go on to college. Do I make myself clear? One more incident—just one—and you can both look forward to receiving F's on your report cards."

Marla dropped her hand and threw a sober glance at Nancy. Marla's father, Harold Mingee, was one of the three attorneys in Sharon Valley, and she felt free to hurl this fact in the face of a variety of dangers, including threats from teachers. She countered Montgomery's flagrantly unethical ultimatum with, "You can't flunk us for an attitude problem, sir. We make the grades. You try something like that and my dad will see you in court."

"I'll see both of you in the principal's office first thing tomorrow morning!" Montgomery thundered, incensed at the calling of his bluff. "We'll see if a three-day suspension won't do something about your attitude problem! Now get out of here!"

He turned his back to them and began to viciously swipe off the equations on the blackboard with an unclapped eraser, producing a thick cloud of chalk dust which made him sneeze like a trumpet.

The girls angrily gathered their books and homework assignments, pausing to glare daggers into Albert's back before leaving. Nancy silently reached over and swiped his favorite writing tool, a gold-plated fountain pen, from the holder on his desk and stuffed it into her purse. Satisfied with her small act of defiance, she marched ahead of Marla from the room and slammed the door behind them so fiercely that the glass in the long narrow window shattered. Giggling, they ran down the wide-tiled corridor, empty but for Harry Bellows, the custodian, who leaned on his mop handle and watched their fleeing figures with disgust.

Outside the building, in the student parking area, they found Marla's boyfriend, Dennis Bloom, lounging against the driver's door of his blue '83 Monte Carlo, which was parked beside the new cherry-red Cutlass Marla's father had purchased for her sixteenth birthday. Dennis's size and build marked him as a linebacker for the football team, which he probably would have been if his grades hadn't been so deplorable. He had straight, dark brown hair which he wore short on the sides and top, down to his shoulders in back. His face had a false look of maturity, his hazel eyes always suggesting possession of some arcane philosophy.

Dennis grinned as the two girls approached. "Montgomery again, eh? I was beginning to wonder if he was going to keep you all night."

"That bastard," Nancy seethed. "He's going to try to get us suspended tomorrow for three days. If he does, my mom will have a shit fit."

"I'll probably lose my allowance for a whole month," Marla lamented. "Or worse—I'll get my phone disconnected. Rick brought two D's home on his report card the first quarter, and I thought Dad was going to tear his head off and stuff the rest of him down the garbage disposal. He doesn't go berserk very often, but when he does—look out. That damn Montgomery! I'd like to stuff him down a disposal . . . he even threatened to flunk us if we broke any more of his stupid rules."

Dennis took a cigarette from his jacket pocket and lit it, with some difficulty due to the cool gusts of wind whipping around them. "Well, what did you do this time?" he asked finally through a belch of smoke.

"Nothing worth getting suspended over," Marla snapped, irritated that Dennis hadn't offered to relieve her of her burden of books. "Nancy slipped me a note is all."

"It was a bad one for him to catch, though," Nancy added, smiling at the memory of Albert's face when he'd first read it. "I asked her when she thought he'd last had a piece of ass."

Dennis nearly choked. "Jesus—he caught you with that?"

Marla sighed. "What I wrote back was even worse. I said if he'd ever had any at all it was from eating a rump roast. I also mentioned something about his playing pocket pool. He does it all the time, the slimy pervert. Uh, these books are getting heavier by the second, Dennis."

Dennis ignored the hint, musing how stupid the two girls were for passing comments like that in writing, and right under the nose of the man those comments pertained to, but he knew better than to say so. Even though he disliked Montgomery as much as anyone else, he thought the actions of his steady and her friend were deserving of whatever punishment was dished out. Such idiocy begged for retribution. "Well, you wanna go to the drive-in for a Coke?" he asked.

Marla was thoroughly peeved at his apparent lack of concern over their dilemma, in addition to the fact he'd still made no move to take her books, even after being slapped with such a strong hint. "We don't have time for a Coke—the jerk gave us enough homework to keep us busy until the year 2000," she responded coldly, and added with an extra dose of venom, "As if you really care."

"So when have you ever done your own homework?" Dennis shot back accusingly, readily on the defensive whenever anyone spoke to him in less than magnanimous tones. Being his girlfriend didn't give Marla any special privilege to slide. "I thought you always paid that geek friend of your brother's to do your homework for you."

Marla's anger deepened. "He said he wasn't going to do it anymore."

"Well, that's too, too bad," Dennis retorted with mock empathy.

"It sure is," Marla shot back, moving past Nancy to get to the driver's side of her Cutlass. "Too bad for you, because obviously I'll be too busy to see you this weekend. And if I get suspended, you'll be lucky if you ever see me again!"

Dennis brayed laughter. "Lucky? You think my life's gonna end if I can't see you? Don't bet on it." He tossed the remainder of his cigarette down on the gravel and jerked his car door open, angry at himself for waiting almost two hours on such a spoiled, conceited ingrate. Moments later he was blasting out of the parking lot, leaving Marla and Nancy behind in a cloud of gravel dust. Marla shot him the finger before getting in her own car, and as soon as she'd leaned over to unlock the passenger door for Nancy, she turned on her stereo—the best that money could buy, and the most important feature of the car, in her opinion—and cranked it up full blast.

Nancy got in and grimaced. "Do you have to turn it up

so loud?" she yelled over the reverberating sound of electric guitars.

Marla rammed the key in the ignition and fired up the engine, gunning it several times for effect. Like her father, she rarely lost her temper, but when she did . . ."As a matter of fact, *I do!*" she yelled back.

They were two blocks from Nancy's house on East Pine Drive before she finally turned the radio down low enough to allow conversation, having convinced herself that she didn't care whether or not Dennis was even alive, and that Montgomery's attempt to get her and Nancy expelled from school could prove to be the worst mistake he'd ever made. After hearing the embellished story she was thinking of later telling her father, he would get on the phone and call his good friend Judge Campbell, who in turn would have a little chat with his brother, the principal of Sharon Valley High. Montgomery would be damn lucky if he didn't lose his job.

She smiled at Nancy. "We could have that dick Montgomery over a barrel if we wanted to. If we tell the same story."

Nancy's eyes widened. "Same story? What are you talking about?"

"What do you think I'm talking about? He kept us after school for two hours. We could say he tried to talk us into doing him . . . certain favors. And if we really want to hang him, we can say that he succeeded."

They were in front of Nancy's house; Marla pulled up to the curb and parked. Nancy was eyeing her friend with genuine admiration. "You're a genius, Marla. We could. We could get the bastard fired. We'd be heroes."

"My dad would kill him," Marla mused, creating the entire scenario in her mind to search for any possible defects in the plan. Harold Mingee's reaction would be nothing less than explosive. Yet there was a small but dangerous hitch . . . Dennis. He knew the truth, and since he was mad at her, there existed the possibility of his blowing the charade. Also, now that she really thought about it, she didn't know for certain if her and Nancy's popularity would survive the fire of such a scandal; some things were acceptable, some weren't, and being linked with the likes of Dr. Doom in a sexual manner definitely wouldn't be. The last thing they'd want would be the rest of the seniors to start calling them Dr. Doom's whores. She quickly began to backpeddle.

"Well, maybe I should just call Montgomery at home tonight and tell him we will do that if he takes us to Greer's office in the morning. If he buys the threat, that'll take care of our problem without creating any new ones. I just realized a thing like that could really get out of hand. I think we could do without the additional hassle."

Nancy expelled a long breath, a mixture of anger and disappointment. "I should've known you'd back down. You always talk big, but when the curtain goes up, your butt is nowhere on stage. I'll bet you even chicken out of going to the graveyard Saturday night . . . but I tell you what: if you do, then I'll just go by myself. And I, Nancy Snell, will be the most famous person at Sharon Valley High."

Marla gasped. "Hey, we can't tell anyone about that! I'm serious, Nan. You know how much trouble we could get into for breaking into a tomb? Plenty, I promise you. Don't be stupid."

"I can't even tell Jay?" Nancy pouted, thinking how impressed her boyfriend would be. "What trouble can we get into anyway, with your dad a lawyer and the judge his hunting buddy? Oh my. We might get out little hands spanked, but that would be about the extent of it. What fun is it going to be if nobody else knows we did it? You are going to back out, aren't you? I knew it. Call me stupid, but at least I'm not a chickenshit. If you won't even try to get Montgomery fired, I know you won't go through with something like that."

"I'm not backing out of it," Marla insisted heatedly, qualifying her statement with, "out of going to the graveyard, I mean." Nancy, in her opinion, was far too impulsive, and she had a bad habit of doing before thinking, which was the cause of many of their troubles. Stupidity was Nancy's middle name, whether she admitted it or not. Marla wasn't afraid to do anything, but she couldn't just throw all precaution to the wind, unless of course the consequences of getting caught were minimal. Most people found themselves in over their heads, she knew, because they acted on plans that had only been hatched, not carefully thought out. Just because she was careful didn't mean she was a chickenshit.

"If it ever got back to my dad, he'd kill me, Nancy. Don't you know how embarrassing that would be to him? I promise I'm not going to back out, but it would really be a stupid move on our part to let anyone else know about this. We're doing it for us, for our own curiosity. We'll find out things—maybe—that nobody else will ever know. Isn't that enough for you? And as for Montgomery, I would love to see that jerk get fired, or run over by a Mack truck, for that matter, but you're not looking down the road at what could happen. I know it was my idea, but it was a bad one and I should have just kept my mouth shut until I thought it through. If we say he actually did something, they might make us get physicals, in which case they'd find out we lied. They might make us all take lie detector tests, and how's it going to look when Montgomery passes with flying colors and our graphs look like the Grand Tetons? That's what it would boil down to—our word against his. This thing could backfire on us really bad. I think the best we can do is try to bluff him."

Nancy shrugged, unable, as usual, to defy Marla's logic. "I guess you're right. Well, before I go, I meant to ask you . . . did Stevie really say he wasn't going to do your homework anymore? We won't have time to go to the bathroom this weekend if we have to do all this crap Doom assigned us. Jay sure won't help me. But if we get suspended, I guess it won't matter if we get it done or not."

"I just told Dennis that, since he was acting like such a turd." Marla smiled. "For a dollar an hour, Stevie will do anything I tell him. Maybe everything will work out. It sure as hell better. If we do end up getting suspended, I wonder if there's some way we could keep our parents from finding out. If the school just sends a notice in the mail or something, we could maybe snatch it out before they see it. But if they make a phone call, I guess we're nailed. We'd better prepare to meet our doom."

Nancy's expression turned sour. "Not me, M and M. If worse comes to worse, I'll just run away for a day or two.

My folks would be so glad to see me when I came home, they'd forget about punishing me." She opened the passenger door and got out, giving Marla a brief wave as she headed up the sidewalk in front of her house, a brown clapboard with white trim. Nancy's father was a watch and jewelry repairman, and had transformed the garage into his shop. His meager income dictated that the Snells had to live on the eastern side of the valley, where the homes were smaller and older and generally run-down. Nancy's mother worked, but only as a volunteer at the small local hospital. It was the inheritance Nancy had gotten from her maternal grandparents that would soon allow her to walk the halls of Princeton.

Marla tapped her horn and drove away, knowing exactly where Nancy was planning to hide out if worse came to worst, and wondering what would happen if on top of getting suspended she was caught harboring a fugitive from parental justice.

Pamela Mingee, Marla's mother, nodded at the RN behind the nurse's station as she turned the corner of the nursing home lobby. She walked, as always, with her back straight and her chin slightly uplifted. A single glance told anyone who looked at her that she was a woman of class who occupied an enviable niche in society. No K mart fashions for this one; only the best could be good enough, even if that meant a shopping trip to Paris. Nature had apparently foreseen her elevated station in life and accordingly granted her a face and complexion worthy of the finest makeup and jewelry, and similarly a full head of glossy black hair which demanded carefully maintained coiffures in the latest styles.

"She's had a pretty bad day," the nurse warned Pamela with a frown. "Threw her oatmeal on the wall this morning, cursing a blue streak at someone who wasn't there. We finally got her calmed down, but she started up again this afternoon. Thought you'd better know."

Cold fingers of sorrow clutched around Pamela's heart, and she almost changed her mind about making the visit. Seeing her mother behave in such a manner was almost more than she could take. "What's she upset about this time?" she asked wearily. "It's not the alien thing again, is it?"

On several occasions during the past few months, Jasmine Colter had sworn that men from outer space had been talking to her through her radio and were threatening to come get her. Pamela had sought to end the problem by taking the radio away, but that only served to transfer the alien signals to the television set. Pamela gave up; she imagined that even in a completely bare room her mother would manage to "hear" strange messages, through the walls if nothing else.

The nurse, Meg Boyd, shook her head. "No, it's not that . . . she's back on Morganna Ober again. Said she's been coming to her room all dressed in black and wearing a witch's hat, trying to make her drink bat's blood."

Tears sprang to Pamela's eyes; the nurse saw them and realized how callous she'd been, how careless of the woman's feelings; Jasmine was, after all, her mother. "Oh, I'm so sorry, Mrs. Mingee! Lord, I have such a big mouth sometimes. I understand how upsetting this is; really, I do. I went through pretty much the same thing with my father. After being retired from the postal service for twenty years, he all of a sudden thought he was back on the job, and we'd catch him going up and down the street sticking Mama's recipes in people's mailboxes. I guess I was just thinking it would be better if you were prepared. Try not to take it so hard, dear. It's just part of growing old." Behind the thick round lenses framed in pink her eyes were full of sympathy.

Pamela nodded and swallowed the lump in her throat, an unbidden vision of herself in a nursing home one day causing her to shudder slightly. She decided to go on to her mother's room; another part of growing old shouldn't be getting deserted by your own children. Pamela's two older brothers, now living in other states, hadn't been back to visit their mother in over two years.

Jasmine was propped up on her pillows, her gnarled hands clutching tightly to the railing on her bed although she appeared to be asleep. She looked so tiny and frail to her daughter; it seemed that time had withered the once-robust woman away to almost nothing, yet none of her former spunk and surprisingly little of her strength had been lost with age. A broken hip, stubbornly refusing to mend, had made her a prisoner of her own body, but her mind and mouth remained unquenchably active. Pamela stepped quietly into the anticeptic-smelling room and whispered softly, "Mama?"

The old woman's faded blue eyes flew open. "Close the door!" she rasped desperately. "Hurry, close the door before she gets in! I can hear her coming!"

"Don't get upset, Mama; I'll close the door." Pamela released the stop at the base of the door and closed it just as one of the nurse's aides walked by. Was that who her mother had feared would come in? No, she was talking about Morganna again. Morganna, the wicked witch of Sharon Valley.

Pamela felt her chest tighten as she walked toward the bed and sat in the green vinyl chair next to it. "How do you feel today, Mama?"

"Did you lock the door? Did you lock it?" Jasmine shrilled hoarsely, spraying spittle on her daughter's arm.

"Yes, I locked it," Pamela lied, fighting to keep her voice light. "Just relax, Mama. You're perfectly safe."

"No, she's going to get me. Morganna's going to come back and pull me right into—oh look, Pammie, a butterfly."

Pamela glanced around the room. There was, of course, no butterfly. Her mother appeared calm for a moment, watching the insect only her eyes could see. But it must have disappeared, because the look of alarm returned and she whispered frantically, "She told me never to tell her secret, but I'm a'tellin' it, and I just know she's not gonna stand for that." Her withered hands clutched at the covers, the large blue veins webbed on their surfaces protruding more than usual in her state of excitement. "She's a witch, I tell you! They were all witches," she continued, shaking her head. "Took Sarah Kennedy's baby and sacrificed it to the Devil. Drank its blood . . ."

Pamela covered her face with her hands. "Oh Mama, please. Don't . . ."

"You think they done that for nothing?" her mother

asked despairingly, wagging her finger at Pamela's chest. "You think that was the end of it when they—"

"That was the end of it, Mother. That was a long time ago. It's over," Pamela said, lowering her hands to reveal the tear tracks etched in her makeup. Her voice cracked with strain. "Please just forget about it. Everyone else has."

"Everybody else didn't get befriended by Morganna Ober," Jasmine said stubbornly, her toothless lips laboring to form the correct sounds. "Only me, but I couldn't tell you why. I was afraid, but so help me God A'mighty, I couldn't tell her to leave me alone. I couldn't, Pammie. I'ze afraid of what she'd do to me if I got her mad. I knew what she could do. I never brung up what happened on the hill that night, but she said to me one day that her mother'd had the consumption, and she couldn't get her body rid of it. That's what I figure that devilment they done was all about. Little Jeremy's life in exchange for hers . . ."

Pamela burst into loud sobs. "Stop it! I can't stand to hear any more of this! There are no such things as witches, Mother. That's just a bunch of old silly superstition. Do you hear me? Myrantha and Nathaniel Ober have been dead for seventy years, and Morganna . . . just forget about her. She doesn't even live in this town anymore. And she hasn't been coming to see you . . . my God, she's at least as old as you are, and probably in a wheelchair. She can't harm you, Mama. What the Obers did has nothing to do with you or me or anything else. Not then, today, or ever. That's all in the past."

"Oh no, Pammie, you're wrong about that," Jasmine sputtered, her ancient heart beating with dread. "Myrantha never got what she paid for, and I—"

"I'm sorry, Mama, I have to go." Pamela stumbled from her chair and rushed from the room, the rantings of her senile mother following her down the hallway.

Three

Lana sprawled out on the living room carpet to rest, and was soon joined by her mother, who preferred the couch, and her twelve-year-old brother Luke. All their possessions were now in the new house, but most of the boxes still needed to be unpacked, the contents put away. No one seemed exactly anxious to jump into the chore.

"I'm so thirsty," Lana croaked. "I'd give about anything for a nice cold Coke."

"Your stereo?" Luke asked hopefully. "I'll go out and get you one if you'll gimme your stereo." His impish face cracked into a wide grin, and with his hair, also blond, cowlicked upward in back, he reminded her of Dennis the Menace. Accent on Menace.

"Oh shut up, you little creep."

"Lana . . ."

"Sorry, Mom."

"I could use a Coke myself," Carol Bremmers sighed, closing her eyes to erase the view of the catastrophe surrounding her. "But I doubt at this point I could even walk out to the car. Bet I wake up stiff as a board tomorrow."

Luke grinned impishly. "Good. Then we won't have to get enrolled in school."

"No such luck, young man. Tomorrow you get enrolled and Monday you start. This isn't a vacation," Carol reminded her twelve-year-old son, who resembled his father so much she sometimes found it painful to look at him. On the other hand Lana had taken after her, and up until the last five years or so they had frequently been mistaken as sisters.

He groaned in protest, but knew there was no escape from the dreaded fate. The fact that he was actually required by law to attend school appalled him.

"I feel so sorry for that guy next door," Lana said, stretching her tired, achy muscles. "I wonder if he goes to my school. He told me all the kids call him Tardo."

Luke cracked up. "Tardo? What, is he retarded or somethin'?"

"Not as much as you, bird brain."

Carol quickly reached the point of exasperation; her children's constant bickering at times had her picturing a noose around her neck—or theirs. The move apparently hadn't helped matters in that regard one whit. "Kids, I'm not in the mood . . ."

"You're the retard, Lana—"

"Shut your face!"

Carol bolted up from the couch, her exhaustion from the physical and mental strain of moving halfway across the country to a town completely unfamiliar to her had tapped her reservoir of patience into nonexistence. She was ready to knock some heads together.

"Listen, you two. Any more of that an' I'm sendin' you both to your rooms. Can't you give me a minute's peace?"

"I still think it's crappy for people like that to get teased," Lana continued, daring her sibling to make another wisecrack. "It's not fair. If he does go to my school and I hear anyone callin' him names, I think I'll walk right up an' slap the snot out of 'em. God knows, if Spiro wanted to, he could knock a person clean into the next county, but I can tell he's too sweet."

Luke started making kissing noises against the back of his hand and taunting, "Lana's got a boyfriend, Lana's got a—"

"That's it, boy, go to your room," Carol barked. "I warned you!"

"But Mom!" he protested.

"Now! March!"

Luke got up and stalked down the hall toward the

bedrooms, stomping on the floor, muttering unintelligible curses under his breath. Lana made no attempt to conceal her glee. "Ah, peace at last."

"It takes two to tango," her mother replied sharply, whipping out one of her many loved clichés. "I don't understand why you two have to constantly be at each other's throats. And don't give me that innocent look, young lady—you start these things at least half the time. Sometimes I think you both do it just to drive me crazy."

Lana rolled her eyes to the ceiling, one of her much loved expressions in response to unjust persecution. "I'm really sure, Mom."

"Then why? Does it really take that much effort to get along?"

"I guess so." Lana stretched again, wishing for the millionth time she'd been an only child. Her mother had once admitted that Luke had been an "accident"—a fact Lana had wasted no time in repeating to her nemesis—so if her mother had just been a little more careful, life, as far as Lana was concerned, would be infinitely more pleasant. Perhaps her parents would even have stayed together. "You mind if I go out for a little walk, see if any girls my age live around here?"

Her mother waved absently. "Go on . . . but save some energy. We're goin' to have to unpack at least some of this stuff tonight. I know I won't feel like doin' any cookin', though, so we'll probably eat out. You gettin' hungry yet?"

"Not really." Lana bounded to her feet, the prospect of getting out of the house giving her a fresh burst of energy. "I won't be gone long."

The late afternoon air was beginning to chill enough for Lana to wish she'd grabbed a sweater, but once outside, she didn't feel like going back in to get one. Standing in the driveway behind her mother's car, she peered down both directions of Cameo Lane, trying to decide which way to head out. But before she took another step, she heard a deep, muffled sob coming from the direction of the backyard. She walked quietly through the shadowed space between her house and Spiro's. Peeking around the rear corner of his, she could see him hunched over on his back porch, his face buried in his hands, his little puppy nipping playfully at his ankles unheeded.

"Hey Spiro, you okay?" she called out softly. She entered his backyard and sank to her knees, encouraging the pup to come to her. He bounded over joyfully and licked at her face, assaulting her nostrils with puppy breath. Lana grimaced and rolled him over on his back to tickle his tummy. Spiro had still not answered or looked up. Lana said a little louder, "What's wrong? Are you hurt?"

The young hulk finally raised his head. The bulbous features of his face were twisted in apparent anguish, his eyes red and puffy from crying. "Mama says . . . Mama says I can't keep Sam."

Lana frowned. "Oh yeah? That's too bad. He sure is cute."

"She says she's gonna take him to the dog pound," Spiro went on in his slow monotone, "if I don't get him another home real quick. I know what'll happen t'him if . . . if he goes to the pound. He'll die. Mama said."

"Maybe I can keep 'im for you," Lana offered impulsively, knowing full well her own mother would probably hit the ceiling like a helicopter. "Then you'd still be able to play with him every day."

Spiro's face brightened instantly, like a child's whose skinned knees had been miraculously healed by the mouth's receipt of a bright red sucker. "Yeah, yeah," he chanted, rocking back and forth. "Yeah. You keep him and I can play with him every day, all right. He can be your dog and my dog too, right?"

"An' Luke's too," Lana added sourly. "Luke's my kid brother. He's a real pain in the ass. Anyway, he'll scream bloody murder if the puppy ain't at least part his. But he'll be nice to Sam, I promise."

Spiro nodded gratefully. His woe vanquished, he tuned in fully to the fact of Lana's presence. She both intrigued and confused him. The possibility that she might really like him seemed too good to be true. Fantasy was safer somehow. He began to feel a little dizzy.

"My mom's gonna kill me for this," Lana mumbled, feeling Sam's needle-sharp puppy fangs sink into her hand. She could well imagine the havoc the fluffy little chomping machine would wreak in the house of a Taurus woman who had an annoying penchant for "nice things." A vision of the pup gnawing on the furniture legs or her mother's Italian shoes inspired subsequent visions of all hell breaking loose, but Lana had already given her word.

"Your mama will kill you?" Spiro asked, shocked.

Lana giggled. "Not really. I meant it'll just take her a while to get used to this idea. But she'll get over it. Don't worry, Spiro. I'll take good care of your puppy."

Spiro nodded and felt his tension relax. He found himself wishing she would sit down the way she had earlier, so he could see . . .

The door behind him suddenly opened. Lana looked up to see an obese woman with gray hair pulled into a severe bun step out on the porch. She was wearing a tight, scruffy blue sweater over a faded flower-print dress, and a pair of black shoes that appeared far too small for her oversized feet. She glared at Lana. "What are you doing here?"

Lana nervously rose to her feet, but was unable to stand still with Sam nipping at her toes through her sandals. "Well, ma'am, I just moved in next door," she explained as she tried to dodge the bites, appearing to be dancing on hot coals. "Spiro was just tellin' me you wouldn't let 'im keep his puppy, so I offered to take it. That's all."

"Then take it," Bertha Guenther spat. "And I don't want to see it in my yard again, you understand? First time I do, I'll call the pound, and I mean it. I don't need no damn dog doing messes over here for me to step in when I go to hang my laundry."

Lana stooped and gathered the puppy in her arms, anxious to get away from the terrible woman as quickly as possible. "Yes'm, I know just what you mean. Well, I guess I'll take him home now. Nice meetin' you. 'Bye, Spiro." She shuffled away at a fast pace, biting her tongue to keep herself from telling the old sow what she really thought of her. Now she felt doubly sorry for Spiro; the poor guy certainly wasn't getting any breaks. With a woman like that for a mother, who needed any additional problems? Before turning the corner in front of her garage, she heard the fat woman yell at her son: "You get in this house, boy! I got supper on the table getting cold as ice . . ."

And then a thud; it sounded like she'd kicked him.

Marla headed north on Bower Avenue, which took her through the main shopping district on her way home. For once she obeyed the twenty-five-mile-per-hour speed limit, being in no particular hurry to arrive at her destination; she knew the minute she walked in the door, her mother would start the inquisition about where she'd been and what she'd been doing in the time since school had let out. The Rule was that after dropping Nancy off, she was to report home before going anywhere else, or in other words, her presence was expected by three P.M. Whenever she broke the Rule, it was usually because she'd had detention, but her lateness was explained with a variety of creative excuses to avoid further hassle. She was having trouble thinking of one for the two hours she presently needed to cover, and decided a little more time wouldn't make any difference; chances were she was already nailed anyway. After this long Pamela Mingee would have called Nancy's mother, who fortunately and unfortunately was one of her oldest and dearest friends, and who undoubtedly would have promised to call back as soon as she found out what was going on. That would have been about five seconds after Nancy walked in the door.

It had been almost a year since Marla had last been in the old graveyard on Beacon Hill. On Halloween night it was tradition for a bunch of the high school kids to take a keg of beer up there and party. After the dancing and necking were finished and the keg drained, they would all sit in the shadow of the Ober House of Death and tell ghost stories. Marla had never carefully studied the tomb's entrance with breaking and entering in mind, and she reasoned that sometime before Saturday night such an inspection should be done to see what sort of tools would be needed.

She turned left on Brookings, which would intersect a mile and a half west with Parish Lane. Parish wound through the foothills and eventually circled around the crest of Beacon Hill. Now was as good a time as any; she still had to give more thought to the incredible story she was going to tell her mother, assuming she would even be given a chance.

She'd never been in the cemetery alone before, but didn't imagine it would be very scary in the daylight, though there wasn't much left of it. There was enough; she wasn't going up there to meditate. The sun wouldn't go down for another half hour. With that in mind, she turned up the volume of her stereo and mashed on the accelerator.

The cemetery was in a clearing surrounded by pine, scrub oak, and spruce trees about fifty yards from the scenic overlook. Marla parked the Cutlass near the narrow path which led down to it and got out, shivering as a gust of cold wind danced around her. Why no one had previously thought to have a look inside the tomb she couldn't begin to guess; the forbidding structure certainly fired the imagination. Perhaps others had tried and had simply failed to succeed. Surely she would have heard about it if the case were otherwise—unless, of course, the perpetrators were smart enough to keep their mouths shut. What a rip-off if someone else had gotten there first and made off with the evidence.

Evidence of what? her mind asked hauntingly, though she already knew the answer. She believed what her grandmother claimed, that the Obers had been practitioners of black magic.

Purse in hand, she entered the shady path, her feet crunching rhythmically on fallen pine needles and dead leaves. The only other sound was that of the wind whistling through the tree branches, the whispers of departed souls. Marla knew she was alone, but imagined —as she supposed Nancy would on such an occasion— that the penetrating stares of a dozen pairs of soulless eyes were burning into her, their moldy bodies hidden from view by the dense foliage on either side of her. In spite of her earlier confidence, she admitted to herself that daylight or no, being alone in such a place was scary as hell, especially having a best friend like Nancy, who always came up with the most godawful "what if" statements Marla had ever heard, and they now echoed loudly in her brain, every grisly one of them, like the voice of a demon.

By the time she reached the clearing, her nerves were completely on edge, and she still had no inkling of the excuse she would feed her mother for coming home so late; she had totally exhausted the supply of believable ones. Even if Nancy had been savvy enough to cover for her, this time she would probably just have to admit to the detention. It might cushion her parents' shock of later learning about the suspension, should that dreaded occurrence come to pass.

Why she didn't just turn around and run back to the car she really didn't know; that was exactly what she wanted to do. What was the hurry on checking out that stupid door anyway? On Saturday she and Nancy could do it together, supposing they weren't grounded for the next four years. But she was already there, and in another five minutes, or less, she could have the duty done, and would be able to proudly tell Nancy that she had (as a matter of fact!) come to the graveyard alone. Let Nancy try to call her a chickenshit then.

Her eyes scanned over the uneven rows of stones, most of them tilted and covered with moss. The one nearest her marked the grave of Jeremy Todd, 1862–1877. Fifteen years old. Marla was sixteen; she couldn't imagine her own life being snuffed out so early. What had Jeremy looked like? What had been the cause of his death? She'd always thought such information should be included on grave stones.

The entrance to the tomb faced east; Marla could not see it from where she was standing. The sun was beginning its descent into the west; soon it would disappear behind the hills. Nancy, naturally, would stick around until the sun did go down, just to turn the pragmatic excursion into a chilling adventure. But that was Nancy. Marla stepped over the graves toward the tomb, drumming up visions of the decayed corpses beneath her feet. She couldn't help it. Was she disturbing their rest? Were the eyes of the dead able to see her through the layers of earth?

She then noticed something peculiar, at the far end of

the clearing; a new grave, not yet marked. Unlike the others, the ground covering it was void of grass, the clods of dirt mingled only with fallen leaves and acorns. Freshly dead was somehow worse than long dead. Marla quickly looked away, pushing down her curiosity about who lay beneath that deep, suffocating blanket. Strange that anyone would be buried recently in the old cemetery, she thought, her eyes falling on the tombstone of Sybil Holmes, Loving Wife and Mother, dead for almost seventy-five years. Everyone who died these days got planted in the new cemetery on the other side of town.

"How are you doing down there, Sybil? Are you having a nice day?" Her voice sounded foreign to her in the desolate place. A crow cawed in response, bringing Marla's heart up to her throat. She hurried over to the tomb's entrance. The door was metal, and covered with a good deal of rust, corrosion, and naked vines. There was no handle, only a small hole on the left side where a key would go. Who would have the key . . . ?

She pushed on the door with both hands; it didn't budge. She was beginning to think they would need a stick of dynamite to get in; an electric drill certainly wouldn't do them any good out there. There were no hinges on the outside to unscrew, no space between the door and the frame to wedge a crowbar into, and neither of them knew the first thing about picking locks. So much for their long-embraced, great idea. Whoever had built the tomb obviously didn't want the Obers to be disturbed.

She stepped back a few feet and gazed up at the engraved names above the door. She called out giddily to taunt her fear: "Hey, anybody home?"

As she would later recount to Nancy, what happened then was nothing short of a scene from a heart-stopping nightmare; too terrible, too frightening to accept as reality. She had been too frozen by terror to scream, as her mind urged her to do when the creaking of metal responded to her mocking words. Her eyes, unbelieving, watched as the door of the tomb slowly began to open. She tried to convince herself that she was having an auditory and visual hallucination, but this was clearly not the case. The door was opening, revealing a widening space of blackness beyond the outer frame.

The Obers were home.

"Then what happened?" Nancy asked breathlessly over the telephone.

"What do you think? I ran like the Devil himself was after me," Marla retorted, shivering convulsively at the memory. "I thought I was going to have a heart attack; by the time I got back to my car, I could actually see my heart beating through my blouse. I know what you're going to say, but I'm not going back there, Nan—ever. What Gramma said was really true. Those people were witches. And I personally don't care to know anything else about them."

"Oh, good grief, Marla. You pushed on the door, right? That's why it opened. It just took a little while, that's all. What . . . you actually think one of the Obers got out of his or her coffin and opened it for you? Get real. But if you really don't want to go back, that's just fine with me. I didn't think you'd wanna do this anyway. I really don't care. But if the door's open, I'm going to go out there tonight, before someone else sees it. If there's anything in there worth taking for a souvenir, it'll be gone if we wait very long."

"We?"

"Well, you can at least give me a ride out there, can't you? My mom's at her stupid cooking class and my dad went bowling. I don't have a car. You don't even have to get out of yours if you're going to be such a baby. I'm not afraid of old bones, and that's all the Obers are by now. Come on; if you won't take me, I'll have to ask Jay, and then it won't be just our little secret anymore."

The only excuse Marla could think of for not taking Nancy to Beacon Hill was that she had to clean up her room, and that if she didn't, her mother would throw everything she found on the floor into the trash. But she'd already confessed that all her worrying about what she was going to say about getting home so late had been a waste of energy, since her mother hadn't even been there when she got home, and was still due to arrive. Her brother had informed her that she'd gone to visit

Gramma Colter at the nursing home, and after that she had planned to do the grocery shopping.

"Look, it'll only take about thirty minutes," Nancy said impatiently. "You can stay in the car, and it'll just take me about five minutes to check it out. Come on, this is our big chance . . . we've talked about doing this forever. And we don't even have to break into the place."

Marla groaned in resignation. "All right, I'll take you up there. I don't see why this couldn't wait until tomorrow afternoon, though. No one's going to go snooping around there tonight."

"No one but me," Nancy quipped. "See ya in a few." The line went dead.

Marla replaced the receiver on her ivory Princess phone and looked glumly at the disaster she called her bedroom. With a defeated sigh, she reluctantly grabbed her purse and car keys and stepped out into the upstairs hallway. The last orange rays of sunlight had already disappeared from the sky. When Marla reached the living room downstairs, a plush, earth-toned testimony to the Mingee's financial success, blackness greeted her through the massive picture window overlooking the front of the estate. Her fourteen-year-old brother Rick sat slumped in the center of the sectional beige couch, watching MTV on the forty-six-inch television screen—which meant that their father wasn't home yet either; Harold Mingee could stand MTV for about 1.2 seconds.

"I'm going over to Nancy's for a little while," Marla informed him. "I'll be back in about thirty minutes. If Mom gets back before I do, I was here when I was supposed to be, in case she asks. Got it?"

Rick dipped into his crumpled bag of Fritos and shrugged. "I dunno if I can remember that, since it's not the truth. What's it worth to you?"

"What's it worth to you if I continue to keep my mouth shut about August fifteenth?" Marla snapped, disgusted by her brother's audacious attempt to extort money from her for such a simple favor . . . totally galling, especially considering the goods she had on him. The previous summer their parents had gone on a three-day trip to Las Vegas, leaving their two children home alone, knowing how responsible, mature, and trustworthy they were, not to mention how much more fun they could have in Vegas without them around. Responsible Rick had snuck his girlfriend, Celeste Johnson, over to spend the night with him on the fifteenth, which Marla had easily discovered.

"All right, all right," Rick said irritably, then grinned before adding, "Can't blame a guy for trying, though. I was just kidding, anyway." He stuffed a handful of Fritos into his mouth.

"Yeah, I'll just bet you were." Marla slammed out through the heavy oak front door and walked briskly to her car, parked in the stone circle drive.

Spiro helped his mother wash and dry the dishes after supper, then went to his bedroom to work on his model airplane, though his thoughts kept returning to his puppy next door, and especially to Lana. Why was she being so nice to him? Other girls had pretended to like him before, but it had always been a mere charade to set him up for a cruel joke. Being mildly retarded obviously didn't stop Spiro from thinking about girls in romantic and sexual ways, but he had no hopes of ever actually becoming involved with one; Beauty and the Beast was just a fairy tale. His fantasies at least partially satisfied his emotional need for a female companion; sexual release, he assumed, would always have to be taken care of in solitude, and only after he was certain that his mother was asleep. She'd caught him masturbating once, and had blistered his hands over the stove as punishment.

But Lana seemed to be fantasy becoming reality, or at least closer to it than he'd ever imagined possible. She apparently didn't mind the fact that he was ugly and simpleminded. He drifted into a daydream in which he was holding her small hand in his massive one as they walked together down the halls at school, seeing the looks of jealousy on the faces of other boys. They wouldn't call him Tardo if a pretty girl like Lana were holding his hand. They would respect him if he had such a beautiful girlfriend, a girl who looked like an angel. Was there even one other more beautiful than she? Spiro didn't think so.

They would wonder what she saw in an ugly lump like himself; perhaps they would assume it had something to do with sex. He would definitely enjoy getting teased about that, being accused of fucking beautiful Lana, sticking his thing between her legs and up inside her, filling her with countless explosions of sticky cream. He would encourage that, all right, with a sly smile and no attempt to deny. That would drive them crazy. And maybe Lana really would let him do things, let him touch her in private places. After all, she'd let him see her panties. And hadn't she asked him if he'd like to touch her . . . ?

Yes, he seemed to remember her saying something like that.

Thinking about such things began to produce the normal physical reaction, and Spiro became increasingly uncomfortable sitting in his chair. He was well aware of what was happening to him, but equally so the unfortunate timing for it. His mother was in the living room watching television, and at any moment she might decide to get up and see what he was doing in his bedroom. Like she wanted to catch him doing something bad so she could punish him, but he knew, deep within his heart, how much she really loved him. She only wanted him to be good. But he couldn't help this . . . it happened sometimes even if he consciously did nothing to cause it.

He looked down at the palms of his hands; the scars he'd received from the hot stove coils were still visible. He didn't want to ever suffer that again. He momentarily considered going to the bathroom to take care of his problem, but that would mean he would have to walk through the living room and expose himself to the scrutiny of his mother's knowing eyes, and he had no doubt whatsoever that she would be able to take one look at him and know exactly what he was up to.

He got up from his chair and began to pace back and forth near the foot of his rumpled bed, on which the stinking, crusty yellowed sheets twisted during the previous night's torrid dreams lured him to come, come and lie down . . . but he had to stop; the rising flame had to be put out before he got himself in trouble. He tried to force his mind on something else. Sam, his puppy. His fluffy, sweet, loving pet . . . but he couldn't think about Sam without picturing him there between Lana's legs.

He thought about school. The hardest part about it was not having any friends, having to eat lunch alone in the cafeteria, knowing that others were talking about him, laughing at him behind his back—or right in front of his face; it hardly mattered to them. Once, a senior named Steve Shadduck had walked up to him while he was eating spaghetti, and had picked up his plate and ground it into his face. The other kids had howled with laughter. Even Mr. Jenkins, who was monitoring the cafeteria that day, thought it was funny and gave Steve only the lightest reprimand. Maybe if Lana would eat lunch with him, things like that wouldn't happen anymore.

Here he was, thinking about her again. And thinking about her made him think about his problem, which only served to make it worse. He kept a small cloudy mirror in the top drawer of his scarred dresser. He took it out and reluctantly gazed into it. This is what she sees, he silently told himself. She sees a Halloween mask that will never come off.

That was another thing he heard fairly often: "Why don't you take your mask off, Tardo? Halloween's over." He'd come very close one day to taking a straight razor and doing exactly that. He'd imagined that beneath the hideous exterior of his skin he would find a handsome face, with intelligent eyes and perfect teeth, a slender nose set in the midst of artistic bone structure. He'd held the blade between his fingers for a long time while he stared in the bathroom mirror and visualized the new face emerging. He became certain it was there. He finally took the blade and cut a deep gash in front of his left ear, and was very surprised to see a considerable amount of blood begin to flow from the wound. The pain was immediate and intense; the razor fell unnoticed into the sink as he cried out, watching in horror as the blood ran down his neck and onto his shirt, and then his mama had pounded on the door, demanding to know what in tarnation was going on in there. When he didn't answer, she came in, and when she saw what he had done, she began to scream. She was angry. After cleaning him up and putting a bandage on his face, cursing all the while, she'd taken him to his room and whipped him endlessly with a wooden hanger. She didn't like for him to hurt himself. She loved him too much.

Spiro put the mirror back in his drawer; it had served its purpose. He went back to his desk to work undistractedly on his model airplane.

Four

The peace was suddenly shattered by a loud crash. Wilma Edwards jumped, the prescription bottle she was holding slipping from her fingers, sending tiny blue and white capsules all over the tray in front of her.

"Colter again," she muttered.

Jane Bellows, the auburn-haired aide who had been chatting with Wilma while she set up the medicine cups, turned and hurried down the empty corridor. When she stepped into Room 128, she just missed getting hit by a flying juice glass, which smashed into the wall inches to her right and exploded glass in every direction.

"Jasmine, just what the hell do you think you're doing!" Jane's sea-green eyes narrowed into slits of anger, accentuating the lines around them.

The old woman clutched her covers up around her chin. "That witch was in here again, Miss Janey! I told you and told you to keep all the doors locked, but you wouldn't listen, and now it's too late! The door's open, you damn little fool. The door's open!"

"Of course it's open," Jane snapped. "We don't like your door to be shut because we might not be able to hear you if you need something. Now just look at the mess you've made. I've got to clean this up, you know. And you'd better watch who you're calling a damn little fool. You hear me? The only witch that's ever been in this room is you. Now I'm going to go get a broom and dustpan, so don't you even think about throwing anything else, or we'll put you in a straitjacket. You wanna be put in a straitjacket?"

42

Jasmine Colter's thin white lips quivered. "No, please
. . . don't put me in a jacket, Miss Janey. Take me to the
church, please. I'll be safe in the church, on holy ground.
I got to go an' pray for my baby and my grandbabies. I got
to throw myself on God's altar, Miss Janey, the
door . . ."

Jane whirled around and left; she had no inclination to
stand there and listen to foolish dribble falling from an
old hag's lips. She wished it were possible to make
Jasmine Colter get out of bed and clean up her own damn
mess. Pinedale Nursing Center didn't really have a
supply of straitjackets on hand, but Jane knew there were
plenty of other things with which Colter's hands could be
tied to her bedrails. The thought of the old troublemaker
being tightly bound had a slightly sadistic though satisfying appeal, but Jane knew she would be fired in an
instant for actually doing such a thing. Unfortunately,
keeping her job was more important than teaching a
much-needed lesson.

Wilma, the RN supervisor for the evening shift, was a
middle-aged, overly plump woman of short stature and
humorless personality. She was ready to make her medicine rounds by the time Jane stalked by the front desk on
her way to the janitor's supply closet.

"What did she break this time?" she asked Jane
tersely, her brow creased with irritation.

Jane paused with her hands on her slightly overpadded
hips. "A juice glass, and she came damn close to hitting
me with it. The first crash we heard was just her tray."

Wilma picked up a pen and jotted a note for herself
about the juice glass; the cost of replacing it would be
added to Mrs. Colter's monthly bill. She'd been breaking
a lot of things lately.

Jane went on to the supply closet and returned with a
broom in one hand, a dustpan in the other. "What are we
going to do about her? She's going to hurt somebody one
of these days, and I for one don't get paid enough to put
up with that kind of nonsense. It's bad enough that she's
incontinent and fights like a bobcat when we go in to
clean her up. Can't you give her a sedative or something?"

Wilma tapped her fingers thoughtfully against the pill

tray. "Well, I should consult with her doctor first, but I don't suppose it would hurt to give her a little something tonight. The other patients on that wing would probably appreciate getting a good night's sleep for once."

"I'm sure they would." Jane's shift ended at eleven, but she'd heard about the two, three, and four A.M. disturbances in Room 128, most of the complaints from other patients with rooms in the same vicinity, but the workers on the graveyard shift were none too happy about the situation either, and had nicknamed Jasmine "Spazmine." Jane suspected that if something wasn't done about the inane fits pretty soon, some morning an aide would go in to deliver Jasmine's breakfast and find the old woman beaten to death with a bedpan or walking stick.

When she cautiously stepped back into 128, she found Jasmine sitting straight up with her King James bible held in front of her like a talisman.

"That gonna keep the witch away?" Jane chuckled, her anger diffused by the comical scene.

The old woman, her long fuzzy white hair flowing over bowed, bony shoulders, lowered the book slightly and peeked over the top. "You won't take me to holy ground, and this is the only holy thing I got. Maybe you would get me some holy water from the Catholic church, Miss Janey? I never been Catholic, but seems I heard once that the holy water will burn a witch."

Jane wondered if her senile ward wasn't just remembering a scene from the *Wizard of Oz*. "Sure, I could get you some holy water." She smiled, knowing full well she would bring nothing but tap water from the kitchen or drinking fountain in the lobby. Maybe the janitor would bless it; the old bag wouldn't know the difference. And as for the reason she was wanting it, it wouldn't matter if it was a cup of urine. Witches!

"My Pammie won't listen to me," Jasmine went on mournfully, resting the bible on her lap. Jane's promise to bring holy water hadn't offered much comfort. It wasn't enough. Closing her eyes, she saw Morganna laughing down at her, her bloodred lips pulled obscenely back on the white face floating near the ceiling, a translucent black cape writhing about the witch's body like a giant stingray. Above the devilish leer, black eyes danced with malefic triumph. The evil was not afraid, and it would make her pay. Jasmine's eyes sprang open, banishing the horrifying vision. She tightened her grip on the bible.

"Pammie thinks I'm just a doddering old fool. She don't believe I know what I'm talking about, but I do, I sure do, Miss Janey, God help me I do. I weren't there that night, but my daddy was. He told me what they done to that Kennedy baby. Sacrificed it to the Devil they did, and I think I know why. You believe in the Devil, Miss Janey?"

"Yeah, I'm married to him," Jane answered flippantly, but she was suddenly uncomfortable. "Now, what are you talking about? Who sacrificed a baby to the Devil?" This was something she hadn't heard before—or perhaps this was the first time Jasmine had said it when she was paying attention—and undoubtedly it was just another facet of the old woman's dementia, but the words nonetheless piqued Jane's curiosity.

Jasmine's beady eyes narrowed within their wrinkled pockets of flesh. Her old heart fluttered with excitement; someone was finally going to listen.

After all the dinner trays had been gathered and returned to the kitchen, the three nurses aides on duty went into the break room for coffee, nicotine, or an update on current gossip. Jane had laughingly recounted Jasmine's story to her coworkers, and had been subsequently shocked to learn from one of them, Cora Yarbrough, that as far as she knew, every word of it was true.

"Yes, that's pretty much what my mom's aunt put down in her diary. All that about the Kennedy baby . . . gruesome. It wasn't just an ordinary murder, for sure—they were doing some kind of ritual, all right. Had a stone slab laid out with weird symbols painted on it, and candles burning all around. They killed the baby on that, stabbed him right in the heart with some kind of dagger. But look, Jane, don't let it get to you. That day is long past. Nothing to worry about nowadays. I don't know what the Obers thought they were doing, but all I know is

45

they did kill an innocent little boy, and if they did that for the Devil, I guess he didn't appreciate it much. But all that's ancient history now. Colter just needs something to rail about. This week it's witches, next week it'll be something else . . . werewolves, maybe. Don't give it another thought."

The other aide, Darlene Lanham, shook her head. "What a terrible shame, though. That poor baby. And his parents . . . imagine what that must have done to them. The evil that men do . . . by the way, did I tell you two what that damn brother-in-law of mine has gone and done now . . . ?"

Jane tuned out, the Ober subject sticking to her mind like an algae-eater to the side of an aquarium. This was something she wouldn't be able to forget so easily, even if Jasmine hadn't shared her hypothesis on the reason for the ritual, and the fact that only one end of the "bargain" had been fulfilled. What Jane wanted to do now—no, what she had to do now, for reasons she didn't care to explain to Cora or Darlene—was to read that diary; see for herself in black and white an original account of the Obers' atrocity. She allowed Darlene to finish her story about what an absolute criminal her sister was married to, gave an appropriate disgusted response, then turned and smiled apologetically at Cora.

"I know this is probably a really nervy thing to ask, but . . . would it be possible for me to borrow that diary?"

Cora grunted. "What's the matter with you, Jane? You still thinking about that? I told you, all that's over and done, and thank God it is."

"I'm just curious," Jane said unconvincingly, her eyes pleading. "I know it's all over and done, like you say, but it's a pretty bizarre piece of history, and it happened right here. I'd just like to read what your mom's aunt said about it, in her own words. Obviously you've read it, so you must have found it interesting."

"I found it pretty revolting," Cora said dryly, wrinkling her wide, flat nose. "But if you want to read it that bad, I guess it's all right with me. I'd rather you didn't take it home, though. You can read it here. There's not really that much in it about that business, anyway. I'll bring it with me tomorrow, if I can find it. I think it's still buried in that cedar chest in my bedroom, unless one of the brats got to it."

Jane squeezed her hand. "Thanks . . . that would be great. God, I thought ol' Jasmine was just pulling all that stuff out of never-never land."

Darlene laughed. "So you really think Morganna Ober's been paying her visits?"

Jane scowled. "Come on, give me a break. What kind of fool do you think I am?"

Five

"**B**ang, you're dead!" Luke squealed for the six hundredth time, according to Lana's estimate. His sentence to solitary confinement had been suspended, and he was "shooting" Spiro's puppy with a finger gun and toppling him over on his back, as a cocker spaniel named Mop they'd once owned had learned to do.

"Would you leave that dog alone?" Lana hissed between clenched teeth. "He's too young to learn tricks, you diphead."

"He ain't neither, donkey face."

"Luke, if I hear you yell bang one more time, you're the one who'll be playin' dead," his mother said irritably, reinforcing her threat with a level stare. "An' that's enough of the name callin', both y'all. Put the dog out in the garage, an' spread out some papers for 'im . . . not that he'll know what they're for. I oughta have my head examined for lettin' him stay."

Lana picked up the squirming bundle of fur and nestled him against her bosom. "Oh Mom, you wouldn't say that if you'd seen the look on Spiro's face when I offered to keep Sam. It was gonna break his heart to lose 'im."

"Boo hoo," Luke blubbered facetiously, wiping nonexistent tears from his eyes.

Carol shot him another warning look. "Cut it out, now, boy, you hear me? All right, let's get a move on. I don't know about you two, but I'm starvin'. Hamburgers sound okay?"

"Could you just bring me one back?" Lana asked, allowing Sam to bathe her chin. "I don't really feel like goin' out. An' I need to write some letters." She was already beginning to miss the best friend she'd left behind in Tyler, and especially her boyfriend, Greg Abbott. When she'd found out that the insurance company her mother worked for was transferring her to another state, clear across the country, she'd started going all the way with him, and that had made leaving him much more difficult. They'd promised each other to always write, but she doubted she would ever see him again. Greg would find a new girlfriend before too long, and she supposed she would meet someone else as well, but she assumed it would be a while before she could put her heart into a new relationship.

"You just wanna stay here so you can play with the puppy," Luke accused poutingly. "I wanna stay too."

"You're comin' with me, young man," Carol insisted firmly. "The dog's goin' out to the garage. I guess we'll have to stop at the grocery store to get him some food too. Well, I need t'go anyway. I just hope he doesn't get very big. I don't want t'be spendin' half my salary on dog food."

"He looks like a German shepherd to me," Luke declared proudly.

"Great, that's just what we need," Carol sighed. "Well, let's go, Sport."

She wiggled into her gray suede jacket and tossed her son his coat. "We'll be back soon," she said to Lana as she opened the front door. "Don't forget to put those papers down, now. I guess you'll have to unwrap some plates and glasses to get some."

Lana forced a smile. "All right, Mom."

After her mother and brother were gone, she dutifully took the puppy straight to the garage, turned on the light and set him down on the concrete floor. Sam immediately began to investigate the new environment.

The garage was cold; besides newspapers, she would also have to put something warm down for him to sleep on. An old towel stuffed into a packing box would make a nice bed, she decided.

Sam seemed quite contented sniffing around Luke and Lana's bicycles while she stayed with him, but as soon as she closed the door behind her to collect the things she needed, he began to whine and yap, loud enough so that she could still hear him when she went down the hallway to get a towel from the bathroom. She hoped he wouldn't keep that up all night; none of them would get any sleep, and although she and Luke would willingly make the sacrifice, their mother would take about five minutes of it before throwing a total hissy fit. The whines soon became frantic howls; Lana strongly suspected she would have to try to sneak the puppy into bed with her.

By the time she got back out to the garage laden with box, towel, newspapers, and water dish, she was certain the whole neighborhood was aware of Sam's demand for company; the acoustics in the garage amplified his piercing wails. She put the box down sideways and bunched the towel up inside it. Sam immediately pulled the towel back out, his stubby tail wagging gleefully. Lana shook her head.

"You're gonna be a real pain in the ass, aren'cha?"

Sam was eager to confirm the accusation; as soon as she put the papers down, he stepped on the water dish, spilling the water and getting most of the papers soaked, then began shredding them with his teeth and paws.

It wasn't until Lana turned off the garage light to go back into the kitchen that she was able to see the distinct shape of a man's head through one of the dusty garage windows. He had apparently been watching her, and even now that the garage was dark, he remained standing there like a Peeping Tom with infrared vision.

Convinced that he had to be some kind of pervert—or worse—Lana backed nonchalantly into the kitchen and locked the door behind her, then dashed through the house to check the front door and windows. Sam began to howl again in protest of being left alone in the dark, which made Lana more nervous, but as far as she was concerned he could yap his head off until her mother got back home.

Only after making sure the house was secure did she dare peek through the living room drapes. The man was not standing on the front porch; she couldn't see him anywhere. Maybe he had gone away.

She let the drapes fall and headed for her bedroom to write her letters when the doorbell rang. It had to be the man she'd seen at the garage window. He hadn't gone away after all.

Pausing in the hallway, her pulse racing, she wondered if murderers or rapists rang the doorbell. She timidly walked back to the living room and leaned against the front door, her ear pressed to the wood. Sam was still yapping away in the garage, adding fuel to the fire of anxiety. Now she was afraid to look out the window. She barked at the door with forced aggressiveness, "Who's there?"

There was no answer; only the shuffling of feet on the other side. It was the last thing she wanted to do, but she made herself step over to the drapes and pull them aside. The sight of the dark, looming shape on the porch initially filled her with dread, but then she suddenly realized who it was. It was only Spiro.

The tenseness rapidly drained from her muscles; Spiro, of course. He'd probably heard Sam's commotion and had come over to check on him, or else had a nasty message from his mother to deliver about the racket. Lana unlocked and opened the door with a sheepish smile. "Spiro! I thought you were some ol' creep . . . you really had me goin' there for a while," she admitted, now feeling pretty foolish.

He kept his eyes lowered, and as she spoke he shuffled nervously from one foot to the other. "I heard Sam, so I sneaked out to see if he was okay."

"Oh, he's just pissed off about bein' left alone. I guess after bein' played with all evenin', he's already pretty spoilt." Lana stepped back. "You wanna come in?"

Spiro shook his head. "I hafta go back home. If my mama finds out what I did, she'll get mad at me. I'm not s'pose to go out my window."

"Well, guess you'd better get back, then; Lord knows I wouldn't want her mad at me. No offense, but . . . anyway, don't you worry about Sam, he'll be just fine," Lana assured him. "He'll probably end up sleepin' with me tonight."

Her last words urged Spiro to steal a glance at her face. His eyelids fluttered as a vision flashed of Lana in her nightgown, lying sweetly unconscious on her bed. He could watch her sleep for hours and hours, study the contours of her body all he wanted while she dreamed . . .

Oh yes, Spiro, any time, any time . . .

"Huh?"

"I said I guess I'll see you later, Spiro." Lana looked away and started to close the door, musing over the strange look on her neighbor's face. Something about it made her a little uncomfortable.

Spiro stumbled backward, eyes still transfixed on her face. "Yeah, later."

"I knew you were going to do this. I just knew it!" Marla crossed her arms firmly over her breast and shook her head stubbornly. "I am *not* going down there. I told you on the phone, I'm staying right here in the car. I think I've had enough excitement for one day, thank you."

"Good grief, what's the big deal? You really think dead people get up and move around? Come on, how dumb can you get? I thought you were the logical one." Nancy poked her friend on the shoulder with the flashlight she had taken from her dad's shop.

"I don't care if I'm being illogical or anything else," Marla responded testily, shoving the flashlight away. "I just don't want to go, and that's final. If you're sure there's nothing to be afraid of, why are you so desperate for me to go with you? Let's just forget the whole thing." She restarted the Cutlass's engine.

Nancy opened the passenger door. "Turn the damn car off—I'll go alone. I'm not afraid, and I'm sure not desperate. I just thought it would be fun to go together."

Marla switched off the engine; the even rumble under the hood fell silent. "Yeah, probably so you can scare the shit out of me. I know you, Nancy Snell. Well, I already got that done this afternoon, so now it's your turn. And don't stay down there too long."

Nancy climbed out of the car and made a production of locking the door before slamming it shut. "Better lock yours too. Zombies can smell fear a mile away." She giggled and turned on the flashlight. After obnoxiously shining it in Marla's face through the windshield, she turned the beam on the trees bordering the path.

The three-quarter moon was shining brightly, but the sky was cloudy and yielded little light from above. Without looking back to see if Marla might change her mind, Nancy set off boldly through the black gape that would take her to the ancient cemetery.

The night was still except for the occasional hoot of an owl and the rustle of tree branches as small nocturnal creatures scurried among them. As soon as Nancy was out of sight of the car, she slowed her pace, her senses honed to absorb every nuance of the experience. In a way she was glad Marla was being such a fraidycat; embarking on such a chilling adventure alone was far more rewarding than having someone else along.

For a few moments the clouds moved away from the moon, bathing the treetops with an eerie glow, accentuating the mood Nancy was creating in her mind. She was a true horror fan, and loved nothing more than to have the crap scared out of her, although such a feat had become increasingly difficult to accomplish. She'd desensitized herself with too many gory movies and bloodcurdling novels. But this, she thought, was nice. She willingly conjured visions of coming to the graveyard and seeing skeletal fingers breaking through the earth's crust, reaching for her, or of having a large pair of dusty black shoes suddenly appear in the lowered beam of her flashlight before she could even get there . . .

It had been her idea to break into the tomb in the first place, and she was glad she hadn't been deprived of the honor of being first to see what lay beyond the metal door. It was strange the way it had seemingly opened by itself in front of Marla, but even though Nancy had a fetish for the supernatural, she didn't really believe in it; she believed in nothing without empirical evidence, and so far her personal experience with such matters had sadly lacked evidence of any sort. The idea of one of the Obers rising from his or her coffin to open the door of the tomb was deliciously frightening, but Nancy knew that no such thing had occurred.

Too bad.

She reached the end of the path and paused, moving the light beam up to illuminate the clearing before her. Shadows stretched beyond the eroding grave markers and fell across brown, needle-covered ground. No corpses reached up to push back their dark blankets of earth, but Nancy found the general atmosphere quite satisfying to her lust for things ominous.

She was aware that her morbid preoccupation with death and torture stemmed from her inability to cope with her own mortality, her own eventual demise; consequently she sought to discover its mysteries beforehand, though such efforts were, of course, frustratingly futile. She had watched hundreds of actors and actresses die in hundreds of different, gruesome ways, the art of special effects making the deaths progressively more realistic, and Nancy had watched closely, raptly, an enthusiastic recruit studying a training film. How else was one to prepare? She had dreamed countless times of embracing the cold flesh of a corpse, looking deeply into its sightless eyes and screaming, *Tell me what it's like! What does it feel like to be dead!*

They never answered her; their bloodless, dry lips hung open but remained silent. She'd heard that mortuaries glued or sewed shut the eyes and mouths of their still, pale customers lest they spring open during the funeral services and thereby cause others to prematurely join the plight of those who no longer breathed. One day she would be the one to make sure such precautions were rendered; she planned to become a funeral director, of course.

She moved slowly toward the tomb in which the remains of Myrantha and Nathaniel Ober lay. They, like the others who surrounded them beneath the ground, knew the secrets of the dead. And possibly a whole lot more. The legend of the Obers having been witches had snared Nancy's attention like the scent of cheese to a mouse. She didn't (yet) actually believe in witchcraft— again, she'd never personally seen it practiced, let alone with results—but it was somehow a part of the vast unknown that encompassed the grave, and the discovery of any truth connected to death would give her a glimpse

54

of what she so desperately wanted . . . *needed* to see before she too became absorbed by it. Her heart quickened slightly as she circled around the entrance of the tomb.

Yes, the door was indeed opened, but just barely. Nancy stepped closer, the beam of the flashlight seeking beyond the crack and revealing a narrow view of some large, dusty object. One of the coffins, on the left. Myrantha's.

She swallowed, forcing down the lump that had suddenly become lodged in her throat. But she was more elated than frightened. It had been almost three years since the idea of getting into the tomb had first occurred to her, and she had feared that her plan would just become one of those things forever talked and dreamed about until it was absurd. Of course, the talking and dreaming and speculating was the guaranteed fun part; she hadn't wanted to rush into action for fear of being disappointed. But wasn't it lucky that, just when she'd decided it was time for truth or consequences, all that had been required was a little push.

She moved up to the door and gingerly began to tear away the dead vines that had prevented it from opening any farther, her eyes still glued to what she could see of Myrantha's coffin. When the impediment was cleared, she pushed the rough metal surface with her hand, the full length of the box coming into view as the door swung inward, groaning on its rusty hinges. It stopped when it came into contact with the coffin on the right.

Everything was coated with a thick layer of dust, but as the light played on the filthy surfaces, Nancy realized with dread that a few places had been fairly recently disturbed: the edges of the coffin lids, the floor. An animal, or . . . ?

She moved the beam of light up to survey the back wall and uttered a gasp of surprise. On it was hanging an inverted black iron cross surrounded by strange symbols painted in red. Whatever they meant, Nancy was already convinced that the rumors about the Obers being involved in witchcraft hadn't just come out of thin air. (She discouraged the nagging possibility that a person had been in here earlier and had hung the cross and painted the markings for a joke.) She shuddered slightly, wondering if just looking at the symbols would invoke some mystical, dark power. The wind whipped up behind her suddenly, as if to say, *Oh, but of course . . .*

Eager to assume the role of idiotic horror movie heroine, she stepped over the threshold of the small chamber and returned her attention to Myrantha Ober's dark narrow coffin. The camera was rolling: this was the moment she had been waiting for. Finally, the payoff (unless the graves had been robbed): to open the lid now inches from her fingertips and see a body that had been dead for seventy years. Would there be anything left of it?

Ashes to ashes, dust to dust. Nancy knew she was going to be extremely disappointed if inside the box she only found something she might have pulled out of the vacuum cleaner bag. The air inside the tomb was heavy, chokingly musty, and hinted vaguely of the stench of decay; she resisted the urge to take a deep breath before opening the lid of Myrantha's eternal bed. She trembled slightly when her fingers touched the wood, hyping herself up with the idea that she wasn't just going to see a dead body.

She was going to see a dead *witch.* Grasping the edge firmly, she began to lift.

Marla glanced at the clock on her dashboard for the fortieth time since Nancy had disappeared into the path; she'd now been gone for seventeen and a half minutes. What was taking her so long? A few horrible possibilities had already presented themselves, and they took turns assaulting Marla's fragile patience.

The worst scenario was, of course, the most unlikely, but in view of what had happened earlier that day, Marla couldn't completely rule it out, insane as it was: Nancy had gone into the tomb, and the Obers had been waiting for her, their mortal bodies revived by the power of the Devil—Gramma Colter had insisted vehemently that all real witches were in cahoots with the Devil. They had enclosed her within giant batwing arms, amused by her vain struggles and muted cries for help; pressing against her, their bloodthirsty lips pulled back over ivory daggers, their excitement grew; the beating of Nancy's human heart, like a fluttering sparrow waiting to be crushed in the tight grasp of an ogre's hand, sounding like sweet music to their hellish souls. Sinking their fangs into the soft flesh of Nancy's shoulder, they had begun to drink . . .

Marla sighed, shaking her head. No, no, that was vampires; witches did something else . . . but what? Maybe Nancy had gone through the metal door of the tomb, and whatever had made it open earlier made it shut again once a victim had been lured inside, kind of like a marble Venice Flytrap. That seemed a witchy sort of thing. Or perhaps the tomb itself had some kind of power, and was hungry for a fresh body in its bowels . . .

Such were the fates Nancy would dream up if she were sitting in the car, waiting for Marla to reemerge from the path. Stupid, asinine notions, really. Hollywood horror. Nothing that would ever actually happen in real life. Still, Nancy could have somehow locked herself in there accidentally, the dumb shit.

Chances were, though, Nancy was playing a little joke, planning to stay down there so long that she would be forced to get out and look for her; and at the worst possible moment, Nancy would jump out from behind a tree, or from the tomb itself—very generously supposing Marla would even go that far without a flashlight—and yell BOO! just for the sadistic pleasure of seeing her best friend fly in several directions at once, and/or scream, wet her pants, and faint in rapid succession. Marla wouldn't put it past her at all. That sort of thing was right up Nancy's alley, which was one of the reasons Marla had refused to go with her in the first place.

Whatever was causing the delay, Marla had no intention of even stepping out of the car, much less going in search of her friend in that dreadful place, without light or weapon. At the most she would wait another fifteen minutes, which would be more than fair, then she would go back home and make an anonymous call to the police and let them go find out what had happened to Nancy.

Another five minutes passed. Marla began to gnaw on her fingernails.

Then suddenly there was movement in the path— something big and black swaying between the trees, barely visible beneath the subtle moonlight grudgingly permitted through the clouds. Marla straightened up in her seat, her eyes riveted to the approaching figure. It had to be Nancy . . . didn't it? But Nancy was wearing a white sweater and blue skirt. Whoever (or whatever) was coming up to the head of the path was totally clothed in black.

Invisible fingers clutched around Marla's throat. The impossible had happened—the Obers had risen from the dead. They had killed Nancy, and now one of them was coming to get her . . .

Seized with panic, she fumbled with the keys dangling from the ignition to start the engine. When it roared to life, the hooded creature began to run—or fly, it seemed —straight for the car. Marla mashed on the accelerator before throwing the transmission into reverse, and in doing so flooded the carburetor; the engine sputtered, then died. She immediately began to wail, her typical reaction in the face of impending doom. She couldn't breathe. The thing was almost upon her now.

She twisted the key again, fiercely, but the Cutlass wouldn't start. The only other thing Marla could think of to do was lay on the horn. The instant the brash sound pierced the outer stillness, the figure raced to the passenger window and drew back its hood. Nancy stood there laughing like a hyena, her face pressed obscenely against the glass. Marla released the horn, her fear turning into boiling rage. She screamed through the glass, "You damn bitch!"

Nancy was far too pleased with herself for the prank she had pulled off to be offended in the least; she continued to screech with laughter.

Marla, gripping the steering wheel, brayed from inside the car: "You think that was funny! I'll show you how damn funny I thought it was—you can just walk back home!"

This sobered Nancy quickly; her face was magically wiped clean of its nasty exultation. "Hey, what are you getting so bent out of shape about? For crying out loud, it was just a joke. Let me in the car. Please?"

It took Marla several moments to decide which was stronger—her friendship with Nancy or her thirst for revenge. Making Nancy walk four miles back to her house would certainly teach her a lesson and even the score, but chances were that even such a well-deserved penalty would permanently terminate their comradery. She finally forced herself to lean over and unlock the passenger door, determined to at least stay mad about the incident for a long, long time.

Nancy got in the car smelling like death warmed over; Marla grimaced and asked scornfully, "My God, did you get that out of the tomb? Off one of the bodies?" She tried the ignition again, this time, naturally, with success.

Nancy smiled secretively, her eyes sparkling with a green hue from the electronic gauges on the dashboard. "Yes, I took it right off Myrantha's skeleton. Isn't it neat?"

Marla was horrified. "Jesus Christ, how disgusting! I can't believe you did that. You actually touched . . . her? It?"

"Sure, why not? Haven't you ever wanted to touch a real skeleton before?"

"If you keep talking about it, I think I'll throw up." Marla turned on the headlights and put the transmission in reverse. As she backed up to position the car in the right direction, Nancy began to giggle.

"Hey, I was just kidding about that. Seriously, the coffins were empty . . . looks like some asshole got in there before we did. Not today, but pretty recently. The dust on the floor was disturbed, and also on the coffin lids. Nothing was in there but this old thing, crumpled up in the corner in front of Myrantha's coffin. That's why the door opened like it did; whoever broke in screwed up the lock, I guess. Wonder who it was?"

Marla's arms and shoulders became gooseflesh. "The bodies were gone? Shit, Nan, remember what Gramma said . . ."

Nancy was staring absently out the window. "Yeah, I know. There were also weird symbols painted on the back wall around an inverted cross. Your gramma did know something, but she's only guessing about what it all means. I don't think the Obers actually walked out of that place on their own two feet. That's a little too far out, don't you think?"

Marla's face had turned pasty white. "But why would someone have taken their remains? What would you do with something like that—put it up on the mantel as a conversation piece? This is just too fucking weird, Nancy. Something's going on."

"Yeah, it's called grave robbing," Nancy said, her tone unaccountably thick with sarcasm. "Don't ask me why someone would want the Obers' nasty old bones . . . why did Michael Jackson want to pay umpteen millions for the Elephant Man's? Go ask a shrink about it."

"It still scares the shit out of me," Marla returned defensively, remembering she was still mad at her friend for the fiendish prank she had pulled. She turned on the radio to an offensive level and erected an invisible wall between the front bucket seats.

Inverted cross, weird symbols . . . sure evidence of witchcraft, all right. But Nancy was right about one thing. It was ridiculous to even imagine that seventy-year-old corpses had suddenly reanimated and hopped out of their coffins, strolled out of their place of interment, finger bones interlinked, their skull faces grinning like dumbstruck tourists'. There was a limit to what even the Devil himself could do. Wasn't there?

The smell of the garment Nancy was wearing, and the strong supposition that it had once been worn by Myrantha Ober, was beginning to make Marla feel extremely nauseated. She rolled down her window to let in some fresh air, her mind spinning with unanswered questions. Who did take the bodies, and why? If they had been after souvenirs, why had they left the cape behind?

And what else might they have left behind?

She glanced suspiciously at the cape and turned the radio off. "That . . . cape was the only thing you found in there?"

Nancy, seemingly offended, lifted her chin with indignance and met Marla's probing stare head-on. "I'm really sure I'd hold out on you, Marla. I thought we were best friends."

Marla, holding fast to her anger, didn't rush to verify the statement. "I was just wondering why that cape would have been left, if someone was after some kinky souvenirs."

"Maybe they didn't want it; who knows? But this is all that was in there besides a lot of dust. And that cross. I know why they didn't take that, though . . . I tried to get it off myself. Impossible."

They rode for a while in silence. Marla, steeped in black mystery, began to have the feeling that another presence was in the car, riding back with them into town. She searched the rearview mirror, half expecting to see a pallid, ghoulish face reflected in it. She couldn't shake off the worry that had sunk poisonous tentacles deep into her peace of mind. She saw again that horrible death's door begin to creak open all by itself . . .

"Are you sure those marks in the dust weren't made today? I mean, how could you tell?"

Nancy tossed her head back against the headrest and expelled a loud breath, knowing what Marla was hinting at, wanting the subject to be dropped. "I could just tell, okay? More dust had collected over the smudges. Probably a month's worth, maybe more. If you want to believe the Obers made them, go ahead, but you can rest assured that they're long gone by now."

Marla wondered what her gramma would say if she knew about the missing bodies. Unless she died of fright right there on the spot, she would most likely begin to rage: *I told you so! I told you that business wasn't over with yet! The Obers have returned from Hell!*

It would serve no purpose for the pitiful, shriveled creature in the Pinedale Nursing Center to be told. "That business" was over with. Someone in Sharon Valley was up to something suspicious, but the Obers were still undeniably, irreversibly, and eternally dead. Jasmine Colter should die in peace, believing that instead.

Marla's mind drifted back to when she was little, and Gramma was her best friend and favorite playmate; they would bake cookies and make paper dolls together, and clothes—Gramma would make the most beautiful little-girl clothes, dresses finer than any store in Sharon Valley had—and other days she would read stories to her with the dramatic flare of an actress, pacing about the floor gesturing with her arms and face as if she were on stage, her wide-eyed audience of one sitting timidly amid the cushions of her great puffy old couch, sucking a lollipop, bursting into frequent high trills of laughter whenever she would make a funny face. Sometimes Gramma would make the stories up, tell tales Marla had never heard before, but always they were just as entertaining, and always had a moral at the end. Then one day she told the story about the witch. Not the witch who kept trying to kill Snow White, nor the one who kept Rapunzel high up in a tower, nor the one who fattened up Hansel and Gretel. This was the one who lived in Sharon Valley when Gramma was a little girl. The moral to this story was that the Devil always kept his end of a bargain, so beware of ever making one.

Marla had suffered waking nightmares and sleepwalking after hearing that story, and her mother had finally gotten out of her what the matter was. Pamela had been so angry about it she called Gramma Colter right then, at three o'clock in the morning, to bawl her out about it. How dare she tell Marla such a story! What was she trying to do, scare the poor child out of her wits?

Gramma never told the story nor mentioned the witch again, except to tell her granddaughter that it had only been a made-up story and that she shouldn't be afraid. Never, that is, until four years ago, after she'd had the stroke. For several months afterward she would talk of nothing else.

"I think I'll wear this to the prom," Nancy said with a short laugh, breaking the heavy silence.

"I wouldn't put it past you," Marla responded sourly. "Maybe you could get Jay to dress up like Dracula. One thing for sure, you'd have plenty of room on the dance floor. That thing smells like it should be crawling with maggots."

"I'll wash it in Woolite, like I do all my fine washables," Nancy quipped with a shrug. "You know, Jay's always said I was a witchy woman."

Marla refused to be wheedled out of her grudge. She responded unsmilingly, "You know what the bible says shalt be done to a witch."

"You preaching to me now?" Nancy snorted. "Don't make me laugh."

They rounded a curve on the south side of the hill; the lights of the valley below sparkled like stars on a blanket of black velvet. Seventy years ago they would only have seen the dim glow of scattered oil lanterns hanging in windows, the activities within the humble dwellings limited by the undiscovered wonders of modern technology. Instead of watching MTV on their color television sets, the kids might have been playing a game of cards, or making paper dolls and toy boats. On this night seventy years ago the people of Sharon Valley would have gone to bed free of worry and slept peacefully through the night, blissfully unaware of the evil that slept with them. Eight days later they would find out, but then it would be too late.

Marla forced herself to think instead of the phone call she was planning to make. She needed to anticipate all of Montgomery's possible reactions, so she would be prepared to respond appropriately to anything he said. In one scenario he gasped and pleaded with her to please, please not publicly accuse him of sexual misconduct, that it would end his career, ruin his entire life, etc., etc. But just as clearly she could hear him say: *We'll see how your little story holds up under a voice stress test, Miss Mingee. Do you know the penalty for falsely accusing someone of that? For beginners, Miss Mingee, I can sue you in civil court for libel and slander; so in other words, your father would probably lose his shirt because of your little indiscretion. I'll see you in the principal's office tomorrow morning—or even worse—and by the way, did you know I have a tape recorder on my telephone?* Then there was the ultimate: *Yes, I have recorded this entire conversation, Miss Mingee, and I believe that you will be dropping by to see me at home about twice a week until after graduation . . . ?*

She turned the radio back on as they approached the bottom of the hill, and said without apology in her voice, "I've changed my mind about calling Doom . . . that could backfire too. We don't need any more trouble than we already have."

Nancy shrugged. "I'm not worried about it."

As soon as Marla dropped her off, Nancy peeled out of the smelly cape and wrapped it in a tight bundle around the other thing she'd taken from Myrantha's coffin.

Marla's suspicion that she was holding something back had been right on the money, and Nancy had come close to confessing, but ultimately decided that Marla wasn't worthy of sharing such a terrible secret. She only flirted with danger and darkness; having an intimate affair with them was out of the question. So it would do no good for her to know.

Hoping that her parents were settled down in the den, allowing her to get to her bedroom without being seen or questioned about the mysterious bundle in her hands, Nancy opened the front door of her house and stepped in, unconsciously cringing as she closed it behind her.

Her mother's voice called out from the den. "Nancy, is that you?"

"Yes," she called back, and holding her new possessions to one side, quickly ducked into the hallway leading to the bedrooms. She'd told her parents that she and Marla were going out for a Coke, and apparently they didn't require a report on the excursion; she continued unhindered to the privacy of her own room.

First she turned on the light and closed the door, then she very reverently unrolled the thin, rough material on her bed. The cape seemed to smell a lot worse indoors, but Nancy didn't think too much about it. She was too excited about what was inside. Her fingers trembled as she exposed the hood and again feasted her eyes on the sinister treasure, an ancient ledger which contained not only the last Will and Testament of Myrantha Ober, addressed to her daughter Morganna, but also the key to her evil power.

Nancy had every intention of utilizing that power, and she knew exactly what she would use it for first. She picked up the ledger as if it were the most priceless object on earth, a wicked smile creeping to her lips.

As usual, Marla pulled up in front of Nancy's house at 7:45 the next morning and honked the horn. Several moments later Nancy bounded from her house wearing a black sweater and navy-blue slacks, her hair pulled back in a ponytail with a blue ribbon. Marla, too fretful about what was going to happen when they got to school to remember she was supposed to still be mad at her, smiled when Nancy got in the car. But the smile fell flat when she saw Nancy's face.

"Crap, Nan, what's wrong with your eyes? Didn't you get any sleep?"

"What's wrong with them?" Nancy snarled, flipping down the visor mirror in front of her. She studied her reflection. "I don't know what you're talking about . . . there's nothing wrong with my eyes. But I guess I didn't get that much sleep last night. I had some pretty bizarre dreams."

"Yeah, tell me about it." The Cutlass moved forward through the residential street, between identical rows of cigar-box houses, most of them shamelessly unadorned, paint cracked and peeling, yards veritable weed gardens, the poor hillbilly cousins of the plush showcase estates of Cameron where Marla lived. The two girls' friendship would have been unlikely if their mothers had not been best friends. Pamela and Beth still carried on ingrained traditions, but the bond between them had grown lukewarm, which might not have happened if they had married men of equal income and status.

"I dreamed Montgomery was chasing me all night," Marla elaborated, "with a big, gigantic piece of chalk, if you know what I mean. What did you dream about? The tomb?"

Nancy hesitated. "Well . . . oh, never mind. I had several dreams, and they were all just weird. I can't really remember any details." She looked away, concealing the lie. She remembered the dreams quite vividly. They had both terrified and awed her. They'd seemed so real. She'd come face to face with the Devil. And he had been so indescribably beautiful . . .

When they pulled into the student parking lot, they saw Dennis getting out of his car near the west fence. He noticed Marla's Cutlass at about the same time, and pointedly looked the other way, then disappeared into a huddle of fellow smokers.

"That bastard," Marla growled. "I can see he's wanting to play games. Well, we'll see who winds up crawling back on whose knees to make up."

"Yeah, probably you," Nancy remarked idly, obviously preoccupied with other thoughts.

"I can be just as stubborn as Dennis," Marla insisted. "Honestly, Nan, I'm not giving in this time. He was the one acting like a jerk. He has to apologize to me."

"Sure, Marla."

They went on into the school building behind a clique of giggling freshman girls smelling like a chemical floral arrangement. Marla and Nancy turned to each other and did the "Aren't they simply deplorable" eye roll while holding their noses. On the surface it might just have been another Friday morning, but there was a strong undercurrent of tension running beneath the outer jovial layer. As they weaved through the throng of noisy students, Marla brought it to the surface.

"I don't suppose we'd be lucky enough for Doom to forget about telling us to meet him in Mr. G's office this morning. You know, maybe it was just an idle threat, intended to scare us into shaping up . . . or at least making us lose some sleep. Maybe he wasn't really serious."

Nancy rolled her eyes again and shook her head. "He was serious as a heart attack, Marla. That guy's got it in for us. We could act real sweet and smile real pretty and promise him we'd never give him any more trouble if he'd let us off the hook this time, and he'd turn right around and burn our butts." She smiled and nodded at the kids popular enough to merit her attention—the fact that she'd achieved socialite status riding along on Marla's coattails didn't humble her a bit. Her expression revealed nothing of the fearful turbulence churning behind it. *What if, what if, what if . . .*

She suddenly halted, her face etching into a mask of surprise. "Oh, shit."

Marla followed her friend's gaze. "Yeah, shit is right; make that with a capital S."

They were approximately fifteen feet from the offices, and Albert Montgomery could clearly be seen through the glass walls. He was talking to the principal's secretary.

Nancy muttered something under her breath, but Marla didn't catch it.

Assuming it had only been more profanity, she said, "Maybe we should just ditch." She pulled Nancy against the wall behind a water fountain. "We can go to a pay phone and call ourselves in sick, pretend we're our mothers."

Nancy frowned. "That'll never work, how stupid. They can tell if they're talking to an adult or not."

Biting her lower lip, Marla tried to think of an alternate strategy. She was angry at herself for not already considering plans A through Z, as she normally did in such situations, but instead had allowed herself to be influenced by Nancy's flip statement, "I'm not worried about it."

Well, she looked worried now. And bewildered and terrified all at the same time. They simultaneously peeked toward the offices again; the clock behind the secretary's desk warned that the first bell would ring in five minutes.

Sue Clark, one of the Sharon Valley Cougar cheerleaders, stepped up to the fountain with an armload of books. After taking a few sips of water, she smiled widely at Marla and Nancy, showing a deep set of dimples. "Hey, you two—you look like you've just seen a ghost. What's up?"

Nancy's skin had just turned a sickly gray-white, effectively masking the sparkle of triumph in her eyes; Marla's mouth hung open in wonder.

"What—What is he . . ."

Sue turned to look in the direction of the offices. Albert Montgomery was now leaning over Phyllis Jenkins's desk, clutching his chest and apparently gasping for air. Phyllis was watching him with a stunned expression on her face, as were the other people standing inside the glass enclosure. Except for Montgomery, they all seemed suspended in time. But when the algebra teacher fell to his knees, the mannequins rushed forward to offer their assistance. Someone shouted, "Call an ambulance!" Suddenly chaos had replaced administrative efficiency; the orderly anthill had been kicked by a giant boot.

Sue gasped and said to Marla, "Gosh, wonder what's wrong with Mr. Montgomery?" They glanced over their shoulders to get Nancy's appraisal.

She was nowhere in sight.

Six

There was an orange and white ambulance parked in the circle drive in front of the school building when Carol and her two children arrived at Sharon Valley High to get Lana enrolled. Luke leaned up from the back seat.

"Wow, an ambulance! Wonder if somebody had a heart attack?"

"You'd probably hope so," Lana said grumpily. Sam had kept her awake most of the night, nipping and pawing at her through the blankets. Whenever she'd tried putting him on the floor, he'd begun to whine. And when she'd awakened, she'd found a smelly wet spot near the footboard of the antique four-poster bed she'd inherited from her paternal grandparents, and naturally on the quilt Mamaw Lizzie had painstakingly made for her. She wasn't in the cheeriest of moods.

As Carol pulled into a vacant parking spot, two ambulance attendants wheeled a stretcher through the front glass doors into the portico, followed by a host of curious onlookers. A woman wearing a lime-green dress climbed into the back of the emergency vehicle, the attendants chasing her in with the stretcher. The victim appeared briefly as a blur of white face covered with an oxygen mask, his body wrapped in a dark green blanket laced with straps. One of the attendants followed the stretcher inside; the other closed the rear doors and rushed up front to the driver's seat. Blue and orange lights swirling, siren blaring, the vehicle sped off. Luke, fascinated, followed it with his eyes.

"Mom, will you make Luke stay in the car?" Lana cast a scathing glance in her brother's direction. "He'll go in there an' act like a jerk, an' I don't want anybody to know I'm related to 'im. Please?"

Luke had every intention of seeing what the inside of the high school looked like. "Hey, that's not fair!"

"It's after eight," Carol said dryly. "I'm sure most of the kids are in class by now." Obviously all were not; there were several teens standing among the adults in the portico, still staring after the ambulance as if reluctant to accept that the show was over; their faces bore looks of anticipation, perhaps revealing morbid hopes that the speeding truck would overturn rounding a corner. "An' he won't act like a jerk," she continued, "because if he does, he can spend the rest of the weekend in his room."

She caught her son's reflection in the rearview mirror. "That understood, boy?"

In lieu of a verbal response, Luke jerked the left rear passenger door open and bolted for the glass entrance. Lana moaned. "Why can't he ever just walk?"

Carol and Lana followed the small crowd back into the building; Luke had already found his way to the offices. The buzz of conversation within the heart of the educational facility simmered down in the presence of the three strange faces, but a young girl sporting a bonnet of blond ringlets, whom Lana judged to be a snotty office aide/lifelong teacher's pet, continued in a high-pitched, airy voice: "He just couldn't breathe . . . oh my gosh, it was just horrible. I thought he was going to die, right on the spot!" Her audience murmured softly in agreement.

A short, beefy man with a pleasant face and an obvious toupee broke away and strode up to greet the Bremmerses. His skin was etched with a good number of laugh lines, but his usual smile was hidden behind a cloud of concern.

"Hello, I'm Richard Greer, principal. You must be Mrs. Bremmers." He held out a pudgy hand and gave Carol's a brief, clammy squeeze.

Carol nodded bleakly, empathizing with the tragedy. "I guess we could have come at a better time. We saw the ambulance . . . was it a student?"

Overhearing her heavy southern accent from across the room, the teacher's pet and one of her fluffy friends began to giggle.

Greer rubbed his bloated jowls, his bushy eyebrows furrowing. "No, one of our teachers. Don't know what happened, really—he was fine one minute, then the next . . ." His voice trailed off as he puzzled over the bizarre occurrence. "Don't think it was a heart attack. Just couldn't seem to get his breath, and I guess his stomach was cramping—"

"Did he eat some poison?" Luke blurted with his usual diplomacy. Lana jabbed him with her elbow.

"Shut up, you little creep. They don't know what happened. Didn't you hear what the man said?" She cast a withering look at the two socialites who were now giggling at her, whispering behind their hands, branding her with the name HICK. It was all over their faces.

"Mom, she hit me!"

Carol sighed with exasperation. "My children get along about as well as two pit bulls. But I trust you'll find Lana acts her age when she's in school."

Incensed that she had been placed on the same level as her brother, Lana sulkily turned her attention to some bulletins on a wall behind them, her arms crossed, foot tapping impatiently on the tiled floor. Unmistakable body language. Screw you, Mom. Screw this new school too. Carol pretended not to notice.

Luke, feeling triumphant, skipped out into the hall to examine some trophies in a glass display case. Greer excused himself to collect the papers he needed Carol to sign; his secretary had gone to the hospital with Montgomery. Lana's school records had already been transferred by mail from her previous school, Edgewater High, thus making the Bremmerses' appearance little more than a formality.

Lana wondered what Greg was doing at that moment back at Edgewater. She'd written him a nine-page letter the night before, sprinkling some of her favorite perfume on it before sealing it in the envelope. It was in her purse, stamped and ready to go; the obituary of a love that wasn't meant to be. She'd decided to be adult about the situation, to cut the cord cleanly so they could both get on with their lives. No doubt he was going to have an easier time of it.

Her mother was ready to leave. Mr. Greer walked with them to the double doors facing the faculty parking lot, his face still pinched with worry. He was concerned, of course, about Albert Montgomery, but he was also aware that upstairs in Room 208 there were thirty unsupervised teenagers. Picturing a human missile being ejected from one of the upper windows, he ushered Carol, Lana, and Luke to the door without offering the standard tour. Priorities. Human life outweighed protocol.

Outside, Carol handed Lana her schedule. "They pretty well matched the classes you were takin' at Edgewater . . . I guess some of the time slots will be diff'rent, but Mr. Greer is certain you'll be able to adjust to the transition easy enough, considerin' your SAT scores. Your teachers will issue your books on Monday."

Lana, still miffed by her mother's earlier comment, jabbed a finger at some figures penciled on the bottom of the paper. "That my locker number?"

"Yes, they have combination locks. Yours is—"

"I can read, Mom."

Carol's jaw set. "Watch your tone, Lana."

"Yeah, watch your tone," Luke echoed tauntingly.

With the Bremmers, it was business as usual.

Someone was knocking on the trailer door, impatiently, relentlessly. Jane finally gave up trying to ignore it and pulled herself out of the lumpy double bed she had shared with her husband for fifteen years. Theirs was a perfect marriage: he worked days and she worked nights, so their affection had not suffered the bitter erosion often seen when couples endured too much time together.

It seemed she had heard him get up and leave for his custodial job at the high school only minutes before, but a sleepy glance at the alarm clock on the nightstand revealed he had been gone for over two hours. She languidly pulled a beige quilted robe over her cotton teddy and dragged herself through the tiny cluttered room. The mirror over a dresser that had seen better days had no reason to feel shame in the presence of the human standing before it; Jane had also seen better days. She still hadn't quite come to grips with the lines that had become a permanent part of her once-flawless complexion, but she'd ceased to agonize over them. Her auburn hair, once the envy of her school chums, now looked as though she'd spent several hours with her head in the microwave oven. The years spent living in high altitudes had certainly taken their toll.

Whoever was knocking also kept trying the doorknob, which narrowed guilt for the intrusion down to two suspects: Jane's mother, or Edna Crassfield, next door neighbor and world-class gossip monger. Yawning, Jane peeked through the faded print curtain over the door's window. Suspect Number One was getting red in the face. Jane wearily opened the door.

"Hello, Mother."

Rose Hester heaved her balloon breasts in relief. "Mercy, thought you never was gonna get up," she sputtered as she propelled her massive figure toward the narrow doorframe. Jane scuffled into the kitchenette to make a pot of coffee.

"What are you in such a tizzy about? You know I'm always asleep at this hour."

"Let me sit down an' catch m'breath," Rose huffed, her sight set on her son-in-law's favorite chair. She plopped onto it like a wet bag of cement. Her first words, as always, were, "Aren'cha never gonna get a phone?"

Jane knew if she had one, it would be constantly glued to her head; between her mother and Edna Crassfield, she'd never get anything done. "You know we can't afford one," she answered, her standard response to the telephone issue. Rose dropped the subject with a grunt.

"Had prayer meetin' las' night. Brother Gibson had a message for you."

Jane gritted her teeth. Her mother was a faithful member of a small fundamentalist church whose members' main objective was to convert the "lost" of their own fold before moving on to save the world at large. Jane was the last survivor.

"Oh, really? And what did God have to say this time?" Brother Gibson's last message from "On High" was that if she didn't repent, something very terrible would happen to her. The next day she'd received a pay raise at the nursing home.

Rose looked at her daughter sternly. "He says you're a'headed right for the pit, Jane Rachel. God's warnin' you. The evil days are upon us, and whosoever's not a'washed in the blood of Jesus is a'goin' into the pit."

"You want some coffee, Mother?" Jane reached into the cabinet for a coffee cup, her mother's warning shooting through her head like a greased spear without leaving a trace of residue. She might just as well have told Jane that the valley was about to be squashed underfoot by Godzilla or King Kong; Jane would have been every bit as worried.

"My baby's goin' ta be lost forever," Rose blubbered. "It were my only wish on this earth that my children would go to their graves right with Jesus. I pray ever' night He'll soften that hard heart of yours. You don't know the tears I've a'cried."

Jane estimated that her mother's tears over her hard heart could just about fill the Yankee Stadium by now. "Listen, Mother, I'm happy just the way I am, okay? I don't think I have to spend twenty hours a week in church to go to Heaven. Don't you worry about it; I'm sure we'll be together in Eternity."

A comforting thought . . .

Rose took a yellowed hanky from her oversized purse and honked into it loudly. "You gotta give your whole heart, girl, not just a little piece," she argued, weeping. "An' when you do that, you'll wanna be in church gettin' fellowshiped."

A lewd picture formed in Jane's mind. She brushed it away. Carrying her steaming cup of coffee with care, she sat down at the Formica dinette table which still contained dirty dishes from her husband's breakfast and last night's dinner. She was thankful they were both slobs. They excused their slovenly domestic habits as an occupational hazard, since their working hours were spent cleaning up other people's messes. It took away the zeal for wanting to come home and do more of the same.

"You're wasting your time, Mother. I'm thirty-nine-years old, and I've got the right to make my own decisions. I believe in God and everything, but I just don't feel the need to make religion that big a part of my life. And nothing you or dear Brother Gibson or God says is going to change that. Besides, if I suddenly got a dose of the Holy Ghost, Harry would leave me. You know how he feels about all that. Is that what you want? You want me to get divorced?"

Rose shook her gray head and remained silent with her eyes closed, her lips forming unspoken words. When all else failed, she always started praying.

Jane's lips curled up in a slight smile as she sipped her black Sanka. The evil days are upon us . . .

When had they ever not been?

Third period, study hall in the cafeteria. Marla and Nancy, unable to get a table by themselves, endured the presences of three other seniors: Jess Staples, Brad Hendrickson, and Lisa Chambers. But since talking wasn't allowed anyway, the two friends passed their comments back and forth on notebook paper. Marla had written first: *What do you think happened to Doom? Did he have a heart attack or something?*

Under which Nancy had replied: *Who cares? Just be happy about it.*

Marla read the reply, then looked across the table at Nancy's face. Somehow it was different, but Marla couldn't quite decide how so. Harder, maybe. Like she was angry about something but trying not to show it. Perhaps Jay, her boyfriend, had said or done something to upset her during the previous class period; the two had biology together. Marla wanted to ask what the matter was, but Nancy suddenly seemed interested in actually doing some schoolwork. Marla tucked the note in her English textbook and turned to her reading assignment, trying to take her friend's advice and "just be happy about it."

Mr. Montgomery had been rushed off to the hospital that morning, saving them from possible suspension. How terribly convenient for them.

Dr. James Prescott studied the constricted pupils of his lethargic patient before returning his attention to the medical chart he held before him. His expression hinted only vaguely of his puzzlement; Albert G. Montgomery was exhibiting all the signs of cyanide poisoning (sans death): blue lips, breathing difficulty, numb extremities, severe headache—but not a trace of the poison had been found in his bloodstream. It didn't make sense.

Montgomery's lungs, even with the aid of an oxygen mask secured to his face and air tubes running into his nose, labored erratically for breath; the chronic headache had been eased by Percodan, but his limbs continued to feel like dead logs. He lay terrified in the body that had suddenly turned against him, not understanding, only knowing it was a fight to the death.

Prescott hung the chart back on the foot of Montgomery's bed and left the intensive care unit, stuffing his hands into the pockets of his lab coat. A pretty candy striper named Cindy nearly bumped into him.

"Oh, excuse me, Doctor. Guess I wasn't looking where I was going."

Prescott smiled tiredly, his steel-gray eyes moving perfunctorily over the girl's form. "Quite all right, Cindy. Just don't let it happen again."

She giggled and hurried away, her cheeks flamed with color. It occurred to Prescott that with very little effort he could have his way with her, but the idea didn't appeal as much as it would have in his younger days, when his sexual appetite and yearning for variety was seemingly insatiable. For the past few years he had been sticking mainly to his wife.

Montgomery's case crept back into his consciousness, retarding the growth of further fantasy. Prescott didn't like mysteries, and especially didn't like to say the words "I don't know," which was all the answer he presently had for Montgomery's condition. But he would hardly admit to that in writing. His prognosis on record was Acute Stress-Related Trauma. Let any of his colleagues study Montgomery's test results and argue with that.

Seven

By two P.M. on Saturday the Bremmerses' new home was in acceptable order, the empty packing boxes stashed in the garage. They were now officially "planted," and the absence of Hugh Bremmers was far less noticeable in surroundings with which he had never been associated. Carol was thankful for that; she'd requested the transfer, hoping it would aid in her emotional recovery. She was still absorbing the impact of the divorce, that forbidden cutting asunder of what God had joined together. They had vowed "Till death do us part." She wasn't dead, and neither was Hugh. Why had they even bothered to say the words?

Her husband of twenty-one years hadn't handled his midlife crisis with the greatest of ease. It had been his fortieth birthday, Carol had decided, when the simmering pot finally started to boil. Following a week of severe depression, he had suddenly come to the conclusion that what he needed to lift his spirits was a new sports car. The payments were no problem, so Carol hadn't given him any hell about it, although she'd been far from crazy about the idea. She knew his ego was suffering; he was going through that universal—and hopefully brief—stage in which he would have to face the fact that he would never again possess the body of a twenty-year old, nor would he accomplish all that he'd aspired to in his lifetime. But Hugh Bremmers became obsessed with cheating fate. Next it was the longer, more contemporary hairstyle. Then the weight lifting, jogging, and tennis lessons. Gambling. Questionable business deals. It was only a matter of time before a mistress entered the picture.

Four months, to be exact.

All at once Hugh wasn't joking anymore about trading her in on two twenty-year olds. She didn't know it yet, but he had already done it: he'd compromised, though; his mistress turned out to be only one twenty-four-year old.

Two months later he moved out, after making a torrid confession that Carol had barely heard. Only later was she able to reflect back and recognize the logical chain of events spelling out the doom of her marriage. She should have been well-prepared for the end, but she had denied everything, effectively burying her head in the sand and convincing herself that all was well in her perfect little world. He'd never stopped making love to her; in fact, their sex life had been on the upswing . . .

Surprise, surprise. That was only because his new little love muffin was teaching him new tricks and refiring his zest. Welcome back to the single scene, Carol. Your perfect little white-picket world was just an illusion.

After three months of mourning, she'd tried to date, but began to shy away from men when she realized how depressing an investment of time they were. Half of it was spent listening to the bitter ravings of men who had been "screwed over" by an assortment of ex's, the other half defending her position on not going to bed with someone she didn't love—forget the variety of diseases she might be subjecting herself to. The idea of sex for mere orgasm's sake repulsed her; she was a human being, not an alley cat. So what if her values were archaic? She was the one who had to live with herself.

She parted the orange curtains with brass kettles printed all over them to observe the activities going on in the backyard. The giant from next door had come over to visit his puppy, and between him and her kids, the little mongrel was being run ragged. The last thing she had needed was an unhousebroken Tasmanian Devil who was also teething. Why hadn't she just put her foot down and said no? Guilt?

Studying Spiro, she became aware that she was gritting her teeth. Maybe he was technically only a boy, but there was nothing about him physically that looked like one. He wasn't the ugliest thing she'd ever seen, but he was certainly the biggest. His hands looked like hams; his bone structure resembled a gorilla's. His shoes most likely had to be custom made; his feet were absolute ships. Was he stable? If one of her kids inadvertently (or otherwise) made him mad, would he grab them without warning and snap his or her neck like a dry piece of hickory? She imagined he was capable, if not inclined. Watching him lumber awkwardly after the puppy, she fervently hoped he would not be spending very much time over at their house, and that Lana—her too-trusting, too-generous daughter—never invited him over for lunch. He could probably eat a week's worth of groceries in one sitting.

Lana was getting bored. What she really wanted to do was cruise the neighborhood in search of a girlfriend; it would be nice to have at least one before starting school on Monday. But she stayed and played Trip the Puppy and Run for Your Heels, fearful that if she left, her squirrel brother would start asking Spiro all kinds of personal, tactless questions; for example, Why do you look so weird? There was a croquet set in the garage, and Lana supposed she could get into a game if they could keep Sam out of the way. She got up and brushed the dry grass from the knees of her faded 501's.

"I'm goin' to get the croquet set out. Y'all wanna play?"

"I do!" Luke piped up immediately. "An' I get the red mallet. That's my lucky mallet."

Spiro looked darkly confused and a little suspicious. "What's croquet?"

"You don' even know what croquet is?" Luke guffawed, clutching himself on the ground. "Boy, are you dumb."

The confusion and suspicion previously displayed on Spiro's face disappeared, his expression turning disturbingly blank. He pulled himself up and turned to go home.

Behind him, Lana's voice shrieked, "You moron! I

oughta cut your tongue out! Spiro . . . ?" Her words fell uselessly on his back. He kept moving away.

Seeing that he wasn't going to come back, Lana glared at her brother with raw contempt. "You hurt his feelin's, you assho'!"

Luke shrugged; what did he know about feelings? "You still wanna play croquet?"

"I think I'll go get your lucky mallet and smash your brains out with it," she retorted, and stalked off toward the house with half a mind to actually carry out her threat. How could she be related to someone who had the sensitivity of a dog turd? Much to her disgust, she immediately proceeded to step in one.

Jane clapped her hands with girlish excitement when Cora withdrew the small white book from her sweater pocket. "You found it!"

"Yeah, bottom of that chest, like I thought." Cora smiled. "Going through all that stuff was a trip down Memory Lane, I'll tell you. Not a pleasant trip, I might add. Anyway, here it is; be careful with it, it's about ready to fall apart as it is. Most of what she wrote was personal mushy stuff, gets a little disjointed toward the end 'cause of her . . . well, you'll find out. The first entry you're interested in was written November first, the day after it happened. There's a little more later on, but I'm not sure where. I guess you'll find it."

Jane held the tattered diary like a rare jewel. "Well, I'm due for a break right about now. Care to join me?"

Cora declined. "It's my turn to help Weaver in the laundry room," she said, smiling evenly to show how happy she was about it. "Just don't let anything happen to that book. If old Mr. Dobbs gets hold of it, he'll eat it."

Jane laughed. "And ask for seconds. Don't worry. I'll read it and get it right back to you." She turned and headed for the break room.

"Remember now, all that happened a long time ago, so don't upset yourself over it," Cora called after her. "Don't pay it any mind at all, hear? I don't wanna be responsible for your shrink bills."

Jane dismissed the warning with a wave. The diary

would no more affect her than the articles she read in the *National Enquirer*, which she admitted to no one—especially Harry—that she bought. It was the same petty curiosity that prompted her to fork out sixty-five cents for the cheap rag with its incredible news stories (REAL VAMPIRES STALK SMALL MIDWESTERN TOWN—WOMAN GIVES BIRTH TO REPTILE) that now drove her to read this diary, or so she told herself. She would dismiss its contents with the same ho-hum she gave the stories in the *Enquirer*. But she still wanted to read it.

No one else was in the break room. She sat at one end of the rectangular table and carefully opened the small book, realizing then how truly fragile the thing was; the pages had turned to brittle leaves. Even handling them as gently as she would butterfly wings, occasionally a corner would break off or a page would come loose from the binder, making her feel guilty for touching it at all. But she was almost . . .

there . . .

29, 30, 31 . . . November 1. The woman's handwriting was tiny and precise, and slightly angled to the left. The pages were also badly yellowed, and some of the ink had been smudged in spots, making a few words illegible.

Jane perched the book on the edge of the table and began to read, her brain sucking in the narrative like a vacuum cleaner.

> *Father came home last night long after Winni and I had gone to bed. We didn't leave our room, for we could tell that he was terribly upset; but though our door was shut, we could still hear what he was saying to Mother in the sitting room. He had gone with some of the men to track down the kidnapper who had taken Sarah Kennedy's baby. Sarah had heard little Jeremy crying, and thinking it was time for him to feed, went to the nursery to get him. But when she got there, Jeremy was no longer in his bassinet. The window of the nursery was open, and the curtains were blowing in. Sarah said she could hear the footsteps of someone running away, and little Jeremy crying.*
>
> *She then screamed for her husband, who upon*

learning of the horrible news, bolted from the cabin with his rifle and a lantern, but could not find a trace of his son or whoever had taken him. He then began to gather neighbors to help him look, and they presently came to induct Father, who did not hesitate to gather his own rifle and lamp and leave with them.

I remember that after he left, I immediately envisioned the strange family who three months earlier had moved into the old Ackley place near the base of Beacon Hill, a couple and a daughter aged about twelve, all of them with hair and eyes like pitch. I wondered at the time why they should have come into my mind, and decided later, when I learned the truth, that an angel must have whispered to me.

And so it was that when I heard Father in the sitting room declare that they had been responsible for the kidnapping, not the girl, but her parents, I was not greatly surprised. But when he told Mother that they, the men, had found little Jeremy pierced through the heart with an engraved dagger, a tool of Satan, I most nearly fainted, and Winni got up and joined me in my bed, and we wept together in each other's arms.

Father said that the baby had been sacrificed to the Devil; that clearly the strangers had performed an evil ritual, an act of witchcraft. They'd killed Jeremy on a stone altar upon which devilish markings had been painted; with blood, according to Lionel Coombs. A multitude of candles were burning all around, which was how the scene was discovered.

When Father and the men entered the clearing, the murderers were just standing there over the body, staring straight ahead, like they were waiting for something. Their faces were grave, but their eyes gave hint of some strange, heathenish satisfaction. They didn't even seem to care that they had been caught; contrarily, it was as if they had expected it.

It was strange, Father said, how the two seemed to cast a host of shadows, a trick of the candlelight, he supposed, but as he stepped through the trees, he could have sworn that there were at least a dozen people gyrating 'round the altar on which poor little

Jeremy lay. And so said all the other men later, after the hanging was done.

As for the hanging, he said there seemed, at the time, nothing else to do; the Obers, as they called themselves, had been caught red-handed. Amos Tulley had brought along some rope, as though he had known beforehand what would have to be done. Tobin Kennedy watched as the bodies were hoisted up, holding his dead baby in his arms, and crying, Father said, like a wounded animal. The wind rose up high and blew out all the candles, and a foul odor could be strongly smelled in their midst. This frightened all the men considerably, but they had to stay and make sure the job was completed; not one of them dared to let the Obers breathe a moment longer. The Obers had said nothing when the nooses were placed around their necks; whatever their last words were, they had already been spoken. Father said they hardly kicked at all.

Jane drew a ragged breath and let it out slowly. There wasn't much there that Cora, or Jasmine Colter, hadn't already told her, but seeing it in black and white had served up one hell of a graphic vision. Her fingers trembling slightly, she searched for the follow-up entries Cora had mentioned. She found the first one under November 14:

The jury has been selected for the trial, but Father is certain it will go in their favor, as they had only done what the Holy Word of God commanded, saying, Thou shalt not suffer a witch to live. He told Mother after supper that Morganna, the daughter, has been taken in by the Widow Symes, much to everyone's surprise, but also great dismay. They fear the girl now, as do Winni and I; is not the branch the same as the tree? She spends every night in the cemetery with her parents' tomb, which all still wonder how she afforded, speaking strange words to the wind, and few doubt but that she is talking to devils.

The last was under November 22:

Without meaning to at all, I tripped Morganna this morning as she was making her way up the aisle to recite her memorization of poetry. She said nothing to me at the time; only gave me a sore look. But later, at the noon recess, she drew me aside and told me I would be gravely sorry for what I had done. I told her I was already sorry, that I hadn't meant to do it, but she would not accept my apology, nor believe it had been an accident.

This evening while I was carrying a log to set on the fire, my legs buckled out from under me, and I have since been unable to stand on my feet. Father called Dr. Tippitt over, but he could find no reason for the paralysis. He believes I have been smitten by a disease, but I know what has truly happened. Winni knows too, but I have made her promise not to say anything to Father or Mother, lest something even more terrible should transpire, perhaps to all of us. I am hoping against hope, and praying with all my heart that the condition is a temporary one.

Scanning over the following pages, Jane learned that the writer's condition had worsened rather than gotten better. Along with the paralysis, she suffered tremors and fever, and nightmares from which she would wake screaming, her blankets soaked with cold sweat. The entries grew shorter, revealing with heartbreaking clarity the tortured girl's deteriorating mind.

On December 21 the writing stopped mid-sentence.

Jane closed the diary and shuddered. Had the girl died while making her last entry? She carried the grim book to the laundry room, located at the end of the south wing, ignoring the imploring faces of the wandering, discarded souls she passed in the corridor, unaware of their silent pleas for reassurance that they were still worth something. They were only a job to her.

She handed the diary back to its current owner without comment. Cora took one look at her face and laughed.

"Gawd, you're white as a sheet, Jane. I told you, don't pay any attention to that stuff, now. My mom's great aunt died of polio, plain and simple. I'm not saying there's no such thing as witchcraft, mind you, but the polio was bad in those days, and I'm sure her getting it when she did was just a coincidence."

Jane nodded numbly. "Of course." She glanced briefly at Norma Weaver, chief executive of the laundry room, who was eavesdropping in on the conversation. Norma gave her a wide smile, revealing ugly black gaps on either side of her eyeteeth; she reminded Jane of a hamster. The rest of the teeth were jagged, rotting protrusions that kept Norma's breath smelling like an outhouse.

"That li'l story git t'ya, hon?" She turned to pull a wet load of sheets from a front-loading washer; her question required no answer.

Jane grinned weakly and left. As if drawn by an invisible force, she found herself walking toward Jasmine Colter's room. The problem was, Jane desperately needed to believe the whole Ober thing was nothing but bullshit, but she wasn't doing a very thorough job of convincing herself. She hadn't been prepared for all that she'd sat down to read. It had affected her more profoundly than she could ever have guessed.

Jasmine Colter was hardly a logical source to turn to for negative reinforcement—au contraire, she would try her bloody best to sway Jane to the superstitious side of the fence, pump her full of shivering dread and have her dashing to the local Catholic church for some genuine holy water. Still, Jane felt the need to talk to her. There had to be more to learn—actual information, not speculation—and only by knowing all the facts could she lay to rest the rising tempest in her mind.

She quietly stepped into Room 128; Jasmine, a white shrunken husk on the pillow, opened her eyes. Her bible lay facedown on the floor; she had apparently dropped it.

Jane moved closer, apprehension closing in on her like a shroud. Jasmine was much quieter now that her medication included mild tranquilizers, but this afternoon she appeared two miles past the brink of peace, hovering precariously over the chasm between life and death. Only a minute spark in her eyes gave any indication that she wasn't quite ready to let go.

"Morganna's comin' for me," she whispered hoarsely, barely above a breath.

Jane touched the old woman's cold, papery hand. "No, Jasmine. Even if she could, she'd have no reason to."

Terror leapt on the old woman's face. "But she does, Pammie, you never knew . . ."

Pammie? Jasmine thought she was talking to her daughter. "Mrs. Colter, I'm not—"

". . . what I done," Jasmine sighed, sinking farther into the pillow. Her lips parted slightly and froze.

Leaning over the bed, Jane saw that the faded blue eyes were fixed, pupils dilated. Jasmine Colter was dead.

Pamela hung up the phone, too numb for the time being to let the tears flow. It was over. She turned to her husband, who was watching an NFL game with their son.

"Harold, my mother—"

"Just a minute, Pam. This is a very crucial play." Harold Mingee leaned forward on his elbows in preparation to cheer or curse, depending on whether or not the field goal was accomplished by his team. Harold's looks were at complete odds with his personality. He looked soft, with almost embryonic facial features; a doughboy with bug-eyes and a serious overbite, no chin to speak of, thin brown hair. But within this mushy exterior beat the heart of a barracuda.

Far be it from Pamela to intrude with heartbreaking news on thoughtless pleasure. Her mother wasn't going to get any deader. And even if Pamela's husband had allowed her to speak, all his response would have amounted to anyway was something along the lines of, "Jesus, Pam, I'm really sorry. Could you make us some more popcorn?"

Shoulders slumped, she slid back the patio door and stepped into the warm sunshine. The pool had been drained and covered for the season; brown and yellow leaves covered the tarp. She stared at them for some time, thinking that her mother was now very much like them.

After a while she noticed the absence of rock music blaring from the clubhouse. How could a group of teenagers get together and resist a perfect opportunity to worsen their hearing loss? Jasmine had been fond of classical music, in particular Beethoven and Wagner. She would never hear them again. Total sensory shutdown. She would simply never anything.

Memories . . .

Jasmine young, vibrant, bustling around the kitchen preparing meals fit for a king. Cutting fresh flowers from the garden for the dining table, wearing a wide-brimmed straw hat. Singing to the birds. Kissing skinned knees.

Talking about witches in her bedroom.

Pamela shook the thoughts away. She would have to teach herself to forget the later things, the doings of the shriveled old woman Jasmine had somehow mysteriously turned into, seemingly overnight. Time would, on its own, weed those memories out, and all that would remain would be the glory of a soul who gave, without reservation, gifts of love in everything she did for her family.

Inside the clubhouse, Marla, Nancy, Nancy's boyfriend Jay Gorman, and Jennifer Parks, a peripheral member of Marla and Nancy's clique, were playing an unenthusiastic game of Liar's Dice. The one-room cabin was twenty by fifteen feet, the lower walls lined with cedar storage compartments that doubled as seats, the removable cushions covered with genuine leather. Shelves on the rear wall contained a small television set and stereo system, a few albums, a wilting Wandering Jew. Yellowing ferns hung from thick redwood beams below the slanted roof; in the northwest corner an old fishing net was spread out like a spider's web, dipped in strategic locations by the weight of conch shells. In the northeast corner was a door that led to a bathroom equipped with sink, toilet, and shower, cabinets full of fluffy beach towels, bathing suits, and tanning products. Money couldn't buy happiness, but it could buy the kind of misery the Mingees could live with.

They'd set up a green card table in the center of the

room, and sat around it in uncomfortable wrought-iron garden chairs. Jay pushed the overturned cup under which three dice were hidden toward Jennifer and announced dryly, "Three kings and two aces."

Jennifer, an anorexic with dark blond hair and sharp, birdlike features, studied the dice he'd left out in the open with a doubtful expression. "I know you're lying bigger than Dallas." After a moment's deliberation, she swooped up the cup, challenging his claim. "I knew it!"

Jay left off picking at his face, scowled, and tossed her a penny. "I've had enough of this stupid game. Let's go to the park; it's too nice to be cooped up in here."

"We could go visit Montgomery in the hospital," Jennifer said snidely. "Take him a get-well-soon card."

"How about a die-real-soon card?" Jay snickered.

Everyone laughed, Marla somewhat nervously, Nancy much too loudly.

"Your mom know anything about what's going on?" Jennifer asked Nancy when the laughter died. "She volunteers up at the hospital, doesn't she?"

"She told me it had something to do with stress," Nancy answered, her eyes vacant, the hint of a smile on her lips. "That's what the chart says, anyway. She asked one of the nurses."

Jay slapped himself. "Stress! That bastard only dishes it out!"

"You think it could be something else?" Marla leveled her gaze at her best friend.

"How would I know?" Nancy shrugged, avoiding eye contact. The hint of smile vanished. "All I know is, I'm glad it happened."

"I wish it would happen to the coach," Jay said half-jokingly. "I think he used to be an army drill sergeant. His workouts are pure hell."

Nancy lifted an eyebrow. "Do you really wish that?"

"Nah." Jay pumped his biceps proudly. "It's been worth it."

"What if Jay was serious?" Marla said accusingly, forcing Nancy to look her in the eye. "Is that something you could arrange?" She didn't know why she'd said it, and was a little surprised she had, but there it was.

Nancy gazed back at her coolly. "Don't be ridiculous, Marla. And I'd watch that mouth if I were you."

After wandering aimlessly all over town, glowering at all the passersby he encountered—and oh, couldn't he scare them with just a look when he wanted to; what a joy to discover—Spiro finally went home, completely unsuspecting of the assault that would greet him. His mother had found the picture he'd drawn of Lana the night before, after he'd come back from checking on Sam. He had done a particularly good job, and so hadn't torn it up into tiny pieces as he usually did with such artwork.

A grim mistake.

She was sitting in her favorite rocking chair, rocking furiously. The picture was laid out in her lap. Her eyes were shooting sparks of outrage. "Git in here and close the door," she said promptly, her voice a jagged blade. "You're in mighty big trouble, boy. Mighty big trouble."

Spiro was certainly smart enough to comprehend the circumstances quite clearly. He'd been caught drawing dirty pictures. A picture of Lana naked with her legs spread apart. By his mama. Was there anything worse?

She shoved it in his face. "Who is that? That little tramp next door, th' one you gave that damn puppy to?"

She received no answer.

"Speak to me boy," she hissed, "or it's just going to go worse for you. Who is this a picture of? That yella-headed slut next door?"

Guilty nod.

"I knew it, I just knew it," Bertha spat, wadding the paper into a tight ball. "Did she take her clothes off for you? Did she let you see her naked?"

"No . . ."

"Don't you lie to me, boy!" She rose to slap him, paused, hand raised. "She let you see, didn't she?"

Spiro flinched. "Just her panties, Mama."

The open palm crashed against his cheek. "Filth! Go to your room!"

She came in with the iron a few minutes later and plugged it in. Spiro heard a hissing sound and trembled on the bed. He was sitting on the edge, clasping and unclasping his hands, subconsciously rubbing the scars. She slapped him again.

"I burned that filthy picture of yours. Now you know what's going to happen to you."

"Please Mama, I promise I won't do it no more," Spiro pleaded in vain.

Bertha tapped her toe on the dusty hardwood floor, the iron in one hand, the other settled impatiently on an oversized hip. "I know you won't never do it again, 'cause I'm fixin' to make sure you've learned your lesson." She moistened a finger with her tongue and touched it to the iron; a light sizzle could be heard.

She smiled. "Almost ready. Give me your hand, boy. The hand you done it with."

He closed his eyes and gave her his right hand, wetting his pants in fear, shuddering from head to toe. She held his hand open by the tips of his fingers, watching them twitch in fearful anticipation. She saw that he had peed himself and slapped the iron down.

His scream shook the walls.

Hours later Spiro stared at the swollen, fiery blisters on his right hand and fingers, which were still throbbing unmercifully, his face settled into an expression of peace. She was singing to him now from her bedroom, her voice sweet and gentle. She really did love him.

He soon closed his eyes and fell asleep.

Eight

Harry was still awake when Jane got home at eleven-ten. He didn't have to work on Sundays, as she usually did, and would stay up so long on Saturday nights that, unable to get up and walk back to the bedroom, he would fall asleep in his easy chair and sleep until Jane left for work the following afternoon.

He was working on his fifth Coors tallboy, his stock-inged feet propped up on the weary ottoman, his mind attempting to focus on an old Philip Marlowe mystery on the black and white television screen. Jane leaned over and gave him a peck on the cheek. "Hi, hon."

He looked up and smiled blearily. "Have a rough shift, ol' gal? Ya look like hell."

"Thanks a lot. By the way, you don't exactly have room to talk." She patted her husband's protruding abdomen to emphasize her point, then kicked off her shoes and cleared herself a place to sit on the couch. She flopped down on it with a groan. "Jasmine Colter died today. I was with her. She thought I was her daughter."

Harry belched. "So your job's gonna be a li'l easier now, huh?"

"I suppose so," Jane replied softly, the memory of preparing the shrunken, wrinkled corpse for the mortuary resurfacing, making her feel anew the revulsion she'd experienced in the performance of her wretched duty. "I wanted to talk to her," Jane went on, needing to discuss the other thing that was haunting her. "A few weeks ago she started up with this witch thing again, I probably mentioned it—"

"About two dozen times."

"Anyway, she added some details to her story the other night that got my curiosity up, mainly that the Obers had killed a baby in some kind of witchcraft ceremony. I mentioned it to Cora, and she told me it was true—that her mom's aunt had kept a diary, and all that stuff was in it. She brought the diary to work with her today and let me read it. I wish I hadn't. It's been bugging me ever since."

"Why? That was a long time ago. Nobody believes in that stuff nowadays," Harry declared scornfully, sucking down the beer that had grown warm in his hand. He crumpled the can, tossed it toward an overflowing trash can four feet away, missed.

Jane squirmed on the couch. "There's a lot of people who believe in it. Cora believes; she told me so herself. And remember that album Mother kept trying to get us to listen to? That Mike Warnke album? He's a preacher now, but he used to be a high priest of a satanic coven in California that had over three thousand members. And I'm sure there are plenty others. You know how this town is."

"So what? A bunch of idiots believing in something makes it true? Why's this all the sudden buggin' you, anyway?" Harry hoisted himself out of his chair and padded over to the refrigerator for another beer.

"I don't know," Jane lamented, trying desperately to find an answer. "The girl who wrote the diary accidentally tripped the Obers' daughter, Morganna, who told her she would really be sorry. She was stricken with polio that very night."

"Just like she'd been anyway, if that other girl hadn't opened her mouth."

"And the polio . . . she was crippled. Couldn't walk. That seems to tie in with getting tripped . . ."

"Mother fuck," Harry muttered, popping open the lid of his beer can and taking a long swig. " 'Fore I know it, you'll be goin' to church meetin's, then comin' home preachin' to me. I can smell it coming, with this kind of talk. I'll tell you right now, I think it stinks."

Jane stiffened. "I'm not getting religious on you, Harry. It's just that too many coincidences stack up to a big question mark, and I'm having a little trouble ignoring it. I know the answer I want, and it isn't yes. But I won't be satisfied until I've proved to my own mind, beyond the shadow of a doubt, that the answer is no. And I will, I'm sure. Eventually."

"Why the hell don'cha just forget about it?" Harry grumbled, weaving back to his chair. It was the evil that mortal men did, in his opinion, that people should be afraid of, not fairy-tale devils. "Bad things happen to people all the time—you gonna try to blame all that on the goddamn Devil, or witchcraft? Like yesterday morning, one of the teachers had this sudden attack while he was waiting to see Greer about something, got rushed off in an ambulance. Greer's seckatary said he was fixin' to get a couple of girls suspended. I suppose you'd think they put a hex on 'im so he couldn't do it."

"Why can't we discuss this without you trying to make me look like an idiot?" Jane said, pouting. "If anything else was bothering me, you'd help me work it out. Don't worry, I'm not going to turn into my mother on you, physically or mentally. By the way . . . she came over late this morning, got me out of bed. She had an urgent message for me from Brother Gibson; he says I'm headed straight for the pit. Doesn't that put your mind at ease?"

They laughed together, the tension between them dissipating.

"I'm sorry, hon," Harry apologized. "It's just . . . you know how I feel about religion. I had it crammed down my throat same as you did, and by a bunch of no-good hypocrites. Daddy preached those fire and brimstone sermons loud enough to raise the dead without blinking an eye, but I knew what he was up to with that cute li'l church seckatary of his, Miss Paulette Pringle. I think she was screwing half the deacons too. Imagine Mama's surprise when the saintly li'l slut turned up knocked an' started pointin' her finger. Out come the bottle Mama thought she'd been keepin' such a big secret. Baptists, they're the worst." He said the last as if something bitter had just landed on his tongue.

His wife smiled and gave him a hug. "Yeah, that's the kind of thing I need to be reminded of. Lord, I'm hungry. Did you eat up all the leftover meat loaf?"

Harry confessed with a look of embarrassment. "I think I pretty well wiped out all the leftovers, darlin'."

"I guess I'll just have a sandwich then." Jane wearily propelled herself into the kitchen, thinking that if she had the energy tomorrow, she would clean the trailer before going to work; decaying food clinging to the piles of unwashed dishes was beginning to smell.

She opened a lower cabinet and took out a can of sandwich spread, frowning at the horned image holding a pitchfork on the red and white label. Jasmine's final words echoed in her ears: *Morganna's comin' for me . . . but she does, Pammie, you never knew what I done . . .*

What in God's name could that have been? Jane's mind refused to fill in the blank. She replaced the can of spread and shut the cabinet, her gut suddenly full of lead.

Lana had finally coaxed her mother into letting her take the car out for a sightseeing spin. She had driven around for almost half an hour, checking out the bedroom town she would be living in until she left next year for college. She looked forward to it for one reason only—she would no longer have to live with her toad of a brother.

Earlier that afternoon she'd gone over to Spiro's to apologize to him for what her dippy sibling had said, but his mother had told her—in venomous language and tone—that her son was not at home, but as soon as he did show up, he was really going to get it. And whatever he was going to get it over apparently had something to do with her, but the insinuations had left Lana more confused than informed.

Before going back home, she decided to stop at the Tastee Freeze drive-in for a Coke. She pulled up next to a blue Monte Carlo and smiled shyly at the two boys sitting in the front seat. The one on the passenger side whistled softly.

"Hey babe, where did you come from? Never seen you around here before." He had frizzy brown hair that might have last been combed several months ago, dark, hawklike eyes, flat nose, and a set of yellowed, crooked teeth in a mouth intended for a catfish.

"Never been around before," Lana answered, now

self-conscious of her accent. She looked past the frizzy-headed boy at the one sitting behind the wheel. He was strikingly handsome, and like his friend, seemed totally interested in her.

Dennis was angry that Marla hadn't called him yet to patch up their fight, and pride prevented him from calling her. It was the standard adolescent Ego Vs. Ego impasse which could well last for a century or two. But Dennis had just seen the answer to his dilemma drive up in a gray Buick sedan. The minute he took up with a babe like that, Marla would have to relent—jealousy would leave her no other choice. She might not think she wanted him now, but she'd damn sure go to Hell before she'd let someone else have him. A delicious plan. Perhaps there would even be additional fringe benefits . . . the blonde looked like she knew how to have fun.

"I just moved here Thursday," she was saying, "from Tyler, Texas. My mom's an adjuster for State Farm, an' they transferred her up here. You guys go to high school, right?"

Dennis moaned inwardly; she was nothing but a dumb country bumpkin. But that wasn't altogether bad news . . . he'd heard a few stories about homegrown Southern Belles. Typically they were hot.

Dennis's friend, Wayne Forrester, laughed abrasively, and began to mock her: "Wahl, wahl, from Tahler, eh? Yeah, war hah school stewdents. When wey fail lahk it."

Dennis poked him in the back and muttered, "Cool it, shithead." He smiled at Lana, who looked ready to hurl cow chips at both of them. "Please excuse my ill-mannered friend here, he has neither class nor brains. He wasn't making fun of you, really. He was just trying to be friendly. Weren't you, asshole?"

Wayne had gotten the message. "Exactly. Why don'cha come over and join us. We've got all kinds of room over here."

Lana's anger melted quickly, and as she scooted toward the passenger side of her car to get out, the driver's door being blocked by the menu and speaker pole, Wayne turned to Dennis and grinned.

"Hot damn. Southern Comfort."

"She's mine," Dennis whispered, as if there was really

a contest. "For a while, anyway. You can have her when I'm through."

A silver-tongued manipulator like Dennis had little trouble convincing Lana to go for a ride with him, but first he had to get rid of Wayne. Half an hour later the two lit up cigarettes as they walked up Wayne's weed-veined sidewalk, purposefully knocking into each other and laughing, Lana having been left behind in the car. Wayne's laughter didn't come from the heart, but he didn't want to look like a hangdog. So he was getting dumped off early because there was only one girl and Dennis wanted her. No fucking big deal.

He puffed furiously on his smoldering "coffin nail," his father's nickname for cigarettes. Of course, he had every right—he was dying of lung cancer, the direct result, his physician said, of his twenty-four-year, three-pack-a-day habit, and why his son should continue to smoke in light of that was beyond him. But Wayne figured his deadly habit was a slow enough bullet, and who wanted to live past the age of forty anyway? "So you think she's hot to trot?" he whispered to Dennis when they reached the porch.

Dennis blew a lacy stream of smoke from his lips and nostrils, a wolfish grin appearing on his face. "Guess I'll find out pretty soon. Want me to call you later with the final score?"

Good-Sport Wayne smiled and said, "Might as well. I'll just be sitting around beating my meat."

Dennis laughed, tossed his cigarette down on Wayne's porch and crushed it out with his boot. "Heard you can go blind doing that."

"I'm just going to do it till I need glasses," Wayne said, recalling the old joke. He kicked Dennis's crushed butt into the grass and went in.

Dennis returned to the car with a confident stride.

Lana had finished the Coke Dennis had bought her, and was munching on the ice. She offered some to him, but he politely declined the offer. He had a fever, all right, but ice wasn't the cure for it. He'd been a "good boy" for too long—and doing a lot of what Wayne had jokingly mentioned, though he would never in a million years admit it to anyone, even in jest—and it was just about time he got some real action. Marla was a regular ice maiden, which in Dennis's book gave him unspoken permission to go for any available strays he came across, whether Marla and he were fighting or not. He smiled innocently at the sweet piece sitting next to him. After Marla got him back, no doubt Lana would have trouble making any worthwhile friends at school, generously supposing anyone would want to hang around with a hick in the first place.

"Been up on Beacon Hill yet?" he asked, pulling into the street.

"I don't think so. Where is it?"

"North end of the valley. There's a scenic overlook on top, where you can see all the pretty lights down here over the treetops. Big deal, huh?"

Lana smiled. "Oh, I think it'd be real pretty."

"There's something else up there too," Dennis continued in a deeper voice. "Spooky old graveyard. We all go up there on Halloween in costumes and party. You'll have to come. It's really a blast."

"Count me out on that one," Lana said with a shiver. "I'm not a big graveyard fan, an' I sure wouldn't be caught in one at night. Especially on Halloween."

Dennis gave her a sidelong glance. "You're not superstitious, are you?"

"Totally," Lana confessed. "You won't catch me walkin' under any ladders, and I've thrown a fair amount of salt over my shoulder. An' there really are such things as ghosts, you know. I've seen pictures of 'em. At least two famous actresses I know of lived in haunted houses, Elke Sommer an' Linda Gray. What reason would they have to make up stories like that?"

"Publicity?" Dennis ventured.

"No, because things really were goin' bump in the night," Lana countered. "Or growlin' behind a basement door, like in Linda Gray's house." Lana tapped the upturned Coke cup to get the last few melting squares of ice to slide into her mouth. Dennis turned on the radio.

"Well, I don't believe in any of that shit myself. There's got to be a logical explanation for all that, and pictures can be faked real easy. But, people like to believe in stuff like that, so they don't go to a lot of trouble to figure it out. When a tree falls in the forest and there's no one around to hear it, does it make any noise?"

Lana's brow creased with confusion. "What does that got to do with the price of eggs in China?"

"Noises are in our heads," Dennis said impatiently, wanting to turn the conversation toward more intimate matters. "And nobody really knows what the brain's all about." He left the explanation at that and began drumming his fingers on the dash in rhythm to the ZZ Top tune rattling through his speakers. *She's got legs . . .*

Lana let the subject drop; he obviously wasn't interested in sharing speculations about the supernatural.

After turning onto Parish Lane, Dennis turned the music down low. "Anyone ever tell you you're a very pretty girl?"

The compliment quickened Lana's pulse. "Once or twice," she answered modestly. Actually she'd been told dozens, maybe even hundreds of times—including ego strokes from relatives—but she thought it would sound conceited to say so. If she'd known Dennis better, she might have told the truth anyway—she was naturally cocky—but she didn't yet feel comfortable enough around him to flop out her whole personality. The great teenage dilemma: Who am I with this person?

"I'll bet a lot more than that." Dennis winked. "You know you kinda look like Jodie Foster? Ever thought of becoming an actress or model?" He was launching into his favorite tried-and-true strategy: pump up the girl's ego, make her feel good in one way—and more than likely she'll return the favor in another way. Simple psychology. Or was it biology . . . ?

Lana dismissed his question with a laugh. "Are you kiddin'? I can hardly memorize my own phone number, let alone a whole script. An' I'm too short to be a model. I'm only five-four."

"Well, I bet you still had about a hundred boyfriends back in Tyler, huh? Am I right or am I right?"

"Only one, actually." Lana sighed. "Greg Abbott. We used to write songs together . . . well, I'd write poems an' he'd put 'em to music. He played the piano. You should hear him do some of Elton John's stuff. He's really good."

Dennis nodded as if impressed, but what he wanted to know was how far Greg Abbott had gotten with his girlfriend, not how well he played the piano. "So you two really liked each other a lot, huh?"

Lana wasn't sure what Dennis was getting at, but she didn't want to spend the time talking about her lost boyfriend. "Sure, but now he's there an' I'm here, an' that's just the way it is. I mailed him a letter yesterday, tellin' him I thought it best if we just go on with our lives and give other people a chance. We can't change the situation, so we might as well. You think that sounds cold?"

Dennis didn't answer. They were approaching the top of the hill.

Carrying the squirming rabbit against his chest, Jay followed Nancy down the forbidding path to the grotesque garden of death. After several minutes of milling around, seduced to one spot after another by Nancy's flashlight beam, they stopped before a flat stone marking the grave of Earl James Cunningham, who had died only two days after his forty-eighth birthday.

"We'll do it here," Nancy announced, lowering herself to a kneeling position. Jay, already feeling guilty about the rabbit's fate, did likewise. Nancy set the flashlight down on the stone and took ten items from a large cloth tote bag: a grease pencil, her father's hunting knife, five short candlesticks, a lighter, the black-hooded cape, and finally, the ledger.

Jay watched in uneasy silence as Nancy ceremoniously donned the cape, opened the ledger, and began to duplicate the markings within it onto the headstone with the grease pencil. As she worked he began to sense another presence very near—not just one, but several presences—surrounding them as shadows, observing their activities with keen interest. He started to say something about it to Nancy, but he couldn't find his voice.

When she was finished drawing, Nancy took the lighter and began burning the bottoms of the candlesticks so that they would stand upright in pentagram formation on the stone. That done, she lighted them and sighed with satisfaction, then smiled up at Jay, looking very much the witch she was aspiring to be. Jay didn't return the smile. He looked down at Thumper, who had suddenly become statue-still, as if he too were aware of the phantom spectators.

"Put him in the inner circle and hold him down," Nancy commanded.

Offering the helpless creature silent apologies, Jay did as he was told, wanting to close his eyes until this was all over, but he was too afraid. If the outer circle of shadows started closing in on them, he wanted to know.

The flames began to dance wildly on their wicks as Nancy began reading the incantation from the ledger, her voice taking on a foreign, almost hypnotic quality. Jay didn't want to hear the sounds being intoned: they made up the language of Hell and spoke entreaties to the damned. Beneath his hands, Thumper still seemed paralyzed, and probably was, by fear. On some instinctual level he might know more about this infernal ceremony than they did.

There was one other vehicle parked on the scenic overlook, which Dennis recognized immediately as belonging to Jay "Pizza Face" Gorman, Marla's best friend's boyfriend, nicknamed Pizza Face (behind his back) because of his severe acne problem. There were no occupants in sight, but he thought he could see the Dodge Charger rocking slightly. Choosing a spot on the left, he pulled in and switched off the engine. He needed another cigarette. "Let's get out and take a little walk," he suggested, grabbing his pack off the dash.

They got out of the car, and Dennis made sure he was downwind from Lana—who'd earlier informed him she was allergic to cigarette smoke—before lighting his Marlboro. He puffed on it greedily for several moments, then nodding toward the Charger and smiling, took Lana's hand and pulled her with him, his intention to intrude on the illicit activities in the backseat quite clear. Lana shook her head emphatically and tried to break free, but Dennis refused to let go. He wanted her to get an eyeful; maybe it would arouse her lust.

But the backseat—as well as the front seat—of the Charger proved to be empty. Lana finally succeeded in yanking her hand away. "It's not nice, trying to sneak up on people. Why would you wanna do that?"

He looked around at the shadowy shapes of the trees, listening for the sound of nearby moans. He heard one, but it came from Lana.

"What's wrong?"

"I'm cold," she complained, wrapping her arms around herself. "An' I really don't like this place . . . it's spooky. Now why did you pull me over to this car? You thought we were gonna see some people naked, didn't you? Were you tryin' to embarrass me, or what?"

Dennis heard nothing but the invitation to share his body heat. "Come here, stand next to me if you're cold," he suggested softly, moving up to her and enfolding her in his arms. She tensed noticeably, but didn't try to pull away.

He stroked the small of her back. "You miss your boyfriend?"

Lana could feel his heart beating, faster, faster. He was obviously getting turned on. *Red Alert. Do you miss your boyfriend? Translation: Do you miss his touches, his kisses, his whatever else you'd gotten used to? ARE YOU HORNY?*

"No," she lied, attempting to put some distance between their bodies.

Dennis clutched her tighter. "Hey, there's no reason for you to fridge up. I'm not gonna bite."

"That ain't what I'm worried about," Lana snapped, breaking free from his grasp. "I don't know what you had in mind when you brought me up here, but all I'm interested in is talkin'. I don't even know you."

Dennis now grimly realized that the fringe benefits he'd hoped for wouldn't be so easily obtained. But what the hell; his main purpose in being with the hick anyway was to make Marla jealous. Some kids at the drive-in had watched her get into his car in front of the printer's across the street, but for all they knew, she was going to be with Wayne. (At least some were undoubtedly stupid enough to think that.) Dennis wanted to find Jay and whoever was with him—probably Nancy, which would be absolutely perfect—and let them see him with a strange girl at the overlook. Nancy would break her neck rushing home to call Marla. The clincher, though, would be for him to have his arm around Lana in the hall at school when Marla walked by. "Hey, what are you getting so upset about?" he asked innocently, spreading his palms in a pretentious gesture of confusion. "I was just trying to keep you warm. Jesus."

Lana didn't quite believe him, but she felt stupid nonetheless. "Sorry, I don't want you to get the idea I'm a prude . . . I'm not. But we did just meet, you know, and I thought you were gettin' some funny ideas. This place . . . and here we are all alone . . ."

"Forget it." Dennis puffed some more on his cigarette, soothing his nerves with the drug. So he wasn't going to get his rocks off—he didn't need to hear the bitch expound on her virtues and sob about being afraid he was going to rape her. "Anyway, we're not alone—there should be at least two other people up here. Wanna go look for them? I'll introduce you."

Lana shrugged. "I guess so, long as they're not, uh . . . busy."

Jay realized that Nancy had stopped speaking, and when he looked from the sacrificial animal to her hood-framed face, he saw by the candlelight that it was sheened with sweat. She had put the ledger aside and had taken up the hunting knife, clutching the handle with both hands, the gleaming tip pointed downward. Jay imagined he heard a dozen intakes of breath as their corrupt audience anticipated the plunging of that razor-sharp blade. Jay held his own breath, and at the moment of the blade's descent, involuntarily squeezed his eyes shut.

Accompanied by a shuddering jerk, there was a squeal of pain from Thumper, and warm blood splashed on Jay's left hand. He immediately withdrew both hands from the rabbit, his eyes reopening just in time to see a brilliant blue flame flash around and through the rabbit's body. A second later something hot and wet smacked into Jay's face.

* * *

Lana came to a stop and hung her head. "On second thought, I really oughta get back to my mom's car. If you want, you can follow me back to my house and—"

Her words were cut off by a distant terror-filled scream followed by abrupt silence. Lana jumped about two feet in the air, a surprised shriek escaping her own lips. Dennis felt his guts tighten. "Jesus Christ. What was that?"

"I think it was just a screech owl." Lana gulped, her heart pounding. "But it's kinda hard to tell 'em apart from a real person screamin'. Which do you think it was?" She wanted to discuss the matter sitting safely in Dennis's car with the doors locked, but her feet were cemented to the ground.

"It came from the cemetery." Dennis took a final deep drag on his cigarette and let it fall to the ground. "I've got a flashlight in my glove compartment. I'm going to go check it out."

Lana shuddered. "You've gotta be kiddin'. Let's go call the police an' let them check it out."

"Fuck the cops," Dennis muttered, heading back toward his Monte Carlo. "You just sit tight, lock yourself in the car if you want to, but I'm going down there . . . that scream sounded pretty human to me. It was probably just Jay and one of his football buddies playing around, jumping out from behind tombstones at each other, yelling boo and shit. But you never know." He tossed the keys down on the front seat and grinned. "If I'm not back in an hour, then you can call the pigs."

Lana balked. "An hour!"

"All right, ten minutes," he amended. "Fifteen tops."

He took his flashlight from the glove compartment and headed for the path.

Kneeling among the tombstones in the moonwashed cemetery, Nancy removed her hand from Jay's mouth. He maintained his silence with difficulty, because he could still feel the hot, wet slap on his face, like an echo of touch. Nancy quickly put everything back into the tote bag and was now rising to her feet. "Come on, we've got to get out of sight. Someone might have been on the overlook and heard you scream."

Jay clambered to his feet, looking morosely at the rabbit's still form. "We just gonna leave it there?"

"Forget about the stupid rabbit," Nancy hissed over her shoulder as she hurried for cover. "Come on, we've got to hide. Now."

Jay didn't think he could stand to touch Thumper now anyway. Suddenly he wanted to vomit, but he hurried after Nancy instead, in no way inclined to touch his own face either. The last thing he needed right now was to learn that his brother's beloved pet had died for nothing.

Lana was about to beat it for the nearest phone when she finally saw Dennis emerging from the trees fourteen minutes later, holding the flashlight in his left hand, a large white object dangling from his right. She rolled her window down and leaned out.

"What's that? Did you find anybody?"

"No, just this," Dennis answered thickly, lifting the thing higher. Something was dripping from it.

Lana stared, horror-struck. "Is that a rabbit? What—"

"Found it laying on one of the flat grave markers. It's still warm."

It was then that Lana realized what was dripping on the ground—blood. She thought she might puke. "Oh, that's horrible! An' it's not even a wild rabbit. That's the kind they sell in pet stores."

Dennis considered telling her about the strange markings he'd found on the stone surrounding the animal's body, but decided against it. That would only bring up the subject about spooks again, and he still didn't care to discuss it. He didn't even want to think about it. If Jay and whoever wanted to get their kicks by killing white rabbits in the old cemetery, that was their problem. He tossed the limp body into some underbrush and walked around to the driver's side.

"Why would somebody do that?" Lana wailed as soon as he got in the car. She stayed well over on her side this time, scrunched against the door as if trying to sink into it.

"Kinky thrills," Dennis shrugged. "You name it, somebody out there does it for kicks."

Lana wanted to find whoever had killed the rabbit and

103

kick their heads off, which would be no less than what they deserved. She and Dennis hadn't heard a screech owl. They'd heard the scream of a human being, not emitted from personal injury, but expressing a primitive conquest over a defenseless animal. The idea disgusted her totally. She clenched her fists. "Got any idea who it was?"

Dennis shook his head. "Nope. Just drop it, okay? We're outta here."

Lana pulled into her driveway at 11:55; five more minutes and the Buick would have turned into a pumpkin. She sighed and turned the key. The living-room curtains were ablaze with light.

Her mother was alone in the living room watching a late horror show. Luke was already in bed asleep; even Sam was being quiet out in the garage, dreaming his puppy dreams. When she timidly walked in, Carol smiled, an unexpected surprise. "I take it you made some friends tonight."

Relieved, Lana closed the door. "Well, sort of . . . a really cute guy named Dennis. He an' his friend Wayne were at the drive-in. We took Wayne home an' went up this hill where you can see over the whole city."

Her mother's eyes narrowed. "You went off like that with a total stranger? My God, Lana, you haven't got the brains God gave a turnip. Where's your head?"

"Last time I checked, it was still on my shoulders," Lana said defensively, reminding herself that it never paid to be too honest. "I've got good judgment. Plus, he's only a high school kid."

"So that makes him all right? You know better'n that," Carol challenged her daughter. "Nice" girls didn't go for rides with strange boys. And boys knew that. When a girl said yes, it gave them instant ideas. Ideas were like matches. Nice girls didn't play with matches either. Carol couldn't stand the thought of Lana losing her virginity. Ever. She would be better off becoming a nun, forgetting about love and romance and other such illusions.

"Nothin' happened, Mom." Lana went to the kitchen in search of a snack, hoping the issue would be dropped.

It was, after Carol's final comment: "You were lucky this time, but make it a habit an' some night I'll be gettin' a call from the hospital. Or the police."

"Mother," Lana called wearily from the kitchen, "I'm not gonna make it a habit. 'Sides, Dennis is s'pose to call me. I might have found myself a new boyfriend already." She sauntered back into the living room munching on an apple she'd taken from the basket on top of the refrigerator. Her mother was again engrossed in her movie. Lana sat next to her on the couch. "Did you hear me? I said I think maybe I've found a new boyfriend. He's got a few faults, but all in all I think he's pretty nice. Not as nice as Greg, though."

"Hmmm."

Lana bit off another chunk of apple and mumbled between chews, "Aren'cha even interested?"

"I'm watchin' the movie, Lana. Can't we talk about it later?"

"Sure." Sulkily, Lana reverted her attention to the television screen. A vampire was silently gliding toward his sleeping victim, a buxom brunette. The scene reminded Lana of the bloody rabbit, which made swallowing the piece of apple she had chewed somewhat difficult. The vampire's fangs plunged, white ivory daggers sinking deeply into milky flesh. Trickles of blood seeped from the wound as the immortal leech drank. Lana got up and headed for her bedroom. "I'm gonna have nightmares as it is. Guess I'll see you in the mornin'."

It didn't occur to Carol to ask her daughter why she thought she was going to have nightmares. She blew her an absent kiss. "All right, night, honey."

The vampire raised his ashen face, his black eyes gleaming evilly, his crimson lips dripping the coppery elixir of life. A lone wolf howled in the distance, a lingering, pitiful wail. "Ah, the children of the night!" Dracula hissed, bringing both sides of his cape up like giant bat wings. The girl on the bed below him groaned softly. Dracula shrank to the size of a coat hanger in a cloud of special-effects vapor and flew awkwardly out the window.

The children of the night fell silent.

Nine

Lana woke to the smell of bacon cooking, the aroma teasing her nostrils until appetite forced her heavy eyelids open. She dragged herself into the kitchen, the dust of dreams still waiting to be swept under the rug of consciousness. Her mother was bustling in front of the stove. "Mornin', sleepyhead."

"Mornin'." Lana pulled herself up on a bar stool at the counter and rubbed her eyes. "Aren't you up kinda early for a Sunday?"

"Your dog started yappin' about six o'clock this mornin'. I guess you didn't hear 'im, but I did, unfortunately. I finally gave up tryin' to go back to sleep aroun' seven, which was about the time Luke got up. I guess he took the li'l pest for a walk. They don't seem to be here now."

"Sam's not a pest," Lana argued. "He's just a puppy, Mom. He'll outgrow his bad habits."

"Well, I know something he won't grow out of, and there's about ten piles of it out there on the garage floor. You're gonna have to train him, Lana, or we'll have to find him another home. The garage smells like . . . well, you know what it smells like. I can't tolerate that. It's disgustin'."

Lana rolled her eyes and sighed heavily. "All right, I'll clean it up today, but Luke's gonna hafta help me. If he wants Sam t'be half his dog, then he's gonna hafta clean up half the messes. But Mom, I don't know the first thing about trainin' a dog. What am I s'pose to do?"

"You should never have taken him without checkin'

106

with me first," Carol said, lifting the browned strips of bacon onto a paper towel with a fork. "We're not equipped to have a dog, mainly. We don't have a fenced yard, or a doghouse, or the money t'be spendin' on vet bills. I don't s'pose he's even had his shots yet?"

"I thought Daddy was payin' you five hundred dollars a month," Lana said sullenly.

"Yes, he is," Carol agreed, "but guess who's gonna be payin' for your and Luke's college educations? Your daddy informed me that if I moved away with you kids, we'd be on our own 'cept for that damn monthly check."

Lana felt a little sick. "Doesn't he . . . care about Luke and me anymore? Why did you leave, then?"

"I had no choice . . ."

"Liar!" Lana jumped off the bar stool and ran back to her bedroom, slamming the door almost hard enough to split the doorjamb.

Carol stared bleakly at her perfectly crisped bacon. "Damn." She went after Lana, still clutching her fork unawares, her intestines knotting with turbulent emotion. Tapping Lana's door lightly, she called out in a strangled whisper, "Lana? Let's talk about it, okay honey?"

From the other side, bitter, insolent: "I don't wanna talk. Go away. I tried to talk to you las' night, but you were too busy watchin' your stupid vampire movie. You don't care about me an' Luke either, or you would've turned down the transfer. You probably asked for it so you could get away from Daddy. You just couldn't take seein' him around town with his new girlfriend. It didn't matter that I had to lose Greg and my other friends, that me an' Luke would have to start a new school in the middle of a semester. You can't have Daddy, so we can't have him either. Thanks, Mom. You're a real carin' person."

Carol couldn't speak; she was drowning in a tidal wave of guilt. She went to her own bedroom and shut the door, leaning against it with a despairing sigh. How could she have been so selfish? Now, besides her husband, she'd also lost her daughter.

The reason she and Hugh had gotten married in the first place.

But nice girls don't . . .

She crawled back into bed and covered her head with the pillow.

The phone rang shortly after one. After several rings Lana realized that her mother was not going to answer it. She threw down the pen she had been holding over a blank piece of paper for nearly two hours, waiting for the wretched prose to flow. She supposed it would help if her brother didn't run in and out of the house every five minutes—with the sole purpose of distracting her, she was sure. She rushed into the kitchen and breathlessly picked up the wall phone. "Hello?"

Just as she'd hoped, it was Dennis. "Yo, Lana."

She felt her spirits begin to lift. "Yeah, hi. I was hopin' it would be you. I'm goin' crazy over here. Why don't you come rescue me?"

"That's why I called," he said. "I was wondering if you'd like to go to the park. Everybody usually hangs out there on the weekends. I could introduce you around."

"I'd love that," Lana responded warmly. "I can be ready in five minutes."

"See you in ten."

"Great. 'Bye." She hung up, her earlier cloud of depression all but gone. A trace lingered, but she decided to ignore it. Accept the things you cannot change, her father always said. A great piece of wisdom if one can manage to appropriate it. But coming to terms with the idea that her father no longer wanted to be a part of her life would take some doing. Maybe he hadn't really meant what he'd said.

As she got dressed, she wondered if she should bother to tell her mother she was leaving. No. Why should she? What consideration had her mother shown for her? She frowned at her reflection in her dresser mirror. Her hair needed to be shampooed; due to its fineness, it had to be washed every day to look decent, but she didn't have enough time. She'd chosen a black long-sleeved jersey over white slacks because Greg had always said she looked good in black. She tried on a pair of white dangly earrings, decided they looked too something or other, and took them back out. Under close scrutiny her eyes appeared too small; she took a tube of mascara from her makeup case and applied it to her lashes, then blushed her cheeks with a fat, tangled brush and smeared her lips with tinted gloss. Dabbed on perfume. Fluffed her hair with baby powder. Puckered her mouth like models often did on the pages of magazines, then stuck out her tongue. Impressing people was such a hassle.

Dennis arrived at one-fifteen, announcing his arrival with a blast of his car horn. Lana thought it was a little crude, but she bounded out cheerfully to greet him. Luke was playing in the front yard of a house several lots down; he had found a couple of friends his age. The three were flinging a hot-pink Frisbee back and forth, a jubilant Sam scampering around their feet.

Dennis gave Lana an appreciative once-over when she got in the car. "You sure look good. Smell good too."

Tingles. Lana smiled. "Thanks. You look good too."

"But I smell like an ape, right?"

She laughed. "Oh, no, no. I didn't mean that. You . . ." He smelled like cigarettes, but she didn't think he would appreciate being told that, so she lied and said, ". . . don't smell like anything, really. You don't stink."

"Whatever." Dennis backed out and headed west. "Nice day, huh? It usually stays fairly nice until November. Takes forever for summer to come, though. Guess it's a trade-off."

"I've never been in snow," Lana mused, looking through the window at the cloudless blue sky. "It does snow here, right?"

"Up to your ass sometimes. Never seen it snow, huh? That's weird. You'll hate it . . . at least I do. I don't much like anything that falls from the sky. Except stars, maybe. I get off on falling stars."

Lana had a romantic vision of the two of them star-gazing together. "Oh, so do I. An' I know you'll probably think it's dumb, but I still make a wish whenever I see one, like I did when I was a little girl. Those wishes never seem to come true, but I do it anyway."

"Maybe you're aiming too high," Dennis said, as if he really cared.

Lana felt a tightening in her chest. "Maybe so."

Marla's Cutlass was nowhere in sight when they arrived at the park, Dennis noted with silent anger. But Jay Gorman's Charger was there, and that was good enough. He parked beside it and stepped out as Lana did, and they slammed their doors in unison. Meeting in back of the car, he asked her politely, "Is it okay if I hold your hand?"

Smiling shyly, Lana answered by proferring her right hand. Dennis took it firmly in his left and they sauntered toward the small group of teenagers hanging around the gazebo. Other groups were scattered here and there, playing Frisbee or bouncing Hacky-sacks on their feet, tossing sticks for dogs they'd brought along, flirting, running, walking in aimless circles puffing on cigarettes. Heads turned to look at the approaching couple. Whispers flew.

Jay and a boy named Bruce Meadows were arm wrestling on the round white iron table set in the center of the gazebo. Bruce was winning, but Dennis's attention was drawn to Jay, old Pizza Face, whom he barely recognized because the severe acne that had acquired Jay his nickname had suddenly and completely cleared up. Jay's arm was finally pinned, and those watching the spectacle cheered.

Then all eyes were on Dennis and Lana, and the group fell silent. Most of the attention was focused on Lana, the two other girls present taking an immediate and obvious dislike to her, the two guys scoring her on the one-to-ten scale, wishing they had X-ray vision.

Jay was the first to speak. "Well, who have we here, Dennis?"

The unspoken question hung in the air, which only Lana was unaware of: *And where, pray tell, is Marla?*

"This is Lana. She just moved here from Texas. She a fox, or what?"

Lana blushed, shyly dipping her head in embarrassment. "Stop it, Dennis."

She ignored the guys and sought acceptance in the eyes of the two girls. They were glaring at her. Lana's ears prickled with heat. What was the deal? Why were they looking at her as if she were their enemy?

Dennis couldn't help but remark about the dramatic change in Jay's complexion. "Hey, doesn't look like I'll get to call you Pizza Face anymore. You finally get laid, Gorman?"

The dark-headed girl standing behind Jay spat, "You watch your mouth, Dennis."

Jay looked equally peeved; he apparently didn't appreciate such a personal question, especially voiced in front of his peers. "I just quit eating so much chocolate," he growled, reaching up to squeeze his girlfriend's hand. Nancy stopped hurling mental darts at Lana long enough to bend over and kiss him on the cheek.

The rebuke didn't bother Dennis, who had the sensitivity of a clump of crabgrass. "Well, you sure look a lot better. Just think of all the money you'll save, not having to buy gallons of Clearasil."

Jay's eyes narrowed into slits.

Dennis shrugged and went on, "Say, did you hear a scream up on Beacon Hill last night? We were up there and saw your car."

Jay and Nancy both reacted like he'd just thrown a bucket of ice water in their faces. Lana immediately realized that Dennis had lied to her when he'd said he had no idea who might have killed the rabbit. Now she had a reason of her own to glare, and did so. The two certainly looked guilty about something.

"We didn't hear anything," Nancy said coldly. "We hiked down the north side of the hill to where the Boy Scouts usually set up camp."

Jay confirmed with a nod.

"You both must be going deaf, then," Dennis declared. "Anyway, it came from the graveyard, so I went to have a look. All I found was a dead rabbit somebody had just killed."

Bruce Meadows leaned forward, his brows knitted in disbelief. "Say what?"

"A white rabbit," Lana said, her heart sinking at the memory of the poor bloody creature. "The kind they sell as pets, with pink eyes. Somebody stabbed him." She turned an accusing stare on Jay.

"Hey, don't look at me. You don't know that it was a person, anyway. It could've been an animal. You must have scared it away from its supper. It was probably an owl or a hawk."

111

Dennis knew of no animal that painted strange symbols around its prey, but he didn't want to bring that up.

"I have to go home, Jay," Nancy said suddenly. "My mom's taking me shopping this afternoon for some new clothes. They're having a sale at Woolworth's."

The girl standing next to her, Jennifer Parks, whispered something in her ear, and both girls giggled. There was no doubt in Lana's mind that they were laughing at her—at the way she talked—which inflamed anew her anger at her mother for setting her down in a place where she was an outsider. She'd never been treated this way in Tyler, where everyone talked just like she did. She'd been able to empathize with Spiro's plight before, but now she was learning firsthand what it felt like to be shunned. It didn't feel very good. But she hardly wanted to be friends with rabbit killers anyway.

Jay stood up. "Yeah, and I have to help my dad clean out the garage. He's been on my case for weeks."

The mention of garage cleaning reminded Lana that her own was still mined with Sam's droppings; after the incident with her mother, she hadn't given any more thought to her promise. But her mother was feeling guilty now—as well she should—so she wouldn't get rid of Sam, at least not until everything had been patched up. And if possible at all, that was going to take some time.

Jay, Nancy, and Jennifer muttered their good-byes— to Dennis and Bruce—and walked toward the parking lot in a conspiratorial huddle, exchanging comments in hushed tones. Dennis flicked his tongue against his bottom teeth with satisfaction; in ten minutes or less, Marla would be fully informed. He led Lana into the gazebo, and they sat down across from Bruce, still holding hands.

Bruce was still thinking about the rabbit. "Hey, like maybe the Obers did it, you know?" He transformed his face into a good likeness of a werewolf, jutting his jaw forward, curling his lips back, plunging his brow. "Could be they're up to their old tricks."

Lana giggled, having no idea what he was talking about, but she found the face he was making quite comical.

Dennis scowled. "Yeah, right. Don't tell me you believe in all that horseshit."

"What horseshit?" Lana sobered and looked from one face to the other. "Who are the Obers?"

"Dead people." Dennis laughed. "Fucking dead people. They're in a tomb up there in the cemetery, and the date on it says they both died on Halloween about seventy years ago. So, you can imagine the dumb-shit things people like Bruce here come up with because of that. Died on Halloween, so they had to be witches, right? People just love to believe in crap like that." The image of the strange markings he'd seen around the rabbit's body resurfaced again, but he shoved it back down.

Bruce accepted the ridicule good-naturedly. "Yeah, it is fun to believe in the boogeyman. I wasn't really serious, though. I just don't think Jay would've done something like that. Not anybody, really. It probably was another animal."

Dennis nodded. "Yeah, probably."

Lana wasn't so sure. She would have an easier time believing it if those two hadn't acted like they'd been caught with their pants down.

"Let's talk about something else," Dennis said, uncomfortably aware of his need for a cigarette. He always had to have one when he was nervous. And he was very nervous now, though he refused to consciously acknowledge it.

"Well, we can talk about this." Bruce grinned, reaching into his shirt pocket. He pulled out a joint. "I just happen to have a little rocket fuel on me. Care to go on a jaunt through outer space, Major Tom?"

Dennis nodded enthusiastically. "All-fucking-right. Where'd you get it?"

"My cousin mailed it to me from Boulder. Tells me he gets it from his psych professor," Bruce said proudly. "Bitchin', huh? I can't wait till I go to college . . . if I get to go," he added somberly. Then his face brightened; he wasn't going to allow his mood to be dampened. "But hey, why worry about tomorrow, right? How about you, Lana? You like to get high?"

She looked uncertainly at the thin white cylinder between his fingers. She'd never thought that sending smoke of any kind into her lungs was a very good idea—breathing secondhand cigarette smoke was more than she could tolerate—but desperate to be "in," especially after the two girls' rejection of her, she altered her attitude for the occasion. "I've never tried it before, but I guess I'd like to."

Bruce looked amused. "I like the way you talk."

"You do?"

"Sexy, isn't it?" Dennis said, putting a hand on Lana's knee. He was glad she was going to try the marijuana; it frequently had the side effect of making people horny.

"Probably won't do anything to you, if you've never smoked it before," Bruce informed her. "Pot has what they call a reverse tolerance effect, just the opposite of alcohol. You have to get it built up in your system a little bit before it'll do you any good. But you might get a buzz. It's pretty potent stuff; pure Colombian bud, no shake."

Unfamiliar with the terminology but unwilling to appear ignorant, Lana nodded as though she had understood; apparently, appreciation was called for. She smiled, appearing duly impressed, picturing the look on her mother's face should her daughter come stumbling home stoned out of her mind.

Bruce lit the joint and inhaled deeply, then passed it to Dennis, still holding his breath. When Bruce finally let it out with a vague cloud of smoke, he explained to Lana, "Try to hold it in as long as you can."

Dennis took a hit, passing the joint under his nose for an additional whiff, then handed the joint on to her. She tentatively raised the foreign object to her lips and began to suck. A blowtorch suddenly fired down her throat, exploding in her lungs, and she began to hack violently. Bruce and Dennis cracked up.

"Maybe you're not cut out for this," Dennis said, conscious of the precious herb she was wasting now that he was aware of reverse tolerance.

"You can't take too much in at once, especially if you're not used to it," Bruce cautioned too late. Lana handed him the joint, her face a deep red. She continued to cough, and feared for a moment she was going to gag. All she needed was to have to throw up in front of Dennis.

When the joint came around to her again, she had pretty well gotten things under control, but she passed on the offer with a wave and croaked, "No thanks. I think that'll do it for me."

Dennis and Bruce continued to pass it back and forth until it was too small to handle without burning their fingers, at which point Bruce put out the flame with a wet finger and dropped the roach in his shirt pocket, his hazel eyes floating blearily in rosy, glazed cream. He smiled dreamily. "Hits the spot, huh?"

Dennis grinned back. "Makes me want a cigarette like hell. Left my pack in the car. Es'scuse me while I float on over to get 'em." He rose in an unseen fog and moved in slow motion away from the gazebo, swaying like a reed in a gentle wind.

Bruce chuckled. "He's fucked up."

Lana glanced back in Dennis's direction. "Yeah, I'd say." But her mind was now on something else; on the subject of the Obers and their alleged connection to witchcraft. She'd wanted to find out more, but Dennis had quickly stomped the life out of that little conversation. Now he was gone, but he would be back soon. She leaned forward and searched Bruce's eyes, aware of the admiration that was showing in them. She pretended not to notice. "What was that you were sayin' about the Obers? Do people think they were witches just because they died on Halloween, or was there something else?"

Bruce gazed back at her reflectively. For a moment he didn't answer; he was on a different channel completely. She looked like an angel to him, all softness and sweetness with no trace of the artificiality normally associated with girls so pretty. She probably knew she was gorgeous, but the fact hadn't gone to her head. Rare. But what was someone like that doing hanging around with a skunk like Dennis? Bruce liked Dennis, to some degree, but that was only because Bruce had the ability to accept people at face value, no personal standards imposed. He lived and let live. He liked everybody, had no enemies.

Perhaps that was because he was fairly adept at keeping a protective amount of space around him at all times.

Her question made a leisurely stroll through his brain, then exited his left ear. The subject of the Obers was far too removed from what his tongue was arbitrarily inclined to discuss. Diplomacy laid waste by the marijuana, he said, "I don't mean to change the subject, but did Dennis break up with Marla?"

Lana felt something like a brick come down on her head. "Who's Marla?" Her voice was clipped.

Bruce, aware that he'd just committed a grave faux pas, colored instantly. "Oh, uh, never mind. She's just this other girl he used to go with. Guess they must have broke up and I just didn't hear about it yet. Well, uh, the Obers. Don't know much about that, just that they both died on Halloween, like Dennis said. Maybe some older people around here know more, but if they do, they're not talking about it. I haven't heard anything anyway."

Lana barely heard him. "How long ago were they still together?"

Bruce shrugged, dismayed that she wasn't going to let him off the hook. "I dunno. Saw 'em together in the halls last week and everything seemed okay, but they must've had a fight, right? Otherwise he wouldn't be with you."

This being what Lana wanted to hear, she accepted the rationale. "I would hope not. So what do you think about that rabbit? You really think another animal killed it? Those two friends of yours sure looked guilty."

Bruce thought for a moment. "Yeah, they did, didn't they? Well, they could've been up to something else they didn't want everybody knowing about. Nancy's pretty paranoid about her reputation. I can't—" He stopped, his eyes trailing upward. Dennis had returned, happily puffing on a cigarette.

"I think," Dennis said airily, sitting back down next to Lana, "that if everybody in the world smoked pot, we could get one hell of an orgy going. Doesn't it make you hornier than hell? Sure does me."

Lana shot him a warning glance. "Don't go gettin' any wild ideas."

"Oh, don't start that shit again," he scoffed. "I

could've raped you last night if I'd wanted, but I played Mr. Nice Guy, right? So why would I get any ideas now? Think I'm gonna spread you out right here on the table in front of Bruce?"

Lana stared back, open-mouthed, at a severely tarnished image. She had imagined this vulgar, foulmouthed jerk as her next steady boyfriend. She felt like a complete dunce. If he was talking to her like this just one day after they met, what sort of things would he say once they were really familiar with each other? Suddenly the little faults she had whitewashed stood out with stark clarity. The smoking, the rude way he had pulled her over to that car on the hill, hoping to embarrass her. His suggestiveness, way out of line when he barely knew her name. He was a pretty cake, all right. But beneath the icing he was crawling with worms. "I'd like to go home, please," she said stiffly.

Dennis nodded in the direction of the street beyond the parking lot. "Then go. I'm not driving in this condition."

On the verge of tears, Lana rose and stalked out of the gazebo, feeling like an insect under the curious stares of those she passed on her way out of the park. The sound of running feet caused her to imagine that Dennis was coming to apologize, but she didn't turn around. It wasn't Dennis anyway. She could hear him back in the distance, laughing. At her, no doubt. For being such a gullible little fool.

Through a blurred haze she walked numbly past a succession of tar strips between the asphalt squares of the sidewalk, being sure to step on every one, chanting a silent, incessant, *Step on a crack, break Dennis's back.* So childish, but somehow placating. He had just been using her. He'd probably had a fight with his girlfriend, his pretended interest in her motivated either by revenge or a plot to make Marla jealous. No doubt the conflict between them would be resolved within a short period of time, and she would have been left standing alone, a heartbroken idiot trying to figure out what she'd done wrong. Just like her mother. The bastard!

The rumbling of an engine slowed beside her. She

glanced up to see a primer-red pickup with only traces of blue paint still visible above the rear panels. The driver was grinning at her. Lana wiped her eyes and managed to turn up the corners of her mouth.

"Hi."

"Need a lift? Sorry about Dennis being so rude. He gets that way sometimes when he gets high." Bruce was, he knew, being generous toward Dennis, and getting high was no excuse for anything. But he didn't like to get radical with opinions.

The pickup came to a halt. Lana got in the reeking cab, recognizing the pungent-sweet smell of marijuana. It reminded her of a sweaty tennis shoe. "I appreciate your pickin' me up. But if you don't mind, I'd rather not talk about Dennis. I know he's your friend an' all, but I've decided I don't like him very much. At all."

Bruce pressed on the naked gas pedal, propelling them forward. "Well, we're not really close friends. He mostly hangs around with a guy named Wayne when he's not with, uh, Marla. Guess they really didn't break up after all. He told me after you left that they'd just had a little fight. He was gonna use you to try to make her jealous. I think that's pretty rude. People shouldn't treat other people like that. But, the world's full of that crap . . . takes all kinds, right? Nothing we can do about it, 'cept get high and try not to think about it." A flash of teeth. "Right?"

Lana's suspicions confirmed, she felt the heat of hatred rise up within her. "Why did he drop me so soon, then? Marla hasn't seen us together yet, has she?"

With a heavy sigh, Bruce shook his head. Buoyancy in this atmosphere was getting hard to maintain. "No, but just as good as. The girl that was there with the shoulder-length black hair . . . Jay's girlfriend? She's Marla's best friend. Dennis knew she'd run home to call Marla, tell her about seeing him at the park with another girl."

"Oh, great. So I haven't even started school yet an' I've already got an enemy?" Lana groaned, tossing her head back against the seat. So that's why the two girls had hated her before she'd even opened her mouth. They were friends of Marla. The bastard's girlfriend.

"Ah, don't worry about it. You'll make plenty of

friends, I'm sure. You've got me, if that's any consolation."

Lana smiled. "Thanks. It is a consolation. What's your name, anyway? I don't guess we were formally introduced."

"Bruce Meadows. Hey, wanna go get a Coke? I've got a really bad case of cotton mouth."

Lana didn't care to know what that meant, but she was more than willing to go for a Coke with him. "Sure, that would be nice."

Sipping their Cokes through candy-striped straws, sharing idle conversation about school subjects and tastes in movies and music, revealed that Bruce and Lana had much in common. Bruce wasn't as good-looking as Dennis; his nose was a little too thin and pointed, and his lips appeared hard, not exactly inviting. But his eyes were large and thoughtful, ginger-brown flecked with specks of green circling the pupils. His hair was shaggy but clean, a light brown, and hinted of natural curl. He was okay, Lana thought, already at work considering new possibilities. She was more emotionally dependent than she'd realized. An inherited trait, no doubt. She concluded that looks really weren't that important anyway. It was the asshole that counted. Unlike Dennis, Bruce didn't seem to be one.

It was four o'clock before they knew it. The old adage, "Time flies when you're having fun," certainly applied in their case. "I guess I'd better be gettin' on home," Lana said regretfully. "I ran off without doin' what I promised my mom I'd do today."

"What is it? I'll help you," Bruce offered, stuffing the last of the french fries they'd shared into his mouth. He was in no hurry to go home.

Lana shook her head, her expression doubtful. "It's cleanin' up dog poop in the garage."

"Oh, I love to clean up dog poop!" Bruce exclaimed exuberantly, his features arranged in an exaggerated expression of delight. "It's one of my favorite pastimes. Ask anybody! I'm always walking around looking for fresh piles."

They laughed together like old companions, the relaxed, easy music of a relationship long sealed. Finally

Lana, teary-eyed and plagued with a sudden case of hiccups, said, "Well, far be it from me to deprive you of—*hic*—your favorite pastime."

When they pulled up in front of Lana's house, she was thankful of the empty driveway, a testimony that her mother, and most likely her brother as well, were gone, probably shopping. She wasn't quite ready to face her mother again, though her anger toward her had mellowed into ambivalence.

Next door, Spiro was sitting on his front porch staring at his feet. He didn't look up when the pickup stopped in front of Lana's house, nor when the two people stepped out of the cab.

Lana turned to Bruce. "I'll be right back. I have to go talk to that guy for a minute. My dipshit brother really hurt his feelin's yesterday, so I guess it's up to me to apologize."

Bruce peered in Spiro's direction. "Hey, that's Spiro Guenther, isn't it? Everybody at school calls him—"

"I know. Tardo." Lana frowned. "He told me. I hope you don't participate in any of that."

"Hey, not me," Bruce replied truthfully. "I don't get off on things like that. I'm one of the good guys. Promise."

"I believe you." She walked toward the lone creature hunched over on his front porch. "Spiro, about yesterday—"

Her words were cut short by the sight of Spiro's lobster-red, blistered right palm, which lay turned outward beside his right foot.

"My God, what happened to your hand? Is it—*hic*—burned?" She cursed at her malady under her breath, as if doing so would make it go away.

Spiro remained silent, his eyes fastened to the shoelaces of his worn-out tennis shoes as if at any moment he expected them to crawl up his legs.

"Hey, are you okay? Spiro?"

He finally raised his head, slowly, beads of sweat shining on his Cro-Magnon brow. Looking past Lana, his dark gaze fell on Bruce, who stood waiting in Lana's yard. "Who is . . . that?"

"His name is Bruce. Now tell me, what happened to your hand? How'd it get—*hic*—burned like that?"

"Bruce." Spiro repeated the name as if it were a dirty word. His facial muscles twitched. He looked like a boxer after the tenth round, contemplating how he might annihilate his opponent in the next. His expression chilled Lana. She remembered referring to him as "sweet." He certainly didn't look sweet now. His face personified raw hate.

She glanced nervously back at Bruce, half inclined to just walk away; she couldn't deal with this. She wondered what could possibly be going on in Spiro's mind, that he should cast such a murderous glare at Bruce. Surely Bruce had never done anything bad to him. She felt she already knew Bruce pretty well; he wouldn't have lied to her. He wasn't the type to pull cruel jokes on the underdogs of society. She faced Spiro again and spoke softly. "Listen, if you don't wanna talk about your hand, fine. I came over here to apologize for what Luke said yesterday. He can be a real jerk sometimes, but he really didn't mean it. He's called me worse things. I . . . I came over yesterday to tell you that, an' your mother . . . I really didn't understand—*hic*—what she was sayin', but I got the idea she was super pissed-off at me about somethin'. Somethin' about a picture. You know what she was talkin' about?"

Spiro returned his attention to his feet, and what had appeared on his face as fierce anger seconds before was now replaced with shame. Lacking the sophistication to create a lie, he allowed the truth to fall from his trembling lips. "I drew a pitcher of you. Naked. Mama found it."

Lana felt herself flush with embarrassment. She was too stunned at first to speak. What on earth was the proper response to a confession like that anyway? Finally she stammered, "Well, that, uh, explains that, I guess." Her hiccups were suddenly cured.

Her eyes fell again on the burned hand, a terrible suspicion rising. And how possible it was! She remembered her first impression of Bertha Guenther. Hateful, cruel. Treating her son like a dog . . . worse than a dog.

Would she have? Lana didn't want to think so, but the idea wasn't totally absurd . . . "Spiro? I want to know about your hand. Did your . . . did your mother do that to you? Was that your punishment for drawin' the . . . the picture?"

Spiro jerked as though she'd slapped him. "Mama loves me."

"Well, she sure has a funny way of showin' it, from what I seen. Did she burn you, Spiro? Did she burn your hand? 'Cause if she did—"

At that moment Bruce strode up behind Lana and nodded amiably at Spiro. "How ya doin'?"

Lana compulsively put her hand on Bruce's skinny bicep before realizing she'd just slid into premature intimacy, but the action felt natural, and Bruce didn't react with any surprise. "Look at his hand, Bruce. He won't say, but . . . I think his mother might have done that to him on purpose. What do you think we should do?"

Bruce leaned over, squinting, and inspected Spiro's palm. Spiro bristled noticeably and shrank away, his expression returning to chiseled granite. An art study in primeval rage.

Bruce had no idea the animosity was directed at him. "Wow, bummer. Why'd she do that?"

Hoping that question wouldn't be answered, Lana knelt in front of the folded human skyscraper. "If your mother did this to you, she oughta get in a lot of trouble for it, Spiro. That's not right. That's called child abuse, an' there's laws against that." Even as she said it, the word child applied to the hideous giant before her seemed a ridiculous misnomer.

The skyscraper began to unfold. Lana rose to her feet and took a few nervous steps backward. His height raised even more by standing on the last porch step, Spiro towered over the couple like a deadly Philistine. Bruce wondered stupidly why there wasn't a slingshot in his hand. "Hey Lana, I think, uh, I think this dude would just like to be left alone, you know?" He started doing a little backward two-step in the direction of Lana's driveway when the front door behind Spiro opened.

Bertha Guenther heaved her tent-covered bulk across

the threshold to stand behind her son, nostrils flaring, giving Lana the impression of a rhino getting ready to charge. "You little slut. You git away from here. Leave my boy alone," the fat woman hurled at Lana with a poisonous glare.

Lana turned to Bruce for support, but he was already safely perched on her front porch making an intense study of the clouds.

Several appropriate retaliatory remarks popped into Lana's mind, but she managed to hold them in check. She didn't want to get into a name-calling fight with the fat old witch, especially not in front of Bruce, in front of Spiro, and the whole neighborhood for that matter. The hell with throwing sticks and stones anyway. She brought out the heavy artillery. "I know what you did to Spiro, and I think maybe I'll just give the police a call. I think they'd be interested!"

Bertha's mouth worked in furious twitches, a scathing rebuttal attempting to escape its chapped white confinement, but for all she knew, Spiro had already spilled his guts. She would deal with his treacherous mouth later. She hissed at him to get in the house and wait for her in his room.

Spiro's chin sank until it was nestled against his breast. He was no longer a thing to be feared; only pitied. He turned around slowly and waited for her to move away from the door so he could pass. He disappeared behind her, becoming a dissolving shadow in the room beyond.

Bertha crossed flabby, tintless arms under huge sagging breasts and turned a woeful glance to the sky. "It's been hard on me, raising a boy like that without no father. And what can I do? He can't be smart and so he'll never come to much of anything, so I figure the best I can do is make him good. That's gotta count for something. Once I'm gone, he'll be all on his own, and he's gotta have at least one thing right with him." She made her lower lip tremble, and willed some tears to the corners of her eyes.

Lana wasn't quite buying the performance—there was no way burning your kid's hand as a punishment could be justified in her mind—but she did soften somewhat. "I don't think you're bein' fair to him. I think he's just a lot more naive than he is . . . well, I don't wanna say dumb, but you know what I mean. But that's not the point. You can't do things like that to him, no matter what he's done. An' what he did wasn't all that terrible, which, by the way, I sure had nothin' to do with it, so you can watch who you're callin' a slut. But if you ever hurt him like that again, I will call the police, an' that's a promise."

Bertha's eyes flashed with momentary anger, but then, as though she were seized with a pleasant idea, an ugly smile appeared on her lips. Her eyes became almost droopy. "You won't have no reason to call the po-lice, missy," she said, and went back into her house, closing the door softly behind her.

Lana trudged over to her own porch, where Bruce stood smiling sheepishly. "I'm some knight in shining armor, huh? Sorry, but when I think Godzilla wants me the fuck out of his face, I book."

"That isn't nice, Bruce. Callin' him that," Lana reproved.

"I know, but did you see the way he was looking at me . . . ?"

She shuddered slightly. "I wish I hadn't, but I think I know what his problem is. Not that I've encouraged it in any way, but he seems to have a . . . some sorta crush on me, I guess. So your presence wouldn't exactly be appreciated."

"Well, that sure makes my day." Bruce frowned. "That dude could pick me up and squish me like a bug. You don't think he will, do ya? I kinda planned on being around here a lot. That is, if I'm wanted."

Lana patted his cheek. "'Course you're wanted. An' don't worry, he'll get over it. Please don't make any change in your plans."

The moment seemed right for a kiss, but feeling suddenly awkward, Bruce didn't pounce on the opportunity. Instead he rubbed his hands together with gleeful enthusiasm. "Okay, point me to the dog poop. I'm rearin' to scoop."

They entered the house laughing.

* * *

Albert Montgomery still labored for breath; his lungs had become burning coals which drew in mace and exhaled fire. Even under his medication, the pain was excruciating. His body convulsed with violent spasms, every organ twisting, shrinking, wrenching itself out of place. His skin was clammy and smelled of death. Drifting in and out of consciousness, he began to hallucinate.

The white wall in front of him, as he watched it, moved ever so slowly away, until Albert was certain he was staring at it from a great distance. He wondered for a moment if his bed were actually being rolled back, but a painful glance over his shoulder revealed that no one was there. Only machines blinked around him, attached to tubes or wires that were affixed to various parts of his anatomy. A heart monitor beeped erratically, giving its uncertain testimony to life. The sound was driving him insane.

Suddenly he saw a tiny figure standing against the wall, a figure in black, an upright cricket posed behind a concave lens. As it moved toward him, its features began to haze and spread out.

Montgomery blinked; the thing did not disappear. It kept spreading in proportion as it drew nearer, the distorted features of a malevolent face coming vaguely into focus. A curved plastic tube had been forced into Albert's throat and secured with tape around his mouth, feeding oxygen to the furnace in his chest. His hands had been strapped to keep him from pulling such things out of his tortured body. He couldn't speak, or cry out in terror; he could only watch the abomination approach, and listen as the beep on the heart monitor became faster and more erratic.

Then a door burst open and he was at once surrounded by angels in white with starched halos encircling their heads. One of them inserted a needle into his arm while another rolled a defibulator forward, shouting for someone to page Dr. Prescott, alert Code Blue.

Albert heard the long, even shrill of the heart monitor and felt a cold rush of air. He squeezed his eyes shut against the blackness encroaching on his soul.

Ten

Marla slammed the receiver down, causing her mother, who sat at the kitchen table playing a thoughtless game of solitaire, to jump. "Careful with the equipment, Marla. What's the matter?"

"That was Nancy," Marla seethed. "She said she saw Dennis at the park with some girl who just moved here from Texas, and he admitted he had her up at the overlook last night. A hick! That rat. I'd like to punch him right in the nose."

"You know how boys are," Pamela said gently. "You're too young to be getting so serious anyway. And you know Dennis won't be following you to Princeton. Don't upset yourself. It's not worth it."

Marla gritted her teeth and sat down across from her mother. "I know, but . . . we aren't officially broken up, you know. He has no right."

"You don't own him, honey. One thing you'll eventually have to learn is that men are not, by nature, monogamous animals. They're biologically programmed to be just the opposite . . . it's healthier for the species. Of course, we've structured a society in which such behavior is condemned, but we are what we are. They can't help it, really."

Marla gasped. "Has Daddy . . . ?"

"I wouldn't be surprised," Pamela said casually, as if adultery were no more serious an infraction than cheating at a game of solitaire, which she proceeded to do by shuffling the remaining cards in her hand. "Now, I'm not saying that he has, I just don't worry about it. Why should I? I can't follow him everywhere he goes. If he wants to cheat, he'll cheat. What am I supposed to do about it? Scream and throw things, give him ultimatums? I'd probably wind up in divorce court." She looked around appreciatively at her sparkling pastel-green kitchen filled with every modern convenience, none of the appliances over five years old. The oak cabinets were supplied with the most expensive cookware money could buy. "I'd rather not. I have a comfortable life. Why rock the boat?"

"I don't think I could live that way," Marla said, picturing Dennis with a broken nose. "If that's the way it is, I don't think I'll ever get married."

"Some men have a little more self-control than others," her mother offered consolingly. "Just choose carefully. There are some faithful ones around, I suppose."

Marla nestled her chin against the palms of her hands, elbows on the table. Her troubled expression deepened. "I wonder why Nancy didn't call and tell me they were going to the park today. She's been acting kind of weird lately, but she keeps insisting nothing's wrong. But ever since—"

"Ever since what?"

"Oh, never mind." Marla forced a smile to conceal the fact she was trying to hide something. Her mother absolutely hated to be in the dark about any detail of Marla's life. They were supposed to be "friends" more than mother and daughter, "good buddies" who didn't keep secrets from each other. How very strange her mother was. One would think she was refusing to recognize her age. "I guess she didn't call because of, you know, Gramma and all. Do I have to go to school at all tomorrow?"

Pamela, again defeated in her game despite her cheating, swept the cards together in a pile. "No, of course not. I'll excuse you for a couple of days, unless you feel like going back earlier. You might not want to get that far behind."

"I couldn't care less about school right now." Marla glanced toward the living room at the various flower arrangements on the coffee table, sent as consolations by friends and relatives. As a means of comfort they were totally inadequate. If anything, they increased the sorrow. The largest one, a tall white basket bursting with Easter lilies, had been sent by the Snells, the card signed by Roger and Beth. The absence of Nancy's loopy scrawl seemed terribly conspicuous.

"Mom, is Gramma in Heaven?" Marla's fear of death was a child of the possibility that such places as Heaven and Hell did exist, and how did one really know for certain one would end up in the right place? As for herself, she knew if she should die the next day—or today, or within the next five minutes—her bad points would almost surely outweigh her good.

A tear trickled down Pamela's cheek. "I'm sure she is, honey. Your grandmother was a very good woman. You know that."

Marla nodded. "I'm sure going to miss her." She was thinking of the old days.

Pamela was too. "So will I, honey. We all will."

After hanging up the phone, Nancy rejoined Jay on the bed, a malicious glint in her eye. "Dennis is in for it now."

"Why won't you let me see it?" he asked testily, reverting back to their previous argument. "You afraid I'm going to steal your secret or something?"

"I'm telling you all you need to know about it," she said, standing firm on her resolve to keep the ledger Eyes Only. "But if you keep bugging me about it, I won't tell you anything."

"All right," he sighed. "Go on."

"Like I said, somehow they knew they were going to get caught and hanged, so Myrantha wrote everything down for Morganna about what they were going to do, and why; she didn't tell her beforehand because she was afraid she'd want to go with them, and someone they could trust had to stay behind. Myrantha was going to die anyway, but she didn't want to be separated from Nathaniel. He agreed to make a pact between themselves and the Devil, that would allow them to return together from the dead to possess new bodies."

"Why couldn't Myrantha just get rid of her cancer?"

"The message doesn't say," Nancy snapped, impatient

to get on with her story. What she was repeating to Jay had been written in the back pages of Myrantha Ober's accounting ledger, and later additions had been made by Morganna Ober. The reason she'd taken so long getting back to Marla's car was that once she began reading her discovery, she couldn't stop. She'd gone into that place looking for souvenirs and clues to death's secrets. What she found was more than she could ever have hoped for. The key to immortality. Every human being's deepest hidden desire.

"So when is this gonna happen?" Jay asked nervously, all skepticism destroyed by proof; he'd seen the blue flame erupt from solid stone, felt the hot, wet slap over his entire face, which was now as smooth as a rose petal.

"Well, when Myrantha wrote her part, she didn't know how long they were going to have to wait, because that decision wasn't up to them. It was up to the baby."

Jay's face screwed up in confusion. "Huh?"

"For every breath he took after they stuck the dagger in him, they had to wait seven years. Myrantha told Morganna to look at their bodies after they were dead, and there would be marks indicating how many breaths the baby took."

"What kind of marks?"

"Puncture wounds. Teeth marks."

Jay turned a little green, requiring no elaboration. "Oh. So . . . how many . . . were there?"

At this Nancy smiled widely. "Morganna wrote that there were ten. She couldn't believe there were that many, that the baby could've lived that long, but there were exactly ten on both bodies, down by their thighs. Ten times seven is seventy, Jay. You know what that means?"

"Seventy . . ." Jay's eyes grew wide. "This year?"

"Halloween night."

"Where? How?"

"In the place up on the hill where they were hanged, on the stone slab they sacrificed the baby on. I'm pretty sure they're talking about Digger's Bonestone. Myrantha called it the Gate. Morganna was supposed to get two people up there, a male and a female, for Myrantha and Nathaniel to enter when the Gate is opened. According to Morganna, the men who hanged the Obers said it was between nine-thirty and ten when they did the lynching, so on next Halloween night, between nine-thirty and ten, they'll return."

"And you want us to go watch?" Jay asked, terrified.

"Watch?" Nancy laughed. "We'll do a lot more than that, Jay-Jay. The Obers probably never dreamed they would have to wait so long, until their daughter was too old to play her role, or even dead. But Morganna knew, and that's why she put the ledger in the tomb, so the right person would find it and do what had to be done."

"She said that?"

"Well, no, but what other explanation could there be? She was twelve when it happened, so she'd be eighty-two now if she's still alive. How would she manage to get two young people up there?"

"How did she know anyone would find it?" Jay countered, not certain at all he wanted to be a part of this.

"If there's anything Myrantha made very clear to her daughter," Nancy said patiently, "it's that if the Devil agrees to a bargain, he always keeps his end of it. Look at the way things have turned out. I'm sure Morganna wasn't worried about it."

"So you're actually going to get two people to go up there . . ."

"You'd better believe it," Nancy declared. "I want to know everything the Obers know. If I help them, they'll give me what I want in return."

"You sure of that? After spending seventy years in Hell, maybe they're not in such a good mood. Don't you know enough?" He couldn't believe they were actually having this conversation, even though, after what he had witnessed Saturday night, primarily the flaming acceptance of their sacrifice, his mind had quickly learned to accept the impossible, the incredible, with surprising ease, like a dry sponge in water. And now they were planning to involve themselves in what was surely ultimate evil. Wasn't that begging for eternal damnation?

Nancy's eyes narrowed, her jaw set with determination. "I'm going to do it, Jay, with or without you. But I'd much prefer *with,* and after what I did for you, I don't see how you could refuse."

He remembered his first glance in the mirror that morning, and then his elation, nullifying the terrors and regrets of the night before.

"I don't know nearly enough," Nancy went on, perceiving his acknowledgment of indebtedness. "All I've got is that thing Myrantha wrote at the end of her instructions, that incantation. I didn't have the slightest idea what would happen when I said it, but luckily I got exactly what I wanted both times. There wasn't anything in there about using those symbols I found on the back wall of the tomb, by the way . . . I thought of that myself." She beamed proudly.

Jay felt dizzy. "I don't know, Nancy. I think you're assuming an awful lot. I'm still wondering what happened to the Obers' bodies. Doesn't that make you think there's maybe more to this than you're aware of?"

"Which is exactly my point," Nancy said, poking a stiff finger in Jay's shoulder. "There's a ton of things I'm unaware of, but not for long. You with me or not?"

Jay rubbed his sweaty palms together, his eyes fixed on the floor. At last he muttered, "Guess it's . . . with."

Eleven

The bell rang, ending Lana's first day at the new school. She gathered her books and merged with the flow of students toward the door. She was feeling tense; the day had been a rough one, and she was completely bogged down by the amount of catch-up work she had to do. Her social life was going to suffer drastically. So much for the smooth transition.

Bruce was waiting by her locker. She had no classes with him, but Dennis, unfortunately, was in her second-hour geometry class. She had glared daggers at him throughout the whole period, but he hadn't seemed to notice.

Bruce saw the glum look on her face and offered a pitying smile. "Somebody step on your bottom lip?"

"That obvious, huh?" She managed a weak grin. "Maybe I'll have time to see you again on Christmas break. I can't believe all the homework I've got. You guys are way ahead of Edgewater."

"Oh, blarney," Bruce said, punctuating his statement with a raspberry. "With me as your tutor and scholastic assistant, you'll be caught up in no time. They don't call me Apple Head for nothing."

Recalling an earlier conversation they'd had about school, Lana asked suspiciously, "What's your grade-point average?"

Bruce shrugged. "Oh, 1.5, 2.0, something like that. I didn't say they called me Apple Head because I'm smart."

Lana giggled as she tugged her locker open and

grabbed the rest of her books. "Guess I'd better get a backpack to carry all this crap in." She groaned, the weight of the tomes causing her to stoop. Bruce removed the top three and piled them on top of his remedial English book.

"Beast of burden, at your service."

"Thanks, Bruce. If it weren't for you, I think I'd go home an' hang myself. Hardly anyone spoke to me today besides teachers. The kids just stared at me like I was a bug under a microscope or somethin'."

Her comment about going home and hanging herself, even though she obviously wasn't serious, left Bruce with a heavy black ball in the pit of his stomach, but he tried not to show it. "Hey, they're just checkin' ya out, that's all. Trying to decide if you're a good witch or a bad witch."

In a duet of laughter they sauntered down the hall to the stairwell, buffeted on either side by students who seemed to think the building was on fire. Bruce bellowed after a chubby boy who had nearly knocked them over, "Hey, like it might be just a fart, you know!"

The stairwell rang with derisive tittering, and above the descending sea of heads an index finger was raised. Bruce yelled in response, "No way! I'm not that kinda guy!"

Lana was laughing so hard her sides began to ache. "Please, gimme a break," she pleaded breathlessly. "I'm about to split a gut."

Bruce beamed, pleased with himself for his success in snapping Lana out of her depressed mood. He had dreamed of nothing but her the night before, and in the morning, when he woke up, the front of his shorts had been wet and sticky. He hadn't felt terribly embarrassed about it—that happened fairly often anyway—but it had been a little frightening, because it confirmed how much he really liked her. He'd never allowed his emotions to go very far out on a limb. But they were crawling out there now, despite his warnings, in defiance of his attempts to rein them back in. Soon, he knew, he'd hear that thin branch begin to splinter, and nothing he could do would stop the plunge.

Outside, a circle of teenagers had formed near the

motorcycle lot. Amidst the jeers and catcalls and mild obscenities, Lana could hear someone shouting, "Lick it! Lick it good!"

Sparks of anger flared in Lana's eyes. She wasn't certain yet, but she had a pretty good idea of what was going on. She muttered to Bruce, "I think they're doin' somethin' awful to Spiro. Let's stop 'em."

Bruce was compassionate, but he had no desire to play champion of the underdog. He preferred to keep a low profile. "Listen, they do it all the time, all right? You can't stop them, Lana. All that'll happen is they'll start giving you a lot of the same shit. Spiro's big enough to defend himself if he wants to. He won't ever learn if somebody jumps in to rescue him every time the bullies decide to have a good time with him. Really, you wouldn't be doing him any favors."

Lana turned her head, her eyes squeezed shut, wishing she had both hands free to cover her ears. Moments later she whispered hoarsely, "I guess you're right. Come on, let's get outta here. I can't stand this."

Behind them the taunting voices suddenly became a chorus of fearful screams. The crowd dispersed quickly, running in every direction. Lana and Bruce whirled around together just as Spiro catapulted the flailing body of a terrified teenage boy about fifteen feet through the air.

Tardo was learning fast.

The white casket was surrounded by elegant funeral wreaths, displaying a collage of harmonious colors in the form of flowers and satin bows. It was the kind of beauty that made one want to vomit.

A staunch, middle-aged woman with a wavering soprano sang "Rock of Ages" to conclude the service. A few old women in the small Episcopal chapel were weeping, one of them as if expecting to win a prize for mourning the loudest. The lament certainly had volume, but it totally lacked the quality of true sorrow. Marla sat wishing the stupid old bag would just shut the hell up.

The people around her were rising. Marla stood between her mother and brother and stole a glance at an auburn-haired woman whom she'd caught staring in their direction throughout the service. The woman's face was familiar, but Marla couldn't place it.

The Mingee family made their way toward the casket to say a final farewell to the lifeless, waxy figure within. Marla felt her stomach lurch as her mother, in line before her, stooped over to kiss the cold marble flesh of Gramma's forehead. Surely she wouldn't be expected to . . . ? No, no, she couldn't. That thing in the box was no longer Gramma Colter anyway. It was just an abandoned, wrinkled shell that would, in time, decay and fall apart. Marla refused to touch it. She stepped up after her mother had passed and stared for a few stricken moments at the shriveled husk; the bony hands, gnarled and liver-spotted, placed in restful repose upon a breast that would never rise and fall again. The small, pinched face, an empty oval of ghoulish hue, would never smile again, give butterfly kisses, read storybooks. Marla numbly followed her mother back down the aisle to the front porch of the chapel.

They were immediately joined by the auburn-haired woman, who put a comforting hand on Pamela Mingee's shoulder and said, "I don't know if you remember me, but I'm Jane Bellows. I work the night shift at Pinedale. We met last Christmas Eve, I think."

Pamela nodded bleakly. "Yes, I remember. It was good of you to come."

Jane paused, searching for the right words, if there were such things in a situation like this. "I was with her when she . . . passed on," she said carefully. "She, ah . . . she thought I was you."

Pamela grappled at the black wrought-iron railing for support. When the swoon passed, she looked back at Jane with tears in her eyes and asked quiveringly, "What did she say?"

Jane saw the deep pain on the woman's face and felt an immediate rush of sympathy, yet she knew she was going to go right ahead and pour salt into the wound. "Well, I don't think you would have known what she was talking about; apparently it was something she never told you," she answered, ashamed of her impropriety, feeling like a

135

crass intruder, even a rapist, on such delicate, deep intimacy, but she couldn't stop. "She said she did something. She didn't say what, but I'm sure it had something to do with Morganna Ober. That's why she was so afraid of her. Do you . . . have any idea . . . ?"

"How dare you?" Pamela spat, her sorrow turning to hot indignation. "You leave my mother's memory alone. And mind your own damn business!" She grabbed Marla's arm and whisked her away to the waiting limousine.

Inside the limo Pamela said to her husband, "That woman, Harold, had the nerve to suggest that Mother did something she couldn't tell me about except on her death bed. I can't believe the nerve of some people. I suppose she wants to exploit Mother's ravings about witches and bat's blood and—"

She burst into angry sobs. Harold Mingee blinked, patted her knee, and looked away. Pamela's brothers seemed lost in space, wondering, perhaps, if they would catch their flight out on time. Rick looked inquiringly at Marla, but she shook her head. Now wasn't the time for questions.

Jane remained on the porch as the other mourners shuffled past her toward the parking lot, shoulders hunched in apparent grief, embroidered hankies soaking up an impressive amount of tears. She felt like a complete boob. What had she expected? She should have waited at least a couple of weeks before even thinking about hitting Pamela Mingee with something like that. But no, she had to ask right at her mother's damn funeral. Why did she feel such a sense of urgency?

It was her own impatience; selfishness. She wanted to put this thing away, just as Jasmine Colter's body was being put away, and forget about it. So she could go to sleep at night without being subjected to one horrendous nightmare after another. Now she'd blown it. Even if Pamela Mingee did have any answers, Jane knew she would never hear them. She was on her own. With a despairing sigh, she proceeded to her car. She'd already missed an hour of work.

* * *

They were halfway up the north side of Beacon Hill when Nancy ordered Jay to pull off the road and park. He did as he was told, his eyes darting about nervously, like a rabbit's upon picking up the scent of a nearby wolf. They got out and locked the doors of the Charger. Nancy headed into some thick underbrush. "Come on, I think it's this way."

Afraid to do otherwise, Jay followed.

They fought their way through prickly brambles, broken branches, and overgrown weeds, following a path that time had all but erased. Jay's heart was thumping "In a Godda Da Vida" at 78 rpms. But he couldn't turn back, not now. She'd made him say a vow, and guaranteed that if he broke it he'd really be sorry. He believed her. What he couldn't believe, now that the realization of what he'd so impetuously done had fully sunk in, was the fact he'd actually pledged allegiance to the fucking Devil. But he had. She'd dangled immortality before him, and like a fool he'd grabbed it as greedily as he had the offer of a clear complexion.

He hadn't totally believed that she could do that for him, at first, and was in fact humiliated that she would even bring up an issue he was so sensitive about. But he was willing to try anything to put an end to his tormenting acne problem. She could heal him, she said. She told about Montgomery and what she had done to him. She claimed she was in control of true magic.

Jay didn't spend a lot of time reaching a decision. He envisioned no more dismay at looking in the mirror mornings to discover a fresh crop of angry red pustules. No more nicknames like Pizza Face or Strawberry Patch. Clean, clear, smooth skin—sure, you bet. Do your hocus-pocus, Nancy. Slaughter my kid brother's pet rabbit. Whatever it takes.

She'd told him how lucky, how privileged he was to receive her trust. She wouldn't even share her secret with her best girlfriend. Marla was nothing but a chickenshit. She would get scared and go running to blab everything all over town. Nancy couldn't have that.

A zitless face and immortality. That was worth his soul, wasn't it?

They finally came to a small clearing, at one edge of which stood a towering lodgepole pine. Nancy studied the area for a few minutes, then finally decided they were in the right place. She pointed to a thick overhanging limb on the pine tree. "I think that's the limb they hung the Obers from."

Jay nodded slowly. What was he supposed to say—Wow, far out? His tongue was lodged somewhere near his larynx. He made a funny gurgling sound in acknowledgment.

After turning around in circles, scouring the forest floor with her eyes, Nancy walked to the center of the clearing and began kicking at fallen leaves. She glared up at Jay. "Well, don't just stand there. Help me clear it off."

He obediently joined her in dislocating the brown, rotting cottonwood and scrub oak leaves. After a short while his foot struck something hard. "Hey, what—"

"Keep going," Nancy barked, kneeling to pull the sodden blanket away with her hands. When they were finished, they were staring at a dirty stone slab approximately six feet long, four wide. Jay remembered it; he had seen it before. Years ago his Boy Scout troop had come upon it during a hike. Nancy was right—it was Digger's Bonestone. A lot of kids knew about it; they supposed it covered some gold miner's grave. If he remembered correctly, Neil Henderson's oldest brother had given it the nickname. But Jay knew now it was something much more than everyone else supposed.

It was a doorway to Hell.

Nancy was rocking back and forth slightly, her eyes wide and glazed as she stared at the blackened stone. The surface seemed in motion. Jay bent over to take a closer look and saw that it was covered with maggots.

"This is it, this is the place," Nancy intoned reverently. "This is where they sacrificed the baby. This is where they'll return."

Jay's expression revealed total disgust, but Nancy was unaware of it. At last able to make his tongue work properly, he muttered, "And we're supposed to get two people to stand here next Friday night. What happens to them?"

"Who cares?" Nancy smiled. "I suppose their poor, displaced souls will find somewhere else to go, or maybe they'll get sucked right into Hell. I couldn't care less."

Jay crushed some of the squirming maggots with his boot. "C'mon, let's get out of here."

Twelve

Not caring to make another thirty-five mile jaunt back into Rapid City to see her uncles to the regional airport, Marla asked to be dropped off at the house after the graveside ceremony. No one argued.

The first thing she did was to run up to her bedroom and grab the telephone from her nightstand. She fell across the bed with it, determined not to start crying. She didn't want Dennis to get the mistaken impression that she was crying over him. She didn't care to stroke his ego any more than she had to.

She pushed the correct series of buttons with trembling fingers, listening to the familiar tune his phone number played, the first seven notes to "Mary Had a Little Lamb." After three rings the line was answered by Dennis's mother. "This is Marla, Mrs. Bloom. I was wondering if I could speak to Dennis, please."

"Of course, dear," the lilting voice came back softly. Florence Bloom reminded Marla of a powder puff, all soft edges, skin like fresh cream, a voice made for recording children's books, politely telling the little brats to turn the page after each beep. Exhale too strongly and she would blow away.

". . . and I'm terribly sorry about your dear sweet grandmother. I saw in the paper that she'd passed away."

Marla cleared her throat. "Thank you." She waited for Dennis to be put on the line, wondering how he was going to respond to her attempt to make up with him. Surely he didn't really like that girl he'd been with, judging from what Nancy had said of her. At any rate, Marla didn't plan to do any groveling. When she heard his voice, she was suddenly without vocal cords.

Dennis repeated impatiently, "Hello? Who is this? Mom, who did you say it was?"

"It's Marla, Dennis. Remember me?" Her voice, once she'd found it, carried a hint of sarcasm she'd intended to suppress. Dennis was silent for a few moments.

"I remember," he answered casually. "So, what's up?"

She was tempted to slam the receiver back into its cradle, let him go ahead and live happily ever after with his little blond hick, but instead she forced herself to say sweetly, "Come on, Dennis, let's stop this. I don't even remember how this fight started, but let's end it, okay? I'm willing if you are."

Dennis was satisfied. His plan had worked beautifully, just as he'd known it would. With a triumphant smile that Marla couldn't see, he said, "Sure, why not. But just to set the record straight, you started it, babe."

Marla clenched her teeth to keep herself from debating his ludicrous claim. "Whatever. Listen, I just got home from my gramma's funeral and I'm really depressed. You want to get together later with Nancy and Jay, maybe go to the Elk or something?"

"I'm broke," he lied, going for every ounce of contrition he could squeeze out of his hot-tempered girlfriend. She always had more money than he did anyway.

"I'll pay for it," she said grudgingly.

"Okay," he agreed quickly. "Pick you up around six-thirty."

"Oh, one more thing, Dennis." She asked herself: Now, over the phone, or later, face-to-face? Dennis had some explaining to do about Saturday night. She decided face-to-face would be better; then she might be able to tell if he was lying when she asked him if he'd gotten into that girl's pants. "Never mind. It can wait."

He arrived at 6:45. Marla let herself in on the passenger side of his Monte Carlo, smelling of a generous application of White Linen. "You're late," she said tersely, "but I guess it doesn't matter. When I finally got hold of Nancy, she told me she and Jay had already made other plans. Her and my parents are going out together for dinner tonight, then probably to the Gold Mine to get drunk on their asses."

"Which means," Dennis grinned, "that Nancy and Jay's plans are to boff each other's brains out."

Marla slammed her door shut. "Wouldn't surprise me, even though Nancy really doesn't even like Jay that much, she just goes with him because he's captain of the football team. She told me once she could hardly stand to kiss him. But don't you dare tell him I said that, though."

"Sounds like you're pissed at Nancy."

"I am." Marla closed her eyes for a moment, nervously biting her lower lip. "She's acting like we aren't even friends anymore, which is fine with me . . . what do I need her for? I don't know what her problem is . . . I haven't done anything to her. Yet. But ever since she . . ." Marla paused, her eyes boring into his. "Can you keep a secret? I mean it, Dennis. You can't say anything to anybody. Though I guess the way it worked out, we didn't really do anything wrong. I mean the door did open by itself. We didn't break in, you know, but I doubt that makes it all right to just go on in and take whatever you want . . ."

Dennis cocked his head; he hadn't the vaguest idea what the hell she was talking about. "What door? Where? Mind giving me a few more details?"

"The Obers' tomb," she answered tersely. "Nancy and I talked about breaking in that place for about three years, ever since I told her my gramma's stories about Morganna Ober, their daughter. You should've seen Nancy's eyes light up. Anyway, we just talked about it for a long time; I think Nancy was too afraid she'd get disappointed. As long as we were in suspense, without knowing for sure what was in there, she could come up with all kinds of possibilities. I never really thought we'd actually go through with it. If nothing really unusual was in there, then the fun would be over."

Dennis sighed. "Are you making a long story longer, or what? Just spit it out."

Marla pursed her lips and shot him a dirty look. "We made definite plans to do it last Saturday night—all of a sudden she decided it was time, since next year we'll be away at college. So Thursday I went up there by myself to check it out, see what kind of tools we would need and stuff. That was the day we got in all that trouble too, so I wasn't in a big hurry to get home. So I got up there, and it looked like there really wasn't any way to get in without dynamite. I pushed on the door, and it was solid—didn't budge. Then I stepped back a few feet and about fifteen seconds or so later the door started opening by itself. About scared me to death."

Dennis chuckled slightly and stuck a cigarette in his mouth. "You girls are so stupid. I've been in that tomb before; you think you were the first to come up with that idea? Me and Wayne got in there a couple of years ago, just fucking around. No big deal."

Marla gasped. "How did you get in? Did the door just open for you too?"

"Nah; Wayne picked the lock. He's good at shit like that. I think he boogered it up, though; we couldn't get it to stay locked when we left. The door must've just gotten rusted up or something, and came loose when you pushed on it. What did you think, that one of the Obers got up and opened it for you?" His eyes danced with ridicule as he puffed on his cigarette.

"So it was you," Marla shot back accusingly. "What did you and Wayne do with the bodies?"

"We didn't do anything with 'em," he said defensively. "What are you talking about?"

"They're gone, that's what I'm talking about. Nancy said the coffins were empty."

"Well, they sure as hell weren't empty when we were there, and we didn't touch 'em. Wayne wanted to take the skulls home and make candle holders out of 'em, but I said no. You get caught with something like that and you're up shit creek. So what, you didn't go in? Just Nancy?"

Marla's eyes were round as saucers. "So what the hell happened to the bodies?"

"Fuck, I dunno. Somebody else came along later and stole 'em, I guess."

Dennis was getting tired of the conversation, and he

still didn't know what any of it had to do with Marla being pissed at Nancy. "What's this all about, anyway? What's the big deal?"

"I had a strange feeling that Nancy found something she wasn't telling me about. Something about the look on her face, and she kept her right hand hidden under that awful cape. I forgot to tell you, she found a gross old cape in there, wadded up on the floor, she said, in front of Myrantha's coffin."

Dennis found this slightly interesting. "Both the corpses had black capes on when we saw them," he commented dryly.

"Did you see anything else? Anything unusual?"

"No, Marla, just a couple of dead people. What did you think there'd be, a goddamn spell book?" He sprayed laughter.

"Spell book." Marla tried the words on her tongue. After being in the tomb, Nancy hadn't seemed so distraught about the trouble they were in. Said just not to worry about it. And the next morning, of all the luck, Montgomery had a mysterious attack and got taken to the hospital. Nancy's face, when she'd first spotted Montgomery in the office. No dismay, no anger. Surprise. She'd been *surprised* to see him. Proof positive in Marla's book; she'd been right on target.

"I know something really bad is going on," she said finally. "I want to go in the tomb. I want to see for myself if those coffins are really empty."

"Whatever turns you on." Dennis fired up the Monte Carlo and peeled out of the circle drive just as Roger and Beth Snell pulled up in their white Volvo at the opposite end.

Even though Dennis was fairly muscular and could hold his own in a fistfight, his presence was little comfort to Marla in such a dark place of death. Chilled wind rustled through the treetops, swayed branches, gave motion to ominous shadows. She could hardly believe she had come back, and after the sun had gone down, no less. But she had to know now. She clung to him as they approached the tomb's metal door, looking like the very doorway to Hell in the impotent glow of Dennis's flashlight. At every sound other than their own footfalls, Marla's heart leapt into her throat. She longed for extra eyes in back of her head so she could see in every direction at once. But most of all she longed to get the hell out of there before she had a massive coronary. The place reeked of evil.

Dennis might have been taking a stroll through Disneyland in broad daylight. He knew with comfortable certainty that dead things stayed dead. Now if they were trolling through some place like Central Park in New York City at night, that would be something else. Living people could do all kinds of damage to their fellow beings. But not the dead. They could only lie there and rot some more, send up more stink. And that's all they would ever do. There were no homicidal lunatics in the graveyard, or residing anywhere near Sharon Valley. If anyone else did appear, it would most likely be a high school or junior high kid, a familiar, friendly, thrill-seeking face. Nothing green or red-eyed or fanged. The only animal life they were likely to encounter would be a deer, perhaps a raccoon.

He pushed the door open, illuminating the cracked concrete floor. "I suppose you want me to go in with you?"

"Hell yes, I want you to go in. I'm not going to touch those horrible coffins."

Dennis led the way with a grunt of disgust. A coyote howled in the distance, turning Marla's blood to ice. "Hurry, please. Let's get it over with."

As Dennis brought the flashlight up and around to shine on Myrantha Ober's coffin, Marla caught a glimpse of some figures drawn on the back wall. "Shine it over there again," she commanded, pointing. "I thought I saw something."

"What?" Dennis bathed the wall in mellow light, then froze, a shuttered memory colliding with his present vision.

Marla clutched him tightly. "Look at that, Dennis. And the inverted cross . . . that's the sign of the Devil. At least Nancy wasn't lying about that." Her words echoed in the small chamber; even their breathing seemed far too loud. Marla's heartbeats were cannon explosions.

"It looks like the same—" Dennis began.

"Same what?" She shook him roughly. "You act like that wasn't there when you were in here before. Was it, Dennis? Was that there a few years ago?"

He shook his head slowly. "No, it wasn't. But just the other night . . . I was up here, on the overlook, and heard somebody scream. Found a dead white rabbit on one of the flat grave markers down near the end, and those same markings were around it. I think. They look the same. Anyway, it doesn't mean jack shit."

For a moment Marla thought she was going to faint. "You didn't . . . didn't see anyone?"

"No. But Jay's Charger was parked up there. That's why I stopped. I asked him about it the next day, and he said he hadn't heard anything. Said he and Nancy were down the other side at the Boy Scout camping place. I'm sure somebody's just playing a joke. Jay and Nancy, probably."

"I don't believe this is a joke, Dennis. Open the coffin."

Dennis opened the lid and shined the light inside. Marla forced herself to look, then let out the breath she'd been holding. "Well, that's something else Nancy didn't lie about, but after what you just told me . . . take me back home, Dennis. I've got a phone call to make."

Lana shoved the pile of textbooks onto the floor and muffled a scream in her pillow. When she lifted her face, Bruce patted her on the head.

"Feel better now?"

She smiled. "Much."

He glanced blearily at his Mickey Mouse watch. "It's getting late. I'd better—"

"Oh please, you can't leave yet. We haven't really had much time to talk about anything but this crappy schoolwork. I want to know more about you. I don't even know if you have any brothers or sisters."

"I've got twin sisters four years younger than me," Bruce answered with a sour look on his face. "They drive me nuts. My stepfather is a Forest Ranger, and my mom's a bookkeeper. We're what you call lower middle class. Or is that upper lower class?"

Lana pressed a finger to his lips. "Don't say things like that. You don't have anything to be ashamed of."

How little did she know . . .

"Well, you haven't seen me naked yet."

His quip hung in the air for an interminable length of time; Bruce flushed with embarrassment. "Hey, I didn't mean—"

"I know, you were just bein' Mr. Funny again." Lana giggled, but her heart was mysteriously pounding.

Bruce wasn't sure if that was entirely true, but he wasn't prepared to deal with a subject like that in seriousness. He was still a virgin, and naturally wanted to rid himself of that plague, but he was afraid. Afraid he might fuck it up. If anyone could fuck up fucking, he probably could. He didn't do much of anything else right.

His only escape from the subject was a leap into absurdity. "Have you ever seen an elephant barf?"

"Oh Bruce, yuck." Lana screwed up her face. "Why? Have you?"

"Yeah, fed one a bunch of cotton candy at the circus when I was a kid. Out came this huge, pink gooey mass . . . turned out to be the lady that rode around on his trunk."

Lana's gullibility had its limits. "Would you lie about somethin' like that?"

"Yeah." His ridiculous dodging maneuver hadn't worked. He could still feel the reverberations of his previous comment; they continued to bounce between the two of them in tangible waves. There seemed only one sensible thing left to do: slay his dragon. He cupped his hand around her neck and drew her toward him. Her eyes fluttered, then closed. Her lips parted. Bruce's body flooded with excitement. Lips touched, tongues probed.

The door flew open.

"Ommmm! I'm tellin'," Luke declared loudly. "You're s'pose to be in here doin' homework, an' all you're doin' is kissin'!"

The couple instantly disengaged themselves and sat

bolt upright, both glaring at the unwanted intruder. Lana shouted, "Luke, you know good an' well you're s'pose to knock on a door before BARGIN' on in, Creepo! Now what the . . . what do you want? An' for your information, we have been doin' homework, up till just about thirty seconds ago."

Bruce made the Boy Scout sign in support of her testimony.

Luke sneered. "Yeah, sure you have. Well, what I want is Sam. An' also Mom said to tell you, it's time for your friend to go home."

A slight look of alarm crossed Lana's face. "Sam's not out in the garage?"

"No, I thought you had 'im in here. Great. You don't know where he is?"

"You were the last one playin' with 'im, Luke Bremmers. If he's gone, then it's your—"

Carol appeared in the doorway behind her son, her wire-rimmed hexagon reading glasses perched on her nose. "What's all the shoutin' about?"

"Sam's gone," Luke wailed. "An' Lana says it's my fault. It's not. I put him back in the garage 'fore supper, an' now he's just gone. I thought Lana had 'im in here."

"Well, go check outside," Carol said, silently adding a prayer of thanks. It would be nothing to her if the dog was never found. "But stop the yellin', okay? I've got a headache."

Luke dashed off down the hallway. Carol gave Lana a fleeting, guilty glance and said with challengeable authority, "I think it's probably about time for your comp'ny to go home."

"Just as I was saying," Bruce said cheerfully, sensing the tension, like a Bengal tiger preparing to spring, rising in Lana. He didn't want to be the cause of a mother-daughter blowout.

Lana opened her mouth to argue, but quickly snapped it shut again. Not in front of Bruce. She silently scooted off the bed and put her shoes on, intending to walk him out to his pickup. Carol disappeared like an unpleasant thought. The way Lana saw it, her mother's simpering actions of late concretely proved her guilt; Lana had hit the nail right on the head. Her mother had actually asked for the transfer. All she cared about was herself. She probably wanted Bruce to leave simply because she was jealous of the fact her daughter had a boyfriend. Misery loves company.

Luke was frantically whistling for Sam up and down the block, dashing in and out of shadows, occasionally calling out in a loud, harsh whisper, "Sam, Sam! C'mere boy! Here, Sam!"

"If that dog's gone, Spiro's gonna be real upset," Lana said, remembering with dread the scene she'd witnessed in the school parking lot earlier that day. "I told him I'd take care of Sam. He's gonna hate me." The thought made her shudder.

They stood in the street, leaning against the left bed wall of the pickup. Bruce put his arms around her, shielding her from the cold wind. "If he's got a crush on you, I doubt you have anything to worry about. Jeez, I couldn't believe him throwing that guy today, though." He remembered too. "He's never done anything like that before that I know of . . . I've seen people spit right in his face, and he'd just turn around and walk away."

"How awful."

"Yeah, well, I don't think anybody's going to try something like that again, unless they have a fervent death wish. Word will get around pretty fast."

"You really think Spiro could . . . ?"

"Somebody like that, who the hell knows?" Their eyes met; the subject of Spiro dispersed like a vapor. Now there were only the two of them in the entire universe, nothing to worry about, nothing to do but explore and enjoy.

"Kiss me," Lana demanded softly.

Bruce slowly lowered his face to hers, but instead of kissing her, for which she was prepared, he whispered teasingly, "What will you pay me if I do?"

Lana's eyes flew back open, unable to focus with Bruce's only two inches away. "Are you ever serious?" she grumbled.

He shrugged. "From time to time." He buried his lips on hers.

* * *

A tearful Luke came through the front door after a fruitless twenty-minute search. His mother was sipping a glass of milk on the couch while flipping through the *TV Guide*. The shower was running; Lana was in the bathroom.

Luke closed the door and flung himself into a chair. "I couldn't find him anywhere, Mom. Sam's flat gone."

Carol shook her head with pretended sympathy. "That's too bad, honey. Well, maybe he'll show up tomorrow."

"He won't," her son sulked. "We won't never see him again, I just know it. I think somebody got in the garage an' stole 'im."

"I don't know . . . I guess that's possible." Carol frowned, upset by the idea that someone would steal anything—including a pup she didn't want anyway—from her property. One of the reasons she'd chosen Sharon Valley was because of its incredibly low crime rate. "Do you think maybe one of your little friends came over to get 'im, you know, just to play with 'im or somethin'? At any rate, it's past your bedtime. We can worry about this tomorrow."

Too dejected to argue, knowing full well that neither of his two friends would have taken Sam without asking, Luke silently headed for his bedroom, dragging his feet on the carpet. Carol picked up the remote control and switched channels. A man and woman were passionately engaged in a kiss. She quickly switched to another, damning Hugh Bremmers under her breath. He hadn't even called to see if they'd gotten here safely. She supposed bitterly that he now had more important things to think about than his own children. And what was happening between her and Lana was really his fault, when you got down to the root of the matter. If he hadn't been so obsessed with satisfying his precious ego—*not to mention a certain twenty-four-year-old!*—then none of this would be happening. They would all be living happily ever after.

Lana stepped out of the shower and rubbed her hair with a towel, then wrapped it around herself, picked up her discarded clothing from the floor and went across the hall to her bedroom. After closing the door, she tossed the clothes over a chair and let the towel fall from her body. Moving toward her dresser, she studied herself in the mirror with satisfaction. The first time Greg had seen her naked, he had candidly exclaimed that she looked just like she'd walked out of a *Playboy* magazine.

She wondered what Bruce would say. (What would her mother say if she knew her sweet, innocent little daughter wasn't a virgin anymore? And who cared?) When (not if) she and Bruce did it, he would probably say something along the lines of, "Haven'cha got anything a little more interesting?"

She cupped one of her breasts, allowing the other hand to slide over a flat abdomen to her golden pubic patch. Greg had known instinctively just how to touch her. She'd heard some girls say that their first sexual experiences had been awful. Not hers. She'd gotten a headful of lice from doing it in a hayloft, but she'd climaxed three times.

Sighing wistfully, she opened her top dresser drawer and pulled out a cotton nightie. She slipped it over her head, then turned off the overhead light and crawled under the covers on her bed, unaware of the shadow that suddenly moved away from the crack between her rosy curtains outside the window.

Nancy reached over and sleepily picked up the jangling telephone. She had gone to bed early—after boffing Jay's brains out, as Dennis had suspected—untypically exhausted. The excitement was wearing her out. She hadn't been sleeping well lately either. "Hello?"

The voice on the other end was so angry it sounded strangled. "I've figured it out, Nancy. And don't tell me you don't know what I'm talking about."

"Marla?" Nancy laboriously raised up to support herself on an elbow, her eyes narrowing into dark slits. The man in the moon frowned at her through the part in her curtains.

"You know it's me. And I know you found something in that tomb besides that raunchy old cape. You found some kind of book, didn't you?" Marla's knuckles turned white as she gripped the phone tighter, waiting tensely for Nancy's reply. It came swiftly, edged with sharp sarcasm.

"You don't know a goddamned thing, Marla. Fuck off."

The line went dead.

Thirteen

Jane was about to enter Goldie Bradshaw's room to see whether or not her bluepads needed changing when Wilma waved to her from the nursing station at the end of the hall. Jane gladly postponed her duty and padded down the tiled corridor, her rubber-soled shoes squeaking rhythmically.

"Phone call, line two," Wilma said disapprovingly. Personal calls were strongly discouraged.

"Harry?"

"No, some young girl, sounds like."

Curiosity creating additional lines on Jane's face, she stepped around the desk, pushed the lighted blinking button on the telephone and picked up the receiver. "This is Jane."

As she listened, her eyes grew wide. When she finally had a chance to reply, she cupped her hand around the receiver and said softly, "I think we ought to talk about this tomorrow, when I'm off work. Can you come over to my place after you get out of school? Great. I live at the Timberline trailer court on Third, near the—Oh, okay. Number twenty-four. Right. Yes, that would be fine. See you then."

She hung up, her hand trembling visibly. Wilma eyed her with concern. "Something wrong?"

"I don't . . . know. I hope not," Jane mumbled uncertainly, clumsily stepping through the low swinging door and around to the front of the desk. "Never mind. I'm all right. Need to go check on Mrs. Bradshaw . . ."

She trudged away woodenly like a sleepwalker, words

batting around in her mind like marbles in a blender. *Ambulance! Tomb! Rabbit! Strange markings!*
SPELL BOOK!

Marla, having been excused from school for another day by her mother, drove over to Jane's trailer house at 9:45 Tuesday morning.

A zombie answered her knock. Jane had hardly slept a wink the night before, and the few winks she did get were spent in a labyrinth of nightmares, horrid apparitions chasing her, catching her, locking her up in a cold, gray, smelly dungeon full of bones. In one heart-stopping scene the ground before her began to crumble upward, like a slowly erupting volcano, and bright, effervescent lava oozed up red through the cracks, black smoke billowing into a starless sky overhead. Then a head began to appear, a flaming crown under which eternal, evil eyes glittered, locked into hers, and destroyed her with a split-second's contact. She had bolted upright in a silent scream, her gown soaked with sweat, not knowing at first if it had really happened or not. Then she'd heard Harry beside her, snoring contentedly, assuring her that she was still in the land of the living.

She couldn't bring herself to close her eyes again. Not after that. To take her mind off the terrible visage, she had gotten out of bed and actually cleaned the trailer from top to bottom. It gleamed like a new penny.

Marla entered, nodding with approval though she thought the place a hovel. "This is cute. I don't think I'd like to live in a trailer, though. Aren't you afraid of tornadoes?"

"It usually looks like one's been through here," Jane admitted tiredly, not giving the question any serious thought. Twisters were the least of her present worries. God, how she wanted to sleep, escape into deep, black, dreamless paradise. She shuffled into the kitchen to pour her ninth cup of coffee. "Want some coffee? If not, I've got Pepsi and orange juice . . ." And plenty of beer, of course. Harry was never without a good supply of brew. But she didn't think it appropriate to offer that, although the teen looked like she could use a double scotch.

Marla seated herself on the edge of the couch. "No, thanks. I'm fine."

Jane poured her coffee, left it black, and joined her nervous guest in the living area. They stared awkwardly at each other for several moments, both wondering how to start such a conversation. Finally Marla started at the beginning and told Jane about seeing the tomb door open, and the events that had transpired since. Jane listened with growing tension, her muscles tightening into rigid cables. By the time Marla was finished with her story, Jane's jaws were aching from clenching her teeth. She hadn't even been aware of doing it.

"I really, really don't want to believe any of this, you know," Jane said. "I've run from this kind of thing all my life, and I never expected it to catch up to me. What scares me the most is finding out . . . finding out it's real. Because if witchcraft is real, then I've got the damn Devil and Hell and mortal sin to deal with, and I don't want to deal with any of it. I will help you . . . if I can. I honestly don't know offhand what I can even do. But I'm involving myself to prove that all of this is just a bunch of ancient mumbo jumbo and superstition. That's what I want it to be, you understand?"

Marla nodded. "Well, I sure as hell don't know what to do. If I tell my mom, she may or may not slap my face, but I doubt very much she'd talk to Beth about it . . . that's Nancy's mother. She and my mom are friends from way back. Anyway, you saw how my mom was at the funeral. One word about anything like this and she'll fly right off the handle. You know, because of Gramma. By the way, why were you asking what Gramma had to do with Morganna Ober? That's why I came to you. You don't think Gramma was just senile, do you?" And what am I doing here? she thought. What could this hag do to help me? How could anyone help me if Nancy knows how to use the power of the Devil? The woman before her was a fool, thinking it could all just be a bunch of nonsense.

Jane told her about the diary. Marla's jaw set, but her knees began to shake slightly. "My boyfriend, Dennis, thinks it's all just a prank, but after what happened to

Mr. Montgomery, and now this diary stuff . . . I'm *totally* convinced Nancy found some sort of book in the tomb, and it does tell her how to . . . how to hurt people with black magic. And she did take Mr. Montgomery's pen."

Jane blinked. "What?"

"She stole Mr. Montgomery's favorite pen off his desk, the day this all started. Haven't you heard the stories? They have to have a personal belonging of their intended victim. Nancy used that pen somehow . . . oh shit, she's got a million things of mine . . ."

Jane put her coffee cup down and looked at Marla sternly. "I think you're—"

"We've got to tell the police. Do you think they'd believe us? If we could just get them to search Nancy's room—"

"Are you kidding? The police? They'd lock us up if we told them what we—"

"She's going to do something to me, I know it! I should never have told her I suspected—"

"Marla, please! You're getting hysterical," Jane said sharply. "I'm sorry, but I'm just in no mood for that. We've got to stay calm, rational. We don't know for sure if such a book even exists. Now what I want you to do, if you can, is take a look through your grandmother's things. Maybe she kept a diary too, or some sort of memoirs. Will you do that? If there's any answers to be had, I think that's where we'll find them."

Marla wasn't listening; she was too busy trying to keep herself together. It was all she could do to keep from screaming, running out of the trailer, and burning rubber all the way to Nancy's house to retrieve her various possessions. She knew, in her heart of hearts, that her ex–best friend was invoking ancient evil, manipulating the material world with deadly spiritual forces. And the bitch had told her, the previous night, to fuck off.

How the hell did you fight something you couldn't even see? What weapons were effective against a witch— or a girl who was playing the role of one?

An urgent knock at the door startled them both. Jane got up to answer it, walking on legs weighing a hundred pounds each. She wanted more than anything at that moment to just crawl back into bed and sleep for a hundred years, have pleasant dreams about finding suitcases full of money, recapturing her youth, landing the starring role in a Broadway musical, dying and finding out death is just a trip into wonderland. No judgment. No books. No show and tell. Just an eternal amusement park.

As soon as the trailer door was opened, a chattering gadfly swished into the room smelling of rose essence, her old-fashioned red-and-white-checked cotton dress, inappropriate for the season if not the decade, hanging loosely on a tall, willowy frame. Mousy brown hair streaked with ribbons of gray was pulled up in a well-sprayed French bun. Cat-eye glasses perched on the end of a long, twisted nose. Quick, probing eyes examined Marla through them, and revealed a hint of disappointment. Edna had seen the Cutlass parked behind Jane's Volkswagen, and had gleefully surmised that Jane could be found in the arms of a virile young lover. God knew it wouldn't be much of a surprise, considering the potbellied slob she was married to.

Jane suddenly realized what she'd done: she'd just let in Edna Crassfield, president of Gossip International, without first warning Marla to keep her mouth shut about things supernatural. About anything, really, except maybe the weather. But it was too late now. She shut the door with a despairing sigh. "Edna, this is Marla. Marla, Edna Crassfield."

Edna extended a bony hand. "Well, so very nice to meet you, Marla. But my, shouldn't you be in school today? Are you sick, dear, or perhaps in a pinch of trouble . . . ?" Her voice sounded hopeful.

Marla released the dry, grasping fingers with a dour smile and, in spite of Jane's frantic signal to Zip Up, spilled out, "Everybody in this town might be. I think my ex–best friend found a book in the Obers' tomb about how to do black magic. Mr. Montgomery was going to suspend us, but the very next day he had to be rushed off to the hospital in an ambulance, and I saw her take his pen off his desk the day before, the same day she—"

"We don't know this for a fact, now, Edna—" Jane interjected desperately.

Edna ignored her and lowered herself slowly into Harry's favorite chair, her eyes riveted to Marla's face, her mouth open and rounded as though waiting for a banana. "Now, what's this? Tell me all about it, dear."

Jane slapped a palm against her forehead and groaned, picturing the headlines of the next morning's Sharon Valley *Gazette:* Woman Claims Witch Hunt Now in Progress. Harry would see his wife's name listed as a source, and would absolutely blow a gasket. But telling Edna to keep her mouth shut about this would be like telling a waterfall to reverse its course.

She hoped Marla would find something in Jasmine's belongings that would quickly put the whole ugly thing to rest. In the meanwhile Jane knew of only one person she could go to for advice in such a matter, much as she hated to admit it. Her mother.

The girl halted Lana in the hallway by reaching out and grabbing her jean jacket. Lana whirled around and recognized her as one of the two she'd met at the park on Sunday. She had been hostile then. Now she was smiling. "Hi, remember me?"

Lana nodded warily. "Yeah, the park."

Nancy's dark eyes glittered like wet onyx. "That's right. Sorry I wasn't very friendly. I was . . . jealous, I suppose."

"Jealous? Of me?" Lana was surprised at the admission. Finding such open honesty in a teen was pretty rare; she thought of herself as rather unique in that respect. But she remained slightly suspicious. The girl was, after all, Marla's best friend, and the rabbit business was still unsettled. "Hey, you don't have any reason to be——"

"It was petty of me, I admit," Nancy interrupted, glancing up at the clock above their heads. "Damn . . . I've gotta run. Bunch of crap that we only get five minutes between classes, huh? Anyway, my name is Nancy. What was yours again?"

"Lana. Lana Bremmers."

"Lana . . ." Nancy repeated the name with an approving nod. "Well, Lana, we'll have to get together sometime."

Lana thought she smelled a rat, but she heard herself

responding, "Sure, that would be great. I haven't made any girlfriends yet. Ever'one here seems to be so——"

But Nancy was gone, disappearing in the throng of students. Lana finished to herself, "so stuck up."

Bruce and Lana ate their lunches—chips from the cafeteria vending machine—at the park. She'd just told him about her earlier encounter with Nancy.

"So what's goin' on, you think? Am I bein' set up?"

Shaking his head at the autumn-gray sky, Bruce answered, "Dunno, but I'd be careful if I were you. I saw Dennis earlier and he said his plan worked great. But Marla didn't even say anything to him about you—had something else on her mind, he said, and that kinda twirked him off—he was wanting to rub it in. So maybe she's just gonna blow it off. Then again, she might be planning to lure you up in the woods so she can shave your head and spray-paint your whole body green." He grinned widely, showing golden flecks between his teeth.

"That's all I need." Lana recalled Nancy's face as she'd grabbed her in the hall. Had the smile been real? Or had it been bait on a hook controlled by Marla, a girl Lana had never even seen as far as she knew, but who probably hated her guts. High school games! Her shoulders slumped, a heaviness settling over her. "I hate crap like this. Good grief, I didn't even kiss Den—well, I guess I did once. But that was all. An' he's the one who asked me out—I didn't go chasin' after him. What am I s'pose to do? Run from Nancy if I see her again?"

Bruce grinned. "Nah, might give her a complex. Just take it easy . . . even if Marla does hate you, that doesn't mean Nancy's got to. She's got her own mind, she can like anybody she wants. Could be they had a fight, and now Nancy is shopping around for a new best friend."

"An' what would make Marla madder than for Nancy's new best friend to be the girl who'd gone out with her boyfriend. I'd just be gettin' used again, only this time by a girl," Lana said, jabbing the toe of her shoe at a stone. "But frankly, I don't know that I'd wanna be Nancy's friend anyway. I still think she had somethin' to do with that rabbit."

"I wouldn't presume guilt on such circumstantial

159

evidence," Bruce cautioned, though he had done some serious presuming of his own in that regard. "But there's two things in this world we can pick: our noses and our friends. Hard to find good ones at this age. Friends, I mean. Ah, the trials and tribs of a teen." He stuffed some more Doritos into his mouth and added between chews, "We die a million deaths before we even get out of high school."

Lana looked up, surprised. "Do you write poetry?"

Bruce took an oratory stance in front of the bench. Lifting his bag of Doritos high, he began: "Roses are red, violets are blue—"

"Bruce." Lana rolled her eyes.

"And I got a worm hanging out my kazoo."

"Bruce, how gross!" Lana crossed her arms and glared at him hotly. "You have to make a joke out of everything, don't you? Are you tryin' to insult me?"

He dejectedly returned to the bench. "Hey, no way. You looked like you were getting all bummed out, so I was just trying to make you laugh. Why would I try to insult you? I like you . . . a lot. This much—" He held his hands as far apart as they would go.

Lana's anger quickly melted away. She mischievously tossed him back a little of his own medicine: "Oh, is that all?"

"My arms won't stretch any further."

"Well, next time you wanna make me laugh, don't tell me about the worm you got hangin' out your kazoo . . . yuck. You were just makin' that up, weren't you?"

Bruce forged a look of embarrassment. "Gee, I hope so. I don't check it out very often."

Lana grimaced.

It was time to go back to school. They tossed their empty chip bags into a trash container bearing the inscription Fuck It, which someone, obviously in need of an attitude adjustment, had scrawled with a sharp object into the white paint. They sauntered lazily toward Bruce's pickup, merging slowly together until their fingers brushed, and then it was only natural that they should join hands. In spite of what Nancy and Marla might have up their sleeves, Lana felt happy. With Bruce around, she doubted she could stay depressed about anything for very long. Except, perhaps, Sam's disappearance. The pup was still missing as of the time Bruce had picked her up for school that morning.

When they got back in the truck, Bruce removed a small brass case from his glove compartment and removed a neatly rolled joint. "I've got a test next hour," he explained, "and I'll never pass it if I'm not stoned, 'cause I was stoned when I studied for it. I can't cross-reference different states of consciousness."

Lana shook her head, trying to look disapproving but unable to keep the smile off her face. Bruce was so crazy. "Whatever you say."

Fourteen

Rose Hester began to tremble like a massive bowl of Jell-O, fat fingers clutching the garish gold cross that hung from her wattled neck. The most apparent emotion on her face was fear, but beneath it surged passionate zeal, the natural response of the Born Again to the onset of spiritual battle. Onward Christian soldiers! Far too much time was spent sitting idle in the reserves.

"I'll call Brother Mitchell right away," she said gravely, gray eyes twinkling. "This is a serious matter, as I'm sure you know. Next prayer meetin' isn't till tomorrow night, so he'll probably call a special one, seein' as how this is an emergency. You two will be there, won't you?"

Jane had finally managed to get rid of Edna—it wasn't hard; after Marla had told all there was to tell, the urgent need to get to a telephone was clearly visible on Edna's face—and Jane had afterward told Marla she was going to her mother's house for advice. Marla had wanted to go along, in spite of Jane's warnings.

Marla now curled her lips in an attempted smile. "I have to go to a church meeting?"

"Land sakes, you gotta get under God's protection," Rose declared, laying a hand on her breast. "Lest you're a'covered by the Blood, you got no defense against the Prince of Darkness, and that's exactly who's behind this thing, as God's my witness. Otherwise you'll be out there like a little lamb without no shepherd, and that ol' wolf's a'gonna eat you alive. Mark my words."

Jane fought the urge to bolt from her mother's house

and run until there were no soles left on her shoes. "Mother, don't scare her like that." How many times had that analogy been pushed in her own face? A thousand, ten thousand? "We don't know for sure this is anything but a prank. If it's not, well . . . we'd just like to see it stopped. We really don't want to get personally involved, if we can help it."

"Anybody who still has breath is involved, whether they like it or not!" Rose retorted. "If you don't cast a vote, then it's cast for you—an' I don't think you're gonna like who yer electin'. You remember what Brother Gibson warned you, Jane Rachel, about a'goin' into the pit. This is just what he was talkin' about," she prattled fiercely, her jowls becoming flushed. "You gonna take this young girl with you? You gonna close the door of eternal salvation in her face?"

Jane wondered which would be worse; leaving Marla defenseless against the jaws of the Wolf (a.k.a. Satan, Lucifer, Belial, Beelzebub) or the jaws of her determined mother, a black belt in gospel karate. "Mother, leave Marla alone. If she wants to go to church, that's up to her. I'm not going to talk her out of it any more than I'm going to let you harangue her into it. The only reason I came to you is I didn't know what else to do. But if this is the help I'm going to get, I'm sure I can think of something else." *Yes, officer, I know it sounds crazy, but do you think you could get a search warrant anyway . . . ?*

"You can't fight the Devil on your own." Rose lowered herself to her overstuffed Early American couch with a sniffle. "Only the mighty power o' God can fight against that evil, and you know what happened to those men in the bible who tried to cast out a devil without bein' saved. It tore 'em to pieces."

"Which is exactly why we don't want to get involved." Jane sighed with exasperation, signaling Marla to head for the door before they were both forced to convert for the sake of peace. For her, the years were flying backward; the scene was beginning to reek of a déjà vu sewer, relentless sermons, WARNINGS, thou shalt nots, and bucketfuls, truckfuls of wonderful guilt, guilt, GUILT—

She got herself and Marla safely outside before she

actually started screaming. Blackness threatened to usurp her consciousness; she had to sit on the front porch with her head between her knees to recover. Too much caffeine, she decided. And not enough sleep.

Marla squatted down beside her. "Hey, are you going to faint or something?" She was already regretting her involvement with Jane; what was she to do if the woman fell unconcious? Give her mouth-to-mouth? No way in hell.

"No, I'll be all right." Jane took a few deep breaths and tried to relax. She felt like a telephone pole vibrating with the current of deadly voltage.

Marla glanced at the closed door behind them, afraid Mrs. Hester would come after them to continue her campaign. "So what's your mother going to do? Just have a prayer meeting? What good is that?"

"The way I see it," Jane said sickly, "is, if this witchcraft thing is real—God forbid—then their prayers just might do some good. If this is a contest between two fantasies, then nothing is going to happen and you and I can have a good laugh about this later. But if we're talking about a clash of two opposite and very real powers, then we've done the best that we can do. My mother's church is about as religious as you can get."

Marla needed no convincing of that. "I won't argue with you. But I just can't sit around and do nothing . . . there's got to be a way to find out for sure what's going on. Maybe Dennis can get something out of Jay."

"Couldn't hurt to try. And like I said earlier, try to get a peek at your grandmother's things." Marla nodded, though she would never get around to it. Jane rubbed her forehead and cautioned finally with a weak smile, "And watch out for the big bad wolf, of course."

Pamela Mingee stared at her shape beneath the crisp beige sheet, trying to remember how it had looked twenty years earlier. Roger Snell traced a forefinger around the outline of her navel.

"Ready for another round?"

"You're a fiend," Pamela accused, then added with a wink, "but that's what I like about you. I'm still hurt, though, that you and Beth didn't come to Mama's funeral. How could you forget a thing like that?"

Roger pulled his lower lip down. "I thought being horny meant never having to say you're sorry."

"That's being in love. Which has nothing to do with us."

He leaned over to give her a lingering, wet kiss, his tongue probing deeply into her mouth. She moaned when he started down her neck, the movements of his tongue sending electric thrills down the entire left side of her body. Roger always joked about her left side being more sensitive than the right; he called it her 220 outlet. Harold had never noticed any difference.

He lingered at her left breast, sucking gently, nipping playfully with his teeth as he kneaded the other. She tugged at the hair on his temples. "Easy, easy."

He pushed the sheet down farther, his hands exploring supple, perfumed flesh, the scent of sexual release mingled with an exotic fragrance he knew had cost Harold Mingee a small fortune. But, of course, the pompous bastard liked to brag about how much his possessions were worth. His favorite T-shirt to wear fishing proclaimed, "He Who Dies with the Most Toys Wins." Harold had a lot of expensive toys. But Roger had his wife at least twice a week.

The fact that she was also his wife's best friend didn't cause him much added anxiety. Though she would never admit it, he knew that deep down, Beth despised Pamela. The two had always been fiercely competitive, but there had only been one brass ring. One Harold Xavier Mingee, Attorney at Law. Roger had been the booby prize. And Beth never let him forget it.

Pamela closed her eyes and relished the sensations coursing through her body. Roger wasn't much of an intellectual, but he was good at what she needed him for. Today she not only needed him for sex, but as a distraction, something to get her mind off her mother's death, the funeral, the fact that her own life was little more than a paper cutout. There was comfort in it, in a one-dimensional sort of way, but few real joys. A world painted in very pale pastels with no vivid colors or shapes. Just one wild streak of purple, hidden offstage, named Roger. Physically speaking, he was everything that Harold wasn't: attractive, hairy, muscular, sexually well-endowed. His face evinced both toughness and sensuality, an irresistible combination. Her affair with him kept her going. Surely Beth wouldn't really mind, if she knew. She had a lot in common with Harold.

When Roger and Pamela again lay spent in a panting heap, her mind drifted, rebelliously, into memories of the dream she'd had the previous night, the dream that had sent her rushing to the telephone to call Roger that morning the moment her daughter had left on some unexplained errand.

Her mother—not the wrinkled, lifeless thing she'd seen in the white satin-lined casket, but the former Jasmine, plump and full of energy—had suddenly appeared in her bedroom, wearing her red paisley-patterned apron over a pale green frock. She held a spatula in one hand, a large iron crucifix in the other. She asked Pamela if she would like some pancakes. In the dream, Pamela sat up and pointed to the cross. "What's that for?"

"Demons been in the pancake mix again," was the irritated reply. "Don't do a bit of good to fry 'em . . . they'll go down hot right into your belly. Then they'll just take over and push your soul right out through your eyes. Dad-gum witches been foolin' in my kitchen again, puttin' demons in the cereal boxes and everything else. Have to stick this cross down in there to drive 'em out."

The next moment, Pamela was sitting at the breakfast table in pigtails, a stack of pancakes dripping with butter and syrup on the plate in front of her. Breathing, those pancakes. Yes, ever so slightly . . .

"Mom, are you sure you got all the demons out of this?"

Jasmine, busy over the stove, called back to her, "Of course I did, sugar. Now eat 'em up before they get cold."

The first forkful made its way down Pamela's throat like a glob of scalding fat, the sweetness instantly turning bitter. Then the fire began to spread and she was on the floor, kicking and screaming as her eyes began to bulge and expand like water balloons, bursting at last in an excruciatingly painful spray of blood which splattered clear up to the ceiling. And then she was looking down at her body on the floor, into the empty eye sockets through which a hellish fire began to glow . . .

"I need a drink," she said to Roger, banishing the memory with a violent shake of her head. Roger snorted; he was sound asleep. She shoved his weight off her and got up to mix herself an anesthetic. The phone rang. "Roger, your phone is ringing."

He grunted, "You answer it. I can't move."

"And suppose it's Beth?"

"You came over to get a new battery in your watch. I went to the john. No big deal. Take a message."

"I'm your lover, not your secretary," Pamela complained, but she stepped over to Roger's nightstand, naked, to stop the dreadful ringing. "Snell residence."

She listened in shocked silence as the caller, assuming she was Beth Snell, proceeded with the message. Pamela felt the blood draining from her face. As the voice rambled on, she slowly replaced the receiver.

Roger rolled over and cracked an eyelid. "Who was it?"

"Just an . . . an obscene phone call," Pamela whispered hoarsely, staring at the instrument as if it were a tarantula.

"Make you horny again?" He chuckled sleepily, following his question with a stretch and a waking yawn, a suspicious lump rising under the sheet. Pamela didn't answer. She was already reeling down the hallway toward the den and her best friend's liquor cabinet.

A familiar voice was calling her name. Lana turned in the crowded corridor and saw Nancy waving at her. Battling her way through the oncoming human traffic, Lana approached her with a guarded smile. Beware the Ulterior Motive. "Hi. What's up?"

"Friday night is Halloween," Nancy replied in an almost reverent tone. "You have any plans?"

Lana shrugged, a small alarm going off somewhere in the back of her mind. She immediately associated Halloween with the cemetery, then the rabbit. She had to know. "Listen, Nancy, I want to know the truth. Did you or your boyfriend have anything to do with killin' that white rabbit?"

"The truth?" Nancy's smile widened. "You want the honest to God, cross-my-heart-and-hope-to-die, stick a needle in my eye TRUTH?"

"Yes."

"We didn't have anything to do with it. So what are you doing on Friday night?"

"I don't know . . . Bruce hasn't said anything about it." Lana wondered how many people vowed to stick needles in their eye and lied anyway. Nancy certainly didn't look guilty now. Maybe she wasn't, after all. If she was, then she was one of the most convincing liars Lana had ever met. Second only to Dennis Bloom.

"If you're askin' me to that graveyard party I heard about . . ."

"No." Nancy placed a possessive grip on Lana's arm. "It's a private party, very exclusive. Just you, me, and our dates. I heard you were going with Bruce now. That true?"

"Well, not officially." Lana blushed, casting her eyes downward. Nancy's intense stare was disturbing. "But we like each other a lot. Anyway, I'd better head on to class. We can talk about it later, after school. Thank God it's almost over for today, huh?" She glanced back up in time to see darkness flash over Nancy's expression.

"Tell me your phone number. I'll call you."

Lana quickly recited her phone number, having an unexplainable urge to transpose the last two digits, but she didn't do it. The correct number could be obtained from directory assistance anyway. Nancy repeated the number, smiled tightly, then turned and blended in with the eastbound flow of bodies.

After the final bell, Lana hurried to her locker, where she found Bruce waiting faithfully. His eyes, bloodshot and glazed, settled appreciatively on her face after quickly scanning the rest of her body. "Hey fox, you willing to go out with a nerd like me?"

"I don't know." She giggled, twisting the combination dial on her locker. "Gimme a month or two to think about it."

Bruce scowled. "Damn. That's what all the foxes say."

A tall, heavy-set boy with the nose of a platypus walked by and clapped Bruce on the back. "Hey, Apple Head, how'd you do on the test?"

Bruce grinned weakly. "Don't ask. Hey Dave, this is Lana. Lana, Dave. Or if you prefer, you can call him Duck."

Lana didn't have to ask why the nickname Duck. "Nice to meet you, Dave." They exchanged nods. Lana nudged Bruce with her elbow. "So you flunked your test, huh?"

"I'd have done good if it had all been multiple choice," Bruce whined. "But the schmuck put about ten essay questions on it. No fair."

Dave the Duck laughed abrasively and moved on. Lana took out the books she needed and handed half of them to Bruce.

"Your friend has some nose."

"Yeah, picks it with a shovel."

Lana was getting used to his unique sense of humor. "How nice." She could hear Dave saying to him later, when she wasn't around, Hey, your girlfriend sure talks funny, and Bruce would say, That's nothing, you should watch her eat. He would just be kidding, of course. As usual.

"Well, I think you'd be better off doin' a little more studyin' and less smokin' of Mother Nature, Apple Head."

"Nag, nag, nag."

"You wanna spend the rest of your life in the twelfth grade?"

"No, Mommy."

Lana gave up. "Okay, it's your life." They walked together toward the stairwell. There was a man on his way up.

Bruce stopped abruptly. "Hey, Mr. Montgomery. When did you get out of the hospital?"

The man didn't acknowledge him; he kept slowly

ascending the stairs, his gaze fixed straight ahead, his right hand gripping the rail. His skin was pale, almost translucent, but there were dark circles under his darker-than-usual eyes. He passed them without answering.

Bruce shrugged, guiding Lana down the stairs. "Guess he's still not feeling too good. Looks like he died a couple of days ago."

"Was that the teacher who got taken away in an ambulance last Friday?" Lana asked, glancing nervously over her shoulder.

"Yeah, had an attack of some kind in the office. Wonder what he's doing here now? Classes are over for today."

Lana hurried him along. "Maybe he needs to take some papers home with him or somethin'."

The sky was overcast with a blanket of gray clouds, but the October air was dry and warm. After emerging from the school building, Lana took a deep breath. "Freedom, an' eight more tons of homework. It's not fair. They screw up a kid's life enough makin' 'im sit in a classroom for six hours a day. That oughta be the extent of the torture."

"Just be glad you're not living in Japan. They have to spend a lot more hours in a classroom than we do. That's why Japs have slanty eyes—too much reading. You know they're smearing us in technology. Their brains are getting too big, stretching everything out. Ever notice how tight their faces look?"

"You're really weird, Bruce." Lana shifted her load from one arm to the other. "An' speakin' of weird, Nancy waved me over in the hall this afternoon an' invited us to an 'exclusive' party Friday night . . . just you, me, her, an' her boyfriend. What do you think?"

Bruce arched an eyebrow. "Exclusive party, huh? Sounds ominous. Where's it gonna be?"

"I don't know yet. She's s'pose to call me."

They reached Bruce's truck in the parking lot, and Lana got the feeling that someone was watching her closely. She looked back toward the school building and saw the familiar lurking shape of Spiro's body on the other side of the darkened glass, stooped and pressed against the wall. Was he spying on her?

She found the idea very disturbing. She hated it when someone she had no interest in, besides friendship, had a crush on her. For some reason it made her feel guilty for not reciprocating. She had already spent a little time trying to imagine the picture Spiro had drawn of her. In her mind it had been fairly graphic, though she didn't think Spiro was all that familiar with the female anatomy or that good an artist. She wished he hadn't told her about it.

Bruce was saying that Friday night was up to her; he would go along with her decision about Nancy's little "party."

"I'll see what she says," Lana replied absently, pulling her eyes away from the shadowy figure behind the glass. Maybe now that Sam was gone, Spiro wouldn't come over anymore, supposing that his mother would even allow it. That would be a relief. She wouldn't have to feel she was being stripped every time he looked at her, and maybe not just stripped. But Spiro still didn't know about Sam. No telling what his reaction would be when he found out.

Dennis was surprised to see Marla's Cutlass parked next to his Monte Carlo in the school parking lot; he knew she'd been absent from school that day. She was sitting behind her wheel with the window rolled down; seeing his reflection in the rearview mirror, she stepped out, smiled thinly at Wayne, then pulled Dennis aside. "Get rid of him, okay? I have to talk to you."

Dennis frowned. "We were gonna go to the park for a while. What's the deal anyway? You in more trouble or something?"

"Can't you just take him home?" Marla growled. "This is important. I know you won't think it is, but . . . it is. Real important."

Wayne, feeling miffed, strode up to them and ribbed Dennis roughly. "You know it ain't nice to tell secrets in front of somebody. What's going on over here? Or is it, like, totally none of my business?"

Marla was about to tell him how extremely perceptive he was, but Dennis spoke first: "Can't you tell Wayne

171

about it too? He's cool." He avenged the ribbing by punching Wayne on the shoulder.

Marla could already hear the two of them laughing their butts off after she shared her news. She didn't want such a serious matter to be turned into nothing but a joke. But she could sense that getting rid of Wayne would be no easier than getting rid of cockroaches, and she didn't want to have to sit on her request until Dennis was good and ready to hear it.

She gritted her teeth. "If either one of you laughs, I'm going to slap you both," she warned. "Come on, let's get in your car, Dennis. I don't want the whole school to hear this."

Just then Nancy and Jennifer Parks strolled by on their way to Jennifer's car. Nancy was staring straight ahead. Only Jennifer, her dishwater-blond hair fluttering in the mild breeze, glanced in their direction, and immediately looked guilty for doing so. But she saluted Dennis and Wayne anyway, muttering a rhetorical, "How's it goin'?"

"Same as usual." Dennis grinned, amused by the fact that Marla and Nancy still weren't speaking to each other. Girl fights, he thought, were utterly ridiculous; the backstabbing, glaring, silent treatments, divvying up of mutual friends, on and on and on. Guys just punched it out and that was that.

Wayne said hi to Nancy, but she either didn't hear him or chose to ignore him. He shrugged and lit a cigarette. "Well, let's get on with the conference. We've got a football game to do. Can't make the school team, gotta play somewhere."

"You could be on the school team if you did something about your grades," Marla said snidely. "Both of you could. But that's not what I want to talk about. Let's get in the car. And remember, no laughing."

They didn't laugh, but their mouths were twitching so wildly Marla knew it was all they could do to hold it in. Wayne finally expelled a loud sigh and said with mock gravity, "Wow, that sounds pretty heavy, girl. So, let me get this straight. Nancy can stroke-out teachers now?"

Dennis trumpeted a short burst of laughter through pursed lips, his cheeks puffing out like balloons. Sticking to her promise, Marla's hand shot out and deflated one of

172

them. Wayne immediately put as much distance between himself and Marla as he could, hunkering against the driver's side in the backseat.

Dennis, both surprised and enraged, slapped Marla back. "Don't you ever hit me again, goddamnit. You wouldn't even have made us promise not to laugh if you didn't know how fucking stupid this is. I should've known this was what was coming . . . I could see it on your face last night. I told you, somebody's just playing games. And you're falling for it, hook, line, and sinker. I don't give a shit what somebody wrote in a diary a hundred years ago, and I don't give a fuck what Nancy found in that stupid tomb. There's no such thing as fucking witchcraft."

Marla held her cheek where Dennis had slapped her, her eyes hot with anger, her breathing shallow, rapid. She wanted to jump out of his car and never speak to him again. But the last thing she needed was for him to go blabbing all over school her suspicions about Nancy. If Nancy wasn't already planning to do something awful to her, she certainly would after discovering what the grapevine had been turned on to. She managed to calm herself down without inflaming the situation any further. "Listen, I'm not asking you to believe it. I just want you to talk to Jay, when Nancy's not around, and see if you can get anything out of him. If he has seen Nancy with a book—"

"Who do you think I am, fucking Colombo?" Dennis sneered. "I'm not going to make an ass out of myself because you've got paranoid, ridiculous ideas about Nancy and can't see a joke for what it is. Even if she did find some kind of book in the tomb, it wasn't in there two years ago, so it damn sure wasn't buried with the Obers, which means somebody around here planted it for a joke. And maybe Nancy did do some weird hocus-pocus, but it didn't have anything to do with Dr. Doom stroking out. Pure coincidence. I can't believe you're really serious about this."

"Besides," Wayne piped up, "I saw Doom going into his classroom today after school let out. He didn't look too good, but he's walking around on his own two feet. Guess Nancy needs to polish up her act."

Marla turned to the backseat, horrified. "You saw Mr. Montgomery? Here? Today?"

"That's what he said," Dennis said scornfully. "So what do you think of your little theory now?"

Marla slunk down in the front seat, dizzy with confusion.

Fifteen

They were gathered together in a circle, holding hands, their heads bowed, eyes closed. Brother Carl Mitchell, pastor of Faith Tabernacle, rang out in a deep, clear voice: "O God, our blessed Savior, grant us Thy wisdom. Evil hath reared its ugly head in our very midst; tell us Thy servants how to fight against it, O Lord. We know we wrestle not against flesh and blood, but against the rulers, the principalities, spiritual forces of evil in heavenly places. We commit ourselves to do Thy will, dear Jesus. Guide us we pray."

Brother Timothy Gibson opened his mouth and began to spew out a litany of meaningless sounds, his voice continually rising in pitch. The group listened with growing excitement; God was speaking to them. One of them would be given the interpretation of the message delivered in tongues, and then they would know exactly what to do. Brother Gibson, who might have just recited the Chinese Pledge of Allegiance, finally fell silent. The rest waited in tingling anticipation for the Spirit to move. Finally Cornelia Mitchell, the pastor's wife, lifted her head and said boldly, "Thus saith the Lord: the girl hath been infested by a might demon, an agent from Hell who existeth only to steal, kill, and destroy. I have already given thee the power over this enemy. In my name thou shalt cast him out and sendeth him back to the pit from whence he came. Thus saith the Lord."

The small mildewy sanctuary rang with praises and moans of ecstasy. A couple melted to the floor "slain by the Spirit" and began to vibrate as though their bodies

175

were being electrocuted. Hands were lifted up in thanksgiving.

Rose Hester shuffled over to the front pew and lowered her heavy body onto it, weeping openly. Mitchell and Gibson, awed and overcome by the message, clung to each other like magnets. They had never before come up against an actual demon, let alone a mighty one. The aspect of confronting such a thing and commanding it to leave its host body was rather frightening, but God would be with them, and the Holy Spirit would protect them.

Pamela put down the phone receiver and shuddered, then reached for her brandy snifter. What in God's name was going on? First at Roger's, a phone call from Edna something or other, blathering some of the same insanity Pamela had heard from her mother, except that now, somehow, Nancy Snell had entered the picture. And now one of Pamela's neighbors, Renee Klingerman, calls her at home with a load of the same garbage, asking, "Isn't that girl a close friend of Marla's?"

Pamela couldn't, of course, say anything about the call she'd received at the Snells'; that would possibly open the floor for questions she didn't want to answer. But this was different. Taking another gulp of brandy to bolster her courage, she left the library in search of her daughter. She finally found her alone in the clubhouse, thumbing through a bible, the white pocket-sized King James with a zip-up cover she'd gotten for Easter almost a decade earlier. Pamela had never seen her open it before.

As if caught red-handed with contraband, Marla quickly hid the book behind her back. "What's the matter, Mom? You look upset."

Pamela stared down at her, unable to completely focus. She weaved slightly from side to side. "What's going on with Nancy?"

Marla's face went ashen. "Oh crap. How did you find out?"

"I just got a call from Renee Klingerman. Don't ask me how she found out—I have no idea. But I have the distinct feeling you started this. You did, didn't you?"

Marla put on a look of defiance. "I was afraid . . . I had to talk to somebody. But maybe I was wrong. I could have sworn . . . but Mr. Montgomery's okay, I guess. I would have talked to you about it, but I know how you feel about things like that. I couldn't—I felt I had to do something, just in case . . ."

"Just in case Sharon Valley was about to be overrun by witches . . . or is it demons? I can't seem to keep them straight," Pamela cackled drunkenly. "I see you've got your bible out—what's the matter, still not convinced? Think you're gonna find the answers in that stupid little book? That book was written two thousand years ago, Marla! It has nothing to do with today. What they thought was demon possession was nothing but epilepsy and lunacy! I find it simply amazing that twentieth century modern men still hang on to that . . . that fairy tale. They drive Lincoln Town Cars and fly in Learjets, but they think there's a demon behind every bush! Don't you find that extremely amusing?"

"Mother, you're drunk."

Pamela began to cry and laugh simultaneously. "You're damn right I'm drunk. And I've also had it up to my ears with this . . . this witchcraft business. I don't want to hear any more about it, you understand me?"

Marla tossed the bible across the room. "There, are you satisfied? You don't have to get hysterical, Mother. It's over now, so just leave me alone."

Across the street and one house down from the Snell's residence was a nondescript white house with light blue trim and sagging eaves under which hung empty wire flower baskets. The flowers had long since died. It was a house typical of the east side of the valley; nothing, in fact, set it apart from any of the others. At least, nothing outside.

Inside it was not so typical. The walls were painted black, and on them, painted in white, were the same markings that were on the back wall of the Obers' tomb. By night the rooms were lighted with candles placed on the various pieces of mahogany furniture that smelled of dust and age. A grandfather clock ticked loudly in the living room, a heartbeat in the silence. Tonight, as always, a chair rocked back and forth on a handwoven rug in sync with the ticking.

The sixty-nine-year-old woman cocked her head and listened. There were footsteps coming up her sidewalk. A familiar pain tugged inside her chest: fear. She was well-acquainted with it. She had been born into it.

She should never have come back to Sharon Valley. But her mother had insisted that she come, to help; for the time was at hand. Living temples had to be provided for Myrantha and Nathaniel.

At the age of nineteen Morganna Ober had moved to Rapid City, where she wasn't known as "the witches' daughter." She never worked, for she had learned her childhood lessons well, and there were several good spells for cultivating generous benefactors. One of them had given more than money. He'd given his seed, and nine months later Eliza was born. But from the time Eliza understood what her mother was, she had secretly abhorred her, her and her deplorable craft, and had often desired to leave. Why she never did was still a mystery to her. Perhaps spells had been used on her as well. So in the later years, as Morganna planned festively for her parents' return, Eliza considered how she might bring those plans to naught.

Together they had returned to Sharon Valley a couple of months earlier, Morganna calling herself Maude Chandler to avoid any unwanted attention that the name Morganna Ober would surely attract. For all anyone knew, they were just two average elderly ladies, the same typical gray matrons you might expect to meet at any quilting circle.

She should have just burned the infernal ledger, in spite of the curse. Eliza had a terrible feeling that what she had done to stop the return of her evil grandparents hadn't been enough: killing her mother along with her power to invoke satanic assistance; scattering the remains of Myrantha and Nathaniel within the same grave she'd dug for their daughter and sprinkling the foul lot with blessed water; painting the symbols on the tomb walls, which would bind any spiritual entity that entered there to retrieve the ledger. She'd also tried to turn the inverted cross, but had found it impossible.

Now there was a knock at the door. It wouldn't be a neighbor, she knew. She was hardly acquainted with any of them. They thought she and her mother were strange but uninteresting recluses. And they had kept to themselves, going out in public as little as possible, and only to buy food and supplies. Eliza had no friends here. Never had. So who could it be . . .?

Ever since she had performed her deeds in the old cemetery, Eliza wondered what might happen. On the worldly side, there was the possibility of someone discovering the grave. A hungry animal could dig it up. Maybe the neighbors were more observant than she suspected, and would note the unexplained disappearance of the eldest "Chandler." But even the worst she could suffer at the hands of the law couldn't compare to the terror of what might happen on the otherworldly side.

The caller knocked again. Her fingers twitched on the smooth arms of the chair. Perhaps, if she just sat very quietly, whoever it was would go away and leave her alone. But she didn't think so. No, she had been right to fear. It was almost time. From the depths of Hell, they had sent someone . . .

Slowly, the doorknob began to turn. The door was locked, as always, and the caller became frustrated. The mechanism jangled as the intruder tried to force it. Trembling, the woman rose to her feet. But before she could reach the door, blue sparks burst from the keyhole in the knob, accompanied by a crackling sound and the smell of ozone. She recognized the odor immediately. It was inseparably linked to the fear. The door began to open.

The face was unfamiliar but the presence was unmistakable. Her mother had summoned it many times. It stepped in, dark eyes glittering in the candlelight. The door closed behind it of its own accord. "Good evening, Eliza."

"Go away," she whispered, arthritic fingers digging into the flesh of her forearms. "Leave me alone. I command you to leave."

It laughed, a deep, guttural sound, almost a belching. The stench of ozone became stronger. Taking a step forward, its eyes locked defiantly into hers. "Is that any way to treat an old friend? Besides, I can't leave yet . . .

179

the bungling novice who summoned me directed me to this flesh using the Ixantra pentagram, of all things. Ah . . . I see your interior decorator appreciates the same design. Or are you perhaps inclined to keep your guests in bondage? How rude. Come now, Eliza, let's sit and have a chat. I command *you.*"

Her bones became rubber. Eliza felt herself sinking to the floor. The thing caught her and helped her to her chair, its touch scorching her through her sweater, its strength making her weaker, as if her energy were being sapped from her body into its borrowed mortal flesh. How could such a thing have happened! Who . . .?

It sat beside her on the black velvet settee, striking a gentleman's pose. Behind the piercing black eyes, sapphire flame danced. The rest of the features were dead. Its hands were folded calmly over a crossed knee. "Dear, dear Eliza. What have you done?"

She shook her head. "Nothing. Nothing."

"Nothing?" One eyebrow arched. "Come now, Eliza, you know better than to try to lie to me. Your mother is with us. Did you really think killing her would do any good? That destroying the High Priestess and her consort's bones would nullify their contract? What a fool you are. It is the Gate incantation you should have destroyed. Why didn't you destroy it, Eliza?"

"You know why," she hissed.

The demon smiled slightly, apparently enjoying its game of cat and mouse. "Ah yes; Myrantha's curse. To destroy the incantation was to die forthwith . . . your mother's little insurance policy. She never trusted you, you know. Didn't it ever occur to you to bury it in a strongbox of some sort in hallowed ground? I suppose not . . . you always were rather dull. Well, I must say your actions have made us very unhappy with you."

"What would things like you care?" she asked, her pulse beating visibly at her temples and throat. "What is it to you if they don't come back?"

"What!" The demon drew back, its voice a reprimand. "What, you assume that the Master thinks nothing of it when his promises go unfulfilled? He honors all of his contracts, my dear. The last thing he would do is disappoint a High Priestess. He wouldn't dream of it. But there is another reason. Thanks to you, dear Eliza, we now have the opportunity to reclaim what is rightfully ours. You should never have hidden the book in the tomb. You might just as well have placed it right in our hands." It laughed and leaned closer.

She began to cry. "I did what I thought was best. I didn't think anyone ever went near that place. I don't want innocent people to die. I refuse—"

The blue flame darkened to indigo. "If you truly hadn't wanted, as you say, innocent people to die, Eliza, you would have burned it. You're really not much of a heroine; you were far more concerned about your own welfare, weren't you? But believe me, there are no such things as innocent people, my dear. If nothing else they are thieves, every last one of them. And once we have our freedom, we shall rid this world of them once and for all. Excluding our converts, of course. But those who worship the Master will no longer pull us through the cunt of physical existence and send us on petty errands. They will dance when we pull the strings; and ah, Eliza my dear, we have such delightful entertainment planned. Sodom and Gomorrah were nothing compared to what will be."

She clutched the arms of her chair and trembled, knowing what it was going to do. She was a confessed traitor, and of no use whatsoever to it. The infernal being stood up slowly and looked down at her without mercy. Its civility gone, the wicked glory of its innate evil shined through.

Unable to bear the sight of it, Eliza turned her head, which was suddenly gripped in an unseen vise. Beyond the point she could turn it herself, it continued to be twisted. With a blast of incredible pain she could hear an odd snapping sound. For a moment she was looking straight at the back of her rocking chair. Then came the final savage jerk in which the epitome of torment was abruptly ended and her head, turned a full 180 degrees, fell limply on her right shoulder.

Nancy came back to the dinner table looking quite disturbed. "That was Jay's mother. She said he started having some kind of seizures, and they had to take him to the hospital."

Beth put down her fork and laboriously swallowed an unchewed piece of Swiss steak, unaware that her husband was making an unfavorable assessment of her physical appearance: the lifelessness of her dark brown hair, adhering as usual to the nape of her neck; her rounded peasant features, and too-pale skin still plagued by occasional blemishes; gray-green eyes too closely set, which held a perpetual look of disapproval whenever they were turned on him.

"Oh God, how terrible," she said, gaping slightly. "He's never had one before, has he? Do you want to go up to see him?"

Nancy shook her head nervously. "There's nothing I can do." She stared at her plate now without interest. Surely what she had done had nothing to do with it . . .

Her father drained his glass of California white wine and poured another. "He's not into drugs, is he?"

"Not that I know of, Dad."

"Well, you never know. Kids nowadays think their bodies are experimental labs. They drink Lysol, sniff anything that comes in an aerosol can, eat any pill they can get their hands on . . ." He lit his pipe and blew a cloud of cherry tobacco over the table. "I hope you have better sense than that."

Beth irritably waved the smoke away from her face. Roger knew she hated for him to light up before she was finished eating. He only did it to antagonize her, she was sure of that. But she wouldn't make an issue of it now, at the dinner table, in the presence of their impressionable daughter. She would bring it up again later, specifically, when he reached for her after all the lights were out.

"How's Marla doing?" she asked her daughter. "Haven't seen her lately. She's still upset about her grandmother, I'll bet. Poor dear."

"Marla's no poor dear," Nancy said hotly. "We're not even friends anymore. I hate her."

Beth wasn't really that surprised; it was bound to happen. Sooner or later the jealousy had to creep in. Nancy couldn't compete with Marla's clothes, or her car, or her fifty-dollar-a-month allowance. Fifty dollars!

Pamela had to rub it in, all right. This is how the Upper Class lives. Nancy had no more stomach for it than she had. "Well, that's too bad, I guess. What happened?"

Nancy looked sulkily at the wine bottle in the center of the table. "Don't wanna talk about it."

"All right, you don't have to." Beth searched for a different subject. Let well enough alone. "Oh, by the way, Mr. Montgomery got out of the hospital today. They thought they'd lost him Sunday; Dr. Prescott had even pronounced him dead. But then he started breathing again, and seemed to be just fine . . . no more pain, nothing. They kept him a couple of extra days to be sure, but . . . Nancy? Are you all right?"

Nancy's face had gone paler than her white stoneware plate. She pushed it away and stood up. "I'm . . . sorry. I guess I'm not very hungry. I think I should go lay down."

"Are you sure you're all right?" Roger asked around his pipe, squinting with either concern or smoke in his eyes, Nancy wasn't sure which. And either her nerves or the smoke was going to make her vomit in the next minute or so. It didn't matter which. She could feel it coming.

"She's fine, Roger. She's just upset about Jay, aren't you, sweetheart?" Beth likewise pushed back her plate and rose from the table, initiating the Cold Shoulder ritual. Because of the smoke, she was not able to finish her dinner. It had probably made Nancy sick as well. He knew how much it bothered her when he did that. How could he be so inconsiderate? And speaking of inconsiderate, why did he insist on operating his business in the garage? An office downtown would attract a lot more customers. Didn't he want to get ahead, if for no other reason than his family's happiness? Didn't he ever want to take his wife and daughter on exotic vacations or buy them expensive clothes or a better house to live in? Did they mean nothing to him? She was rehearsing.

Nancy hurried from the kitchen with one hand on her stomach, the other over her mouth. Beth began clearing the table. A few minutes later there was a knock on the front door. Trudging like a mistreated slave for Roger's benefit, she went to answer it.

There were two strange men standing on the front

porch. They looked like salesmen. Beth's expression and tone were less than encouraging. "Yes?"

Brother Mitchell cleared his throat, hoping fervently that as he and Timothy Gibson had prayed, God had already prepared the hearts of the girl's parents to receive their message. "Yes, ma'am. You're Mrs. Snell?"

Beth nodded slightly, still unsmiling.

"Well, we're from the Faith Tabernacle Church," Mitchell went on solemnly. "I'm the pastor, Carl Mitchell; this here is Timothy Gibson."

"What do you want?" Beth asked coldly, now wishing she hadn't answered the door. Almost nothing bothered her more than religious fanatics barging into people's houses trying to make new converts. She was Catholic, and highly resented anyone who tried to sway her from the beliefs she'd embraced since childhood. Some fundamentalists had told her once that Catholicism was a cult. The nerve!

"We need to talk to your daughter, ma'am. Is she home?"

The question both surprised and confused her. "Nancy's not feeling well . . . she's lying down. What do you want with her?"

Mitchell sucked in a deep breath and briefly, silently, prayed for God's assistance before answering, "We are convinced beyond a doubt, Mrs. Snell, that your daughter is in need of a demon exorcism."

Beth blanched as though he'd hit her in the face with a frying pan. As soon as the shock subsided, she bellowed over her shoulder, "RO-GER!"

Mitchell and Gibson exchanged worried glances. This was not how they had pictured things going.

Roger appeared several moments later wearing his work apron, his pipe clenched between his teeth. He peered curiously at Mitchell and Gibson over his wife's shoulder. "What is it?"

She turned back to face the two men and growled, "I'd like you to tell my husband exactly what you just told me."

Brother Mitchell reluctantly repeated the message. Roger's face immediately became crimson with rage.

"What kind of a nut are you, anyway? You get off my property right now, and I don't want to see your faces around here again. And if you so much as even approach my daughter, I'll have both your asses thrown in the can. Got that?"

"God has commanded us to do this," Gibson complained in his nasal tenor. "We have to obey Him. Don't you understand the danger your daughter is in? That all of us might be in? Sir, I beg you, please—"

The green plywood door crashed forward in his face, cutting off his plea with a thunderous crack. He shook his head sadly and turned to Mitchell. "I think we need to pray about this situation some more, brother."

Nancy, having heard the commotion, peeked out the bathroom window. She watched the two figures, one tall, one short and stocky, slowly descend the porch steps and merge with the shadows on the sidewalk toward their car, a dented yellow monstrosity parked against the curb in front of the house.

As they got in, a movement beyond the car caught Nancy's eye. A door was opening across the street. Maude and Eliza Chandler's house. They were strange old women. An aloof spinster and her prehistoric mother, both hardly ever seen since they moved in a couple of months ago, but Nancy on several nights had seen candles burning through the lace curtain over the picture window in front. She'd noticed strange odors about the place too, and for some reason it gave her the creeps to be very near it. Which was why she sometimes snooped around anyway.

She squinted, attempting to sharpen her vision. Someone was coming out the door, but it didn't seem to be Eliza, certainly not her mother. No, it was definitely a man, and something about his shape seemed familiar. She couldn't see his face so she couldn't possibly be sure, but a name came to mind; she quickly dismissed it. She was only being paranoid. What would he be doing over there? (What was he doing *anywhere*? He was supposed to be dead!) The fact that they'd had a visitor at all was strange enough.

Suspending her wonder at that, she moved away from

the window and went back to her bedroom, her stomach voided of her supper, and sat on the bed. The ledger was lying open on her pillow.

Across from it, on the nightstand, was the bloody crystal ashtray in which she had killed a white mouse two hours earlier. The ashtray was positioned in the center of a piece of red construction paper on which she'd drawn the same symbols she'd copied off the wall of the tomb. The mouse was now wrapped in an old newspaper and stuffed in the bottom of her trash can; she had planned to take it out after her parents went to bed. She couldn't remember any of the words she'd spoken, as if that mystical language refused to make an impression on her brain. She only remembered her wish concerning Marla.

She realized she was trembling. In the hallway she could hear her parents arguing over whether or not to question her about something. Nancy snapped the ledger shut and tossed it under her bed. Marla had probably started something. Well, Marla would be going down very soon—

Oh, by the way! Mr. Montgomery got out of the hospital today!

and there was nothing at ALL to worry about

Nancy, this is Jay's mother. Something terrible's happened . . .

and her plan was running quite smoothly, oh yes, it was all so easy. That dumb hick was so unbelievably trusting . . .

Something went wrong. Maybe she'd mispronounced some of the words. Maybe the sacrifice had been unacceptable . . . maybe it had to be a human baby, like the Obers had used. Why the hell wasn't Montgomery dead? And why was Jay in the hospital having seizures?

She curled up in a tight ball under her blanket and eventually fell into an unsound sleep, her nightstand lamp burning brightly.

Sixteen

The puppy had grown tired of pawing against the walls of the small box in which he had been imprisoned. He was also weak from lack of food and water; it had been almost twenty-four hours since he'd had any of either.

When a small strip of light suddenly fell across his forepaws, he lifted his head and emitted a low whine. Footsteps approached. Sam's tail thumped softly against the cardboard wall. At last, at last.

The flaps above him were pulled open, temporarily blinding him with harsh light. He blinked rapidly and pulled himself up, searching for friendliness on the unfamiliar face hovering over him. There was none.

He began to whine in earnest, anxious for the hands that had closed him up in the cruel box to reach in and lift him back out. He pounced against the wall in an attempt to climb out and nearly tipped the box over. The person righted it, then reached for the back of his neck and roughly clutched the soft, loose skin before yanking him up by it. The pup yelped in pain.

He was savagely thrown to the floor of the fruit cellar. His breath knocked out of him, he lay still and wondered why he was being hurt. He didn't understand; he had never experienced torment before. He tried to get up, but a foot came down on his back. His large brown eyes rolled upward and caught the glint of something shiny being positioned horizontally above him. He didn't know what it was, but it didn't look like something to eat.

The shiny object plunged down, and Sam's world became silent and black.

Lana watched from the front yard until Bruce's taillights disappeared, then turned to walk slowly back to the house. She was past the initial liking stage and into heavy infatuation now, and her step was light, her feet seeming to land on springy clouds instead of solid ground. Her first poem for Bruce had already begun writing itself on the tablet of her mind . . .

You reach, we touch and blend, I take a breath, you . . .
Got a worm hanging out your kazoo . . .

Movement at a dark curtain next door captured her attention. Was someone watching her? Spiro again . . .? She frowned deeply, hoping her expression was visible in the dim light. It also occurred to her to lift her middle finger, but she really didn't want to be mean to Spiro— supposing he would even know what the gesture meant —she just wanted him to leave her alone.

She couldn't be friends with him anymore, even if his mother hadn't forbidden it. Because of that, for a while at least, she didn't have to deal with telling him about Sam, unless he should happen to catch up with her at school. She wouldn't make it easy for him.

The curtains ruffled again, indicating that whoever had been peeking out had moved away. Lana sighed and went back into her house.

Luke, still mourning Sam's disappearance, sat glumly on the couch watching a sitcom, the canned laughter in response to horrendously unfunny lines having no effect on him. Normally he would be laughing anyway, or berating the show and switching channels. Carol was at the dining table writing a letter. Lana ignored her and plopped down on the couch beside her brother.

"You still depressed about Sam?"

"Just lemme alone," he pouted.

"Well, it wasn't my fault—"

He punched her on the leg. "I said lemme alone!"

Lana reflexively whacked him back. "You don't have

to hit me, turd face. I'll gladly leave you alone." She escaped to her bedroom before the Referee could step in, and slammed her door, thinking how too damn bad it was that Luke hadn't disappeared instead. What had she ever done to deserve a bratty brother like him?

After clearing the textbooks and papers from her bed, she stretched out on it, the twinkly ceiling plaster above her head soon marching in patterns as she continued to stare at it with unfocused vision. An entertaining hallucination. Heart shapes swirled, cupids arrows pierced them through. Bodies entwined, rose and fell in sultry rhythm. The room began to feel stuffy.

Moving dreamily, she got up and opened her bedroom window to let in some fresh air. The frigid breeze blew against her face and neck, feathered her hair. For the moment it felt good.

You reach, we touch and blend, I take a breath, you . . .

She closed her eyes and smiled as the words, like honey, dripped into her consciousness from the hidden hive of creativity.

You sigh:
Then through your eyes I see, and together we fly;
One mind, One body, One dream . . .

She could see Bruce's eyes, the jester's mask laid aside. Even if he refused to admit it to himself, he had a lot to give.

The shining, gold-flecked eyes in her daydream began to stare at her more intensely.

Through your eyes I see . . .
See what? What?

Suddenly the eyes became scarlet, the color of blood. Lana gasped, her lids fluttering open in dismay. That hadn't been Bruce. The face, yes, but the eyes . . . definitely no. They hadn't even been . . . human. Why should she have imagined such a thing?

Through her bedroom wall the raucous laughter from

189

the television seemed to mock her. She stormed back into the hallway and yelled for Luke to turn down the volume, initiating another name-calling contest that quickly sent their mother slamming out of the house.

At 11:15 Jane stepped into the dark, silent trailer and quietly made her way through the living room. She stumbled into a pile of beer cans by Harry's chair and cursed softly, hoping the sound hadn't wakened him. If he woke up, he'd more than likely need to have sex before he could fall asleep again, and Jane was far from being in the mood for that. She had the sinking feeling that she'd started a rock slide of sorts, and the entire load was threatening to crash down on her and bury her forever. And for what? The girl had called around ten-thirty and said it was all a false alarm. Call off the Witch Busters. Forget the whole thing. Just like that. Sure, right.

In the bedroom she set her purse on the dresser and began to unzip the back of her white uniform when Harry turned on the bed, weary slats groaning beneath him, and muttered groggily, "You've started some shit, haven't you?"

She froze. "What are you talking about?"

"Don't give me that," Harry's voice answered thickly in the dark room. "I stopped at the bar after work for a few beers and got an earful of rumors. You've got some people just about pissing in their pants, Jane. Maybe it wouldn't happen in a bigger town where folks aren't so superstitious, but with the dumb-shit folklore that's been hanging over this place for so long . . ."

"Please, let's not get into it." Jane tiredly slipped out of the uniform, leaving it crumpled on the floor.

"You're already in it up to your eyeballs," Harry shot back. "And if something happens to that girl, I'd say you'd be responsible. No doubt the high school kids will get onto this pretty damn quick."

"What was I supposed to do, Harry? Her friend came to me for help. She was scared, and I have to admit I was too . . . still am, if you want the truth."

Harry was silent for a few moments. Jane slipped under the covers in her bra and panties, too drained of energy to put on a gown or wash her face and teeth. She wanted to sleep for a million years.

Finally her husband said tersely, "All I gotta say is, you'd better get your shit together in a hurry, and things better settle down, or I'm moving out."

Jane sat up on her elbow, alarmed, and searched the shadowed features of his face. "My God, Harry, you'd divorce me over this?"

He turned his back to her. "I could strangle you over this."

Seventeen

Dawn seeped into Spiro's bedroom in subtle shades of blue and gray. Night's darkness shied into the corners, unable to dispel the sunlight. He cracked his eyes open, his nostrils picking up the scent of something cooking in the kitchen. Normally his mother only fixed him lumpy oatmeal for breakfast. Curious, he got out of bed and dressed himself in the same clothes he'd now worn for a solid week. The aroma was activating his salivary glands, and a thin line of drool made its way from the corner of his mouth to his chin. Unaware of it, he shuffled barefoot out of his room and followed his nose to the kitchen. "That smells good, Mama. Can I have some?"

She turned from the stove and smiled, which was also unusual; she usually greeted him in the mornings with a scowl on her face. But when he wasn't looking at her, she would always whisper *Good morning* and *I love you, son.* "Of course you can have some, Spiro. I made it especially for you. Sit down, sit down."

He obediently sat at the peeling Formica-topped table, his eyes alight with anticipation. The string of drool reached the end of his jaw and oozed itself onto his shirt. "What is it, Mama?"

"Never you mind what it is, boy," she snapped, her smile vanishing. "It's good for you, so you just eat it all up. Every bit." A few moments later she carried a large steaming bowl over to the table and set it in front of him. Handing him a spoon, she commanded, "Eat up."

He studied the dark, stewlike substance, and after

glancing up gratefully at his mother's face, dipped his spoon into the bowl and delivered it, full, to his waiting mouth. Bertha smiled again after he had swallowed. "That's a good boy. Every drop, now." She remained standing by his chair, apparently intent on watching him eat the entire meal. When the bowl was empty, she took it back to the stove and filled it again. "Here, this is the last of it. Is it good?"

Spiro nodded happily. "Good, Mama. Can I have it every day?"

"No, just today, boy."

Clearly disappointed, Spiro ate the second bowlful a little more slowly, savoring the spicy meat with every chew, because he would never have it again. Just today. Was it his birthday already?

After fishing out the largest chunks, he lifted the bowl to his lips and sipped the rest, spilling the last drops of it on his shirt. His mother uttered a sigh of disgust. "You can't wear that shirt to school now, you clumsy idiot. Can't you do anything right?"

He lowered the empty bowl and shook his head slowly. With the intention of going to his room to change shirts, he started to rise from his chair. Bertha forced him back down. "Look at me, boy."

Flinching as if expecting a slap, he looked up. But his mother didn't appear to be angry. Instead, she seemed in a particularly good mood. She asked him cheerfully, "You wanna know what you just ate, boy? You want me to tell ya?"

Something about the question scared him, but he didn't know why. She'd asked pleasantly enough, but there was a taunting quality in the tone . . . he'd heard it too many times before not to recognize it. He glanced nervously at the empty bowl. "I . . . guess so, Mama."

Bertha tilted her head back and brayed sadistic laughter. "You jest ate that goddamn puppy, boy! You ate your puppy! How d'ya feel about that? You gonna rat on me ever agin?"

A shattering eruption occurred in Spiro's brain; for an instant he saw nothing but bright red webs before his eyes, and his only impulse was to claw through them. He realized, vaguely, that his body was moving—moving fast—but he had no idea what it was doing. The webs were bursting all around him as he fought his way out. Then there was a terrible sound, the sound of a ripe cantaloupe hitting the sidewalk. Soon afterward his vision cleared, but the world remained seriously out of focus. His mother was half sitting, half lying against the front of the stove, her chin resting on her breast.

You ate your puppy! Ate your puppy! Ate your—

His gorge rose with lightning speed, and he knew he would never make it to the bathroom. Being careful not to step on his unconscious mother, he groped for the sink, spraying vomit all over the counter cabinets below it.

They sat hunched down in the seats of Mitchell's yellow Cadillac, which he had parked half a block down on the opposite side of the street from 2314 Glenwood. Mitchell kept glancing nervously at his Timex and asking, "Are you sure this is what the Lord wants us to do?"

"I heard His voice plain as day," Gibson insisted for the fifth time in as many minutes. "Whether she wants to go or not, we've got to get that girl on holy ground and cast that demon out of her. We can't just sit back and let Satan march on to victory. Bless God, it's our duty to fight, tooth and nail, if we must. I don't want to have to stand before the throne on Judgment Day and say, 'Well, I'm sorry, Lord, but it seemed the laws of men were more important at the time.' I want to bow before Him and truthfully say, 'I have done what the Lord my God commanded me to do,' and to hear Him say, 'Well done, thou good and faithful servant.'"

Mitchell nodded bleakly. "Amen, brother. Amen."

The front door of the house opened, and a young dark-headed girl wearing a white turtleneck sweater and green skirt stepped out. Since the split with Marla, Nancy had started riding to school with Jennifer Parks. But Jennifer had called this morning and said she was sick and wouldn't be going to school today, and Jay was in the hospital, so Nancy had to ride the bus. The stop was two blocks away.

"That's got to be her," Gibson whispered, his gray eyes bulging behind his tortoiseshell glasses. "Demon-possessed. Lord have mercy."

The girl closed the door behind her and stood on the porch for a few seconds, looking up the street. Mitchell and Gibson dipped farther in their seats.

"Should we do it now?" Mitchell asked, somewhat tiffed that he, the pastor, was having to take instructions from a mere deacon. Why God had chosen to speak to Gibson was beyond Mitchell's spiritual comprehension, but as he reminded himself, the last shall be first and the first shall be last, and furthermore, God could use whomever He'd a mind to.

Gibson began rattling off in tongues (Mitchell could swear at times he'd heard Gibson saying things like "See me on my Honda" and "Shonda like coconut"—he himself had yet to receive that particular gift of the Spirit, a slight heavenly oversight which would soon be corrected, he was sure) then Gibson stopped suddenly and said, "Yes, Brother Mitchell. The Lord says to go."

Just then a red Toronado made a left turn behind them; not wishing to be seen, the two men again ducked toward the center of the car and cracked their skulls together. The Toronado roared past.

Mitchell, rubbing his head, sat back up and said, "I guess He didn't mean right that second."

Nodding in agreement, Gibson opened his door. Nancy was walking in the opposite direction. "Brother Mitchell, I think maybe you should follow in the car. We can't be dragging her all the way down the block to get back to it. If she doesn't want to go, she might make a little noise."

"Or a lot," Mitchell acquiesced, and started the Cadillac's engine.

Gibson shut his door quietly and began jogging toward the unsuspecting Nancy. When he was about ten feet behind her, she turned around, saw what she thought was some squirrelly accountant jogging before work, and dismissed him. But then she noticed the car following close behind, moving very slowly near the curb. Though she was not yet afraid, she began to suspect something was up. The car looked like the same one she'd seen out front the night before. Was it the same two men she'd seen leaving the porch? Surely they wouldn't be kidnappers, though, not at 7:25 in the morning. Gibson caught up to her and she stopped, turning to challenge him with a fearless glare. "Are you following me?"

"Well, uh, guess I was," Gibson politely admitted, signaling Mitchell with his eyes to get ready. "But you see, I was kind of hoping you would follow me . . . to church. You've got a problem we need to take care of."

Now Nancy was afraid, but she cloaked her fear in anger. "Are you crazy? I'm not going to any church with you. I'd say you're the one with the problem."

"Miss Snell, I'm sorry to inform you of this, but you are possessed of a mighty demon. We'll get him out of there in no time, though, if you'll just come with us, please."

Nancy started to run, but Gibson was quick—because the Spirit of the Lord was upon him, he would later tell his wife, just as it had been upon Elisha when he outran a horse to Jezreel—and he caught her before she could get away. Mitchell pushed open the passenger door and Gibson pushed in the screaming girl, whom he soon learned was about as easy to subdue as an angry bobcat with twelve sets of claws. But Mitchell somehow managed to drive them safely to the church without having an accident, which was a miracle indeed.

Marla had still been a little nervous about having to face Nancy at school that day, but she wasn't present in first hour, nor in third. But something worse than facing Nancy was happening. Most of the kids thought she and Nancy were still friends, and under the present circumstances, that was very bad news for Marla. The grapevine was tittering with the message: Nancy Snell is a witch. Two plus two equals nine—Marla, her best friend, must also be a witch. Halfway through the day Marla was feeling like a germ on a petri dish full of penicillin.

Hey Marla, my art teacher's been a real bitch lately. Can you put a hex on her, too?
Hey Marla, can you turn yourself into a black cat?

Do you ride a broomstick?
Got any spare eye of newt?

Her denials, including not being a friend of Nancy's any longer, received derisive responses ranging from disbelieving smiles to loud, ripping raspberries and snide declarations of "Oh, is that so?" Finally her frustration level reached its peak in fourth hour, Mrs. Potter's literature class. Becky Snodgrass, a snotty redhead who had won popularity by virtue of her double-D tits, received a slap in the face after asking Marla if Dennis was a werewolf.

This action landed Marla in Mr. Greer's office, where she sat staring blankly at the glossy sheen of the large oak desk upon which thin strips of light, shining through the Levelor blinds on the window, contorted themselves across the principal's hairy folded hands. His normally gentle features were pinched in irritation.

"Teasing is a fact of life all through your school years," he was saying in a stern fatherly tone. "Kids are cruel . . . sometimes I can't believe how cruel. You should hear some of the labels that were laid on me when I was your age. But you don't solve this problem by hitting people—that's only going to compound it. The best way to deal with it is just to ignore it . . . that sort of thing will die of starvation if it doesn't receive any feedback. It's no fun to torment someone if they don't react. I learned the hard way. You don't have to."

Marla nodded with false contrition. "I know, I know. I did ignore it for a while, but . . . I just completely lost it for a minute. I'd had too much. I should've just kept my big mouth shut. But after what happened to Mr. Montgomery, I was so sure . . . and there were other things too . . ."

"What's that about Mr. Montgomery?" Greer leaned forward on his desk. "What's all this have to do with him?"

Marla felt cornered; the only way to explain herself was to admit Montgomery's intention to have her and Nancy expelled. But she couldn't think of a handy lie, so she went ahead and confessed. If Montgomery was still planning to do it, well . . . then he would do it. Otherwise, Greer knowing about it probably wouldn't make any difference. Unless Montgomery pressed the issue, Greer would just forget about it.

When she was finished, having omitted only the part about the bodies missing from the tomb—that might be begging for an official investigation, which could spell Big Trouble should the police come around asking questions at home—Greer looked down at his hands. "Very interesting. You know, the doctors never could come up with a physical reason for his distress . . . said it was mental. He was even pronounced dead at one point, you know." Then fearing he'd just disclosed confidential information—he had, in fact, been unconsciously talking to himself—he quickly added, "Of course, that's just between you and me."

Marla's mouth fell open. "He was pronounced dead?"

"That's what I understand, yes." Greer suddenly looked very uncomfortable. "But you don't need to repeat any of that, as I said. I was just thinking out loud, I guess."

"Why did you say it was interesting?" Marla queried. "You almost sound like you believe—"

"Oh no, no," Greer smiled, wiping his brow. "I wasn't saying that at all. The only strength any of that nonsense has is a person's belief in it . . . so it's very simple. I don't believe. No, I'm quite certain that we're just looking at a coincidence, and like you say, you don't really even know for sure that Nancy found such an object. And Albert is back on the job, in spite of my insistence that he take another week off, so there's obviously nothing to your fears."

It sounded to Marla as if he were trying to convince himself more than her. She could tell that he wanted to say more—something seemed to be eating him—but why should he discuss it with her, a mere student? And by doing so probably violate some stupid code of ethics. "Well, I'm sure you're right. So . . . can I go now? I'm sorry I slapped Becky. Am I still in trouble?"

"Well, I'd say you're probably still in trouble with Becky, but I think I can drop the issue from this end . . . as long as I have your promise that it won't happen again. Ignore the remarks. Better yet, go ahead and laugh at them. Even if you feel like you're going to explode, keep a smile on your face. It'll blow over. They'll get bored and look for someone else to give a hard time to."

"I hope so," Marla sighed, thankful that he apparently had no interest in the suspension subject. Greer picked up his phone and prepared to make a call; Marla was officially dismissed.

Taking her cue, she picked up her purse and left, leaving the door to his office open behind her. While the secretary was writing her a pass to get back into class, the principal's office door was firmly closed by a very grim-looking Richard Greer.

Entering her final class at 1:45, Marla studiously avoided looking at the desk in front and the man sitting behind it. She was tense to the point of being classified as petrified wood; any moment he would bark out her name and demand that she plan to stay after class. But he didn't.

She took her usual seat on the back row and slid behind the desktop, aware of the empty seat next to her. As the other students took their places, she heard the whispering start again, saw the suspicious glances, the amused smiles. She wanted to get up and slap every one of them off. Ignoring such persecution was much easier said than done. Greer had admitted his own inability to do it. It seemed so unfair. She was popular; a member of the upper echelon, Le Superior Clique; they shouldn't be treating her like this. Not like gold one day and scrap iron the next. Such loyalty she should find in a viper's nest.

The bell rang, and the desk next to her on the right remained empty, as Marla had known it would. Her ex-best friend had either skipped the whole day or had called in sick—Jennifer wasn't there today either, so most likely they'd cut together—or maybe Nancy had heard Montgomery was back, and had caught the last train for Marakesh.

She suddenly noticed that the room had become as still as a tomb. Slowly, tentatively, she raised her eyes to see what was going on. Mr. Montgomery was staring straight at her. At least, something that resembled Mr.

Montgomery. He looked to her like death warmed over thirty times. As dark as the circles around his eyes were, from her vantage point he looked very much like a raccoon. The rest of his skin reminded her of a cheese omelet. And to top it off, he was smiling. Not much, but even a slight smile of the face of Albert Montgomery was the eighth wonder of the world. Marla's hands suddenly felt clammy, her throat dry as old parchment. She became conscious of her heartbeat. Thumpa thumpa thumpa. Too fast. Much too fast. She gave her head a quick shake. It seemed Montgomery had spoken to her, but his lips hadn't moved.

Piss yourself, you little cunt . . .

She tightened her thighs. Her bladder began to ache. What was . . . ? No, *no . . .*

Go on, piss in your pants, you arrogant little bitch. You're no better than the rest of these crawling insects. Do it, do it.

Hot shame flushed over Marla's face as she felt her bladder release, the wet warmth spreading below her. Tears ran down her cheeks. She could hear him laughing, laughing . . .

The boy sitting on her right noticed the urine dripping from her chair to the floor and started to snicker. The rest of the class turned to stare. Some laughed out loud. Someone nearby forgot whose class he was in and brayed, "Look at that! Marla Mingee's pissed her pants!" Only a few were too afraid of the New & Improved Dr. Doom to do anything but keep their eyes glued to the blackboard. The rest had a field day.

Eighteen

Nancy's throat felt like coarse sandpaper had been rubbed inside it for an hour. She could barely talk any more, much less scream. As if any of the screaming she'd already done had benefited her one bit.

They had tied her to a metal folding chair, which had been placed in the center of the platform behind the pulpit. Four men stood around her: the two who had kidnapped her, and two others, a young, stupid-looking one named Daniel, who had yet to outgrow his pubescent body, and an older, somber man with a skeletal frame, named Frank.

Nancy thought if she heard "I CAST THEE OUT IN THE MIGHTY NAME OF JESUS!!" one more time, her internal organs would obey the order and start evacuating her body. Her threats to file charges against the men had no effect, since their teachings convinced them that God's commandments took precedence over the laws of the land, should the two ever conflict. Such as with the case at hand.

She could take the torment no longer. Obviously the only way they were going to let her go was if they believed she had been successfully exorcised. She knew there was no demon in her, but she could show them one, if that's what they wanted to see. Then after convincing them she'd been freed of it, they would take her back home, where she would waste no time in calling the police and having the fuckers arrested.

She narrowed her eyes and hissed at Gibson. "Yer mother sucks cocks in *Hell!*" she spat, lowering her voice.

She'd seen *The Exorcist;* she could do this bit. Too bad she couldn't spray their faces with green vomit.

Gibson, whose mother just happened to be dead, turned green anyway. All of them stepped back, their faces slack with shock. Nancy cackled gleefully. "Whassa matter, you mother-fucking, felching faggots? Fucking cat got your ass-licking tongues?"

Gibson began to tremble violently as his shock turned to horror.

"So, you show yourself at last!" the young man named Daniel declared with booming authority, emboldened by an extra reserve of faith. He held his right hand out toward Nancy. "Release that body at once, I command you in the name of Jesus!"

Nancy had created foam in her mouth with saliva, and allowed it to bubble from her mouth. She snaked her tongue in and out and made hideous faces.

Daniel's faith wavered. "Brother Mitchell! Everyone! Let's say it together!"

"Go FUCK YOURSELVES!" Nancy roared. "I'm not coming out till I'm good and ready! FUCK YOU FUCK YOU FUCK YOU—"

Gibson fell to his knees and all but drowned out Nancy's obscenities with meaningless sounds. Daniel joined him with his own loud gibberish but remained standing. The skeletal man named Frank pulled Mitchell aside and shouted something in his ear.

Then the room fell silent, all eyes on Frank. Nancy seethed venomously, "WHAT the fuck did you say?" It had sounded like he'd said something about dunking her in the baptismal font.

"Do you think that would work?" Mitchell asked uncertainly.

"Of course," Daniel said, slowly nodding his head. "Jesus sent that herd of swine into the sea, and the legion of demons perished . . ."

"Hey, wait a minute," Nancy balked, resuming her normal voice. "I was just putting on a show for you guys. That was me talking . . . *me*. Don't you dare go putting me in that goddamn—"

But they were already in motion, untying the knots,

freeing her from the chair. Each grabbed a limb and carried her, kicking and yelling hoarsely, toward a small set of steps leading down to a pit at the rear of the platform. A mural above the baptismal font showed Jesus in the river Jordan with John the Baptist, a dove preparing to light on the Christ's head as a voice proclaimed from a velvet banner in the clouds: *This is my beloved Son, in whom I am well pleased.*

Nancy looked fearfully at the blue water in the large tub. "Goddamnit, let me go! I was just ACTING, YOU ASSHOLES!!"

The brethren began to pray as they positioned her above the water. "In the name of the Father, Son, and Holy Ghost," Mitchell intoned.

Nancy thrashed wildly as they lowered her into the tub, then pushed her under. She could see their faces above her, distorted by the tidal waves she was creating. Their lips were moving, but she could hear nothing but the blood pounding in her ears. She held her breath. How fucking long did they plan to keep her down? Soon her chest began to ache; she needed air. Panicked, she fought to rise up, but strong righteous hands kept her below the waterline. Her mind was screaming denial. This couldn't really be happening. She wasn't supposed to die. She was going to learn the secret of immortality from the Obers and live forever. This had to end. She would never end. Never, never . . .

But she could no longer restrain her impulse to breathe. Her mouth opened and she sucked in a lungful of water; the displaced air surged to the surface. The men watched as Nancy's body relaxed and sank to the bottom of the tub, her eyes still wide and staring. A few more bubbles escaped through her nose.

"It worked." Gibson smiled, his face glowing. The men hugged each other, weeping with joy, offering thanks to God for their victory. The mighty demon had been destroyed. But just to make sure, they let her stay down for another minute or two. Then they yanked her out and laid her facedown on the floor, whereupon Daniel, who was in the Coast Guard reserves and trained for such procedures, proceeded to push on her back, forcing the water out of her lungs. As soon as it stopped trickling from her mouth he turned her over and gave her mouth to mouth resuscitation.

After a few moments Nancy began to sputter and cough. There was no fight left in her. She stared up at them dazedly. "I was dead," she croaked.

Mitchell nodded, a benevolent smile on his face. "We can't tell you how sorry we are that we had to do that, but it seemed the only way. Demons can't survive underwater, apparently. Fortunately humans can be resuscitated easily if it's done fast enough. But you're free now, and that's what matters. I must warn you, though. In the bible it says, 'When an evil spirit comes out of a man, it goes through arid places seeking rest and does not find it. The demon says, I will return to the house I left. When it arrives, it finds the house unoccupied, swept clean and put in order. Then it goes and takes with it seven other spirits more wicked than itself, and they go in and live there. And the final condition of that man is worse than the first.' Fill your heart with the Spirit of God, Nancy, so that when the demon returns, he will not find it empty."

Nancy paid little attention to the admonition; beyond the drowning, her brief experience with death had not been frightening in the least, and she knew that no demon had been cast out of her, so she was hardly concerned about its return. These assholes, idiots. What did they know? Nothing, nothing at all. She could hardly wait until Halloween.

A fistfight had broken out in the parking lot after school. Lana and Bruce edged up to the small crowd to see who was involved.

"Who's fighting?" Bruce asked someone in front of him wearing a black leather jacket.

"Dennis Bloom and Joel Mintern," the freckled youth replied. "Joel made a crack about Marla in front of Dennis, and Dennis just went berserk."

Knowing that Dennis was involved, Lana was no longer worried about running to find a teacher to break up the fight. She silently rooted for Joel Mintern, whoever he was. Dennis deserved a good beating as far as she was concerned. But she remained curious about the cause of the fight. She had overheard bits and pieces of gossip that afternoon, but no one had completely filled her in. She wasn't sure who they were talking about, but she thought she'd heard Nancy's name mentioned, and she had definitely heard the word witchcraft. Marla had to fit into that somehow.

A strawberry-blond Amazon angrily pushed her way through the crowd. Lana nudged Bruce. "Who's that?"

"Joel's girlfriend. She's probably going to rearrange Dennis's face. She doesn't like her little Joel to get hurt."

The crowd became quiet; only the growls and scathing curses being hurled by the fighters could still be heard. Joel's girlfriend, Michelle Kirkpatrick, watched the struggle for a few moments, then shouted at the top of her lungs, "STOP IT! Stop it right now!"

The fists landed their final blows, the two bodies quickly separating as bloodied faces looked up to see who had shouted the command. Joel said angrily, "I can handle this, Michelle! Stay the fuck out of it!"

Dennis, refusing to be intimidated by a girl—even if she was six-foot-two—was back on top of him in an instant, pummeling away. Michelle glared around at the circle of faces, then turned and stomped away.

"You stupid asshole!" Dennis roared at Joel, now pinned on the ground beneath him. "You really think Marla's a goddamn witch? What is this, the Middle Ages? And for your information, Nancy and her aren't even friends anymore! Nancy told Marla to fuck off! Now take it back, you douche bag!"

Joel dug his thumbs into Dennis's eye sockets. "FUCK YOU!!"

Lana grabbed Bruce's arm. Maybe Dennis was a creep, but he didn't deserve to get his eyes poked out. "Shouldn't somebody do somethin'?"

"Yeah, we should be moving right along," he said, leading them away from the sporting event. "And I hope after what you just saw, you won't think any more about hanging out with Nancy. Look what you'd be doing to me."

Lana wondered if Bruce really would engage himself in a gladiator match for the sake of her honor. Somehow she couldn't quite picture it; his spirit was undoubtedly willing, but his flesh only weighed about a hundred and fifteen pounds, with no apparent muscle. And he wasn't stupid.

On their way to the drive-in for a Coke, she brought up the subject of the rumors. "Did you hear anything about witchcraft today? I guess that's what that fight was all about, huh?" She wondered if Dennis still had his eyesight. A vision of him tapping down the hall with a white cane entered her mind. It actually wasn't that heartbreaking.

"Yeah, sure did." Bruce began shaking the steering wheel, enhancing his action with special sound effects: "OOOOoooooo-eeeee-ooooOOOO." His eyebrows made alternating, rapid bows over narrow, long-lashed slits.

"Come on, Bruce, get real," Lana pouted. "I wanna talk about this. I just wanna know what's goin' on. I wanna know if Nancy lied to me."

Bruce made a stab at sobriety. "Lied about what?"

"About killin' that rabbit. They kill things in satanic rituals, or so I've heard. Maybe that explains it. Maybe the rumors are true."

Bruce resisted the urge to pretend a spastic seizure. "You really believe in that stuff?"

"A'course . . . I thought I already told you that. I thought you were a believer too."

"Okay, I'm a believer." He flashed a toothy grin. "I'll be whatever you want me to be."

Lana rolled her eyes. "All right, I'll settle for that. So how do we get to the bottom of it? Nancy's obviously not gonna tell the truth."

Bruce gulped loudly. "Why do we want to get to the bottom of it? I kinda like it where I am. Uninvolved."

"Bruce, Bruce." Lana slumped down in the seat, not knowing whether to kiss him or knock him upside of the head. "Listen, if somethin' like that is really goin' on, we gotta help try to stop it. Don't we?"

"I don't know how to find anything out," Bruce said uneasily. "Nancy's the only one that would know for sure, and like you said, she's not gonna just come right out and admit it. If there's anything to admit."

"What about Jay?"

"I heard he's in the hospital."

Lana gasped. "Hospital! Well, let's go see 'im. Now."

Spiro felt unusually blessed as he made his way home. Not one person had teased him all day; no one had been lying in wait for him after school to make him lick the spit off their boots, or to sit atop his face and blast him with farts while others watched and hooted with laughter. Amazing what one small lesson taught them all.

He let himself in the house. His mother wasn't sitting in front of the television set as she usually was when he returned home from school. He shut the door and took a left off the living room toward her bedroom at the end of the hall. Her door was still open, just as he'd left it that morning after carefully laying her unconscious body on the bed. He stepped into the doorway and stared. She hadn't moved.

After putting his book bag on the floor, he approached the bed, his heavy footfall creaking the bare wooden slats. "Mama?"

When she didn't answer, he took a thumb and pried open one of her eyelids. Her flesh was cold, and something in the room stunk. He moved his hand away from her face and the eyelid remained open, but she still didn't speak. He covered her with the right side of the bedspread and quietly tiptoed from the room.

The man followed Roger Snell into the house and handed him the ancient timepiece, a pocket watch on a heavy gold chain. "I'll take a look at it in my shop," Roger said, opening the glass casing. "This way, Mister . . . ?"

"Montgomery."

"Ah, that's right. Nancy's chemistry teacher?"

"Algebra."

"Oh yes, excuse me. Say, you're the one my wife was talking about at the dinner table last night; she's a volunteer at the hospital. Said they thought you were down for the count."

The imposter smiled. "Obviously they were wrong."

"Well, my shop is this way—"

"I'll just wait here in the entry hall, if you don't mind."

Roger shrugged. "Fine with me, wherever you want. If it's something simple, I'll have it ready in just a few minutes. Otherwise you'll have to leave it with me, and you can pick it up tomorrow afternoon. Or I can have Nancy deliver it to you at the school Friday morning. It may just need a new mainspring."

"Take your time."

"Have a seat in the living room, if you like. You look like you're still not feeling too well."

"I feel quite all right," the demon Nephyrcai argued, its claim unsupported by the physical appearance of Albert Montgomery's body. But Roger was hardly going to force him to sit down.

"Whatever you say." He went through the kitchen to get to his shop, leaving his stubborn customer in the entry hall. As soon as Roger had disappeared into the garage, the demon turned right down the hall that led to the bedrooms. It felt in no hurry. It was a creature that created fear, never experienced it.

The first bedroom on the right was obviously Nancy's; teen idol posters covered the walls, stuffed animals sat on pink shelves over the standard stereo equipment and rock albums, clothes were strewn on the floor. A vanity next to the nightstand was stocked with makeup articles and perfumes, hair spray, an earring tree. A gum-wrapper chain dangled from the light fixture. Nephyrcai went in. The first place it looked was under the bed.

And there it was.

Nineteen

Bruce and Lana stepped up to the information desk.

"We'd like to visit Jay Gorman," Bruce said. "What room is he in?"

The pale, white-haired prune stared at him through inch-thick lenses, her pale gray eyes magnified six times their normal size. "Eh, what was that, sweetie?"

Bruce cringed at the term of endearment. "Jay Gorman," he repeated, somewhat louder. "Room number?"

"Faye Morgan," the receptionist mumbled, running bony fingers over a Rolodex.

"Gorman," Bruce shouted, drawing the stares of a family sitting in the adjacent waiting room. *"Jay Gorman."*

"Ah Gorman, yes. Room 122."

Jay was in a semiprivate room. The lights were off, but the television was on with the volume turned completely down. He lay peacefully surrounded by white, his mother sitting beside the bed in a chair, holding his hand, staring at the silent television screen. The other bed was unoccupied.

Rita Gorman smiled tearfully at Bruce and Lana when they quietly entered. "He's been in a coma for about three hours," she said, her voice strained.

Lana dropped her gaze to the highly polished floor. "What happened to him?"

"They don't know. He started having . . . seizures, I guess. Last night. They've done CAT scans, X rays, blood tests, everything; they just don't know. They say there's no reason for it. But look at him. He justs lays there . . ." Her voice began to crack. Bruce and Lana waited uncomfortably for her to compose herself, not knowing what to say.

"I guess I need a break," Mrs. Gorman said weakly, dabbing her eyes with a tissue. "I was here all night, and now all day. I should probably go to the cafeteria and get something to eat. Will you . . . would you mind staying with him until I get back? I won't take long."

"Oh, of course," Lana said quickly. "No problem at all. Take your time. By the way, my name's Lana. This here is Bruce."

Rita Gorman nodded gratefully. "It was kind of you to come visit him, very considerate. Well, I'll hurry back."

After she left, the two teens timidly approached the bed. Staring at Jay's serene face in the dim light, Lana whispered, "Well, what do you think? The doctors couldn't find anything wrong with him. You don't suppose . . ."

Bruce slowly shook his head. "I don't know. This is all pretty strange, I gotta admit that. But doctors don't know everything, even though they think they do." He leaned over the bed. "Hey Jay, wake up. I've got a killer joint with me. Let's light up and party, bud."

Lana sighed. "Come on, Bruce, this is no time for jokes. Comas are serious; they can last for years."

"I'm sorry. I just thought if anything would bring him out of it, that would."

"Nice try, but I'd be guessin' he's high enough."

Lana took the chair vacated by Jay's mother, and Bruce perched himself on the windowsill. They passed a few minutes in thoughtful silence. A nurse came in, mechanically took Jay's temperature and checked his pulse and blood pressure, then left, an unsmiling robot. Bruce said sarcastically, "Some Florence Nightingale. Hope I never have to come in here."

Lana sighed. "I wish we could talk to him. I'd sure like t'know what's goin' on. If he knows anything."

"You know what they say about curiosity."

"My daddy says that sayin' was invented by the Nixon administration." Thinking of her father made Lana feel sad. She missed him terribly, and had secretly tried to call him on several occasions, but he was never at home. At his bimbo girlfriend's, probably. Lana had never even learned her name; her mother refused to discuss the affair. Why didn't he call? Did he really not care anymore?

She couldn't allow herself to dwell on that. She would end up crying, and she knew how much Bruce hated to see her depressed. No telling what he might do to try to snap her out of it—put the bedpan upside down on his head and pretend to be Paul Revere? This wasn't the place or time for such frivolity. She returned her concentration to the problem at hand. "I wonder what's goin' on in his mind. Do people in comas dream?"

Bruce shrugged. "Don't ask me. I've never been in a—oh wow, look at his face."

Lana had already noticed, and her lips were pulled back in a grimace. "My God . . . what's happenin' to 'im? Should we call for a doctor?" Large red bumps were beginning to sprout all over Jay's face and neck. Even as they watched, some of the pustules came to a head and broke open, oozing yellow-green pus.

Bruce leaned forward on the sill in shocked fascination. "Talk about a zit attack. Yowza, I've never seen anything like this before."

Lana shuddered. "I think we should go find a doctor. This isn't right at all—"

Jay's eyes suddenly flew open. It so surprised Lana that she uttered a small shriek; Bruce jerked backward and hit his head on the window.

"Bruce, Lana. How nice of you to come see me." The patient smiled. Even his lips were covered with sores. His irises seemed to glow like rings of fluorescent blue paint under a black light. They held a slight sparkle of malevolence. His breath had a strange odor.

Lana covered her mouth and pointed. "Jay, your face . . . I think I oughta go find your doctor . . ."

"Ah, I'm fine, just fine, just the old acne flaring up," he said hollowly. "It doesn't hurt, except maybe to look at, eh?" His smile widened obscenely.

Lana looked away; the sight of him was making her

sick. "Well, if you're sure . . . we, uh, we came to ask you about Nancy. If you know anything about her bein' involved in . . . in witchcraft."

The boy on the bed spewed out deep, gurgling laughter. "Witchcraft? Oh my, that's a good one, gooood one. Have you also heard that I'm a vampire? It's true, you know. Come closer and let me bite your neck."

Lana grinned weakly; only Bruce was amused enough to chuckle. Lana pictured herself wearing a dunce hat; she could certainly run off the deep end on wild-haired ideas. "Okay, okay, it was a stupid question, and I got the answer I deserved. But I just had to make sure. Anyway, that's the rumor goin' around school. I thought we should check it out, just in case."

Jay's body abruptly rose in a sitting position. "You're very conscientious, aren't you, dear girl? That took a lot a courage, I'm sure. But yes, it was a stupid question. Now if you two will excuse me, I'm going to get dressed and out of here before the old lady comes back."

By six-thirty Bertha Guenther had still not risen, and Spiro was getting hungry, although the thought of eating anything was revolting to him. He wondered why that was. He went back to his mother's bedroom and called from the doorway, "Mama, will you fix me something to eat?"

Her voice rang out from the darkness, "You can fix your own supper, Spiro. And you can eat whatever you want."

Grinning, he marched into the kitchen and painstakingly opened a can of fruit cocktail. He ate it right out of the can, sitting in his mother's rocking chair in the living room. He had not cleaned up the vomit in the kitchen—his mother's breakfast must not have agreed with her at all—and the room reeked of its unpleasant odor, so he hadn't wanted to eat in there. When he finished the fruit cocktail, he went back to the kitchen and took the white bread from the bread box, and after eating half the loaf plain, topped off his meal with an overripe banana. Actually, only the thought of eating meat made his stomach feel queasy.

After the banana he was satisfied. Leaving the empty

fruit can, banana peel, and bread bag on the floor beside his mother's chair, he crossed the room and peered through the drapes. The hated pickup truck was parked in front of Lana's house again. That meant she was with him, the boy with the nice face and straight body. The boy she kissed. Spiro wanted to be him more than anything else in the world.

His mother was calling his name. Softly, softly.

He went in to her and turned on the light. The dull eye looked at him with approval. "You can draw another picture of her if you want, boy," she said through still, white lips.

Spiro was overjoyed though not really surprised; he'd somehow known what she was going to say, just as she'd known what he wanted to do. He lumbered back to his bedroom for some paper and a pen. He could draw Lana really good now. He knew exactly what she looked like in the nude.

Harold Mingee had come home early in a rage. They would be lucky, he angrily informed his daughter, damned lucky if this scandal didn't ruin his law practice. She'd had no goddamned business going up to that cemetery in the first place, ad infinitum, ad nauseum. Of course he was greatly exaggerating about being ruined. But he loathed social embarrassment.

Marla had retreated deep into herself hours before, that being the only way she could cope with what had happened to her. She took the verbal lashing from her father calmly, then afterward went upstairs and locked herself in her bedroom, his voice booming after her, "And you can just stay there until I say you can come out!"

Her urine-soaked skirt, panties, and panty hose still lay crumpled on the floor, where she'd dropped them before taking a scalding bath. She was too ashamed to put them in the laundry hamper and let her mother know what she had done. She picked them up and wrapped them in a plastic shopping bag, then stuffed the bag in a corner of her closet. After everyone else went to bed, she would sneak it outside to the trash can.

He made me do it . . .

Impossible! How? You're nothing but slime. Rich slime . . .

She flung herself down on the bed just as her phone rang. She wearily picked it up and sighed, "What?"

The familiar voice on the other line was frantic. Marla gripped the phone, anger rising over her shame as she listened.

". . . to talk to you about something. My dad said Mr. Montgomery was here and he must have gone into my room—"

"Looking for what, Nancy?" Marla cut in, her voice razor sharp. "Something else you found in the tomb, maybe? That you lied to me about having, like that witch's spell book? What did you do to Montgomery anyway? He's not a man anymore, he's something that crawled up out of Hell!"

"Listen to me, Marla—"

"You listen to me, Nancy Snell," Marla hissed. "Right now my whole life is falling apart because of you. I'm falling apart. Besides, now I know what a liar you are, so why should I believe anything you say?"

Now Nancy's voice became heated. "Where do you get off calling me a liar? Can you prove it? Can you prove I put a spell on Montgomery?"

"I don't have to, I know you did and that's all that matters."

"Oh, are you psychic now?"

Marla wished Nancy's head would pop out of the mouthpiece so she could spit in her face. "As a matter of fact I am, and I'm going to give you a free prediction right now. You're going to be sorry, you stupid bitch!"

"Not as sorry as you, BITCH!"

"What's that supposed to mean? Have you put a spell on me too?"

"You're the psychic," Nancy quipped. "Answer your own questions."

Her voice shaking with rage, Marla ended the exchange by saying, "Last time you told me to fuck off, well now I'm telling you to fuck off. So FUCK OFF!" She slammed the receiver down, a resounding ring echoing in her ears. She muttered at the instrument, "Fucking bitch."

Then the cramps hit, as if someone had just rammed a bowling ball into her abdomen. Marla clutched herself, mouth opened in a silent scream. Something was inside her, something hot, and it was pushing its way up. Her spirit clung tenuously to its haven; whatever that thing was, forcing its way up from her—womb?—it obviously had both the intention and the power to squeeze her own spirit out. The thought suddenly hit her like a blow: *Nancy sure as hell did cast some terrible spell on me, and I'm going to die. Right now, right here on this bed. In the next minute or two I'm going to be dead. Or something even worse.*

The ensuing tidal wave of panic triggered the simultaneous release of both bladder and bowels. She tried to scream for help but it was too late; she was no longer in control of anything. A tingly numbing sensation had begun at the top of her head; it was happening, she was passing through. A torrent of foreign images began to flood her mind, hundreds of them in the space of a few seconds, all of them so vile and depraved that she felt as though she were being raped, and all at once she realized that she was; her mind was being purposefully violated by another intelligence, a stupendously evil one. A physical attack by the most despicable man on earth would have been preferrable to this. She saw naked men and women copulating with every inanimate object imaginable and every living beast, mothers and fathers abusing their own children, who screamed and cried and then begged for more; she saw cooked infants on platters with fruits stuffed in their mouths, orgies in human excrement.

Then abruptly the assault ceased and she was looking down at herself, at the face she had seen only in a mirror before. It was now a face upon which the stamp of horror was deeply engraved, but just before Marla's spiraling journey through the black tunnel of death, she saw her brown eyes spark with blue flame, and the gaping mouth curve up in a fiendish smile.

Twenty

The phone rang at 7:35. Several moments later Luke's voice was ringing through the house, "It's Daddy, it's Daddy!"

Lana jumped up from the bed. "I've gotta talk to him. I'll be right back."

Bruce waved her on. "Go on, and take your time. I'm not gonna disappear."

It seemed to Lana an eternity before her brother finally relinquished the telephone. Carol sat rigidly on the couch, silently seething.

Lana listened to her father's voice with a pounding heart. Her mind produced a one-dimensional image of him, an image that was miles and miles away, that couldn't reach out to gather her in its arms, pull her onto its lap, as he had done so often when she was little. That was something, she thought, that a little girl should never have to outgrow. That original source of comfort and protection, of total security, should always be available.

"How's your new school, honey?"

"Hard," Lana replied despairingly. "I wish—"

"I know, babe, I wish too. So are you all settled in the new town? Made any friends yet?"

"A couple . . . I've got a new boyfriend, named Bruce. Oh, an' we had a puppy, but he ran away . . . Daddy?"

"Yes, angel."

"Do you still love us? Me and Luke?"

Hugh Bremmers's voice came back strained. "A'course I do, sweetheart. More than anything else in the whole world, you know that. I said some things to your mother in anger, tryin' to scare her out of movin' away with you kids. But I didn't mean . . . I'm still your dad, honey. I'll always be your dad—" His voice cracked. Lana could hear muffled sobs, the sound tumbling down the dam keeping back her own tears. They flowed down her cheeks unchecked.

"I'm sorry I didn't call sooner," he continued after a while. "I've had so many pans on the fire this past week, I've met myself comin' and goin'. But don't ever doubt that I love you, angel. You'll always be my little girl."

Bursting into sobs, Lana croaked, "I love you too, Daddy," and shoved the phone back at Luke, who was practically doing somersaults wanting to talk to his father again before the connection was terminated. Lana ran back to her bedroom. Bruce held and rocked her gently, for once not turning the situation into a farce. She clung to him tightly and moaned, "It's not fair."

He nodded sadly. "Life's a real bitch sometimes. Go ahead, babe, let it all out." Her pain was seeping into him, oppressing him with its heavy weight. In the emotional atmosphere of the room, he was powerless to fight it. He was usually successful at keeping such darkness out of his system, holding it at bay with jokes and cynical wit, a plastered-on grin, a few tokes of marijuana. He knew he had to keep it away because he knew how deadly it was . . . that if allowed to get a good hold on him, it would probably destroy him within a few days. And he knew where his mother kept her sleeping pills. That scared him the most.

He was the son of a man who had been convicted of armed robbery. Bruce had been only eighteen months old when it happened; three when his mother remarried. The twin girls she had by her new husband were treated like princesses by their father. Bruce, the son of the convict, the loser, was treated like a sack of shit. And he had been told often enough that he was JUST LIKE HIS FATHER and he would NEVER AMOUNT TO ANYTHING, blah de blah de blah, and Hell is just another word for being alive.

His mother, as if attempting to escape the reality of her past mistake, withdrew from him and made no effort to stop the verbal—and oftentimes physical—abuse. Bruce wondered sometimes if she was even aware of it. But what the hey! Eat, drink, and be merry, for otherwise you might just get that bottle of pills out of your mother's dresser drawer and eat every last motherfucking one of them.

Something beyond Nancy's control was happening. Something terrible. She knew it, could feel it. And Albert Montgomery was an integral part of it. She'd made him a part of it. If he had been the only other person in the house today, then he had taken the ledger; a simple deduction. But what did he plan to do with it—the same thing she had? She couldn't let him!

She remembered looking out her window the night before and thinking she'd seen him emerge from the house across the street. Now she was almost certain that it had been him. What had he been doing over there? Did he know the Chandler women? Were those two strange old ladies somehow involved in this too? If they were, maybe they would tell. Maybe they knew what to do. Nancy put on a light jacket and opened her window. The less she had to explain to her parents, the better.

Tonight there were no candles burning on the other side of the lace curtain. Peering through the large window, all Nancy could see was her own black reflection. Apparently Eliza Chandler and her mother had already gone to bed. She almost turned around and went back home, to call the church people instead. But no, those idiots couldn't find their own asses with both hands and a flashlight; they wouldn't know what to do about this. She had only taken a step when she heard a noise inside the Chandler house; a loud thump. Gathering her courage, she stepped up to the door and knocked. "Mrs. Chandler?"

The door swung open on Nancy's third knock. It hadn't been closed all the way. She thought that was strange, because her previous snooping adventures had always found the door locked, even during the daytime. She pushed on the door, opening it farther. The room beyond was a museum of dark shapes. "Miss Chandler?" Nancy's voice bounced off the shadows, stirring the musky air. But there was no reply; only the rhythmic ticking of a clock.

And the rocking of a chair.

She called out again, softly, "Miss Chandler, are you there?"

"Please, do come in," a gravelly voice finally replied. "So sorry about the dark. The candles are all burned out, you see."

"Don't you have any electricity?" Nancy fumbled along the wall for a light switch and found one, but when she flipped it, nothing happened.

"It seems the bulbs are burned out also," the voice said apologetically. "But no matter. Your eyes will adjust. Come closer."

Nancy took a timid step forward. "Am I going to bump into anything?"

She could barely see the shape of the chair several feet in front of her; the woman sitting in it was all shadow. Nancy wondered how she could stand to sit in the total dark like this with no television, unable to even read a book, just rock in a chair and think, think, think . . .

"There is nothing between me and thee," the voice cackled thinly, "except, perhaps, a little fear. But it's not mine. Is it yours?"

Nancy stopped dead in her tracks, gooseflesh charging over her body. "Yes, I'm afraid. I've lost something . . . important. I know you don't know me or anything, but I have to talk to somebody. I thought you might know something because I . . . did I see Albert Montgomery come out of your house last night? He was at my house earlier today, and now the ledger is gone . . . I made him sick, well actually he was supposed to die, but now . . . and my boyfriend's in the hospital, and I did it to my ex–best friend too, and I know something is wrong but I don't know what, and I don't know what to do . . ."

"Why don't you just relax, Nancy."

"How did you know my name?" she asked, surprised.

The voice that answered her was not at all the one that had spoken moments before. The quality was completely different. And though the transition was impossible to fathom, she recognized it immediately as Jay's when he said, "I know a lot of things. Including the fact you're going to die very soon."

Realization hit Nancy like a freight train; this wasn't Jay—she wasn't even talking to a human being. Marla's words echoed in her brain: *Montgomery's not a man anymore, he's something that crawled up out of Hell!* Something had gone terribly wrong with the spells; all she'd done was conjure demons! Her instinct was to flee, but her lower body had suddenly become made of wood. All she could do was whisper through a tightly constricted throat, "Oh, shit."

Deep, guttural laughter filled the room. The demon Azrahoth mocked her, "Power, power, I have the power to heal, the power to kill, the Obers will just *love* me. They'll tell me all their secrets. Well, I've got a little secret for you, Nancy. You're history."

"I'm not afraid to die," she answered as bravely as she could. "I've had a glimpse of the other side. It wasn't anything like I'd expected."

"Oh?"

"I saw a light," Nancy went on, suddenly at peace in her remembrance. "And love was pouring out from it, toward me. I felt safe."

"Ever read something about Satan appearing as an angel of light?"

"But—"

"But nothing, you stupid bitch."

Dread rushed through Nancy's veins. "So there really is a Hell?"

"Of course there is, but you don't actually have to be dead to live there. It's not exactly a place; let's call it a state of mind, for simplicity's sake."

"Well, I can come back here if I want, just like you," Nancy said uncertainly, aware that the shadows surrounding them were gradually lightening with a bluish cast, enabling her to see the pustule-infested horror sitting before her.

"Don't count on it, bitch. You know nothing. Like a child playing with adult toys, you had no idea what you were doing, but you were certainly willing to try anything, weren't you? I must admit you had some guidance, but that was possible only because of your natural propensity for such an experiment. Your creativity went beyond suggestion, however. Not that it posed any real problem, but this clay doesn't keep very well on us. Does get to be a little embarrassing, but we'll manage. But if you think you have the power to escape the realm of the damned, I think you're in for an unpleasant surprise, as you'll soon discover. Very soon . . . feel that little pain in your chest? I would like to thank you, though, for your help before you go, but we can handle things from here on out. Oh—do give my regards to the Master. I haven't seen him in ages."

Too stunned to speak or move, Nancy watched the demon rise from the rocking chair. She couldn't die. She refused to die! Bringing up a fist to the cleft between her breasts, she told herself adamantly that there was no pain, none at all, she was just under a great deal of stress at the moment. But suddenly her heart was clenched between merciless jaws, wrenching a loud groan from her throat as she dropped to her knees, her left arm curled up in a seizure. Falling over on her side, paralyzed by the intensity of the pain in her chest, she was equally tormented by the fact that she had brought this on herself, and tears squirted from her eyes. How could she have been such an idiot?

Then a violent, unseen force jerked her up from the floor and slammed her against the wall, centered over one of Eliza Ober's Ixantra pentagrams, arms and legs spread to match the star's lower points. She watched in disbelief, the demon's laughter barely heard, as the front of her blouse tore open from top to bottom and her bra snapped in two, exposing her bare flesh to an invisible razor that proceeded to carve a deep gash down and through her breastbone, spraying blood up into her screaming mouth. The pain was far past bearable now, but nothing compared to the sight of her own heart springing out from its cavity, beating wildly as it strained against the aorta, nerves, and ventricles connecting it to her body.

"Oh, don't be such a baby," Azrahoth chided. "This is just the sort of thing you loved watching in all those movies, isn't it?"

Nancy had never seen something like this in a movie,

and she thought she'd seen it all. Through the widened crevice in her chest now crawled one of her rapidly collapsing and expanding lungs, immediately followed by her large, purplish liver, the two bloody organs crowding around the still-beating heart. She could feel every organ in her abdomen surging upward for evacuation, just as she had imagined them doing when those religious fanatics had her tied to the chair.

She screamed the word NO over and over, but no one heard. She didn't know it yet, but she was already dead.

The fire blazing in the hearth had made the room too hot; she had started it for atmosphere, not heat. She opened the library window and went back to sit on the Persian rug among the cardboard boxes.

Pamela's eyes were dry now, her emotions numbed by alcohol. Perhaps her world was falling apart at the seams, but with her brain steeped in alcohol, she honestly didn't give a damn. What a perfect time to walk down Memory Lane . . . not her memories, but those of a woman who had written the final chapter, had typed The End on the last page of her life's manuscript.

Jasmine had saved dozens of her grandchildren's scribblings, report cards, homemade Valentines, and other priceless artifacts like the ones Pamela had carelessly tossed away. Locks of hair. Baby shoes. Badly crayoned family pictures.

Once an aging but still graceful woman had rocked a bundle cradled in her arms, cascaded in moonlight, gentle shadows swaying. For hours upon hours. No wonder Marla had grown up so spoiled. But that was a later chapter, not very many years before the plot had turned sour, before a rational, spritely human mind had become ravaged with senility. Too close for comfort.

Pamela opened another box and reached in, drawing out a framed black and white photograph of her parents on their wedding day. Her father wore a high-necked white shirt under an ill-fitting black coat with a carnation attached to the lapel, looking as though someone had just crushed a boot heel down on his bare toes. He had long, bushy sideburns into which merged a thick moustache. His wavy black hair was brushed back, revealing a high, clear forehead above the stricken eyes staring bravely into the camera. A beautiful, slightly plump Jasmine stood proudly beside her captured prey, her expression a mixture of triumph and joy. Her long brunette tresses were covered with white lace that fell below her elbows. In her smooth, unwrinkled hands she held a single long-stemmed white rose.

So much life ahead when that picture was taken. So many blank pages waiting to be filled. The writers, now a team, pooled their dreams and ideas and planned the creation of the greatest love story of all time, as all such couples did when the sun rose and fell in that uncomplicated era. Now the writers are realistic, adaptable to chaos, Pamela thought cynically. The acceptance of divorce was no more significant than having your hair done, the confusion of roles, the competition to succeed, the disintegration of the family unit—best not to count on anything more than a poignant short story.

Yellowed letters in matching envelopes; worn, tattered books; dusty trinkets. Small porcelain dolls, probably worth a fortune in an antique shop. Another photograph, this one of two young girls holding hands. The one on the left Pamela recognized as her mother. Holding the picture up to the fire's light, she studied the features of the other girl. Black hair hanging wildly, dark, piercing eyes, a secretive smile. Black dress. Aunt Jovanna? No, the girl was too young . . .

Pamela's hand began to shake. Morganna Ober.

She tore the photograph to separate the two images, accidentally cutting off her mother's left hand. Growling with wrath, she tossed both halves onto the burning logs and watched through a haze of tears as they curled into meaningless black cylinders.

She was immediately sorry for burning the half with her mother in it. That image of her was now lost forever, as Jasmine was. Turning her gaze bleakly to the floor, Pamela's eyes fell again on the pile of letters. She leafed through them slowly. Most were addressed to Mr. and Mrs. Charles L. Colter, the various return addresses in the upper left-hand corners familiar; other relatives, her parents' close friends. Then she came upon one without a return address, marked only "Jasmine" in her father's handwriting. Tenderly, she opened the loose flap, drew out the single sheet of brittle stationery, and began to read:

My darling wife, I know you won't discuss this with me, so I will tell you in this note what I have to say, and nothing more need be said about it. I know now what's been troubling you because you pored it out last night in your sleep. I understand why you must feel tortured over what you did, but my love, we both were on the brink of desperation, and I myself would have stopped at nothing to save our Pamela. The fact is that she is well now, and that's all that matters. The end justifies the means, as they say. Please don't punish yourself any longer.

Your loving husband, Charles.

The phone rang. Pamela jumped, startled. Her head throbbed when she stood up and weaved toward the desk, answering on the third ring.

Would have stopped at nothing to save our Pamela . . .

"Hello?"

Mother, what did you do?

It was Pamela's oldest and dearest friend, Beth. She seemed upset. "Pammie, is . . . is Nancy over there by any chance? I know the girls have been in some kind of a tiff lately, but . . . we don't know where else she could be. We thought she was in her room, but I stopped to check on her before we went to bed, and she was gone; she'd snuck out through her window. Do you know if Marla picked her up?"

"Marla's been in her room all night, as far's I know," Pamela said thickly.

The end justifies the means, as they say . . .

"But I'll go up and check if it would make you feel any better."

"Please. There were two . . . two men over here last night looking for her. Religious fanatics. I don't even care to repeat what they said, but I'm afraid . . . well, just please go check with Marla."

Pamela put the phone down and left the library, wondering if her dear friend was aware the whole town was talking about her behind her back. She didn't seem to be. That was fortunate. Otherwise she would also know who was responsible for the rumors about her daughter being a witch, and she might not let her husband come over to play anymore.

She was back a few minutes later. "Marla's sound asleep; passed out with her clothes on, and the light . . . guess she was really upset after Harold raked her over for some stupid thing she'd done. She always did that, you know, ever since she was a little girl; if either of us got mad at her, she'd go to her room and fall asleep. Her way of escaping, I guess."

"So Nancy's not there."

It was a morose statement, not a question. "All right, well, I guess we're going to have to call the police. I'll talk to you later." She hung up before Pamela could say another word.

The letter was still in her hand. Half consciously, she walked over to the fireplace, tossed it in, and watched as the orange flames devoured her haunting questions.

Twenty-One

"Please, please, try to calm down, Mother. I can't understand a single thing you're saying." It was only six-thirty in the morning; Harry was still in bed snoring profoundly, the sound ripping through the whole trailer. Jane hadn't slept five minutes the whole night, and she was definitely in no mood for hysterics. It seemed her mother had said some nonsense about her father being in jail, but Jane thought she must just have misunderstood. Her father couldn't be in jail. That was simply ridiculous.

But when Rose Hester was finally able to speak clearly, that was exactly what she repeated, her massive breasts rising and falling in shallow, tremorous heaves. "They came to question him early this morning. Two detectives. They'd already been to Brother Mitchell's house, and he told them what they had done yesterday, admitted to takin' the girl against her will, but explained why they done it and how the girl had got delivered and saved and all, and that they took her back home. But they arrested him anyway, and then went after the others; Brother Gibson, Daniel Laker, and your daddy."

Jane's eyes grew wide. "They took the girl against her will? Mother, that's kidnapping! Daddy could go to prison for that! What in the world were they thinking?"

"They were only doin' what the Lord told 'em to do," Rose blubbered. "And it was a good thing they done it; Frank told me when that demon finally showed itself, it liked to have scared them to death, and spewed out the worst string of profanity they ever did hear. They got her

226

freed of it, though, praise God. We got the victory on that."

"You're saying . . . the girl was really possessed?" Jane clutched at the T-shirt she had worn to bed, twisting it tightly around her fingers as she stared blankly at her mother. She could feel all the repressed fears getting ready to jump in front of her face like a huge, obscene jack-in-the-box.

"A'course she was really possessed, just like the Lord told us. Your daddy said her face twisted up all grotesquelike, and she was a'foamin' at the mouth and everything. Told 'em in this horrible voice that it wasn't gonna leave that body till it was good an' ready. Sounds like a demon to me."

Jane stopped twisting the T-shirt and sat frozen for a few seconds. Then she began to laugh, loudly and hysterically. Her mother was incensed.

"Now just what do you think is so funny about that, Jane Rachel? You stop that right now. Your daddy's up at the jail. This is no time to be laughing."

But Jane couldn't stop. At least, not until a disheveled, disgruntled Harry appeared at the end of the hallway. "What the hell's going on here?"

Jane clapped a hand over her mouth to shut herself up. Rose pushed herself out of Harry's chair and said, "Well, I'm not a'gonna sit around here and listen to a bunch of cussin'. I'm a'gonna get me down to the church to pray for your daddy."

"My father's in jail," Jane explained to her husband with an inappropriate smile, followed by a snicker. "He and some other men from the church kidnapped Nancy Snell and cast a demon out of her." She giggled. "Can you imagine, Harry? A real live demon."

Harry waited to respond until his mother-in-law had lugged her jiggling buttocks out the front door, then turned an icy set of eyes on his wife. "You've fucking flipped out, haven't you?"

"Flipped out?" Jane cocked her head, musing over his question. Her face cracked in a wide smile. "Noooo, I don't think so. I've just finally accepted it, Harry. I've decided to go ahead and swallow the whole can of worms. Mama was right, all those years. Demons are

227

real, witches, angels, God, the Devil—and so I guess UFO's, werewolves, and vampires are too . . . what else? Oh yes, ghosts, zombies . . . I think that about covers it. But that doesn't mean I'm flipped out, does it?"

Little did Jane know she would soon become a patient in the same nursing home where she worked. Oh yes, she was flipped out, all right.

Harry's face was turning quite red; his hands balled into tight fists at his sides. "Goddamnit, I knew you were headed for this. Of all the fucking shit . . . my wife's gone blookers on me. They find out up at the school that my father-in-law's a kidnapper and I'll probably lose my job. So far this day really SUCKS!" He turned and slammed his fist into the wall, breaking three of his fingers.

Jane trilled high-pitched laughter over his howls of pain. "Uh-oh! Devil's got ahold of you, Harry, better watch out! He might make you fling yourself off a building, or onto the railroad tracks when a train's coming! *Devil's got you, Harry!*"

Holding his swelling fingers, Harry glared at her, wanting very much to strangle her, but he'd just made that an impossibility. "You'd better shut up," he growled, supposing the only thing to do now was go next door and tell the gossip-monger to call the psycho squad. His wife's voice followed him out the door, making sound effects for every monster that man's imagination had created.

Half an hour later a dozen or so neighbors had gathered to watch the drama promised by the appearance of the private ambulance. For the last few minutes they had been treated to the sounds of mayhem inside the Bellows trailer, which included much yelling, breaking, and crashing. Finally the star of the scene was dragged out in a straitjacket between two burly orderlies, her hair a total mess, eyes glazed and filled with madness. She struggled vainly inside the jacket as they escorted her to the rear of the panel truck, hissing and gnashing her teeth at her mortified audience, occasionally railing something inane at them along with a considerable amount of spittle: "They're all real!" "There's one behind you!" "Are you just going to stand there and let these devil worshipers take me to Satan's throne?"

Harry had never been more glad of anything than the closing of those rear ambulance doors. His fingers were throbbing badly, and probably needed to be set, but all he could think about now was buying a couple of six-packs and getting stoned.

It was seven-forty, and Marla had still not come down for breakfast. Before going to bed, Pamela had covered her and turned out the light, but otherwise had not disturbed her. Fearing Marla might have overslept— Pamela suddenly realized she had forgotten to set her daughter's alarm—she set her toddy on the kitchen counter and went upstairs to check. Her son and husband had just left.

Marla's bedroom door was first on the left in the hallway upstairs. It was slightly ajar, as Pamela had left it the night before. She gently pushed it open. The bed was tousled; at some point during the night, Marla had gotten into it. But she was not in it now. Pamela took a step into the room and peeked toward the closet, noticing a trace of some foul odor which reminded her of the toilet backing up. The closet door was standing open, but her daughter was not in front of it selecting the day's apparel. Pamela's sodden brain searched for an explanation. Had Marla already left without her knowing it? She could have, possibly . . . might have purposefully snuck out early to avoid facing her father. So then her car would not be in the driveway. Proud of her clever reasoning—it didn't come easy during times like this—she crossed the room and parted Marla's curtains. Looking down over the drive, she could see the sun glinting mercilessly on the polished finish of Marla's Cutlass, still parked in its usual place. Pamela frowned, then walked back into the dim hallway and called out, "Marla . . . ?"

She heard a creak at the end of the hall, where the master bedroom and Rick's rooms were located. Marla was apparently in her brother's room; borrowing something, Pamela supposed. The kids were constantly accusing one another of borrowing things without asking.

Weaving her way down the hall, past the empty bathroom on her right, she said sternly, "Marla, you're going to be late for school. Are you dressed already? Marla?" Rick's bedroom door was shut. A poster taped to it warned: Enter at Your Own Risk. Quite appropriate, Pamela thought with dismay. Stepping through her son's room was like walking through a mine field. One wrong move and you've got an Atari joystick poking through your foot, or you're falling over a football, or sliding on the pages of an open *Penthouse* magazine. Marla's was often the same way, only not quite so dangerous, unless you got tangled up in a pile of clothes. Pamela was getting a little sick of playing maid to her two lazy offspring. They were certainly capable of cleaning up their own rooms. Like she'd told them a thousand times.

She snarled at the poster and, fully aware of her mortal danger, opened the door. The room was a disaster area, as usual. But Marla was nowhere in sight. Through the fog in her mind, Pamela became aware that there was someone behind her. The hair on the back of her neck prickled. She whirled around.

Marla stood in the hallway, having apparently just emerged from the master bedroom. In the shadows, her eyes glowed like sapphires. They bored into Pamela's. "Looking for me, Mother?"

Pamela let out her breath; she'd been unaware until then that she'd been holding it. She nodded, wondering at the strange odor she smelled. "I was afraid you were going to be late for school . . . by the way, what were you doing in my bedroom? Borrowing a pair of my earrings again?"

White lips turned up in a smile. "Just wondering."

"Just wondering what?" Pamela asked irritably.

"Wondering how many times you've fucked Roger Snell on that bed in there."

Pamela was sure she was going to faint. She felt her cheeks burn, her brain turn into a helium balloon. But she couldn't deny. She could only stand there and admit her guilt with an open mouth and bloodshot, stricken eyes.

"What's the matter, Mother? Was it supposed to be a secret? Yes . . . I can see that you wouldn't want Daddy to find out, not to mention your old chum Beth. Or me, you fucking hypocrite." The sapphires narrowed. "Look at you . . . you're disgusting. A secret lush with a secret lover. Looks like your mother lost her soul for nothing. Well, guess I'd better be on my way. See you soon."

Pamela melted unconscious to the floor.

Spiro closed the gap in the curtains and turned to face his mother's rancid mound of flesh, now heaped at an odd angle on the couch. "Mama, do I have to go to school today?"

"No, son. Stay here with me. You can draw pictures all day long."

"Lana just went away in that pickup truck with that boy, Mama. She's always with him. I want to be him."

"No, son, you just want to look like him. And you can, son, you can."

Spiro scrambled over to the couch and sank to his knees. With a gesture of supplication, he pleaded, "Please tell me, Mama. Tell me how."

The dull eye caressed him with affection. "It's very simple, boy. Just put on his mask."

Greer jerked up the phone and punched the correct extension button. "Hello? Dale?"

Dale was his brother, a judge for fifteen years. Surely he had some connections, could pull some strings, get something done. "Yeah, sorry I didn't get back to you sooner. Had to go to Pierre. So, what's up?"

Richard Greer felt beads of sweat pop out on his forehead. He found himself searching for the right words to say, although he had rehearsed his little speech at least two hundred times, and all night in his dreams. It was going to be much harder than he thought.

"Dale, you've known me all my life; you know I'm not crazy, right?"

His brother cleared his throat. "Well now, I don't know that I'd swear to that under oath . . ."

"Come on, Dale, I'm serious. If I told you that I'd seen, with my own eyes, a UFO land in my backyard, would you believe me, or would you think I've gone off my rocker?"

The voice came back incredulous. "You're telling me you saw a spaceship? In your backyard?"

Richard wiped his brow with his sleeve. "No, that's not what I'm telling you. But what I do have to say is going to sound just as incredible. Are you going to listen to me?"

"I think I'd better hear it first, Bubba."

Greer winced at the childhood nickname. He'd hated it then and he hated it more now. At times he wanted to shove it back down his brother's throat with his fist. A difficult feat to accomplish over the phone. He said evenly, "You remember what I told you when I got back from Haiti?"

Silence. Then, "You mean about the voodoo?"

"That's what they call it, yes. There's another name for it over here. Doesn't matter what it's called. The same things do the dirty work."

"Right. Demons, or evil departed souls." A slight cough.

Richard could picture the expression on his brother's face. Amusement. Disbelief. He wore it often on the bench. "Whatever. I don't know what they are, but I know they're real. I came face to face with one—"

"I know, I remember. So get on with it; I need to be at the courthouse in half an hour, and I haven't shaved yet. Get to the point."

Richard swallowed nervously. "I've seen another one . . . recently. Here. One of the teachers."

"Very interesting, Richard. Well, I'd better be going. Why don't you and Lila plan on coming over for dinner tomorrow night? We can tell your little story to the trick-or-treaters; I'm sure they would enjoy it. And you know how Barbara is about things like that; she'd certainly be in the limelight at her next tea."

"You've got to do something!" Richard hissed, gripping the phone. "Set up a bust—get the thing behind bars. I don't know if that would do any good or not, but—"

"Whoa, hang on there. You've got to be kidding. I don't know what kind of shows you've been watching on television, but we don't do that kind of thing around here. No way. Maybe you should be telling all this to Dr.

Shearer, Bub." Shearer was a psychologist. Richard angrily slammed down the receiver.

Lana turned to Bruce in the cab of his pickup. They were at the drive-in eating a breakfast of hash browns and Cokes. "Do you ever think about death?"

He shook his head. "Never. I don't even think about getting sick. Why worry about it? It's not like you can do anything about it. Me, I just party when I can, try to keep a positive attitude in this stinking jungle, and make out with pretty girls like you."

Lana gave Bruce a light pinch on his inner thigh. "Not at the drive-in, unless you wanna go around an' charge admission. No sense puttin' on a free show."

"How much you think we could get?"

"About five cents." What she meant was that so far, the physical part of their romance was G-rated—which was fine—but the words had come out sounding like a complaint.

Bruce donned an expression of despair. "F-Five cents?"

She gave him a quick, consoling peck on the cheek. "Oh, you know what I meant. They wanna see some real action, an' we're not that kind of movie."

Bruce surprised himself by saying, "I wish we were."

Time was suspended for what seemed like a small eternity. Lana felt her body grow warm. The time was right, she finally concluded. Not here at the drive-in, of course, but in the privacy of her bedroom . . . "You wanna skip school today?" she asked, her eyes lowered. Saying the words sent goosebumps up her arms and shoulders.

Bruce's crotch stirred slightly. "You really mean it?"

"Nobody's home at my house. We could . . ."

Bruce's mind reeled. She was actually inviting him to make love to her. He felt his penis shrink to the size of a pencil stub. She was so pretty, and he was so . . . nothing. What a mind-blow. A wavering smile touched his lips. "I guess it would be okay."

"Okay?" Lana crossed her arms in a huff. "Well, if that's all the enthusiasm you have about it—"

"Oh dear, is there trouble in Paradise?"

Bruce and Lana jerked their heads toward the passenger window to see who had spoken. At first glance Lana thought someone was wearing his Halloween mask early. When she realized she was staring at a real face, she thought she might well blow her breakfast.

Jay (or the thing they thought was Jay) leaned in through the open window, smelling strangely of burned electrical wires. "Hey kids, what's the matter? Do I look that bad?"

Bruce nodded. "You really do, man. Maybe you should go back to the hospital."

"What? And miss our little party tomorrow night? Look at it this way—now I won't have to worry about a costume." The malicious creature in Jay's body grinned obscenely. There was not a square millimeter on its face and throat that wasn't oozing pus. Lana couldn't stand to look. She turned her attention to the activities of the carhops.

Bruce couldn't handle it either. Pretending to study his fingernails, he said, "This the private party you're talking about, you and Nancy, me and Lana?"

"The same. You two are still planning to come, aren't you? Don't break my heart."

"Nancy was s'posed to call me to talk about it," Lana mumbled, wishing Jay would go away and gross out someone else. "But she never did. We hadn't really made up our minds. What were we all gonna do anyway?"

She could feel the intense heat of the demon's stare upon her when it replied, "Oh, something fun, I promise. But it's a surprise; I can't tell you."

Lana wasn't very fond of surprises; nice ones, yes, but not any being offered by the creature from the black lagoon. She looked up at Bruce with an expression she hoped conveyed the message: *Get us out of this.* For some reason, she couldn't decline the invitation herself.

Bruce either misinterpreted the signal, or else couldn't bring himself to say no either. He nodded compliantly. "Sure, whatever. So what time and all that?"

"We'll pick you up at eight-thirty. Just say where."

Lana sighed. "My house, I guess." She gave him the address.

The demon Azrahoth gave them a mocking salute.

"Until then, my little beauties. You can go on with your discussion about whether or not to play hookey for nookie." It laughed and strode off.

Lana shuddered. "My God. He's the grossest thing I've ever seen in my life. If I looked like that, I'd sure as hell be in the hospital, or at least in a doctor's office."

Bruce had no stomach for the subject, and quickly changed it. "When I said I wouldn't mind, I was just trying to cover up the fact that I was . . . well, scared. I hope you don't laugh, but . . . I've never, you know, done it before."

How did Jay know what they were talking about?

The insidious, unwanted memory of Jay's appearance melted from Lana's awareness. She looked at Bruce tenderly. "You're so sweet. Come on, let's go to my house."

It seemed only just the next moment that they were standing in the cool dimness of Lana's bedroom removing each other's clothes. Bruce was obviously nervous, and so their actions had begun to seem awkward, mechanical. The suggestive talk, the longing glances were over, and the mystery would soon be. They were actually, really going to do it. All the way. Lana giggled nervously as she fumbled with the last button on his shirt. "Feels kind of weird, doesn't it? The first time?"

"Yeah, a little like falling off the Empire State Building." He bent over and gave her a long, probing kiss. Lana's breath quickened. Bruce guided her over to the bed, feeling too self-conscious about his skinny body to display it au naturel in a standing position in the middle of the room. That was too much like being on a stage with floodlights. He had already slipped out of his jeans, and Lana was down to her bra and panties. They were naked enough for now.

Lying together on the bed, arms and legs entwined, lips joined in a passionate kiss, they both relaxed. The pencil stub began to extend.

He whispered against her neck, "You're the best thing that's ever happened to me, Lana."

The confession touched her deeply. She had imagined he would be making wisecracks, playing his typical clown role. She responded huskily, "You ain't seen nothin' yet."

They quickly dispensed of their lower undergarments and rejoined in an embrace. Bruce positioned himself over her, but suddenly realized their lack of precaution. "I know this is probably a bad time to be asking, but are you . . . uh, on the pill or anything?"

"You're right. It's a bad time to ask."

"You're not? What if—"

"I didn't use anything with Greg," she said with a trace of embarrassment, "and nothin' happened. Besides, I'm sure it's not that time of the month. It'll be okay, I promise. Come on, you're gonna ruin the mood."

But the mood was ruined by something else. They heard a noise at the window, and turned in time to see Spiro's head duck beneath the windowsill. Lana bolted upright, enraged. "That creep! I oughta go out there an' slap the hell out of 'im!"

Bruce quickly lost his erection. "Shit."

"I wonder what he's even doin' around here; he should be at school by now. Well, I will go over to his house later an' tell his mother what he was up to. He sure will get it from her!"

"And so what if he tells her what he saw and she tells your mom that you and me were in bed together?"

Lana doubled over, burying her head in her lap. "Damn. You're right. I can't do anything."

After several moments they got up and began to dress in strained silence, both feeling cheated. Afterward they went into the living room to watch television, though neither of them could recall later what they had seen.

Twenty-Two

Richard Greer pushed the intercom button. "Yes?"

"Marla Mingee wants to have a word with you, sir."

Greer let out a shaky breath. "All right, tell her to come in."

She was seated with the door closed before he looked up from his desk. "Don't tell me you've slapped—" His voice faltered as his pulse began to race. "—someone else," he finished weakly.

Her eyes burned into his like hot pokers. "Oh no; the rumors don't bother me at all anymore, and you should hear the new ones going around. You were right; it's best to ignore them. But there is something I can't ignore . . ."

Greer's eyes darted to the telephone. He licked his lips, which were suddenly bone dry. "What might that be?"

"Oh, don't play games with me, Mr. Greer." She smiled as if remembering a lewd joke. "The phone call you made to your brother. Now, was that very nice?"

"How . . . how did you know?" he asked, but he knew already, yes, he knew; he wasn't talking to Marla Mingee. She had moved with no forwarding address. The thing sitting across from his desk was only renting the vacated premises. He wanted to pull his eyes away, but he was powerless to do so. He wanted to pick up the phone and scream for his secretary to run in and save him—and he was going to need saving, of that he was deadly certain—he wanted to bolt for the door. But he could do nothing but sit like a marble statue and wait.

He was mesmerized by the third demon, Vikael, which

Nancy had unwittingly summoned from the darkest realm of the spiritual universe. It said insincerely, "Too bad he didn't take you seriously; that might have caused a bit of a problem. And we don't want any problems, do we?"

Greer shook his head slightly; sweat was pouring down his cheeks. "Why are you here?"

"Why are you here?" Vikael tossed Marla's head back and uttered a low, raspy laugh. "That's the biggie for your kind, isn't it? Along with 'Who Am I?' and 'Where Am I Going?' Well, you might say I'm here in this capacity by accident, but as it turns out, were it not for the compliance of a certain fool—I'm speaking of Nancy—a couple of the Master's faithful servants might have been very disappointed. I'm sure the Master himself would have been disappointed as well; Myrantha and Nathaniel have added many to our number. And the more the merrier, eh?" More grating laughter.

Greer thought he was having a heart attack. He gripped the edge of his desk, his face becoming mottled. "That's hardly an answer to my question."

"Well, it's all the answer you need, Richard. By the way, I must thank you for being such a constant source of entertainment. Does your wife know you still jack-off with torrid magazines? You like the lesbian photos the best, don't you?"

Greer's cheeks flamed crimson. "Do what you're going to do. Get it over with."

"Oh my . . . I've embarrassed you, haven't I? How thoughtless of me. Just look at what I've done. You're so upset you're getting a nose bleed."

Greer felt a tickle above his upper lip. He touched it with his finger and looked, only then able to break the chilling eye contact. His finger was bloody.

"I believe you're beginning to have a brain hemorrhage," Vikael said somberly. "Tsk, tsk. I imagine you'll be dead before the ambulance can get here. Well, it was nice chatting with you."

The demon rose, turned on its heel and left.

The trickle from Greer's nose quickly became a spurting gush, joined by crimson tears leaking from his eye sockets. He fell across the desk, crumpling papers in both fists. Twenty seconds later he was dead, his face lying in a thick pool of blood.

"I'm sure she's just fine. You know how kids are," Pamela said wearily, still thinking of Marla's shocking confrontation. She and Roger had been extremely discreet . . . hadn't they? How could Marla have known? But it wasn't even that, or the fact that Marla had called her a fucking hypocrite and a lush, that bothered her the most. What bothered her the most was what she'd said about Jasmine losing her soul for nothing.

The letter . . .

NO!

Surely Marla hadn't really said such a horrible thing, such a senseless, vicious thing. Pamela had only dreamed it after she'd fainted. *Yes, try to convince yourself of that . . .*

"I don't know about other kids, but Nancy would never run away from home," Beth sobbed, dabbing her eyes with a frayed, damp Kleenex. Pamela handed her a new one.

"I didn't suggest that she'd run away from home, Beth. Kids just get wild ideas sometimes. Did you check with Mrs. Gorman? If Jay's missing too, then that could pretty well explain things."

Beth resented the implication. "Nancy's a good girl. And I did talk to Rita. Jay got out of the hospital yesterday afternoon. He was home last night when I called over there, which she apparently wasn't too happy about . . . she said he looks terrible. But he said he hadn't seen Nancy."

Pamela forced another swallow of tepid black coffee down her throat. "I see. Well, I guess you're just going to have to wait. Are the police doing anything?"

"They were going to check around that church, and the homes of those four men. But if they'd found anything, I would have known by now. What I can't understand is why Nancy didn't say anything about what they'd done; we thought she was in school all day. They came right out and admitted they'd taken her by force to that church."

"Then it stands to reason they would confess if they knew where she was now."

"Well, they're not getting out of jail before she's found, I can promise you that. Roger's ready to murder the lot of them."

The mention of Roger's name brought a fresh pang of guilt to Pamela's heart. She knew then that she would never see him again. Not in that context, anyway. The affair was over; it should never have begun. She remembered the first time with him. Compared to sex with Harold, the experience had been cataclysmic. She'd had no idea her body could respond in such a way. Perhaps the forbiddenness had had something to do with it, but her best friend's husband was unquestionably a sexual dynamo. Her own husband probably thought cunnilingus was some kind of toe fungus. She brought herself, sadly, back to the present. "Would you like a drink? I think you could use one." She knew she certainly could.

Lost her soul for nothing!

"I was thinking of fixing myself a brandy."

She traded it for your health, you secret, disgusting lush! And guess who handled the transaction!

The leukemia! Remember? The doctors said you had leukemia, leukemia, and there was no hope, none at all, except for Morganna Ober, Morganna Ober and her witchcraft, Morganna Ober and those special pancakes she brought you for breakfast that morning . . .

No! Not true, not true! There was nothing in those pancakes!

"No thanks," Beth sniffed. "I guess I should get back home." She gazed wistfully at Pamela's ultramodern living room and added, "You're so lucky. I wish I could have a home like this."

Pamela almost offered to trade homes with her, if husbands and kids were thrown in on the deal, but she couldn't quite bring herself to make such a stab at jocularity; she was afraid it would sound like a confession of some sort. She said instead, "Let me know the minute you hear anything."

But Pammie's well now, and that's all that matters!

Beth nodded tearfully.

* * *

The fly crawled lazily over the open eyeball; Spiro wondered why his mother didn't shoo it away. He reached over and did it for her, then went back to studying the straight razor he reverently held in his left hand, his right still too tender to handle anything. It was so very simple. Just put on Bruce's mask. Of course. He should have thought of that himself.

He glowered as he remembered the scene he had witnessed earlier through Lana's bedroom window. They had been getting ready to do it, to fuck. The idea angered him greatly. Spiro wanted to do that with Lana. And soon, very soon, he would. When he was wearing the mask. She would think he was Bruce and she would gladly open her legs for him. A smile spread over Spiro's thick lips. His scrotum began to crawl. He could hardly wait.

"You plannin' to put your thing up in her, boy?"

Spiro glanced guiltily at his mother's corpse. "No, Mama."

"Don't you lie to me, boy. I know what you're thinking. You go turn on that stove, now, and get it red hot. Then you're gonna put those lyin' lips down on it."

"Please, Mama, no . . ." He couldn't understand; she had let him draw the pictures. She had even been pleased. It had been her idea about the mask. Why was she going to punish him now?

"I promise I won't do it, Mama. I promise." Gripping the razor, he accidentally cut one of his fingers. He automatically popped the wounded digit in his mouth and began to suck.

"Go turn on that stove, boy, or I'll make you cut your nasty thing off."

Then he suddenly understood. She didn't want him to do it to Lana; she wanted him to do it to her. She always had. He put the razor blade down on the rickety coffee table and began to unzip his pants, which were already bulging in front.

"That's my good boy. You come to Mama now. Mama loves you."

Spiro kneeled on the floor, then slowly shoved his pants down over his pimpled buttocks until they were around his knees, and moved closer. One thing was sure.

In the future he'd have to do his thinking a lot more quietly. He didn't want to make Mama jealous.

Lana glanced at the wall clock over the bookshelves and sighed. "My brat brother will be home shortly. Let's get outta here."

"Where you wanna go? Vegas? My Gramma Meadows sent me an extra ten dollars this month."

Lana snickered. "Ten? Well, let's go to Paris, then. By the way, what's ol' Sharon Valley High do when you don't show up for your classes? My mom'll kill me if she finds out I ditched today."

"Never fear, my dear." Bruce stood up and stretched, thinking of the two joints he had left in his glove compartment. He wanted to get high, but he had promised himself he would save the last of it for his birthday the following Sunday. Happy Birthday to me. "I never did explain why they call me Apple Head, did I?"

"Come to think of it, no. You just said they didn't call you that because you're smart."

Bruce held up an index finger. "Ah, but what kind of smart? Book smart . . . well, I gotta admit I'm kind of low-key there . . . don't want people thinking I'm trying to show off or anything, right?"

Lana tossed a look at the ceiling. "I think you're pretty safe there."

"But in other ways, I have no qualms about showing my stuff, seeing as how it benefits all. You are looking at the number-one admit-slip bandito. I take an accomplice —usually Duck—into the office with me, right? Duck creates a disturbance, which he's really good at, and while Greer's secretary is like, picking up the papers Duck accidentally on purpose knocked off her desk or something, I grab a couple of admit-slip pads from the back shelf. Every sheet is worth a dollar too. We make a killing. You see, they don't call your parents or anything if you're just absent, but the only way you can get back in class is with an admit slip, which normally you can only get if your parents have called the school to excuse you. I think the school nurse will call after three consecutive days or something to make sure you haven't croaked; they wanna be sure to get all the paperwork taken care of.

242

Students kicking the bucket is a real hassle. Anyway, like I said, never fear, the Apple Head is here. Admit slips have a little apple in the top left corner."

Lana thought the scam was hilarious. "And your gramma sends you money every month too, huh? You must be gettin' rich."

A dark aura momentarily settled over Bruce's features. "Yeah, my gramma's one nice lady. Still writes my dad every day. My real dad. He's back in prison."

"Bruce, I'm sorry . . . I didn't mean to—"

"Don't worry about it." He quickly snapped out of his morbid trance and ruffled her hair. "I should have told you before. My Gramma Meadows is the only person that really gives a shit about me. I don't really like taking the money, but it makes her feel good to give it, you know? So I let her give, figure if I don't take it, she'll just send it in to some greedmonger TV evangelist. Come on, let's go to the park."

"Bruce." She tugged at his shirt and forced him to look around. "She's not the only person who gives a shit about you."

He blinked back an embarrassing tear. "Thanks, Lana. That means a lot."

There were three teenaged boys huddled in the parking lot behind Larry Kessler's van. Bruce pulled up next to it and parked. As soon as he and Lana stepped out, Larry waved them over.

"Hey, you guys cut today? Didn't see you in fourth hour, Bruce. Heard the news yet?"

Bruce put his arm around Lana. He saw how the other guys were checking her out. No problem, just as long as they knew she was his girl. "What news is that?"

"Greer, man. Bought it right at his desk this morning. Brain hemorrhage, they said."

Bruce's eyes bulged. "Bought it as in died, man?"

"As in deceased, kicked the bucket, croaked, rubbed out, turned into a stiff—"

"Okay, I get the picture." Bruce and Lana exchanged disturbed glances.

"But that ain't all," Larry went on in a husky whisper. "Guess who was in his office right before it happened?"

"Is this a trick question?"

"Marla Mingee, dude. Marla the witch. I passed her in the hall today, and I thought she'd died . . . looked like she'd had her makeup done at a funeral parlor. And when she saw me, I like, felt this radical electric buzz in my head. She's ate up with the Devil, bad. You saw *The Exorcist* . . . well, we also heard she pissed right in her seat yesterday in sixth hour, just like Linda Blair. We've been talking about maybe, uh, burning her at the stake."

"What!" Bruce and Lana both shouted simultaneously.

"That's what you're supposed to do to witches," said a tall, muscular boy on Larry's right named Matt Lowery. He was the S.V. High Cougar's star quarterback. Lana recognized the other youth as Joel Mintern, the one who had been fighting with Dennis in the parking lot at school. Joel still had a black eye.

As Bruce patiently explained to Matt, Larry, and Joel why they couldn't go around burning people at the stake, Lana remembered the revolting experience at the drive-in that morning. The weird odor on Jay's breath had reminded her of burned electrical wires. The one moment in which she'd made eye contact with him . . . hadn't she felt a slight jolt? And oh God, his face, his face . . .

Matt was voicing his rebuttal. "There isn't a law in this land says you can't kill a witch; that's against the bible. It's our duty."

"We thought we'd get Nancy too, while we were at it," Joel added, "but apparently she's MIA. There were some detectives at the school this morning asking questions about her."

Bruce couldn't believe what he was hearing. Surely they were just shitting him. They couldn't seriously be thinking about burning Marla and Nancy at the stake, for Chrissakes, not in South Dakota USA in this day and age. Sure, that was it . . . let's see how gullible Bruce is today. Ha ha. He decided to play along with the joke. "Well, maybe it's not such a bad idea after all. You gonna burn Dr. Doom too? He looks about as bad as you say Marla does. When we passed him in the hall Tuesday afternoon, his eyes were like laser guns, and when he turned 'em on me, I thought my brain was gonna melt. And I could hear him telling me telepathically to *shit my pants!* I almost did it too."

The three guys seemed genuinely impressed. "Are you fucking serious?" Matt asked, eyes wide.

"Do native Africans have kinky hair?"

"You guys are bein' ridiculous," Lana felt compelled to say, but she wasn't at all sure how true her statement was. She kept seeing Jay and recalling how she'd kept thinking that something was wrong, wrong, terribly wrong with him, and there was more to it than just the way he looked. But witches? No, no . . . witches were only people who worshiped the Devil and practiced black magic. They looked just like anyone else. They could be your next door neighbors or the librarian or the police chief's wife; anybody. They couldn't be distinguished because they looked like corpses or pus factories.

And now she'd learned that Nancy was missing. Jay would have been one of the first to know about it, yet he'd said he and Nancy would pick them up tomorrow night for the party. How could he have said that if he didn't know where she was?

Something was going on. Maybe not what everyone thought, but definitely something, something bad . . . and until she and Bruce found out what was what, no way in hell were they going to that little "party."

Suddenly Larry started laughing. "You should see the looks on your faces, man," he guffawed, and his two companions joined in.

"We were just putting you on," Matt said. "We're really sure we're gonna burn people at the stake. You think we wanna spend the rest of our lives in prison?"

"G'wan." Bruce waved, shaking his head. "We knew you were shitting us. Get outta here." He started leading Lana toward the gazebo. When they were out of earshot of the van, he muttered through the side of his mouth, "I don't think they were kidding at all."

Lana squeezed his hand. "Neither do I."

Twenty-Three

After completing the damage estimate on a late model Mercedes Benz, Carol was asked by the car's owner, Sidney Grace, an attractive, graying man with gentle blue eyes, to have a few drinks with him after she got off work. Her first impulse was to tell him thanks but no thanks, but she found herself answering, "Sure, I'd love to."

Her wounded ego needed CPR, she told herself after he'd left, promising to return for her at precisely five P.M. She wasn't ready to get involved, but the attentions of such a distinguished-looking man couldn't hurt anything, so long as he didn't launch into a bitter spiel about his ex-wife or start groping for her under the table. She found that by the time five rolled around, she was honestly looking forward to the date.

He took her to the Gold Mine lounge, where they found themselves a corner table near the back. The motif inside the establishment was rustic, the walls made of ancient, rough-hewn timber. They were decorated with tarnished vestiges of the big gold-mining days: picks, rock bolts, carbide lanterns, methane detectors, sluice boxes, drill rods, mining hats, frayed coils of rope. A sledgehammer near the exit had a sign underneath that warned it was used on people who tried to walk their tab. Strategic pinpoints of light illuminated the relics, and candles burned on all the tables. Still, the large room was fairly dark.

"Quite an interesting place," Carol commented after they were seated.

Her companion nodded. "It is indeed. I like it; it's

quiet. The younger crowd stays away; that's what I like most about it."

She smiled, absorbing the soft music being piped over their heads, the relaxing atmosphere of the club, the gentle blue eyes reflecting the candle's flame. The scantily-clad cocktail waitress arrived to take their orders. Carol ordered a tequila sunrise; Sid, a scotch and soda.

Two hours passed before Carol realized it. She had become totally engrossed in the man sitting across from her. He made no mention of ex-wives, kept his hands to himself, never steered the conversation toward intimate subjects. He had a broad knowledge of politics, history, and business, and he amazed her with his capacity to remember detail. She partly blamed the alcohol—she wasn't much of a drinker, and three sunrises on an empty stomach had loosened her up to the point of falling apart—but the obvious quality of the man himself had much to do with the fact that she suddenly realized, much to her surprise, that she wanted to go to bed with him. It wasn't her style at all, but she couldn't deny her feelings. And it had been so very long . . .

It was also getting late, but she'd called Luke before leaving the office and had warned him not to expect her home soon, and to have Lana fix their supper. Carol impulsively reached out and put her hand over Sid's and said softly, "Could we . . . go to your place?" She'd actually said it. Her face grew warm. She felt like a wanton predator.

Sid sandwiched her hand in both of his. "I thought you'd never ask."

The sex was wonderful. Sid was gentle, sensuous, and romantic. Carol didn't feel like an alley cat, as she always had supposed she would under such circumstances. She'd dated Hugh a year and a half before they had finally become intimate—and wouldn't you know, she'd conceive that very first time, in the backseat of his dad's Thunderbird—and he was the only lover she'd ever had . . . until now. But thanks to the alcohol in her system, she'd been able to give herself fully, unabashedly to another man on their *first date,* and Sid had made his appreciation known. Several times she had caught herself fantasizing that it was Hugh inside of her, which had brought on mixed, mostly unpleasant emotions, but her body was definitely having a good time, and the bad spells only lasted a few seconds apiece. Afterward she lay spent on Sid's king-sized bed, peaceful and satisfied. Given a little more time, she thought she might actually be able to fall in love with this man.

He gave her an affectionate pat on the rump through the sheet and got up to get dressed. She groaned in protest. "Why are you gettin' up? I'm not finished with you yet."

"I'm sorry, Carol," he apologized, "but my wife's flight is due in about half an hour. I'm going to be late as it is."

Carol felt the blood drain from her face. "Your . . . wife?"

He stopped for a moment and looked at her coldly. "You didn't know I was married?"

She sat up and clutched the sheet around her chin, the good feelings instantly replaced by shame and humiliation. "You neglected to mention that one little detail," she spat fiercely, terrified that she might cry.

He resumed buttoning his shirt and shrugged. "For all I knew, you were married too. What difference does it make? We both got what we wanted. Why should you be upset?"

Carol was too angry to respond. She wanted to grab the lamp off the table beside her and hurl it at him. But instead she just sat there shaking, injecting poison darts into him with her eyes, feeling like the cheapest slut on earth. She would have given her soul for the ability to shrug the experience off, think no more of it than she would shampooing her hair. To say, and really mean it, something like: "Yeah, I got what I wanted, an' it was okay, I guess. I've had better, but I've also had a lot worse." She waited until he had finished dressing and was gone from the room before she crawled out from under the sheet and put her own clothes back on, the effects of the inhibition-killing alcohol all but vanished. Before walking out, she used the bedroom extension to call for a cab. She would be damned before she'd allow him to drive her back to the office where she'd left her car. Damned for eternity! She went into the bathroom and wrote in lipstick across the mirror, YOU WEREN'T ALL THAT GREAT, HONEY. A little message for Sid's wife.

God help any male pedestrians who might be crossing the street as she drove home from the office.

Lana's bedroom door was thrown open with such ferocity that the knob made a dent in the wall behind it. Bruce and Lana both jumped. "God, Mom, what's with you?"

"I believe it's time for your friend to go home," Carol said harshly from the doorway. "An' I would appreciate it if he was over here a lot less often."

Bruce had a revelation; he was being thrown out. And far be it from him to stay where he wasn't wanted. That's why he was hardly ever at home. He released Lana's hand and stood up.

Lana glared at her mother hotly. "How dare you? I can have him over here as often an' as long as I want. An' if I can't, then you're gonna start seein' a lot less of me."

"You talk to me in that tone of voice anymore, young lady, and you'll spend the next month in your bedroom. Don't you dare make threats to me. Until you're eighteen years old I can tell you what you can or cannot do, and you will obey me or you'll be gravely sorry. Do I make myself clear?"

Carol dared her daughter to challenge her authority. The guilt trip was over. It was Lash-Out time.

Bruce hadn't been planning to get in the middle of this, but at that moment his tongue seemed to have other ideas. It said (politely, of course): "Mrs. Bremmers, I guess you might not appreciate this, but you don't own Lana. She's her own person, you know? She's got rights."

Carol lunged forward, her right hand landing with a loud smack on Bruce's left cheek. Lana started to scream.

"I hate you, hate you! I haven't done a damn thing! Why are you doin' this?"

"Get out," Carol hissed at Bruce. "You're quite right, I

don't appreciate some delinquent young smartass tellin' me how to be a mother. Lana's too good for you anyway."

Lana tried to shove past her mother to leave with Bruce, but Carol restrained her with an iron grasp. "You're not goin' anywhere."

Lana was mad enough to strike her mother, but the taboo against it was too strong. She flung herself down on the bed and continued to scream out her rage. Carol pulled Lana's door shut behind her and stalked after Bruce, but he hurried through the living room and was out the front door before she could say anything else to him. As far as he was concerned, she'd already said quite enough.

The night air was chill, almost frosty. Bruce stumbled blindly toward his truck, unable to see clearly because his eyes were stinging fiercely with tears. His cheek throbbed. He got into the cab and closed the door, then promptly proceeded to open the glove compartment. To hell with his birthday. Eat, drink, smoke marijuana, and be merry . . . now, for that is all there is and all there will ever be. Live for the moment, because the next one may be your last.

He and Lana had gotten into quite a conversation before being so rudely interrupted. It had started at the park, and like a snowball rolling downhill, had gotten bigger and more lopsided on the way. They had convinced themselves that people around them had been invaded by alien beings—just like in *Body Snatchers!*—and their only chance for survival would be to run away to an island somewhere in the Pacific. Bruce had saved almost five hundred dollars; that would get them by for a while. What else could they do? Tell a story like that to the police? Not hardly.

Bruce lit one of the joints and dragged deeply. Three hits later he was smiling again. *Invasion of the Body Snatchers.* Now their ideas seemed rather funny to him, all but the part about running away to an island. That he could handle; they could create their own blissful paradise, just like the young lovers in *Blue Lagoon.* Yes, yes . . .

Nobody around to tell him how worthless he was, or that he wasn't good enough for her daughter. Only Lana, her angel face and dazzling smile. That such a beautiful girl as she would actually care about him was so amazing. He still couldn't quite believe it. He only hoped she cared half as much for him as he did for her. That would be more than he would ever need.

He reached into his jeans pocket for his keys and started the pickup's noisy engine, then turned on the custom-made stereo system which he himself had designed, built, and installed. Boston's "More than a Feeling" blared through the speakers. Must be oldie night, he thought to himself. But the tune sank into him, vibrating him with a comforting rhythm. He had to agree; it was more than a feeling. He now felt capable of handling Home Sweet Home.

He put the transmission in gear and drove off, accidentally mashing too hard on the accelerator, resulting in the squeal of tires. Lana's mother would probably think he'd done it on purpose, his last great act of defiance or something. Probably strengthen her resolve to keep him away from her daughter. She was going to have a hell of a time doing that.

He stopped at the corner of Teakwood and Briar Lane behind a battered blue Nova which bore a yellow bumper sticker in the rear window: Shit Happens. Bruce saluted the unknown driver with his joint. "It sure does, buddy. All the time."

The Nova made a left turn and sped away. Bruce pulled to a lazy halt behind the stop sign and decided to finish off the whole hooter before going on. He was almost high to the point of passing out when he heard a scraping noise in the bed of his truck. He jumped, looking over his shoulder through the cab's rear window.

The intersection was illuminated by a single mercury streetlamp on the opposite corner, and only gave him a good view of the tailgate. He raised up and peered into the shadows beneath the window, wondering if a dog or cat had decided to hitch a ride with him. It had happened before; he'd been heading for the park from the drive-in when he'd caught a glimpse of a monstrous black head in his rearview mirror, which had startled him so much he'd jumped the curb and smashed smack dab into a U.S. mailbox. The Labrador had bailed out, leaving Bruce alone to deal with the trouble. He had shouted after the wagging tail, shaking his fist, "Thanks *so fucking much!*" just as a patrol car pulled up behind him, red and blue lights flashing. Damn cops everywhere when you didn't want them, but just try finding one in an emergency. It could have been worse, though. At least he'd been out of pot at the time, or he would have had it on him—and oh, did they search his pickup, hoping to bust him on a DUI. But that hadn't eased his punishment with the belt-wielding maniac his mother was married to. The only time Bruce had received a worse beating was the time he got caught selling raffle tickets for an nonexistent drawing. But hell, what twelve-year-old boy hadn't done something like that?

The truck rocked slightly, as if something heavy in the bed had just shifted its weight. Bruce strongly considered just turning back around in his seat and punching the accelerator, but he was going to have enough trouble trying to drive straight without expecting at any moment to see a hairy apparition pop up in his mirror.

Warily, he put the transmission in park and eased his door open. The street on either side of him was lined with small, identical houses, all brightly lit as families sat around the dinner table to thank God for filling their stomachs, as if He had punched the time clock forty-six times that month.

Bruce slowly moved along the side of his truck, muscles tensed, his legs ready for flight. But he was several tokes over the line, and he doubted his ability to run very far without tripping over his own feet. Not that he would actually need to run, of course.

More noise in the truck bed erased any trace of doubt; something was definitely back there. Heart hammering, Bruce pursed his lips and tried to whistle, but his mouth and throat were too dry, and all that came out was a hiss. He gave up and called out softly, "Hey pooch, why don'cha introduce yourself? I don't usually pick up hitchers, but I might make an exception if you're—"

The word "nice" stuck in Bruce's throat as he watched

the incredibly large, dark mound begin to rise above the bed wall. At first he was willing to believe it was a Saint Bernard, but a slab of pink skin caught in the street light vanquished that idea. It was definitely a biped, good old Homo sapiens. It was—

His good friend Spiro Guenther.

Twenty-Four

Paperwork had kept Detectives Louis Helm and Brent Phelps, his partner, late at the station that night. Sooner or later, they told themselves, they would learn not to let things pile up.

Helm had just hung up from a call that had him looking like he'd been selected by the IRS for an audit of his last twenty years' income. Phelps gazed up through a haze of pungent cigar smoke that encircled his desk like a gray wreath. "What is it, Lou?"

"Damn murder," Helm said, uttering a hearty belch. The Reuben sandwich he'd grabbed for dinner was beginning to avenge itself. "Some kid. You gonna accompany me to the scene?"

Phelps crushed out his cigar. "Damned right. Don't see much of that kind of action around here. Isn't the Snell girl, is it?"

Helm pushed away from his desk and motivated his body up and forward, releasing a puttering burst of flatulence which his partner ignored. Helm had made it clear early on that if Phelps could smoke cigars in the office, he could damn sure let wind whenever the urge presented itself. "No, it's a boy. And unidentifiable, from what I just heard. Gimme a hit of your firewater. I think I'm gonna need it."

Phelps leaned over to slide out the bottom drawer of his desk. He produced a half-empty bottle of Jack Daniel's and a shot glass. "Help yourself. So, what was it? Stabbing, shooting . . . ?"

"You'll see when we get there," Helm muttered, pouring two fingers and tossing it back. "I'm not ready to talk about it just yet."

Bruce's body, naked and shimmering in golden light, was poised over hers; now he entered her body and rocked with gentle motion, his lips nuzzling her neck and shoulders. Lana moved her hips upward to meet his thrusts, a low moan escaping her throat. He whispered, "You feel so good."

Drowning in ecstasy, she opened her eyes to look at him. He gazed down at her adoringly, driving himself in deeper. So perfect, so perfect. But then the picture began to change. His face, as she stared at it, began to crack and peel. Blood oozed from the cracks and fell onto her cheeks.

When his eyes popped out and dangled over her own, she screamed and sat up, her heart jumping madly. Just a dream. Bruce wasn't there; no one was there. She took several deep breaths and glanced at the lighted digits on her clock radio. Ten past midnight.

She listened to the silence. Apparently she hadn't actually screamed out loud. That was good. Wouldn't want the Bitch to lose any of her precious sleep. Nor Luke, the little viper.

She knew why she'd had such a horrible dream. The way Jay Gorman looked. The things she and Bruce had talked about all afternoon and evening. Aliens. Able to assume the guise of a human being by forcing the human soul out. But something about their presence in the earthly flesh made terrible things happen to it; made it look dead or chronically diseased . . .

It was possible, wasn't it? What was a better explanation, especially with all the weird rumors going around? Lana remembered her father's wise words of advice: never assume. To assume makes an ASS out of U and ME. Therefore, an investigation was called for. Or rather, the continuation of the investigation they had allowed Jay to talk them out of persuing.

What better time than the present . . . but she would have to do it alone. She still hadn't the foggiest idea where Bruce lived, and it was too late to call his house. And there was no use looking for his address in the phone book, since the listing was under his parents' last name, and he'd never mentioned what their last name was. But she could do it alone. She was in a defiant mood anyway.

She slipped out of bed and got dressed as noiselessly as possible. She wasn't sure what she expected to find, but if things were as weird as they seemed, she would surely uncover some evidence. Maybe she would find some giant pods. Or a small spaceship. Something.

She groped in the dark until she got to the kitchen, where she located the light above the stove and clicked it on. But by mistake she pushed the wrong switch and the ventilation fan responded with an incredibly loud roar. She cursed under her breath and turned it off, then waited tensely for her mother to come barreling down the hallway wanting to know what the hell she was up to. Carol didn't come. Lana finally relaxed. A little.

She took the telephone directory down from the top of the refrigerator and opened it on the stove, after managing to flip the correct switch for the light under the grease hood. She thumbed through the pages until she came to the ones headed Mitchell-Mooney. Her finger trailed over the column of listings until it stopped in the middle of the first page. Montgomery, Albert T., 2819 Teaberry. Memorizing the address, she turned to the back of the directory to look it up on the map. If something unnatural had really happened, he had been the first victim. And when conducting a serious investigation, it was best to start at the beginning.

She closed the phone book and replaced it, then took her mother's extra set of car keys from the hook next to the garage door.

A block from the house she began to breathe a little easier. The hard part—getting this far without waking her mother—was over. Snooping wasn't so difficult. She drove slowly through the dark, sleeping streets, proud of herself for being so brave.

Teaberry, when she found it, turned out to be a cul-de-sac; Montgomery's house was located at the end. Lana parked in front of a house two doors down and got out.

She'd only worn her jean jacket for protection against

the cold, and it was not enough. Shivering visibly, she crept along the dark, quiet street, the residents thereof all nestled snugly in their beds, and asked herself what in blazing tarnation she was doing out there in the middle of the night, sneaking around a strange man's house. The closer she got to Montgomery's house, the more her bravery began to look like sheer stupidity. Looking for giant pods? Seriously, now. Did she really expect to peek through the garage windows and see a saucer-shaped aircraft hovering about the tire tools, strange lights blinking on and off?

No, but she sincerely hoped to. How exciting could you get? As long as there was no harm to her personally, or to anyone she loved. Not that she would want anyone to get hurt, but it happened anyway, every hour of every day. Someone she didn't know was being murdered or raped, robbed, tortured . . . she mused at how desensitized she had become to such news. It affected her no more than hearing the weather report. Those people weren't real to her. They were nothing but faceless characters who had been written out of a play she had never seen.

But if she found out something terrible was going on, that Sharon Valley was under some kind of alien attack, and exposed it, then maybe she could save a few. How guilty she would feel if she hadn't checked it out when she had the chance, and as a result hundreds of innocent people ended up suffering. Then again, maybe she was under a completely false alarm. It all boiled down to one thing: investigate. Prove or disprove.

Her breath made white plumes in the air as she walked. Slowing to a snail's pace as she reached Montgomery's property line, she gazed up at the house. It was the only two-story on the block, painted beige with burgundy trim. All of the windows were dark. The garage windows had been painted over.

Glancing nervously up the street, she stepped onto the lawn, the dead grass crunching beneath her feet. She was headed for the side of the garage, hoping to find an unlocked door.

When the knob twisted easily, her heart skipped a beat. Now that she was down to the nitty-gritty, she was more frightened than she had ever been in her life. For the first time since this cockamamie idea had occurred to her, she fully realized the personal danger she might be in. If . . . And if the if was true, it was possible that those things never slept . . .

But she opened the garage door anyway. The air that greeted her was warm and musty. The odor was an assault but the warmth an invitation, and she cautiously stepped inside, all senses on the alert. Her eyes swept the darkness which revealed no shapes. Only the smell had a shape; it conjured a vision of something huge and round, like a giant moldy sponge rotting in a corner. Lana swore at herself for not bringing a flashlight. Thinking of one reminded her of watching Dennis disappear into the woods on top of Beacon Hill. She wouldn't have gone with him for a million dollars.

And yet here she was, without light and all alone in what might turn out to be a place infinitely more dangerous than an old abandoned cemetery. Could it be that her mind perceived aliens as that much easier to deal with than dead people? Sometimes she just couldn't figure herself out. Her duplicity, like her dependency, was unquestionably hereditary. But, of course, there was another major difference in the two experiences. She hadn't heard any screams in the house. Not yet anyway.

She groped along the wall for a light switch. She found one and flipped it, even though it didn't seem a very smooth thing to do. A professional sleuth would never do it, that was for certain. A professional would have brought along a penlight with extra batteries. And a camera, and a tape recorder and a gun. Or at least a sharp knife.

Maybe she wasn't really doing this. Maybe she was only dreaming that she was. At this very moment her body could be lying peacefully under a pink comforter, her eyelids fluttering with REMs. Hopefully she wasn't really this big a fool.

But the room before her seemed real enough. The switch had turned on a single bulb near the ceiling. Its glow was dull; probably only forty watts, Lana thought. If that.

It revealed in its subtle way something like a garbage

museum. There were countless stacks of old newspapers, dismantled exercise equipment, threadbare tires, shelves crammed full of every type of junk imaginable. No wonder he painted the windows over, she thought; the place was a pit.

No hovering aircraft, she noted.

No pods. Unless . . .

Her eyes were drawn to one of the far corners. There was a large green lump; something covered by a blanket. She wrapped her arms around herself and slowly shuffled toward it. The smell, the smell . . .

It was getting stronger.

Grocery garbage, that was it. But why would he have covered it with a blanket? He was throwing it away too? It looked perfectly good to her, at least, what she could see of it. (Could be a pod, looks about the right shape . . .) She was close now. Two more steps and the tips of her tennis shoes would touch the blanket's border. Then all she would have to do was bend over, pick up the blanket, and look (and scream) at the sacks of putrid garbage. That's all that was under there. She was sure of it. Sarah Sylvia Cynthia Snout had just not taken the garbage out. Shame on you, Sarah.

Unable to stand the suspense any longer, she stepped forward and picked up the border of the blanket, but hadn't raised it very high when her eyes fell on something that made her blood chill. She froze, her brain frantically attempting to absorb the impact.

This was a only a bad dream. Had to be. Two sets of shoes. Two sets of shoes attached to four white ankles attached to—

"Well, good evening."

Lana felt like she'd just hit the ground after falling off a ten-story building. She spun around, her heart exploding with fear. She'd been caught!

It was wearing a dark suit that Albert Montgomery had ordered from a discount catalog in 1967, its arms folded casually, its body leaned against the doorframe between the house and garage. There was an amused smile on its chalky, grotesque mouth, but all Lana could see were its eyes. They held her spellbound, unable to move or speak. Unable to scream.

Blue flame. Burning, searing, searching . . .

"You were close," it said, its voice a distorted bass, as if it were speaking underwater. "You're a very brave girl, coming here like this all alone, in the dead of night . . . Oh, speaking of dead, those feet you were looking at belong to Nancy Snell and Eliza Ober. Or should I say used to belong? I daresay they won't have any further use for them. But I am being rude. Please, come with me into the house. It's much more comfortable."

Lana no longer had any more control over her body than she did the 747 she could hear flying far overhead. Her brain had entered another state of consciousness altogether. Sometime when she hadn't been paying attention, an invisible doctor had come up behind her with a hypodermic needle and injected her with a big dose of Demerol; it was just like the time she was being wheeled into surgery to have her broken arm set. Her fear had melted into blissful apathy. Montgomery could have been inviting her to her own execution and she couldn't have cared any less.

The demon Nephyrcai backed into the house, keeping her captive with its sparkling, magnetic eyes, and she complacently followed, fully aware of what was happening but unable to bring herself to react in any way.

Twenty-Five

The sun rose with its usual laziness on the morning of October 31. Birds everywhere chirped their usual songs, debating in treetop committee meetings which southern location they would go to this fall. Alarm clocks went off, eyes blinked, bodies stretched.

From an airplane that morning Sharon Valley would have looked like a big bowl of gray soup. A cloud had settled into it like a hen upon her nest, blocking out the sun, making visibility less than five yards. Driving was next to impossible. Standing outside was like being in a cold sauna.

Faces peeked out of windows, mouths opened in surprise. It was not unusual for fog to settle in the valley, but it wasn't often so thick. In cases such as this, the town was virtually paralyzed. The workers would have to wait until the sun burned it off before business could proceed as usual. Many climbed gratefully back into still-warm beds. Those who worked graveyard shifts moaned in despair, knowing their replacements wouldn't be able to come in.

Carol opened her eyes, the depression she'd gone to sleep with returning full force with consciousness. The events of the previous evening, recorded on mental videotape, began the day's schedule of reruns. The cheap little affair she'd had was believable; the way she'd taken her anger out on Lana and Bruce was not. How could she have been such a bitch? Lana might never forgive her—and with good cause—but Carol had to at least acknowledge what a monster she'd been, perhaps even make a

261

confession about the situation that had triggered such behavior.

And let that be a lesson to you!

But she knew she could never bring herself to ever tell anyone about it; she had been humiliated enough. Damn her Victorian upbringing. She swung her legs over the side of the bed and grudgingly sat up. Her room, she noticed, was unusually dark for that time of the morning. Had to be cloudy outside. How appropriate.

After putting on her robe and slippers, she finger-combed her blond wedge and went to beg her daughter's forgiveness. *It's all your father's fault, you see. I never acted that way before the divorce, did I? No, because I was a human being then, with a real sense of self-worth and everything, and a husband to sleep with every night. Just like Barbie and Ken, who lived happily ever after in their Mattel Dream House.*

But Lana's room was empty. Cold fingers of fear crept up Carol's spine. Lana was just up early, that was all. She was probably in the kitchen eating a bowl of Frosted Mini Wheats. She was here somewhere. She wouldn't have run . . . away.

But Lana was not in the kitchen either, or in the garage or bathroom or any other part of the house. And if she was outside, she would be invisible. Carol couldn't believe the view through the living room window; solid white. She'd never seen such a fog in her life.

It increased her panic a hundredfold. If Lana had run off, it would be impossible to even try to look for her. To tell her that Bruce was welcome anytime, hell . . . he could spend the night if he wanted to. Why not? Why should the tradition of prudery and inhibition be carried on? Just please, please come home . . .

Her first course of action should be to call Bruce's house, naturally. Lana was probably there, unless he was also gone, and God only knew where the two of them would have gone together. There was only one problem with taking that first course of action. Carol didn't even know Bruce's last name.

Fighting to stay as calm as possible, she went to wake her son. Luke was a militant sleeper. Carol had always claimed that a bomb could go off in the room where he was sleeping and he wouldn't know it. It took her several minutes to bring him around to the cold, cruel world of reality. He pouted, rubbing his eyes. "I'm still sleepy."

"It's not time for you to get up yet," Carol said shakily, "I just need to ask you somethin', darlin', then you can go back to sleep for a while. Do you know Bruce's last name?"

He frowned with irritation and kicked under the blanket. "No. Now lemme alone, I was havin' a good dream."

Carol patted her son on the thigh before tiptoeing out, now fully overcome with dread and a fresh supply of guilt. She'd been so wrapped up in self-pity that she hadn't even bothered to learn Lana's boyfriend's last name. That was pretty rotten.

So what now? Call the police? They wouldn't be able to look for Lana, any more than she could. With the thin hope that maybe, just maybe, Lana had gone for a little walk and would come back through the front door any minute—if she could find it—Carol went to the kitchen for an aspirin and to start a strong pot of coffee. It was when she reached into the cabinet next to the refrigerator for the Extra Strength Excedrin that she noticed her extra car keys were missing from the pegboard.

Hugh's voice sounded gratingly cheerful. "Carol! Say, if you're callin' about the check, I swear I mailed it two days ago . . ."

Carol clutched the phone, stifling a sob. "It's Lana, Hugh."

The cheerfulness vanished. "What about her? She's all right, isn't she? Carol?"

"I think . . . I think she may have run away. I came down pretty hard on her last night . . ."

"Damn it! Have you called the police?"

"It wouldn't do any good. It's pea soup outside . . . I can't even see the posts on the front porch. If she's out tryin' to drive in this—"

"She took your car?"

"I think so. The extra keys are missin'—" Carol bit her lower lip, trying to stop the flow of tears, but they gushed out in spite of her. She began to sob openly. "I'm sorry, I had . . . had to talk to somebody, but there's nothin' you can do. I don't know what to do. Hugh, I'm scared."

"Do you want me to fly up?"

Carol came close to shooting back, *Would you be bringin' your damn little bimbo along with you?* but she answered calmly instead, "Well, ah . . . that's very thoughtful of you, thank you. I don't know. We should probably wait. Maybe she'll come home after the fog clears up."

"You don't have any idea where she could be?"

"Well, maybe, but . . ." *But I don't know the kid's damn last name! See what you've done to me, you bastard!* ". . . but their phone is busy. I'll call you back as soon as I know anything."

"I'll be here most of the day. If you call an' I'm gone, leave a message with my secretary. She'll know where to find me."

Carol thanked him again and hung up, thinking, *Yeah, I'll just bet she will.*

Her wrists and ankles hurt, and it took Lana a few moments to figure out why. Each limb was tightly secured by a piece of rope that was also attached to each of the four posts of the bed on which she lay. In the cool dimness she could see a doily-covered dresser with a cracked mirror, a wicker fan chair with a stained blue pillow on the seat, a small bookshelf full of dusty books, an ancient Singer, and two darkly-stained doors standing catty-corner on the opposite side of the room. One of them began to open. She shrank back when the shape of a man appeared in the doorway.

"Ah, I see you're awake. You slept well, I hope?"

"What are you gonna do to me?" she asked numbly, flexing her fingers. She tried not to look at the hideous face, but she couldn't help herself. The eyes willed her to look, to submit, to drop all defenses, to relax. They were impossible to resist. The terror she'd awakened with quickly faded away. She watched calmly as the malevolent creature entered the room.

"Your body will serve as the new temple for a High Priestess."

Lana languidly turned her head from side to side. "My body? Are you sayin' I'm gonna die?"

Nephyrcai moved closer to the bed, its reeking flesh fouling the already-stale air of the infrequently-used room, its inhuman gaze sinking more deeply into Lana's mind. "Die? No, not really. You will continue to exist. Consider yourself lucky, my dear. Your departure will be easy compared to those that follow. You see, the High Priestess Myrantha's wish to return gave us an irresistible opportunity to do the same. I'm sure you can understand. Our deepest wish is to destroy the usurpers of our world, destroy the Light. And we will. Then I suppose we will throw a little party. Join us, my dear. I think you could learn to appreciate our ways."

Now she knew. They weren't aliens. They were demons. She accepted the fact without emotion.

Before she could reply to the invitation invading her mind—*Join us, yes, just think of the pleasure*—another shape appeared in the doorway; Lana could see it from the corner of her eye. Only when it moved up next to the bed could she tell that it was Jay Gorman. Or what used to be Jay Gorman's body. Something else was using it now.

Its pitted flesh was crawling with maggots; only the eyes, the fiery blue orbs, remained untouched above the collarbone. When it opened its lips in a smile, a dozen or so ivory worms fell out.

"She's lovely," Nephyrcai commented smilingly to its decomposing comrade, reaching out to pull down the blanket with which Lana was covered. For the first time she realized that she was naked.

Azrahoth reached out to stroke her left breast. "She is indeed. And how sporting of her to come to us; I'm hardly presentable in public these days."

"What about the other? The boy?"

"He can't be found. An alternate selection has been made."

"Very good."

"I suppose it would be a shame not to take advantage of this flesh while I still have it."

"I was just thinking the same thing . . ."

"After you."

"No, go ahead."

"Well, if you insist." Leprous hands pulled down the zipper of Jay Gorman's faded jeans, then reached in and extracted a large flaccid penis covered with open sores, the tip oozing a thick yellow mucous. In an instant it became rigid as an arrow, its weeping eye pointed between Lana's outspread legs.

Her eyes widened. *Think of the pleasure* . . .

She heard the words echoing darkly in her mind, and an unexpected rush of heat flooded her body. Something deep within her cried against this outrage, this abomination of which she was about to become a part, but her flesh was burning; her body said yes.

Remember those three orgasms you had with Greg in the hayloft?

Lana smiled dreamily.

Well, you ain't seen nothin' yet.

Suddenly there was a flash of blue flame at the four bedposts and the ropes holding Lana's hands and feet were severed. A moment later her body slowly began to levitate off the mattress, her legs forced farther apart. She was dimly aware of muscle pain in her upper thighs, but there was a far more demanding ache between them. Its name was lust, and she had never experienced it this strongly before. It was like being in the grip of a powerful drug, and at the moment nothing mattered more than its satisfaction. Absolutely nothing.

She stopped rising when she became level with the jutting, diseased penis aimed at her from the foot of the bed. A leering smile crossed the demon's cracked lips, and a few more maggots tumbled out.

Then Lana was hurled forward, becoming impaled on the fetid erection. She subconsiously released a scream of ecstasy, and the demons began to laugh.

Twenty-Six

There was a tapping sound at the window. At first he thought it was part of his dream, but the persistence of the sound wakened him and he continued to hear it. Muttering "What the fuck?" under his breath, Dennis crawled out of bed for the second time that morning and stumbled toward the curtains covering his window. He parted them with both hands and stared at the face in the mist.

"What the hell are you doing out there?" He unlocked the window and raised it, allowing tendrils of the fog to creep into his bedroom. Clad only in his briefs, he shivered, waiting for her response.

"I need you to come with me, Dennis. Get dressed."

He opened his mouth to protest, but suddenly that seemed an unacceptable thing to do. He should do just as she asked. He got dressed and quietly climbed out the window.

She seemed certain of her step, even though he could barely see his feet. He followed like a trusting sheep being led to the slaughter, his hand locked in hers, his body feeling strangely warm although the air around him was quite cool. Half the time he walked with his eyes closed, and in those moments dreamed that he was being pulled through the outer stratosphere toward the sun. He was not afraid.

When they were about ten blocks away from his house, Vikael began to speak. "You're a real bastard, you know that? You think you're the center of the universe. The only reason you refuse to accept the supernatural is because such power threatens your 'supremacy.' You are the Controller, the User, the Manipulator; there simply cannot be anything in Heaven or Earth that can dictate to *you*. You're such a stupid fool. But a very pretty one, I'll grant you that. I used to be quite beautiful myself."

He felt no reason to argue. He opened his eyes and watched the palpable white mass roll past him; for all he knew, he was walking on another planet, or simply in the sky, over and through clouds, and the journey would last forever and ever. It was possible. He didn't care.

Vikael laughed maliciously. "Finding that dead rabbit sure gave you a run for your money, didn't it? You nearly shit your pants. I'm amazed that you got it under control; but then, your pride wouldn't allow for anything else. We understand pride; it goeth before a fall, they say."

An eternity later they approached the hazy outline of a two-story house. Vikael led him up the porch steps and through the front door. The world came sharply into focus for Dennis, almost to the point of being surrealistic. He stared at his surroundings with vague wonderment. Most of the furniture was old, but not old enough to be given the prestige of being called antique. Just outdated, worn, a sad tribute to the fifties. The couch was green vinyl with cracks along the seams revealing yellowed foam padding. The blond tiered end tables on either side of it were crammed full of magazines, *TV Guides,* folded newspapers showing the crossword section, the puzzles never to be completed. Next to the six-hundred-pound console television was a tarnished brass floor lamp with three bulbs of varied height, all glowing through brass colander shades. The hearth was fake and contained a mechanical pile of burning logs. It was not turned on. The pictures on the wall were mostly faded prints of floral arrangements, some of fruit. It was the living room of someone who refused to change with the times, and who was as miserly as he was stubborn, which was precisely why Albert Montgomery's wife had left him.

There was an uncarpeted staircase on the left. Vikael led Dennis up the creaking steps. When they reached the landing, they turned to the right and were greeted by two figures stepping out of a doorway. Dennis looked up and recognized Montgomery. Dr. Doom. The nickname seemed more than appropriate now; he might have just walked out of makeup to perform a role in a horror movie. But Dennis didn't react. He simply stared with genuine apathy at the cheesy skin turned brown in spots, the sagging nostrils, and the hint of two small lumps on either side of the upper forehead. Nephyrcai spread its palms in a gesture of welcome, and in doing so drew Dennis's attention to its hands. The fingernails were nearly an inch thick and grew to sharp points, giving them the appearance of bear claws. Its voice had become deep, echoing static.

"Ah, I see you've brought a friend over for a visit. How lovely. We must introduce him to our other guest."

"I believe they have already met." Vikael sneered, and Dennis turned to look down at the demon's face. He'd never noticed Marla was green before.

"What in God's name is this?" Beth's features were arranged in an expression of total disgust as she lifted the black fabric from her daughter's bottom dresser drawer. "I knew I smelled something bad in here. This is it. Now what the hell is it and where did she get it?"

Her husband threw up his hands. "Damnit, I don't know. It looks like a cloak of some kind. What difference does it make? It doesn't have anything to do with the fact that she's gone."

Beth dropped the garment on the floor and kicked it toward the doorway with her foot. "Are you so sure? I overheard a little gossip going on at the hospital; they didn't know I was standing just around the corner. What I heard made me angry, of course, but I really didn't dwell on it. Crazy rumors get started all the time, and they always die out. Go making a scene denying them and you'll just fan the fire. So I forgot about it. But now . . ."

"But now what?" Roger asked irritably. He had aged ten years in the last forty eight hours. Nancy was his only child. He'd have much preferred she'd been a boy, but she was doing him proud. Going to Princeton in the fall. Yes, she was one hell of a kid.

"That thing," Beth said, pointing to the cape with a shaky finger, "it smells . . . like something dead. The rumor I overheard was that Nancy had taken something from that tomb on Beacon Hill. Oh, my God . . ."

She suddenly put it together, her mind getting crushed in the process. "Remember . . . oh God, remember she asked if we'd taken anything from her room? An old book? Jesus, Roger, that's what they said she took."

"So that tells us where she is?"

"It might," she quivered. "Roger, we've got to go up there."

"For Chrissakes, why? Besides, we're not going anywhere until that fog clears up. We'd end up in Canada."

"You can do what you want, but I'm going. This is the only lead we've got."

Roger blew out a sallow breath and nodded bleakly. "We'd better wear our coats. We'll have to walk."

They sat across from each other at the kitchen table exchanging glares. Harold took another swig of black coffee and raised an eyebrow. "So where the hell is she? You look like you're hiding something. Is this some little scheme you two cooked up to make me feel guilty for jumping her ass? Well, you're wasting your time."

"Stop thinking like a damn lawyer, Harold," Pamela growled. "I don't know where she is."

"Then what's the big secret?"

"I don't know what you're talking about." But she was unable to say it making eye contact, and averted her gaze, ostensibly to check for tarnish spots on her sterling silver spoon. Harold, professionally attuned to body language, knew instantly she was lying through her teeth.

"The hell you don't. Is it the drinking? Hell, I've known about that for quite a while; no great revelation there."

"My drinking has nothing to do with it," Pamela spat, realizing too late that she'd just made a confession. Her cheeks colored.

"Then what does it have to do with, Pam? Is it the reason Marla took off into that blasted cloud before anyone else got up this morning?"

Pamela shook her head violently. "No! Just drop it,

Harold. My *my mother lost her soul* head is splitting and I'm in no mood *lost it for nothing* for a damn argument."

"I don't care if your head falls off. I've got all the time in the world right now, seeing as how I left all my paperwork at the office, and I want to talk about this. You're making me extremely curious. People normally don't take a defensive position if there's nothing to defend."

"Go screw yourself, Harold."

The game was on. He feigned shock at her language. "I see you've added some new words to your vocabulary. Sounds terribly vulgar, dear, such expletives coming from the mouth of a refined lady like yourself."

She gripped her spoon with rage. "Don't push me, Harold. I know what you're doing. We're in a courtroom, right? And I'm a hostile witness on the stand, and you plan to badger the hell out of me until you get what you want. Until I get so damn mad I'll hit you with it like a baseball bat, at which point you win. Forget it. I won't let you do this to me."

Harold loved a challenge. "Is it your *mother?* This rumor shit wasn't started by Marla—it was started by your mother. Maybe you're just mad as hell at her for getting old on you, eh? You can't take it out on her, so you bury it, let it burn in your guts. Then all this shit hits the fan and the fire gets out of control. You have to lash out at someone. The alcohol isn't doing its job very well. Did you take it out on Marla? Sure, I jumped on her, but I didn't say anything that would make her want to run away. God knows what you might have said."

No, but the Devil knows the Devil knows . . .

Pamela saw red. She couldn't believe he would sink so low as to bring her dead *in Hell!* mother into this. Her husband was colder than she'd ever imagined. And she knew, then, that he was going to get exactly what he wanted. "You're nothing but prestigious scum, Harold. A giant maggot walking around in a three-piece suit. You want to know why Marla left? That secret I'm so viciously guarding? She found out I was *healed by a witch* having an affair with Roger Snell."

The baseball bat cracked into Harold's skull, shattering his objectivity. "You worthless whore! I suppose I

271

shouldn't be surprised—what can't you put past an alcoholic? But your best friend's husband? And I'm scum?"

If there had been a gun in Pamela's hand, she was certain she would have shot him right between the eyes. The charade was over anyway; a little murder conviction wouldn't make that much difference. At least she would have something to look back on with a smile.

Then she remembered there was a gun, in the library, behind some envelope boxes in the left bottom drawer of the desk. She calmly got up and left the table.

"I'm not through talking to you," Harold called after her. "I'd like to hear more about your tawdry little affair with Roger. Have you had him in my bed, you sleazy whore? Have you?"

"As a matter of fact, I have," Pamela answered several seconds later from the library. "Would you like me to draw you pictures of all the positions we tried?"

Harold felt his face flushing from the rage boiling up within him. He stood, knocking over his chair in the process. He'd never hit a woman before, but he was about to introduce himself to the experience. He began skirting the table to follow his unfaithful tramp of a wife to the library, but she reappeared in the kitchen after he'd taken only a few steps, his .45-caliber Smith & Wesson held steadily in both hands.

Harold's flush receded as the blood drained from his face, quickly turning his skin from pink to ivory. His eyes trailed up from the gun's deadly barrel to Pamela's face, where they hoped to find at least an ounce of reason. What they saw was the cool, collected look of a woman who had firmly made up her mind.

Seeing Harold so petrified gave Pamela some satisfaction, but seeing him dead would give her complete satisfaction. It would make up for all the times she'd had to endure his bland, sweaty lovemaking, all the years she'd spent living like a bird in a gilded cage, and for what he'd done a few minutes ago, cruelly dragging her mother into their petty argument.

"See you in Hell, Harold," she said, and before he could lodge any protests, calmly raised the gun higher and squeezed the trigger. The report was deafening, and the discharged bullet made a dime-sized hole in the middle of Harold's forehead, exiting with a tremendous spray of blood, bone fragments, and brain tissue. He was dead before he hit the floor, a look of utter astonishment on his face.

Pamela stared down at the ruined mess of Harold's head for a few minutes, enjoying her brief reward. Finally she whispered, "Here I come, Mama," put the warm barrel into her mouth, aimed it upward, and closed her eyes. A few seconds later she pulled the trigger again.

Twenty-Seven

After an endless walk through three and a quarter miles of cloying mist, Beth and Roger finally reached the base of the hill on Parish Lane. They'd clung to each other like lovers the whole way.

"This is a nightmare," Beth muttered under her breath as they started up the hill.

"I still don't know what you expect to find. Surely she's not up there. What good is this?"

She responded crisply, "It's better than just sitting at home and waiting for a phone call. It's doing something. And at this point, I just don't know what else to do. She could be there, hiding. Maybe the kids from school were giving her a hard time."

"For taking an old book out of the tomb?"

"For practicing witchcraft, Roger."

"For what?"

"Never mind . . . someone just made that part up. Hey, I can see."

As they slowly rose in altitude, the fog became thinner. At the top of the hill there were only stray wisps of white here and there, the surroundings hazy but visible. Roger pointed to some trees on the northern border of the overlook. "The path is over there."

"I know," she said huffily, pulling away from him. She no longer needed his reassuring contact. "I went there a million times as a kid, some of those times with you, remember? Those horrible parties we used to go to?"

"They still do it," Roger mused, taking the lead. "They'll be up here tonight, just after the sun goes down,

I imagine, dragging their beer kegs along. Or whatever it is they get high on these days, all dressed like their favorite monsters."

Beth followed him, their shoes making loud crunching noises on the gravel. The rest of the universe was dead.

They were halfway down the path when, to their left, from about fifty yards away, they heard the staccato cracking of limbs. Something was coming fast in their direction.

Beth rushed forward and grabbed the back of Roger's pea coat. "Oh my God, Roger, do you think it's a bear?"

He started running, pulling her along with him. "I don't know, but I'm not going to stick around to find out. We've got to get to the cemetery."

When they came to the edge of it they stopped, catching their breaths, listening above thundering heartbeats for the sound of their pursuer. All they could hear was the gentle rustle of leaves.

Beth was trembling uncontrollably, her stomach threatening to empty itself on her shoes at any moment. Her teeth chattered in harmony with her knocking knees. "Oh God, Roger, where is it? What is it?"

He clenched his fists, scouring the ground for something he could use as a weapon should whatever it was present itself in an offensive manner. As far as he knew, there were no bears in their part of the hills, but the devils were known to get around from time to time. He located a thick fallen branch and broke off a club with his foot. "Maybe a bear, I don't know; I don't have ESP. Let's get over to the tomb. We can get on top of it and just lay low for a while. Maybe it'll go away."

Joining hands, they cautiously moved toward the tomb, careful not to trip over any headstones. When they got up beside it, Roger put his club down and made a stirrup with his hands. "You go up first. You'll have to help pull me up."

Beth had just stepped her foot in his grasp when a human growl rumbled just inside the trees fifteen yards away. Beth screamed, jamming her foot down so hard on Roger's hands that they broke apart. "Get me up! GET ME UP, GET ME UP!" she shrieked, dancing in terror against the tomb wall.

Roger was fast deciding whether or not he had time to lift his wife to safety. Something was emerging from the dense foliage. Something very offensive. Beth pummeled him on the chest.

"Damn you! GET ME UP, IT'S COMING!"

He made a stirrup again, a surge of adrenaline enabling him to virtually toss her up on the tomb's roof. The instant her foot left his hand, he whirled around and grabbed his weapon, clutching it in a fist of steel. He could see the outline of it now, the face . . .

Oh God, the face!

Looking down from above, Beth began to scream hysterically. "Roger, get *up!* Get up here right now! Don't try to fight—"

But Roger didn't have a choice. The bloody monolith was converging on him like a swift nightmare.

Luke was bored. His mom wouldn't let him go play outside, and the white cloud seemed so inviting. Lana was out in it somewhere, so it wasn't fair that he couldn't enjoy the same privilege. His room had become both refuge and prison. If he went anywhere near his mother, she nearly bit his head off for making too much noise, then would immediately apologize and get all mushy and want to hug him, which bothered him even more than the bitching. He didn't like to be touched. By anybody.

He tossed the crumpled *Mad* magazine which he'd been reading across the room and decided he'd had about enough of this. It was like being grounded, and he hadn't done anything wrong. He got up and listened at the doorway. The television was on; his mother was watching one of those stupid soap operas. He wondered why those shows were called operas; he never saw any fat ladies singing on one.

She wouldn't notice him being gone. He wouldn't stay out very long anyway. He would find his way over to Billy's—which would be an adventure in itself—and then the two of them could play Space Invaders, using their fingers as ray guns, seeking each other out in the eerie mist of Planet Crouton. Without further ado he lifted and climbed out his window.

He had found the street and groped blindly down it for

a few minutes when he became frightened. His fantasies had been far more delightful than the actual experience. He was walking in dragon's breath. And for all he knew, he might be headed right for the gaping jaws of the extraterrestrial beast . . .

He turned to go back home. He could play Dick Tracy instead and snoop through his sister's room, searching for clues to her mysterious disappearance. Boy was she gonna get it when she came home.

Taking baby steps on mulchy grass again, both arms extended, he walked face first into a yard lamp before seeing it. An opportune time to use the new profanity Billy had taught him. He spat out angrily, "Cocksuckin' motherfucker!" and grinned at the feel of the words as they left his mouth. He repeated them again for the sheer pleasure of it.

He moved away from the pole, took several uncertain steps in three different directions, then began walking in a beeline, convinced that he was now heading straight for his bedroom window. Far off course, he walked through the space between his house and the Guenther's, unable to see either structure. He began to panic when he reached the backyard without running into brick, and veered slightly to his right. Seconds later he was tumbling over a trash can, the contents spilling out beneath him. He repeated his profane catechism several more times. When he moved to pick himself up, his hand landed on something soft.

Soft like puppy fur.

Another bucketful of dread washed over him. He picked the object up and brought it around to his line of vision. A hazy Sam grinned at him with eternal blankness, his eyes shriveled like raisins. His pink tongue was black with ravenous ants. Luke tossed the head away and began to scream.

Twenty-Eight

Willard Quincy grumbled as his wife of thirty-two years urged him through the swirling fog, prattling on about the screams she thought she'd heard coming from their next-door neighbor's house, the two-story at the end of the cul-de-sac. After three unanswered phone calls to the Montgomery residence, she'd made up her mind that something was definitely wrong over there, but she'd received only busy signals when she tried calling the police station. Willard, having neither heard nor seen anything unusual, told her to mind her own business, to which she'd replied that anything happening on Teaberry *was* her business, by God, and she'd promptly pulled him out the front door by his ear.

The wide porch steps groaned as they approached the hazy burgundy door. It opened before either of them could knock, although no one was standing behind it. Jeanette Quincy fearlessly led her husband inside.

There was a creaking sound above their heads. "Who's there?" Jeanette called out, taking a few bold steps toward the staircase. "Albert? What's going on over here?" Receiving no reply, she grabbed her husband's belt and started pulling him up the stairs with her.

A shadowed figure appeared on the landing when they were about two thirds of the way up. "That you, Al?" Willard asked uncertainly, having never known his stodgy neighbor to go for costume parties, or parties of any kind, for that matter. But he was wearing one hell of a Halloween getup.

The small bumps on Nephyrcai's forehead had extended about an inch. The shoe-leather skin on its face was gathered up in multirows of wrinkles, and yellow fangs protruded between mummified lips. The lifeless clay was conforming to the nature of the beast within.

It snarled, "Well, well, if it isn't the Quincys. How nice of you to drop by. As a matter of fact, we were just talking about you. What a coincidence." It started down the stairs.

Willard gripped the banister, realizing that a stranger —with a serious vocal cord problem—was behind the hideous mask. "Now hold on there, Buddy. Suppose you tell me what this is all about. My wife seems to think—"

"Your wife is a dirty little slut," Nephyrcai hissed, its green slimy tongue snaking in and out between the fangs. "She was Cunt Queen of the class of 'fifty-seven, remember? But that didn't bother you! You married her anyway, you spineless wimp, made her a respectable woman, riiight?" Malevolent laughter. "Well, she hasn't changed a bit!"

Jeanette gasped. "Willard! Are you going to let him get away with that?"

With uncharacteristic aggressiveness Willard shoved his wife aside and bolted up the remaining stairs to teach the freak a lesson he wouldn't forget if he lived to be a million. His fist was swinging into position when he was hit by an invisible train. With the speed of a bullet his body was knocked down the stairwell and slammed into the wall, his life ended by the abrupt dropping of a dark veil. He bounced off the wall and landed facedown on the floor.

Jeanette appeared to be jitterbugging against the banister, staring down at her husband's body with disbelieving eyes. Nephyrcai slowly descended the steps until it was standing just above her. Its sulfurous breath enveloped her like a smog. "And now you, my dear. I'm wondering how you must feel now that your precious pussy-whipped husband is dead. The only man on earth who ever respected you, including your father. What will you do now? Hubby hadn't earned a full pension. And you're far too old and repulsive to peddle your wares on the street."

Jeanette slowly turned back around, looking dazed. "Willard's dead? He can't be dead. He's all I've got . . ."

The flames into which she stared sparkled with glee. "What a sad little testimony. It gets me—right here." A gnarled, warty hand with two-inch talons unzipped Montgomery's trousers and pulled out a stiff rope of what looked like raw sausage. "Here, would you like to suck on that? I know you sucked a lot of cock in your day; no doubt you miss the variety. Put your lips around this sweet morsel. Let me fill your fat belly with the seeds of Hell."

"You filth," Jeanette spat, refusing to look at it. "Disgusting pervert. If my husband is really dead, you'd better believe you're going to pay!"

Her tormentor grinned, its obscene tongue snaking across its upper lip. "Hey, I was just trying to think of something fun to do; I always try to entertain my guests. Perhaps you'd prefer to get fucked in the ass. Or would you rather have a bath? Remember the ones your father used to give you? Until you were what . . . twelve? Remember what he used to do with the bar of soap? The look on his face when he did it? Oh yes, he knew what he was doing. And later, when you were tucked away in bed rubbing yourself because it itched—and oh, an itch so delicious to scratch—he was in the bathroom jerking off over the toilet, thinking about that precious little gash between your legs—"

Screaming for him to shut up, Jeanette tripped and fell backward down the stairs. Landing on her husband's body, she burst into angry, bitter sobs.

"Take your clothes off, cunt," the demon commanded.

Still sobbing, Jeanette sat up and began to unbutton her blouse.

The walking horror continued to circle the tomb and try to climb up. Beth sat hunched in the center of the roof, her knees drawn up, her arms wrapped tightly around them as she rocked back and forth, blubbering softly. Every few seconds she would see large, bloody fingers pop up and try to get a grip along the edge of the roof, accompanied by the thud of shoes kicking the wall, and the vise around her heart would become another notch tighter.

At one point the deranged creature had burst through the tomb's door, and she had been able to hear it below her, opening and slamming the coffin lids. Looking for a way up so it could get her and tear her apart like it had Roger. Like it probably had Nancy. Beth had forced herself to accept it. She'd found what she'd come looking for. And now it was going to kill her.

But then she could hear the crunching of leaves as it moved away, and soon she could see the back of it appear from top to bottom as its distance increased. It looked somewhat human from the backside. A pudgy giant with short-cropped hair and a hump between the shoulders. From the other side it looked like something walking out of her worst nightmare. A face that wasn't a face . . .

She stared across the cemetery at the base of the path long after the chilling figure had disappeared into it. Finally she stopped rocking. It was really gone. She could get down now, put Roger back together, and the two of them could go home and have lunch. Tuna salad sounded good. She could whip some up in no time.

She crawled to the edge and looked down at the ground where her husband's mutilated body lay in hacked bits and pieces. She thought of Humpty-Dumpty and uttered a shrill giggle. Roger was going to need a gallon of Super Glue.

Jolts of pain shot up her legs when she hit the ground. She stumbled forward on her knees, her spread palms automatically positioning themselves to break her fall. They slid over a bloody mound of sodden leaves. Lying next to it was one of Roger's hands sans the bones; the skin had been pulled off the meat like a sheath. Beth picked it up and carefully arranged the limp fingers between her own, then got up and walked woodenly toward the path, occasionally banging a knee on an upright tombstone from not paying close enough attention to where she was going. She squeezed Roger's hand.

"It's going to be all right, honey. As soon as we get home I'm going to make us some nice tuna salad sandwiches and some iced tea, and after we've finished eating, you can light up your pipe, and we'll go sit in the living room and read, take our minds off our troubles for a while. That sound all right with you?"

She had only walked a few yards into the path when she heard something behind her. Not thinking, her body acting exclusively on its automatic defense system, she shook the hand loose and spurred into a run. She didn't get very far. She was tackled from behind by what had surely been a four-hundred-pound bag of cement. In slow motion she flew through the air, watched as the ground rose up to meet her. A stout twig so perfectly positioned upward entered her left eye and ripped through vital brain tissue. She was mercifully unaware of what happened to her body afterward.

Luke was still sobbing uncontrollably an hour later when the phone rang. Carol left her heartbroken, mortified son on the couch and rushed into the kitchen to answer it, hoping against hope that it would be her daughter calling to say she was at such and such place and would be home as soon as the fog did its disappearing act.

It was Hugh, his voice low and void of amenities. "Have you found Lana yet?"

Carol sighed despairingly. "No. I called the police, but they can't do anything in this fog. And somethin' else horrible has happened. Luke accidentally found the remains of that puppy the kids had in our neighbor's trash can about an hour ago; he's very upset and I can't seem to calm him down. I called the police about that, an' they told me they'd gotten a report from the postman that my neighbor is dead! They told me to just lock all my doors and windows and sit tight until they get things under control. Hugh, I'm scared! I'm afraid that boy— that horrible monster—has gone berserk or somethin'. They told me he's missin'. What if Lana—"

Hugh exploded with anger. "Why didn't you just take the kids an' move in with the Hell's Angels? I'm hangin' up to check the flight schedules right now. I'll call you from Rapid City when I get in. The damn fog should be cleared up by then."

Carol winced as the line clicked and went dead. She'd

never wanted to see his face again. But oh, how she needed him to hold her now. She'd never been more frightened in her entire life. If anything had happened to Lana, she would feel totally responsible. And she didn't think she could live with that.

"It's time we headed for the hills. Our appointment draws nigh," Nephyrcai said, picking up a box of candles Azrahoth had taken from the Chandler residence.

The three demons had fully bloomed into the physical manifestations of innate evil. But they would not remain incarnate for long; the corrupted flesh would begin to crumble, become a heap of meaningless dust. Released from confinement, the infernal creatures would normally return to the metaphysical realm, where their powers were limited to the access of human inclination. From their dark world they could suggest, not control. But a suggestion was all that was usually necessary.

Howbeit this was not a normal occasion. The key was in their hands; with the Gate incantation of the original High Priestess, whore of the fallen sons of God, they could make the ethereal cervix between the spiritual and physical worlds dilate permanently. Except for the Master's relatively small body of mortal followers, humanity would be doomed. The earth would again belong to the creatures of darkness.

Nephyrcai settled its fiery gaze on Lana. She sat on the edge of the bed, dressed and perfumed, her hands folded calmly in her lap. The room was a sweltering, dry sauna, and her skin glistened with sweat. Dennis sat beside her, seemingly unaffected by the heat. His head lolled from side to side as he continued to inspect objects in the room which by now were quite familiar to him.

"Lana, you will walk with me," Nephyrcai said. "I have the honor of giving your body to the High Priestess. I've no doubt she'll be very pleased."

Azrahoth and Vikael cackled gleefully. Vikael hissed through curled, blackened lips, "Do let me offer the boy."

Patting an empty wasp's nest where there had once been a cheek, Azrahoth retorted, "Only if you'll let me recite the incantation."

283

Nephyrcai nodded. "The book is downstairs; you can get it on our way out. Come, children. It is time to fulfill your destinies." It held its hand out to Lana. She took it and slid off the bed.

They followed Azrahoth from the room. Dennis and Vikael, also holding hands, brought up the rear. The procession became solemn, all footsteps in sync. They marched slowly down the steps.

Lana observed the man's body lying against the wall and wondered idly who he was, and if he was as dead as he looked. Not that such trivia mattered. She was going to fulfill her destiny. That was the only thing that was presently relevant.

As Azrahoth stepped across the living room to get the ledger from the television console, Lana's eyes were drawn to another body sitting in the center of the couch. It was a woman, and she was naked. Her eyes were opened wide with unseeing terror, her mouth open in a silent scream. Lana stared blankly for a few moments and then looked away as Nephyrcai lead her toward the open front door.

Twenty-Nine

At last the sun made a belated appearance in the popcorn-dotted sky over Sharon Valley. The halted machine spurred into activity. Automobile engines roared to life, daily rituals grudgingly began. A small portion of the population moved completely unaware that the day was any different than the day before it or the thousands of days before that. They knew nothing of cold-blooded murder and kidnapping, and other acts of violence never dreamed of in Sharon Valley. In their case ignorance truly was bliss, and something of a wonder as well. The police had made a concerted effort to contain the panic by demanding silence from those who were not so blissfully ignorant; mass hysteria was a frightening possibility in a town that size, and one which was inclined to get bent out of shape over small, ridiculous rumors anyway.

Something like this could turn Sharon Valley into a literal war zone. If the people didn't start tearing each other apart, they would swarm to the police department like angry wasps, demanding miracles. But in spite of the department's efforts, the majority was now aware that something was happening, and that whatever it was wasn't good. It was practically impossible to keep a domestic argument a secret, much less something as vile and aberrant as murder. The switchboard at the police station was jammed with calls as one voice after another asked the harried desk clerks: "WHAT THE HELL IS GOING ON?" They wanted answers and they wanted them NOW.

Sharon Valley had become a virtual powder keg searching for a match.

Carol watched through her living room drapes as the two patrol cars converged on the house next door, bright lights flashing impressively, boasting of unquestionable authority. The neighbors who beheld them experienced a pang of paranoia, a conditioned response due to the humiliating times those same lights had appeared in the rearview mirror.

Three officers crept up to the Guenther house, pistols drawn. Carol thought it was like watching a TV movie. Surely this wasn't really happening right next door.

The fourth uniformed cop was headed toward her house, his young, still-immature face grim. The script called for him to knock on her door. Feeling a bit disoriented, Carol went to open it.

He spoke crisply. "I'm Officer Tom Pate. You're the lady that called, ma'am?"

She nodded numbly. "Yes, I'm Carol Bremmers. Would you like to come in?" She stepped back and gestured for him to enter. After tossing a fraternal glance back at the officers still cautiously approaching the Guenther house, he slapped a hand over the firearm on his left hip and bellied into the room. He first noticed the sullen boy sitting on the couch sucking his thumb. The boy looked much too old to be doing that sort of thing. Pate grunted with disgust and turned around to face Carol.

"Normally one of our detectives would be around to ask these questions, but they've pretty well got their hands full right now." He pulled a small pad and pen from his shirt pocket and seemed to search Carol's face for approval. She shrugged helplessly.

"What do you want to know? Please, have a seat. I don't think I can stand on my feet very long, 'specially not discussin' somethin' like this. Luke, why don't you go to your bedroom, honey, while I talk with the officer."

Like a remote control robot, Luke got up and marched stiffly down the hallway, his thumb still planted firmly in his mouth. Carol took a deep breath and ordered herself not to cry. He would snap out of it. She just had to try to be understanding. He was one upset little boy.

"You from Texas, are you?"

Carol managed a weak smile. "How'd you guess?"

They sat on opposite ends of the couch. Pate leaned forward, resting his elbows on the knees of his starched gray uniform slacks, his brow creased with professional concern. "Ma'am, when was the last time you saw Spiro Guenther?"

The name chilled Carol's blood. For a moment she couldn't think. "I believe it was last Saturday. He was out back playin' with my kids an' that . . . dog. You know about that, don't you?"

Pate nodded briefly. "Yes ma'am. But our main concern at this point is who killed Mrs. Guenther. Her husband used to be on the force, so it's possible some creep he busted finally got out of prison and came to get revenge, killed whoever he could find at that residence. But since the son is missing, it might well be him too. We never had any trouble with Spiro before—called him the Gentle Giant—but we knew he had, you know, brain problems, so you never know."

Carol's throat tightened. "I know. I wasn't exactly thrilled about him bein' over here. Do you . . . do you think he might have had somethin' to do with my daughter's disappearance?"

Pate only tapped his pen against his pad, his lower lip sucked in. His refusal to answer stabbed Carol in the heart.

"My God, you do, don't you?" Her hand flew to her mouth, a barricade against enemy tears.

"At this point, ma'am, I really can't tell you much of anything," Pate said truthfully, attempting to make his voice reassuring. "We've got, including your daughter, six teenagers reported missing right now, and one dead. Now if it was only one or two, maybe even three, we really wouldn't think much of it. You know how kids are; they get pissed off at their parents, go hide out at a friend's house for a while, assert their independence, teach their parents a lesson. They usually don't stay gone more than a couple of days. But with this many, and on top of these two murders, we're persuaded there's something bad wrong in this town. Now maybe Spiro Guenther disappeared for the same reason they all did—supposing this is all connected somehow—and is innocent of any crime. But from the report called in by Sam Weaver, we gather Mrs. Guenther had been gone at least a couple of days, which lends credence to the theory that next door is where this whole thing got started. I know that's not encouraging, but that's all I can tell you, ma'am. We're working on it—now that we can. That was one hell of a fog, wasn't it? Heard it's been that bad around here before, but not in my day. Jesus. Well, let's get on with this and I'll get out of your hair. Were you aware of any hostility between Spiro and Mrs. Guenther?"

Carol's tear-brimmed eyes lit with remembrance. "Lana mentioned somethin' about one of Spiro's hands—palms—bein' badly burned. She suspected that his mother had done it to him on purpose, as a punishment for somethin'. But he wouldn't admit it. So Mrs. Guenther came out on the porch an' apparently she and Lana had some kind of confrontation. An' I guess Mrs. Guenther confessed to it, so Lana warned her that if she ever did anything like that again, she'd report it to the police. I know I should've called anyway, but frankly I . . . I didn't really care."

She had to compose herself before continuing. Pate waited patiently. "Come to think of it, the dog disappeared right after that. Spiro gave it to Lana because his mother wouldn't let him keep it. If she was sick enough to burn his hand, maybe she killed that poor li'l dog . . ."

Pate wrote furiously in his notepad, the tip of his tongue protruding from the left side of his mouth, reminding Carol of a five-year-old Luke studiously drawing his first masterpiece with crayons.

Both eyebrows shot up when he finished, and he let out a slow breath. "Yeah, well, no telling what all she could have been doing to the poor schmo all these years . . . maybe he just finally cracked. Happens all the time, I guess, but not around here. Not until now anyway. Anything else?"

Carol shook her head, her gaze settling somewhere in

space. But when Pate stood to take his leave, she came back from her astral voyage and asked meekly, "Do you know if a boy named Bruce is one of the missin'?"

"Bruce . . . last name?"

Her cheeks flushed. "I don't know the last name, sorry."

Caressing the handle of his .357 Magnum, Pate said, "Well, we got so much thrown on us at once, truthfully I don't know any of the names, except your daughter's. Why do you ask?"

"He was spendin' a lot of time with Lana, that's all. Guess that probably makes you wonder why I don't know his last name, doesn't it?" She laughed bitterly. "Never mind. Well, if Bruce is missin', Lana's probably with him, an' I would be very surprised if they weren't on their way to Tyler. But better that than bein' involved with the rest of this . . . this madness."

"Well, if you have a picture of your daughter I could take with me, that would help. We'll also put APB's out on your vehicle and this Bruce kid's, if he had one. You know if he did?"

"Just an ol' pickup, missin' most of the paint. A real horror to have parked in front of your house every evenin'." She left to go get a picture of Lana.

A slight smile touched Pate's lips as he remembered the "horror" he had driven in his youth, and parked in front of Janet Shelby's house night after night. But her parents hadn't seemed to mind.

Carol reappeared a few minutes later with Lana's junior year school picture and handed it to him, her eyes pleading. "Please find her."

"We'll do our best, ma'am." He tipped his hat and left, after cautioning her to keep what she knew to herself.

Thirty

The sun finally yielded its azure brilliance to frothy blackness. A full moon appeared in the center of a massive halo which glowingly displayed the entire spectrum of colors like a round rainbow. To the simpleminded it was a sign in the heavens. To the aesthetically inclined it was a thing of beauty, a natural work of art, and they scrambled for their cameras. To a certain group of teenagers it was the signal to party down.

The usual ritual of Trick or Treat had been unanimously canceled. By sundown very few in Sharon Valley—basically those in the nursing home or too young to understand the English language—remained in total ignorance of the Happenings. Teenagers were ordered to stay at home—and play Monopoly or Trivial Pursuit with the family for once!—but most of them thought not. They had gone to painstaking trouble to create their new costumes, hoping to win the Most Gross title, an unparalleled honor among the juvenile set. Watching their parents strangle each other over pieces of meaningless property, or seeing younger siblings smirk every time they held out their greedy little paws and said *"I own that!"* or even worse, playing a game that made you seem like you had an IQ of minus six, was asking a bit much. Those who didn't retreat to the solace of their headphones, and who had the nerve to do so, snuck out, stuffing pillows under the blankets on their beds to make it look like they'd sacked out early. They hadn't been nailed to the floor. They found ways to get out.

Miss the Halloween party on Beacon Hill? Get real.

They lay on the stone, side by side, surrounded by burning candles. For a moment Lana imagined she was an icing decoration on a huge birthday cake, and pretty soon a giant was going to come along and eat her with one hot swallow. The image evoked no fear, and was soon forgotten.

Directly above them the moon shined brightly, glorified further by the loveliest ring that surrounded it like a mother-of-pearl bracelet. No renegade clouds dared to invade the iris of that perfectly round eye, the pupil white instead of black, and thereby inhibit its vision of the proceeds conducted below it. It stared down at them without emotion.

Azrahoth stood behind their heads. Forming a triangle, Nephyrcai stood to the right of Lana's feet, Vikael to the left of Dennis's, both of them facing Azrahoth, who had just opened the ledger.

"The hour has come for the High Priestess Morganna Ober and her consort to return to this domain," it said with a voice like crackling flames.

As it began to read the incantation, the ancient Open Sesame of spiritual planes, the rectangle of candle flames flickered wildly. The words held no meaning for Lana; she'd never heard any of them before. They certainly weren't Spanish, the only other language she was even halfway familiar with. German, perhaps; the words were harsh and overloaded with consonants.

The halo around the moon seemed to grow slightly smaller, and the stone on which they lay began to vibrate. Like a massage bed, Dennis lay thinking. Someone had just dropped in a quarter. They could also hear, vaguely, the distant sound of music.

The demon Azrahoth eventually finished its recital and fell silent, whereupon Nephyrcai and Vikael lifted their arms and together began chanting solemn praises of Satan. The vibration in the stone gradually escalated to a rumble.

* * *

"Dy-no-MITE!" Jeff Lindy exclaimed at the approach of the best Dracula he had ever seen. "Hey Starkey, is that you, man?"

The green-faced vampire hissed and snaked out a red tongue.

"I am Deraculaaaaah," it boomed darkly, heavily-lined eyes fixed longingly on the throat of Jeff's date, the Bride of Frankenstein. She had painted a temporary silver streak up the part of her naturally wavy hair and had plastered the whole lot upright with mousse and three quarters of a can of hair spray. She had to avoid low-hanging limbs; she was afraid if her hair hit something, it would break off. She returned Dracula's leer with one of her own and wantonly offered her neck.

The party was in full swing, blood alcohol levels respectably risen—several of them had had the foresight to raid their parents' liquor cabinets before dark. The degree of drunkenness one could attain was directly proportionate to the fun one would remember having the next day. When you could remember puking in your pocket, you knew for certain you'd had a gas.

Mike Owen, S. V. High's token black, had brought along his monster boombox, though he still proudly referred to it as his Ghetto Blaster. Through the speakers DJ Duane Gunn played their favorite rock hits, the volume loud enough to wake the dead. Mike's family was one of the richest in Sharon Valley, and the Owens had learned that green covered a multitude of dark pigment. Mike was the biggest teller of nigger jokes in the whole school; he thought they were all outrageously funny because the whites he repeated them to couldn't afford even the steering wheel of his Maserati.

A few couples were gyrating spastically to the music; one of them, a matching set of Egyptian mummies with greatly exaggerated sex parts, slammed against each other like warring pogo sticks. Others sat leaning stuporously against the south side of the Obers' tomb, staring at the small mellow campfire they had irreverently built right on Christina Warner's grave, unaware of the hacked and mutilated remains of Roger Snell scattered on the other side. Someone needed to put more wood on the fire, but it would never get done. Behind the cloak of leaves still others groped and fondled, exchanging wet, sloppy kisses, pausing as little as possible to breathe.

What appeared to be a two-hundred-year-old man wearing a tan trench coat cursed loudly, "Mother fuck, man, the booze is all gone!" He opened his coat and jiggled the obscene foam rubber appendage protruding from his zipper.

There was a consensus of groans. Mike, who had come as a zombie—he'd had to explain a dozen times why he hadn't had to change his normal appearance, always with the same robust laugh—silenced the boombox and rubbed his hands together. "That means it's Gory Story time, kiddies."

The partiers responded in unison: "Ahhhhh!"

The ghosts and goblins, pasty corpses with nooses around their necks or fake knives protruding from their chests above a generous application of ketchup, the Jasons and the Freddie Kruegers, Lizzie Bordens and warty witches, gathered around the fire. Only two, the Cat people, remained in their leafy sanctuary because Gory Story time could in no way compete with Lose Your Virginity time. Their absence was not noticed.

The Bride of Frankenstein, Amy Lusk, giggled nervously. "We don't have to make up any stories this year. We're living a real one."

Heads nodded, bloodshot eyes grew wider.

The male mummy, whose stiff penis suspiciously resembled a paper towel holder covered with papier-mâché, added after a hefty belch, "Yeah, my parents would shit their pants if they knew I was out here."

Jeff Lindy snuggled against his girlfriend, whom he'd encased in his satin cape. When he opened his mouth to speak, his fangs fell out, which brought a short relief of laughter to the mounting tension. He popped them back in and asked in his most otherworldly voice, "But WHOOO are the VICTIMS?"

Everyone looked at everyone one else. No one knew.

"I heard they found somebody that was so messed up they couldn't tell," Cory Fulcher said behind his Freddie Krueger mask. Gasps all around.

Mike said in a deep baritone, "I'll tell you what's happening, my little white brothers and sisters. Just look at the moon."

They all looked up and shuddered appropriately.

"That's what they call a witches' moon," Mike continued, circling the group in a much-practiced zombie walk. "Yes, a witches' moon, children. And we knew before tonight that there were real live witches in our midst, not to mention any names or anything, like Nancy Snell and Marla Mingee; but like fools, fools, we let them continue on their merry wicked way, and now you see what they've done, picking off their victims one by one, all those who might pose a threat to their evil craft. And tonight, under the spell of the hellish moon, they will seek out the rest of their prey . . . I don't doubt that they're on their way down the path at this very moment—"

"Ooh, hey, let's do another story," Amy interrupted shakily. "You're really scaring me, Mike."

He grinned the grin of the dead. "That's what it's all about, my pet, my lovely punk poodle. That's what you came here for; what we all came for. To DIE!" He bellowed out a hollow string of laughter.

A scream punctuated his laugh like a siren, setting off a chain reaction of similar shrieks in the group. Even Mike jumped and turned a few shades lighter, but for ego's sake he composed himself quickly.

He called to the bordering wall of trees, "Very funny, whothefuck ever you are. Come on out now and join the party, we're trying to tell ghost stories here!"

His command was answered by another scream, another voice, with the same genuine-sounding terror. Mike was neither impressed nor amused; someone was stealing the show from him. His audience, now captivated by the unknown screamers, began to scoot together in a tight bunch against the wall of the Obers' tomb, horror stamped on every face. The trees in the direction they were staring rustled and swayed, making way for the mass that was moving between them. There were audible intakes of breath. More than a few were picturing ten-foot Nancys and Marlas appearing before their eyes in the clearing, pointy black hats atop their heads, black robes flowing, fingers arranged in the hexing position, green lips prepared to hurl curses of the worst kind.

The costume disguised him fairly well from the neck up, but the size and shape of his body, the way it moved, and the clenched fists at his sides gave him away very quickly. They all began to laugh.

It was Tardo come to join the party.

Cory Fulcher was first to get up. He pulled off his Freddie Krueger mask and sauntered over to the tree-framed hulk, still snickering. "Hey Tardo, you wanna borrow my mask instead? Yours just doesn't—" His words faltered as he realized that Spiro Guenther wasn't wearing a mask. In fact, he was hardly wearing a face. The muscle tissue, exposed veins, and blood clots bordered by ragged skin flaps were real. "Gross, man!" Glancing toward the group he yelled, "Come check this out! Tardo's cut his fucking face off!"

At that moment the Bride of Frankenstein and Lizzie Borden shrieked in unison, because Spiro apparently intended to cut Cory's face off next. He lunged at the smaller boy with outstretched arms, one hand clutching something that looked like a knife. Acting instantly on the girls' warning screams, Cory ducked, just barely escaping Spiro's mortal embrace. Everyone was on their feet now, the girls screaming for all their lungs were worth, the guys arguing over whether or not to take Tardo on as a team or just play it as every man for himself. After several moments of watching Cory dodge Spiro like a matador dodging an enraged bull, they decided it was every man for himself. The group began to scatter.

"Help us!" Christie Luben screamed through the narrow mouth slit in her mummy costume. She and her boyfriend Bill Roberts were having a hell of a time just standing up. "God, you guys! *Please!*"

Ironically, the only one who paid any attention to her plea was Spiro. He stopped chasing Cory and settled his gaze on the two gauze-wrapped figures making a very slow and clumsy getaway, leaning against each other for support. Still, one or the other fell every few feet.

Spiro smiled, creating a fresh ache in his raw cheek muscles. He'd take off all the faces, all of them, and then he could be anyone he wanted to be. And if they laughed at him then, they would only be laughing at themselves. He charged toward the mummies, who both began to yell and scream with dire urgency, but no one turned back to help. Spiro took the boy first and yanked him away from his girlfriend's embrace, toppling her over in the process. Bill landed on his back, and in the blink of an eye Spiro was straddling his chest and brandishing the straight razor in Bill's bandaged face.

"Don't hurt me, man!" Bill cried in a falsetto voice. "Come on, Spiro! You know I really like you! Chill out, okay?"

Christie continued to scream as she crabbed away on the dead grass, and Spiro turned to look at her for just a second before slicing the lethal blade deeply across Bill's swathed neck. A backup chorus of screams came from the nearest trees, where some of the others had apparently hidden, waiting to see what would happen. Now they'd seen, and were buying more distance wholesale.

Bill made a gurgling noise as the white gauze began to turn red. He seemed to be trying to say something, but the only thing coming from his throat was blood. Christie's screams escalated, and they were beginning to give Spiro a headache. Leaving Bill to finish spilling out his life's blood, he went after Christie. Until the gauze was cut away he wouldn't know if she was pretty or not, but if she was, maybe Lana would like to look like her sometimes.

Seeing Spiro rise to come after her, Christie's overload of fear hurled her into unconsciousness. He knelt beside her still form and began to unwrap the gauze, becoming impatient when it got tangled. With the sound of Bill's death rattle in his ears, he started making indiscriminate slashes, each evidenced by the gradual surfacing of a thick red line.

Now this was a Halloween party. After slicing the girl mummy to a mass of bloody ribbons, he went in search of more fun. He could always come back for his faces later.

Thirty-One

Distant wails of human terror wafted through the continuing praises of the dark god. If the demons were aware of them, they showed no sign; their contorted mouths chanted on with enthusiasm.

An atomic rocket was tunneling its way through miles of compressed earth and stone and would eventually thrust its warhead through Lana's back. She calmly wondered what it was going to feel like. On the other hand, maybe they were just having an earthquake, in which case the ground would soon split and swallow her up forever. She tried to guess who was doing all the screaming and why. There was simply nothing to get that excited about. It didn't seem to last for very long, although Lana's perception of time had become greatly distorted. She could easily believe she had been lying on the cold stone for a whole year.

Cold? No, as she came to think of it, it really wasn't so cold any longer. In fact, it was growing rather warm. The heat seeped into her flesh like a dog's moist, hot breath, panting. She felt the rhythm of a heartbeat—hers?—the mounting tension of a woman in labor. The rumbling continued to grow louder, the vibration sensation more intense. Soon it would happen, whatever it was. Oh yes. Her destiny. The High Priestess was coming to take over her body.

Lana gratefully absorbed the heat pulsating from the stone and waited, realizing with little surprise that the ring around the moon had become so small that there seemed only about an inch of the iris left. The rainbow colors had deepened to glittery brilliance; the eye had become a diamond brooch with a pearl in the center, surrounded by a thin band of onyx. Lana watched it twinkle, spellbound.

Suddenly the demons fell silent. The offerings lay still and ready. The stone grew from warm to hot, the rumble became a roar, the vibration strong enough to jar the entire planet, or so it seemed to Lana.

And then something happened, though it was far from anything she had expected. A deep, mournful voice bellowed out her name as a large shape intruded into the clearing. It was a pathetic sound, the serenade of a desperate, wounded animal. She didn't look to see who it was; she couldn't pull her eyes away from that beautiful, enchanting jewel in the sky. The onyx had just disappeared.

The demons snapped out of their trances and whirled on the intruder in a rage. Their concentration centered elsewhere, Dennis and Lana were freed from their stupor. Dennis instinctively shoved Lana off her side of the stone before spinning off his, toppling many of the candles with them in the dirt. They watched in complete shock as the body of Spiro Guenther was lifted by invisible strings into the air and twisted like a dishrag. He fell to an indistinguishable heap just as the roar reached its crescendo and two human-shaped blue clouds appeared glowingly on the stone's surface, giving off a powerful stench of sulfur and ozone. In the dead silence following, the clouds writhed as if in agony, their vague, watery facial features contorted in vehement accusation, bewildered and beseeching. Making an echoing, hollow gurgling sound as if they were literally drowning in their defeat, they faded until they had disappeared.

The scene had been so spectacular, so riveting, that Dennis and Lana had failed to notice what had happened to the demons during its occurrence. All that was left of them were the clothes they had been wearing. It was as if they had simply evaporated.

Neither of them could speak for several moments; their brains had a lot of catching up to do. When Lana's finally caught up to the fact she was naked, she felt extremely embarrassed, although it wouldn't have made any difference to Dennis at the time if she'd been covered with whipped cream and cherries or wrapped in a parka.

Dennis seemed intent on sitting there with his mouth hanging open until everything he'd witnessed coagulated into some sort of sense. For an instant his mind sought to remind him of what he had done, what he had said. He resolutely refused to acknowledge it.

But you did it, you did, you pledged your soul to the Devil . . .

No way! What Devil?

"C'mon, Dennis, we've gotta get out of here," Lana mumbled, refusing to look at him. She had the impulse to grab her clothes and just start running without him into the darkness of the woods, but she was afraid of getting lost.

He still didn't move. "What the hell happened?"

"Nothin' that anyone will believe in a million years," she muttered, folding her arms over her breasts and shivering. "I don't believe it myself. But let's go now. We've got to get out of these damn woods. I just wanna go home. Which way, Dennis? Which way?" Her heart was thundering, her mind reeling. She would never be able to accept this nightmare as reality, as something that had actually happened.

"They'll be partying at the cemetery. Oh Jesus, the cemetery . . ." Dennis recalled the horrible screams coming from that direction. How little the sound had affected him then. "We've got to go see what happened there. If there's . . . if there's anyone left, they can give us a ride . . ."

Lana looked over at the silent remains of Spiro Guenther. Her heart welled with pity. But the poor bastard had not died in vain. Perhaps no one else would ever know what he had done—inadvertently, yes, but nevertheless, he was a hero in his own right. She at least would honor his memory, if somehow she could ever cope with remembering. She was thankful that his head was twisted in such a way that she was unable to see his face, the dead eyes staring up at her with a primitive, perverted rendition of love. He had intended to save her.

And had done so, plus a lot more. He had possibly saved the whole world.

Dennis noticed the ledger lying on the ground. He picked it up and turned it over in his hands, his face changing to register intense hate. As much as he didn't want to, he began to remember what the creatures had done to him, and the fact that they'd touched him at all, much less sodomized him, filled him with total rage. He started ripping out the pages and touching them to candle flame. "Those dirty motherfuckers."

Lana watched his actions with an intense sense of relief. The Devil's end of the bargain had not been kept, and therefore the Obers' contract, including any secret clauses, was null and void. The light in men's souls would continue to be attacked, but not extinguished, and the earth would not be turned into a seething den of iniquity.

Dennis watched the final page blacken and curl on the stone. He flung the cover away and stood up, still looking like a bloody fistfight demanding a place to happen. "All right, I'm ready. Let's get dressed and get out of here."

After they had self-consciously put on their clothes, Dennis picked up a few candles and handed them to Lana, then gathered the remaining ones for himself. Nodding at the gap through which Spiro had appeared, he muttered, "That way. I'll lead."

They stepped carefully over Spiro's body and began to climb the upward path, branches swatting and scratching them with every step. Lana looked up one last time at the moon above them, now naked of its jeweled halo, void of its entrancing spell. It was just a plain old full moon now, a gentle face frowning in sorrow.

Suddenly Dennis stopped and swayed, clutching his chest. "Oh, shit!"

Alarmed, Lana reached out to support him. "What's the matter?"

"I can't . . . breathe . . ." He sank to his knees, gasping loudly for air. His candles fell from his hand. "My heart . . ."

Lana became hysterical. "Dennis, NO! Get up! You'll be all right!"

But Dennis was not going to be all right; Myrantha

Ober's insurance policy against anyone who tried to destroy the ledger was already taking effect. Even as Lana spoke he uttered a loud, strangled grunt and jerked spasmodically, then lay completely still. She fell over him and began shaking him violently. "Get up, Dennis! We gotta go! Please get up! Dennis . . .?"

It took her a while to realize that he was dead. She checked over and over for a pulse, convinced she just wasn't checking in the right places, thinking when she put her ear to his chest she could hear something, some sign of life. When at last she accepted it, she curled into a fetal position and began to weep helplessly.

Sometime later Lana woke with a start, surprised that she'd fallen asleep. Dennis still lay motionless beside her. She numbly rose and moved on alone, now with only the moon's light to guide her. Her mind obediently stayed on its immediate task, putting one foot in front of the other, warding off scratchy branches, listening for the sound of wild animals. No other thoughts allowed. Not now. Just keep moving . . .

What seemed hours later but was in fact only a few minutes, her body aching from the grueling uphill hike, her legs certain she had somehow been transplanted onto Mount Everest, she could hear the sound of voices. She entered the clearing and was immediately assaulted with blinding lights and a harsh command to hold it right there.

In spite of the way things had sounded, only two of the partiers had been unable to escape the clutches of the driven madman and his trusty straight razor, besides the two he had slashed in the throes of mutual orgasm; the mummies, who were too tightly wrapped to do any serious running. The others had scattered to hide in the safety of the dark forest, and a few had hightailed it up the path and made it to their cars, thus enabled to drive to a phone and call the police. The entire force of nine was present and aiming their weapons on the white-faced, terrified girl.

"It's the Bremmers girl," one of them said.

The guns were lowered, as were the powerful flashlights. They illuminated a red and white form at the officers' feet, and when Lana figured out what it was, she thought she might vomit, but there was nothing in her stomach to heave. A renegade memory flashed. The demons doing all those terrible things to her body . . . and her begging for more.

She swooned unconscious to the ground.

Thirty-Two

The officer who drove her home was the same one who had interviewed her mother, which Lana discovered when he mentioned that Carol Bremmers had reported her as missing. He'd recognized her from the school picture he'd been given. In a gentle voice he told her that in a day or two, when she was able to talk, a detective, probably Louis Helm, would be around to get a report from her. But for her it was all over now, he said, and she should get plenty of rest and some food in her stomach, take it easy, and she would be her good old self in no time. She didn't tell him what she knew, that it was over for everyone. Spiro was dead and the demons were back where they belonged. Hopefully forever.

The police would eventually find Spiro. They would never know he had not been singularly responsible for all the bodies they would find, and Lana saw no real reason that they should be told otherwise. They would never believe the truth anyway.

The sight of her well-lighted home made her at last feel some sort of security, of being tied to manageable reality. There was a strange car parked in the drive; a dark blue sedan. The patrol car eased up to the curb in front of the house and Pate left it running while he helped Lana up to the porch. He needed to deposit her quickly and get back to the crime scene.

Lana noticed that Spiro's house had been roped off with bright orange tape and wondered what it was for, but she was far too weary to concern herself with anything other than her own problems.

The door was opened by her mother, who upon seeing her burst into tears of joy and gathered her in her arms. Pate awkwardly tipped his hat and melted quietly away.

The scene that greeted Lana in the living room was another surprise, this an extremely pleasant one. On the couch, Luke was sitting between two of her favorite people; her father and the ever-smiling Bruce. All four met in the center of the room for a passionate joint embrace, Luke complaining that he was getting squashed. Laughing and crying at the same time, they drew apart and beheld each other with tender gratitude.

Hugh Bremmers was first to break the happy silence. His gaze leveled lovingly on his daughter's face, he announced softly, "Your mother and I have had a long talk, Lana. You're all comin' back to Tyler."

The news made Lana happier and sadder than she could ever remember feeling. She dared not ask if the family was officially reunited—wouldn't that be asking too much?—but at least her father would no longer be countless miles away, unreachable, untouchable. But Bruce would be.

As if reading her thoughts, Carol added, "We've also had a long talk with this fine young man here . . . seems he's dealin' with a pretty rough home situation. We were thinkin' it probably wouldn't be very difficult for your father and I to become his legal guardians."

"And if I ever get caught with so much as a gleam in my eye when I'm looking at you, I won't live long to regret it." Bruce beamed, drawing a warning glance from Hugh. "But anyway, are you okay? What happened to you? They found your mom's car parked over on Teaberry, but none of the residents that were home knew anything about it. They've got it down at the police station combing it over for clues."

Lana was afraid if she recited any part of the truth, it would all spill out, every disgusting, degrading detail of the horrendous experience. She couldn't come to terms with it herself; she could hardly share such horror with anyone else, especially not with her parents, of all people. Or Bruce. She never wanted him to know what had happened to her. What would be the point? Yes, well, there was the matter of four dead people in the house at the end of Teaberry Street, but they would be found sooner or later, regardless of her testimony.

"I . . . I just wanted to drive around an' think," she lied. "I couldn't sleep, I needed some fresh air. But then that awful fog came in an' I couldn't drive anymore, so I parked an' got out. Walked for hours, got lost, somehow ended up in the woods. Then it got dark, an' I couldn't see where I was goin' again. Finally I heard voices, an' I followed the sound. Next thing I knew, I was walkin' into that blindin' light an' the police were tellin' me to hold it right there."

Hugh and Carol hugged their daughter, resisting any urge to voice more questions. She was home and she was safe, and that was all that mattered.

No longer feeling threatened by an impending interrogation, Lana took a few deep breaths and marveled at her blessings. They were going back to Tyler—as a single unit, from what she had gathered—and Bruce would be coming with them. Maybe he could get Luke to mellow out. But what about Greg? She hoped he had already found someone else. That would make things a lot less awkward.

Carol ushered everyone to the dining room table for some celebratory drinks. While she was preparing them, Bruce launched into the story of his misadventure.

"You wouldn't believe what I've been through. That dang Spiro hid out in my truck bed last night, and when I figured out something was back there and got out to see what it was, he came at me with a straight razor and tried to open my jugular. Just about succeeded too. Before I knew it, I was moving air, and he was loping right after me. I couldn't run up to any houses because that would've been the last thing I ever did; I never knew Guenther could run that fast. He must've chased me around for a whole hour, until I thought my sides were gonna split wide open. Finally we ended up clear over by Beacon Hill and I managed to hide up in a tree. He went crazy looking for me; I could hear him pawing branches, snorting like a wild hog. I didn't dare move, not even when I couldn't hear him anymore; I figured he was just laying low somewhere, listening, waiting for me to reveal my location. I couldn't have run anymore anyway. Don't know how long I sat there, but I wouldn't be surprised if it was more than three hours. When I finally got back to my truck, the batteries were dead because I'd left my headlights on. I was surprised somebody hadn't called the cops about it; it was sitting right in front of an intersection. Anyway, so then I decided to come back over here. When I got here, all the lights were off, so I tapped on your window several times, but I guess you were asleep and didn't hear me. I didn't want to wake up your mom and I couldn't handle the thought of walking all the way home, so I just sacked out on your front porch, figured it would take Spiro at least a week to figure out I wasn't still somewhere in the woods.

"I woke up right after you started your mom's car. Wasn't much light, but I looked up and could tell it was you when you pulled out of the driveway and turned on the headlights. I ran after you, but apparently you couldn't see me. I thought you were probably headed over to my house, so I ended up walking home anyway. But you weren't there." He let out a whew. "What a nightmare, huh?"

Lana smiled wanly. If he only knew.

Bruce concluded his story by saying, "By then I knew it was really late, and I wasn't about to bounce in and give my loving stepfather an excuse to turn my buns to raw hamburger; I'd had enough for one night. So I sacked out in the doghouse with Duke, in case you're wondering why I smell like a kennel. When I woke up the next morning, I thought I'd died and gone to Heaven; all I could see was white. I mean I really believed it. I wasn't sure why I was still in Duke's doghouse, but I just stayed in there all day waiting for somebody to bring me my harp or whatever. By the way, I've decided to lay off the, uh, Mother Nature."

"I should hope so," Hugh said, tossing a suspicious glance at Lana.

"Well, imagine my surprise when the fog lifted and there I was, still right in the middle of my backyard. I thought then, oh great, I'm really in for it now. So I said to myself, 'You're already in a hole, dude, so why not just keep on digging?' So I snuck away to come back over here. This time the truck was gone, so I knew right away I'd done the right thing. I didn't expect your mom to be very happy to see me, but I was in for a nice surprise. Your dad showed up about an hour later and we all sat around and talked, worrying our heads off about you. Thank God you're all right."

"You too," Lana said softly.

He continued in a grave tone, "I guess you don't know about Matt. We were right—those guys at the park weren't kidding about trying to burn Marla at the stake. Crazy jerks. Apparently Matt went over to Marla's house last night to lure her out. She's missing now too, by the way, and her mom killed her dad and herself this morning. But they found Matt . . . in a ravine just outside the Mingee property line. Heard the story on the radio about an hour ago. His head exploded or something—"

"I think that'll do for now," Hugh interrupted with a frown.

Bruce grinned sheepishly, thankful that a reproof in the Bremmerses' household didn't include a sock in the ear. "Sorry, Mr. Bremmers."

"Make that Hugh. It's all right, I just think we could talk about somethin' more on the cheerful side. Like how old fools like me can finally come to their senses."

Lana impulsively grasped her father's hand across the table. "I love you, Daddy. You're not an old fool."

"All right, middle-aged, then."

It was just like the 'and they lived happily ever after' ending to a fairy tale, Lana thought, for the moment successfully blocking out the horror of the last eighteen hours. Her mother came in with a tray bearing five glasses of red wine. Luke whooped with delight at his rare opportunity to imbibe; permission was given only on the most special of occasions. For the time being Sam quietly slumbered in a far corner of his mind.

They toasted to health and happiness, clinked their glasses and drank, Bruce chugging his. He lowered his empty glass wearing a dopey smile, his jittery nerves finally calmed by the warm tingly glow quickly spreading through him. But the feeling of peace was short lived.

His eyes suddenly bugged outward, the smile vanishing from his lips. "Lana, what's happening to you?"

All eyes, including Lana's, turned to look at her abdomen, which was inexplicably beginning to swell. Within the space of a few seconds she appeared to be in the third trimester of pregnancy.

"My God!" Carol exclaimed, her wineglass slipping from her fingers and tumbling over on its side, soaking the tablecloth with a bloodred stain.

"She's gonna explode!" Luke yelled, both horrified and delighted. He scrambled out of his chair and backed into a far corner, not wanting to get hit by the spray of guts and organs.

Hugh bolted for the wall phone to call 911, cursing when he got a busy signal.

Lana had dropped her own glass on the floor and was now gripping the arms of her chair, grimacing deeply with her teeth clenched and eyes squeezed shut. Her belly continued to expand, straining against the fabric of her flannel shirt until the buttons popped off, baring the growing mound and her breasts to the shocked stares of her family and Bruce.

"Lana!" Carol sprang from her chair, knocking it over. Her face a mask of hysteria, she rushed to her daughter's side with the intention of pulling the shirt together over Lana's exposed chest, but by the time Carol reached her, Lana's shameful exposure was already covered by her still-growing belly. Standing a few feet away, Hugh again cursed loudly at another busy signal.

Carol clutched the sides of her head, totally at a loss as to what she should do. "What IS that? Why is this happening to her? Oh GOD!"

"Wow!" Luke shouted from the corner. "Her gut's as big as the TV set!"

Carol turned a murderous glare on him. "Shut UP, LUKE! NOT ONE MORE WORD!"

Bruce was about to suggest sticking Lana's stomach with a needle or something just in case this was a freak gas attack that really would cause her to explode when Lana's chair suddenly flew backward, spilling her onto the carpeted floor. Movement could be seen beneath her tightly stretched skin, reminding Bruce of the movie *Alien,* and of his and Lana's ludicrous conversation in the park the day before. He felt his testicles crawl up into his body. Didn't seem so ludicrous now.

"It's an ALIEN!" he yelled, jumping up from his chair. "Run for your lives!"

But no one moved; they only stared with horror-filled eyes as Lana's skin went on stretching to accommodate the writhing bulk inside her. Bruce fully expected to see Lana's skin begin to rip and a slimy green head with two sets of jaws pop out of the hole.

Lana's tortured moans escalated into screams, and Hugh slammed the receiver down onto the hook. "Hell with it, we'll take her to the emergency room ourselves." He strode purposefully toward Lana to pick her up and carry her out to his rented car, but as he was bending over, her 501's were jerked down around her ankles by unseen hands, her knees lifted and roughly parted wide. Driven back by the forbidden sight of his daughter's sex as well as the stench emanating from it, Hugh clamped a hand over his mouth and looked strickenly to his wife.

"Oh Jesus, Jesus," Carol blubbered, groping the table for support. "Something's coming out!"

With Lana's piercing screams resounding in their ears, they all watched in petrified silence as a blood-smeared human hand reached out from Lana's vagina and scrabbled at the carpet. The hand was joined by the crown of a skull, its blond hair pasted down with bloody mucous. The moment the head emerged far enough for the mouth to suck in a lungful of air, Lana's screaming abruptly ceased, her eyes fixed unseeing on the ceiling.

A deep sob wrenched itself from Carol's throat. "No . . . please God, *No!*"

"This can't be happening," Hugh breathed.

Bruce was pretty sure he was going to pass out. Luke already had.

Next came the creature's shoulders with a gush of rank, dark blood, the overstretched tunnel of flesh tearing as they were pushed through. When the posthumous birthing was completed, the newborn creature severed its own umbilical cord with its teeth and stood up between

Lana's legs at a height of nearly four feet, wiping the blood clots from its face. It seemed oblivious to the mortified stares of its observers.

Carol's brain registered the fact that the thing was an hermaphrodite, having both male and female sex organs. It also had cloven hooves instead of feet—and above the shoulders, Lana's face.

My grandchild, Carol thought, and immediately began to scream. The child from Hell looked up at her and smiled. A heartbeat later Carol's eyes exploded, then her body rocketed toward the ceiling, her head and shoulders punching through it. Her arms and legs spasmed for a few moments, then hung limp.

With a cry of rage, Hugh picked up one of the dining room chairs, prepared to hurl it at the unholy creature, but a series of loud snapping sounds brought him to his knees screaming in agony, splintered bones jutting from his forearms and hands.

Bile surged up Bruce's throat as the snapping sound continued and Hugh's head began caving in, skull fragments ripping through his scalp. When Bruce saw brain matter oozing from the splits, he promptly bowed over and emptied the contents of his stomach.

"Major bummer, huh?" the creature with Lana's face said to him mockingly, and Bruce reluctantly raised his head but found that he was too terrified to speak.

The opportunity for last words was soon lost. At first he assumed he was only pissing in his pants—which would be totally understandable—but the front of his khaki shorts was rapidly turning crimson. In blind panic he jerked down his zipper and pulled out his penis to find that blood was gushing from the tip at an alarming if not incredible rate.

"Coming and going!" the creature laughed as Bruce tried desperately—without success—to stop the flow. "Feel good, Brucie?"

Weeping uncontrollably now, Bruce stumbled toward the front door, his thrashing penis spraying blood all over the living room like an unmanned fire hose, going, most definitely going . . .

. . . and gone. He was dead before he hit the tiled floor of the entryway.

As the newborn Nephilim stood gazing at his lifeless form, it began to grow again, reaching its full height of nine feet in less than a minute. It turned to stare down at Luke, who was still lying in an unconscious heap in the dining room corner, and for a moment invaded the privacy of the boy's dream. Surprisingly enough he was having a good one; he and his parents were having a picnic at a beautiful park, and Sam was scampering around the blanket chasing after butterflies. Lana wasn't there because she was dead, having been crushed by a giant television set.

How sweet.

Luke's whole body suddenly burst into flame.

The top of its scalp brushing the textured ceiling, the Nephilim stepped over Lana's right leg and entered the kitchen, where it lowered itself to the floor and lay prone with its legs apart. Later it would go on a fun-filled killing spree, but first there was serious work to be done.

The Master still had a contract to honor.

Its long, massive penis, achieving an instant erection that curved upward to the hairless vagina positioned above it, thrust itself in.

FROM THE BESTSELLING AUTHOR OF
SECRETS OF THE MORNING

TWILIGHT'S CHILD

V.C. ANDREWS™

The V. C. Andrews series continues
with the next mesmerizing chapter in
the Cutler series—TWILIGHT'S CHILD.

At long last Dawn is happy. She's
found her daughter Christy and she and
Jimmy have finally married. The future
is theirs. Yet Dawn's happiness is as
short lived as the dark clouds that have
always hovered above Cutler's Cove.

Dawn's happiness is threatened by her
sister Clara Sue's insane jealously, her
brother Philip's mad love for her and
the return of Michael Sutton her old
love—who may destroy her new world.

TWILIGHT'S CHILD

AVAILABLE FROM
POCKET BOOKS

POCKET
B O O K S

194-02